Praise for the novels of C. Kelly Robinson

The Perfect Blend

"C. Kelly Robinson has created *A Perfect Blend* of humor, drama and emotion. Nikki was too real." –Gloria Mallette, bestselling author of *Shades of Jade, Promises to Keep,* and *The Honey Well*

"What a story! Robinson flaunts his literary skills and spins a tale of love and family that is emotionally riveting and highly entertaining. This is one read you will not want to miss." –Tracy Price-Thompson, bestselling author of *Chocolate Sangria* and *Black Coffee*

"C. Kelly Robinson is a wonderfully talented writer who captured my attention on page one and kept it until the very end. Fast-moving, true-to-life, and most entertaining." –Kimberla Lawson Roby, author of *Too Much of a Good Thing*

"Terrific and entertaining, with a rhythm that draws you in. . . . A winner!" –Victoria Christopher Murray, bestselling author of *Temptation* and *Blessed Assurance: Inspirational Short Stories Full of Hope*

No More Mr. Nice Guy
A Main Selection of the Black Expressions Book Club

"Robinson handles his subject matter with plenty of attitude. As in his debut, brisk plotting, snappy vernacular and resilient characters keep things entertaining . . . this spunky title will please fans of E. Lynn Harris and Omar Tyree." –*Publishers Weekly*

"Funny, nimble, entertaining storytelling with laugh out loud moments. Robinson's characters are easily recognizable." –Marcus Major, author of *A Man Most Worthy*

"Robinson writes another insightful and funny story about black men and the dating scene. Women and men will enjoy this love story." –*Booklist*

"Young, black, single and mad as hell. . . . [A] lighthearted look at the irrationality of dating." –*Kirkus Reviews*

continued . . .

Between Brothers

"Not since Spike Lee's *School Daze* and the much-loved sitcom *A Different World* has the Black experience on campus been this intriguing . . . a spirited tale of four classmates on a mission to save their college while dealing with real-world growing pains."   —*Essence*

"Good, resourceful characters fight back in a vivid narrative . . . a refreshing variety of characters."   —*Kirkus Reviews*

"Robinson has skillfully painted three-dimensional characters that reflect our rich, often misunderstood diversity."
                 —William July, author of *Brothers, Lust,* and *Love*

"*Between Brothers* gives a candid and refreshing look inside the lives of four 'together-brothers' who transcend stereotypes and restore faith and hope in our black men."   —Tracy Price-Thompson

"C. Kelly Robinson has produced an insightful, well written novel. Highly recommended."
                 —Timmothy B. McCann, bestselling author of *Until*

"[*Between Brothers*] is both an exceptionally well written and consummate novel of character studies . . . an engaging, compelling story set in the very real and contemporary world of the Black community."
                 —*Midwest Book Review*

The
*St*rong,
*Si*lent Type

C. Kelly Robinson

 NEW AMERICAN LIBRARY

New American Library
Published by New American Library, a division of
Penguin Group (USA) Inc., 375 Hudson Street,
New York, New York 10014, USA
Penguin Group (Canada), 10 Alcorn Avenue, Toronto,
Ontario Canada M4V 3B2 (a division of Pearson Penguin Canada Inc.)
Penguin Books Ltd., 80 Strand, London WC2R 0RL, England
Penguin Ireland, 25 St. Stephen's Green, Dublin 2,
Ireland (a division of Penguin Books Ltd.)
Penguin Group (Australia), 250 Camberwell Road, Camberwell, Victoria 3124,
Australia (a division of Pearson Australia Group Pty. Ltd.)
Penguin Books India Pvt. Ltd., 11 Community Centre, Panchsheel Park,
New Delhi - 110 017, India
Penguin Group (NZ), Cnr Airborne and Rosedale Roads, Albany,
Auckland 1310, New Zealand (a division of Pearson New Zealand Ltd.)
Penguin Books (South Africa) (Pty.) Ltd., 24 Sturdee Avenue,
Rosebank, Johannesburg 2196, South Africa

Penguin Books Ltd, Registered Offices: 80 Strand, London WC2R 0RL, England

First published by New American Library,
a division of Penguin Group (USA) Inc.

First Printing, January 2005
10 9 8 7 6 5 4 3 2 1

NEW AMERICAN LIBRARY and logo are trademarks of Penguin Group (USA) Inc.

ISBN 0-7394-4902-8

Set in Berthold Garamond

Printed in the United States of America

PUBLISHER'S NOTE
This is a work of fiction. Names, characters, places, and incidents either are the product of the
author's imagination or are used fictitiously, and any resemblance to actual persons, living or
dead, business establishments, events, or locales is entirely coincidental.

For everyone seeking the courage to step out on faith,
with thanks to those who have helped me find it

To keep me from becoming conceited because of these surpassingly great revelations, there was given me a thorn in my flesh . . . to torment me. Three times I pleaded with the Lord to take it away . . . But he said to me, "My grace is sufficient for you, for my power is made perfect in weakness."

II Corinthians 12: 7–9

Before

THE BEGINNING OF THE END

Deacon

I was on the air, my image and my words being broadcast to Fox News's global audience, when it happened.

"Mr. Davis?" On the monitor hanging overhead, Bridget, the pretty, feathery-haired anchor, leaned in, looking confused. I couldn't blame her; our first minute on air, I had held my own, articulately taking on the conservative activist who sat by her side in Manhattan. Now I was struggling to get a single word out. "Mr. Davis," Bridget asked again, "do you have a reply to Mr. Abrams's point?"

Unclamping my lips, I took another run at my previous sentence. "Yes, B-Bridget, I do," I said. "As I was saying b-before, the country needs a political p-p-party dedicated to the interests of minorities. That's not the sole p-p-p-p–" My head filled with bubbles as I realized I had gone off the rails. This was the third damn time this had happened since the cameras in Fox's Atlanta studio started rolling.

Sensing I was incapable of respecting the three-minute time limit for this news segment, Bridget turned back to my opponent. "Mr. Abrams, why don't you sum up your concerns about the American Dream Party? Why is this a bad idea for the country?"

"I'm not done, Bridget," I said, realizing only as I heard my voice that I was yelling. I couldn't go out like this; people were counting on me to make a strong case. "We at the American D-Dream Party are c-c-committed to–"

Pawing at his balding head, the local producer held up a hand. "Mr. Davis," he said, his gruff tone offset by his inability to look me in the eye, "you're done. We had to cut your mike."

Deacon

Ever been invited to resign from your job? For me, the experience went something like this:

Three days after I made a fool of myself on the Fox News Channel, my cousin Errick invited me to lunch at midtown Atlanta's Madison Grille. In addition to being family and my former best friend, Errick was VP of fund-raising for Communities in Action, a sister entity of my employer, the American Dream political party. He was also the assigned "hit man."

I could say that my boss, Miriam Lloyd, the Dream Party's chairwoman, was too chicken to fire me herself, but I won't. The woman's known me since the day I was born; if I were in her shoes, I doubt I could pull the trigger on a friend's kid either. Better to let a water boy like Errick get his hands dirty.

Deke, you have to resign. You know I wouldn't do this if I didn't think it was best, for you and for the party. The words popped out of my cousin's mouth after a half hour of small talk, just after our waitress promised our meals were on the way.

He'd pulled a sneak attack, but somehow I kept my cool. Although Errick had punctured the last, thin layer protecting my self-respect and pride, my real reaction wouldn't come for nearly twenty-four hours. That's usually how it happens when folk lose it. As a brother with five NFL seasons under my belt and a proven track record of community activism, I have to say, failure was a new experience for me.

Protesting at first, I had loosened my tie and reminded Errick why I deserved to continue as the party's executive director. I had the training: a master's in public policy, earned at Carnegie Mellon during my years with the Pittsburgh Steelers. I had the experience: before joining the Dream Party, I had spent three years running education

reform programs for Communities in Action, the empowerment organization my father founded before setting up the Dream Party. I
didn't stop there, reminding Errick that I had trained at my father's
elbow, formally and informally, from the day I was born until his
tragic death in a fire at his Washington, D.C., supper club. Errick,
who like me is twenty-nine and was once more like a twin brother
than a cousin, was touched, but he didn't buy my defense.

This ain't about what I think, he whispered, his eye contact wavering
as the waitress set a sizzling sirloin filet before him.

I wanted to believe him. Errick and I had been yin to each other's
yang for years. I was ruggedly handsome; he was just this side of
pretty. I had the brainpower and the social conscience; he had the
charm and the people skills. Back when we were teenage punks and
my stutter turned me mute, Errick always stepped in and played
Aaron to my Moses, covering for me with his flashy smile and quick
wit. As a team, we'd done it all—seduced women from coast to coast,
raised money for both Communities in Action and the Dream Party,
and helped extend my father's legacy. Damn, those days felt like an-
cient history.

*Don't take this the wrong way, Deke, but Miriam always thought your
stuttering would cause problems. Most people never see you talk like that, but
come on, Miriam's known you since you were a kid. She gave you a shot out
of respect for your dad, but Jesus, after the way you bungled words in that interview? George Bush sounds more articulate on his worst day.*

Momentarily overpowered by my cousin's slam, as well as by the
lingering scent of the waitress's heavy perfume, I reminded Errick this
was my first time "losing it" during a media appearance. The Fox interview had been my first appearance on national television in a
while, but through the years, I'd handled myself perfectly on all sorts
of radio and television shows.

When you lose it one time, Errick replied, *no one remembers the times you
got it right.*

My brain was as good as frozen, but somehow my mouth kept
moving. Defenses, pleas, and threats spilled out of me. I even reminded Errick of my children, not to mention my trusty child-

support obligations. When none of that cracked him, I insisted on a face-to-face with Miriam.

That got nothing but a narrowed stare and an anxious wave of the hands from Errick. *Not a good idea. You know Miriam's just getting over that surgery; she's not at full strength yet. That's why she came to me. This is a crucial time for the Dream Party, man. We have a chance to honor your father's memory, build the Dream into the first viable political party for black folk.*

Like I didn't know that.

Everything has to be executed perfectly, though, starting with our public image. You don't fit, Deke, not when you can't get your words out straight. Miriam needs an executive director who delivers—no missteps or mishaps.

I pushed back from the table, intent on calling Miriam, but Errick's next words welded my ass to my seat.

She's afraid you'll sue her for discrimination, cuz. That's why I'm here, as a buffer. I'm asking you to keep this confidential, do what's best for the Dream Party. Do it for Uncle Frederick's legacy. Miriam won't be in charge forever.

Errick's attempt to use my father's memory against me was too low. I don't recall my exact response, but it involved four-letter words and pointed accusations about my cousin's loyalty.

Deacon, come on. Do you want to be the loser son hanging around his father's organization, even when you're not cutting it?

End of conversation.

Walking the plank at gunpoint left me as cold as a corpse. Humiliation blanking out my thoughts, I went home, packed for a previously planned trip to Chicago, fed my dog, Prince, and strode into the dark night, hoping a five-mile run would transport me to another world.

Fifteen hours and a plane ride later, I pulled up to my son Dejuan's school building. Time had passed, but Errick's words were still there, poking holes into my soul like pins in a cushion. Shuffling my way up Jackson Junior High's front walk, I swept a gaze over the chipped bricks, peeling paint, and windows insulated with duct tape. Compared with Kenwood Academy, my alma mater on Chicago's south side, this west-side school screamed "academic emergency." I couldn't imagine Jackson offered Dejuan an equal opportunity to compete for the American dream, but it was a last resort. I'd helped Candy, his mother, enroll him in two separate magnet schools. The thirteen-year-old fruit of my loins got expelled from both of them.

"Hey! Over here." Candy stood a few feet down the hall from me, just outside a doorway with a generic white sign overhead reading OFFICE. Nodding coolly, I prepared for my first real conversations of the day. *Feel the flow,* I told myself, recalling some of my old speech therapy from childhood. *Feel the flow.* After my recent Fox News debacle, where I'd stuttered my ass off, I was newly self-conscious. Relaxing the muscles around my mouth and letting my words "flow" out in a calm, unhurried manner was my only hope of sounding more like Superman and less like Porky Pig.

I needed to speak fluently today; I was here to protect my son from himself. The night of the Fox News disaster, Candy had asked me to fly up from Atlanta after Dejuan was suspended, *again,* for groping a girl in the hallway without her permission. My boy was turning into a little Arnold Schwarze-Negro. Knowing even then that I was in danger of losing my job, I hadn't felt like playing Father Knows Best, but I had no choice. At thirteen, Dejuan was in a pivotal phase: either I had to help stomp out these antics now, or I'd deal with far worse consequences down the road.

Reaching Candy, I took her into my arms with a quick, tepid hug. Still rail-thin, her figure had hardly changed from the days we cut school to wear each other out on her father's plastic-covered couch. We complimented each other for looking good for "damn near thirty"; she didn't look like she'd ever carried a baby, and at six foot two and two hundred pounds, I was still firm enough to hold my own on the football field.

Candy and I had made the best of an awkward situation for fourteen years now. We were high school sophomores when Dejuan was conceived. A leggy, high yellow honey, Candy was a dancer in the school band, a quiet girl whose rarely used, cautious smile showcased beauty that had survived its share of beasts. Raised in public housing by a gruff but loyal single father, she'd seen her share of abuse at the hands of family "friends" and pretty much equated love with a good orgasm.

On the surface, I may have seemed a little more together—son of a revered civil rights leader, all-American defensive back, earning more A's than B's—but I had my own wounds. My knotted tongue, so rare in my world of high school friends and my high-achieving family, had me wracked with self-inflicted guilt. Candy and I were never in love, but in some ways we were soul mates, sensing and soothing each other's pain.

As I released Candy from my hug, I mourned those simpler days of our youth. Candy wore her Chicago Transit Authority uniform proudly, including the baseball cap sitting atop her shoulder-length, blond-streaked brown curls. "So you know," she said, her gaze hardening, "I didn't appreciate being stood up."

"Trust me," I said, clasping my hands apologetically. "You can't give me any more hell about it than Darlene already has." Darlene, my baby sister, is the only one of us Davis kids still in Chicago. My sister Benet and her family live near me in Atlanta; my brother, Miles, is a proudly rolling stone; and my mother lives in Florida with Roberto, my wealthy and insecure stepfather. A graduate student in chemistry at Northwestern, Darlene lives in our old family home on the south side. When she completes school, we'll either sell the family home or turn it into a historical landmark.

"I know your flight got in late last night, Deacon," Candy said, a smile matching the twinkle in her eyes. "Darlene told me that's why you overslept." I had agreed to meet Candy at nine for breakfast, so she could prepare me for this sit-down with Dejuan's principal. "I was just pickin' with you." Tentatively, she brushed her fingers over my wrist. "I saw you on TV the other day. What happened? Were you feeling all right?"

Now that may sound like a bitchy way to pick with me for embarrassing myself on national television, but Candy didn't have the slightest ounce of attitude in her question. She'd always been a genuine straight-shooter. I smiled and said, "I didn't do anything you hadn't heard before, right?"

The concern in Candy's eyes tapped at the door of my brave facade. "Look, just between you and me, Deacon, if people are talking shit to you about a few stutters, tell them to go to hell." She stuck a thin finger into the center of my chest. "They haven't walked a step in your shoes. It would take a strong man to walk in your father's shoes, even if you spoke perfectly."

The earnest, protective look in Candy's eyes and the slight catch in her voice reminded me that she knew what she was talking about. Because we shared a child, Candy was the only lover from my teen years who was still in my life, and no woman I'd been with since, except my ex-wife, Mercedes, ever knew that I stuttered. Candy knew because when we hooked up, I was still searching for a world where my stuttering didn't matter. She, along with many other pretty young things, helped me find it—in bedrooms, car backseats, and the corners of parks throughout Chicago. No woman worried about the smoothness of my speech once I slid myself deep inside her. In record time, I discovered sensitive spots, pressure points, and creative positions requiring no words at all. The heat of a sweaty, heart-thumping embrace melted every speech impediment I had. Sex became my drug of choice—cheaper than cocaine, more private than beer runs with the boys, and less fraught with danger, as long as I kept Jimmy wrapped in his hat.

Or so I thought.

As Candy and I checked our watches, wondering when Dejuan's principal would call us in, she cleared her throat. "You hear who Dejuan's new principal is?"

"I wouldn't know unless you told me," I replied. I knew the old principal had resigned recently, but hadn't heard about the replacement.

"I saw an announcement with the name a few weeks ago," Candy said, picking at her teeth with a glittery fingernail, "but I just put two and two together with my girl Tiara this morning. Do you remember—"

The sudden creak of the office door interrupted Candy. In my peripheral vision, I saw a bulky brother around my height step into the hallway.

"Deacon Davis?"

I turned and looked into the face of Byron Collins. "That's me," I said, matching his firm handshake. "What's up, Byron? How long you been teaching here?"

"Oh, I'm done teaching, brother," Byron said, stroking his full beard. "I'm Jackson's principal now. Still getting settled in, but already enjoying my mission here." With his short fade haircut, Byron looked like a real man now, not just an oversize hulk of a boy. His face had filled out, too, but through the eyes he still looked like my sarcastic, wisecracking football teammate from Kenwood. A few years back, I had heard that he was teaching, but the brother had apparently come up pretty quickly, to already be a principal.

Byron clapped his hands, then rubbed them together as he glanced quizzically between Candy and me. "Now, uh, Ms. Dewitt, I know you're here to discuss Dejuan's suspension. Deacon, what brings you this way? I thought you'd moved to Atlanta."

Another awkward moment in the life of a single father. Candy and I never exactly broadcast my involvement in Dejuan's conception. Even back in 1990, my father—a one-time protégé of Martin Luther King, founder of a venerable civil rights organization, and the first African American elected to the Senate in twenty-five years—had a reputation to protect. By putting baby making ahead of college, graduate school, and a real job, I had jacked up my parents' game plan pretty good.

As a result, while Frederick and Mother insisted I take responsibility when Dejuan proved to be mine, they were overjoyed when Candy's grandmother insisted he take her family's last name. "He gonna be living with us, anyway," Momma Dewitt had said. "If Deacon's stuttering ass think he too good to marry Candy, the baby may as well have our name. Best way to keep from confusing his teachers and shit."

In my mind I heard my reply to Byron, explaining that I was Dejuan's father, but the next thing I knew, I had slipped into speech limbo again, just like during my Fox News nightmare. When I felt my throat muscles squeeze tight and heard air fill my lungs, I knew I'd plunged into trouble. Couldn't get a damn word out.

A fleeting smirk danced across Byron's face as he turned to Candy. "Ms. Dewitt, uh, I guess the cat has Deacon's tongue, so can you tell me why he's here?"

As Candy began to reply, I patted her on the shoulder. "I'm Dejuan's father," I said, relieved to feel the words slide their way out. "We're very concerned with his recent b-behavior."

Byron took a mental beat in response to my revelation, an "oh, shit" look crossing his face. "Well, I wish I could argue with you," he said finally, "but you should be concerned." Before Candy or I could respond, he stepped aside, holding open the door. His smile showcasing dull yellow teeth, Byron pointed us through the doorway before following behind. "We're headed to the office in the far right corner."

Just as I stepped past Byron, he tapped my elbow. When I paused to face him, he nudged me playfully. "If that don't beat all," he growled in a low whisper. "Little Dejuan Dewitt is part of the world-famous Davis family. You old dog, you." When I acted like I didn't hear him, he tugged at me again. This time, his whisper had more bass to it. "Some things never change. Still get all the women—still can't talk worth a damn."

2

Deacon

Byron's verbal jab yanked me out of my attempt to leave the past in the past. I slowed my strut and let him catch up with me as we trailed Candy toward his corner office. "Grow up, Byron," I said, just loud enough for him to hear. My stomach warming with anger, I nodded pleasantly at his secretary, convincing myself that Byron would back off now. *Feel the flow,* I pleaded as we stepped into Byron's office. *Feel the flow.* This was about Dejuan, not about my history with his principal.

Byron was a star offensive lineman at Kenwood, and the dude had the offensive mouth to match. There were days he seemed obsessed with ridiculing my stutter. In truth, he was the last person to define me as a stutterer, a walking punch line for his latest joke.

For the past twelve years, I had successfully passed myself off as a normal speaker, to the point that I'd thought the shame and frustration of my youth had been banished to the rearview mirror of my life. With that in doubt after my Fox News meltdown and my forced resignation, I had little patience for Byron's antics.

Dejuan sat perched in a low wooden chair opposite Byron's desk, his posture slumped and irritated. With his newly braided cornrows and wire-rimmed glasses, I barely recognized the child from my last visit a few weeks earlier. Lanky and lean, he had Candy's build, but his broad nose and long eyelashes marked him as a Davis. As he coolly nodded our way, showing minimal respect while protecting his teenage pride, I realized that with his deep ebony complexion, my son resembles my father even more than I do.

Byron shut the door behind us, motioned toward the empty wooden chairs, and stepped over to the window behind his desk. Dark and overcast, the sky churned, ready to unleash a late spring thundershower.

"Now, let me just get this straight," Byron said, turning toward us and flipping open a file on his desk. "Dejuan, this is your father? This man, Broderick Deacon Davis himself? The former all-American defensive back, the former Pittsburgh Steeler, the son of Frederick Douglass Davis himself?"

"That's really beside the point," Candy said, her voice just above a whisper. "We're here to discuss ways to correct Dejuan's behavior."

Byron shrugged as if he had barely heard Candy and trained his eyes on me. "Still can't believe this boy's yours. What're you doing in Atlanta again?"

"I'm executive director of the American Dream Party, the same party my father used for his '96 presidential campaign," I said, acting like I hadn't just written my own pink slip. "Before that, I ran the education reform programs for Communities in Action, at the headquarters office here in town." I chose and phrased each word as if my life depended on it. I wasn't losing control of my speech again. As a long-distance father, I knew I wasn't a model parent to Dejuan, but the last thing I wanted was to sound like a stuttering mess in front of him. He didn't need that humiliation any more than I did, least of all from Byron Collins.

Silence filled the room as Byron took a seat and tented his fingers. His brow wrinkling, he sized up my little makeshift family. The situation had to be killing him, because it was driving me nuts. "Well," he said, snapping his suit coat more tightly around his broad shoulders, "we need to deal with Dejuan's disrespectful treatment of his female classmates. I called you in, Ms. DeWitt, because based on Dejuan's overall record at Jackson—his solid attendance, his slowly improving grades, and his generally positive reputation among most teachers—I believe you're doing some good work with him."

"He didn't learn any harassing language from me," Candy shot back. "I've told him," she said, placing a firm hand on Dejuan's shoulder, "that if he gets written up again for saying something that *I* would smack a guy for saying to me, I'm smacking *him*."

"Understood." Byron looked at his desk before smirking at me suddenly. A new glint lit his eyes, one I recognized from our childhood. "Mr. Davis, is it possible Dejuan's disrespect of women is based on your relationships with the opposite sex?"

He got me with that one—he got me good. Syllables tumbled over themselves, trying to escape my lips. "What? Where d-did you get that from?"

Byron's eyes were smiling, nearly winking, though his lips formed a straight line. "We commonly see in these situations that boys act out in response to things they're seeing in the home, Mr. Davis. I know you don't live here, but I assume you spend regular time with Dejuan?" He trailed off, happy to leave an uneasy silence in the room.

My stomach cramped as I answered. "I haven't seen much of Dejuan since I moved to Atlanta," I said, my forehead dampening. "I've been working through some things on my own. B-but before I left, Dejuan stayed with me at least once each week."

Byron frowned. "He never lived with you? I thought he mentioned living with his father briefly, two or three years ago?"

Now Byron had really done it. I leaned forward in my seat, staring past Candy and making eye contact with my son, who quickly looked the other way. Abandoned, I stared back at Byron. "Dejuan lived with me and my wife for a couple of years, yes."

Byron folded his hands, looking at me as if searching my soul. "Was Dejuan exposed to a happy or unhappy marriage while living with you? You're no longer with your wife, are you?"

"We're d-divorced," I said, sighing, "but Dejuan moved back with Candy for different reasons. Mercedes and I were happily married when he left."

"I didn't leave," Dejuan said, his voice squeaking with annoyance. "You all sent me away."

"D-Dejuan," I replied, my cheeks warming, "you know you weren't the problem." I wasn't going to take a walk down memory lane in front of Byron, but Dejuan's attack caught me by surprise. I'd tried to protect him from all the drama that had split me from Mercedes, but I thought I'd made it clear he was not to blame.

"Mr. Collins, this isn't helpful." Candy glanced at our son like she wanted to touch him, comfort him, but knew she couldn't. "I know this man," she said, placing a hand on my shoulder. "He may not be perfect, but he's a responsible father. Dejuan didn't learn this behavior from Deacon."

I leaned forward again, looking past Candy. "D-Dejuan, look, we're going to talk about this later today. I know I haven't b-been there for you lately—"

"Mr. Davis, you're clearly flustered," Byron said, interrupting. "It's best in these situations to keep your wits about you and face the need for change. Dejuan does not act like someone raised to respect women. What would your father, rest his soul, think of all this?"

"What does my father have to do with this?" I nearly leapt out of my seat, sitting there poised at its edge. "You're out of line, Byron." Restraint peeled off me like a layer of dead skin. He had crossed the line with the reference to Frederick. In addition to being a failure at filling my father's shoes professionally, was I really a failure as a parent, too?

Before I could get another word out, Byron switched his focus to Candy. Questions flew left and right about her boyfriends, men in her life, things she might have done to cause Dejuan's behavior. Candy hung tough with him, but the fatigue in her eyes grew by the minute.

Sweat caked my underarms, and the pounding of my heart made me as good as deaf, in addition to being "dumb." Byron had to know what he was doing, needling me in a more sophisticated version of his locker-room taunts years before. *Get it out, Davis. Cat got your tongue, muthafucka? Duh-Duh-Duh-Deacon, c-c-can y-you s-say your o-o-own n-name?* The taunts had flowed from the brother's mouth like lava from Vesuvius, until I got my revenge.

It didn't take much creativity for me to sweep Byron's girl, Lajuana, off her feet. She'd always found me "fine," if the grapevine could be believed. One night after catching three interceptions that sealed our regional championship, I wrote her a letter on parchment paper professing my hidden, undying love. She probably bought it because we'd almost dated during sophomore year, until the news of Candy's pregnancy sidelined me.

When Lajuana read my letter, she dropped into my reach like low-hanging fruit. I left a pair of her panties and a bra nailed to Byron's locker during our next practice, and in the weeks of humiliation that followed, he wound up transferring to a school across town. I don't think he ever lived that down.

In hindsight, maybe I should have pitied the brother. My own life sat a stone's throw from disaster itself, but when I think back on how unprofessional Byron was that day, it's clear he had issues of his own. I should have let his nonsense roll off my back, walked out with dignity, and focused my attention on mending fences with my son.

I might have thought that way, if not for the rank disrespect cascading from Byron's tone. All I needed, as a newly unemployed man, one still stalked by the stuttering gremlin I'd dodged year after year, was some basic respect. Robbed of that, I had only one way to claim it, and I took it.

Byron was still lecturing Candy when I stood and shoved my chair back. "Candy, Dejuan, excuse us. Mr. Collins and I need to speak in private."

Candy clamped a hand on to my wrist and looked up at me with pleading eyes. Behind her, Dejuan stared at me with an intrigued smile.

"I'm all right," I said calmly, gently removing her hand from me. I looked at my son. "Mr. Collins is your principal, Dejuan, and you will obey him. He and I need to straighten one thing out first, though."

Byron popped out of his seat and strode to the office door. "Ms. DeWitt, Dejuan, please wait at my secretary's desk." He held the door open for them, a grim smile on his face, as I remained standing.

He shut the door behind them and walked right up to me, swaying back and forth. "What's the problem?" he growled, blasting me with his musk cologne and tobacco-stained breath.

"Don't put my son in the middle of unfinished business," I replied, flexing my shoulders and taking a step forward.

"See, you got that sentence out nicely," Byron said, a chuckle offsetting the threat in his eyes. "We'll see how you handle the next one. Still haven't licked it yet, huh, Deacon?"

I wanted an answer for Byron as much as I wanted anything in my life, but I had no clue. No clue why my granddad stuttered worse than me for his entire life, while my father spoke with the eloquence of a Baptist preacher. No clue why I continued to struggle with the basics of speech while my brother and sisters were some of the most articulate people I knew. I was clueless, a reality that punched me in the gut.

For some amount of time—twenty seconds, a complete minute, maybe even ninety seconds—I ignored Byron and let the past days' events sink in. I was thinking about Granddad.

Henry James Davis was the first person to acknowledge my stutter. "We're different, you and me." That was his loving warning to me at ten years old, as we stood picking fat, purple grapes in his backyard. When I looked up in confusion, he patted my head playfully, though he had a faraway look in his eyes. "Sometimes it's hard g-getting words out, ain't it?"

"There's nothing wrong with b-being different, Deacon," Grand-dad continued, his eyes shutting as he squeezed my name between trembling lips. He knelt down so we were eye to eye. "Some of these Negroes out here don't realize that, though. They think folk who talk like us are c-clowns." He cupped my chin, raising my eyes to meet his urgent stare. "You may need a thick skin someday, little one. Just re-member, you're not normal, so don't t-try to be. Be yourself."

I wish I had been strong enough to absorb Granddad's advice, but the truth is when I started choking on words while answering teach-ers' questions and butchering jokes by sounding like a broken record, I wanted nothing more than to be normal. If I were normal, I could introduce myself to my father's famous and powerful associates with-out embarrassing him. If I were normal, I wouldn't have to run from the reporters who chased me with those dreaded microphones after each football game.

Determined not to be mocked for the rest of my life, I picked up a few coping tricks from my school's speech therapist and began "passing" as a fluent speaker. In time, I developed a sixth sense for each stutterer's approach. In those moments, I adopted a new persona—the mysterious man of few words, the strong, silent type. For over twelve years it worked, but the chase had finally ended in the hot glare of that Fox camera, and the world stood ready to judge me.

Byron interrupted my thoughts, and to this day I say he shares the blame for what followed. "Deacon, come on," he said, tapping his watch. "We don't have all day. I know you need extra time, but if you have something to say, spit it out."

No respect. Just like Miriam and Errick. Just like I could expect from whatever companies I'd be begging for employment now.

Byron was still chuckling when I shot my right hand out and grabbed him by the throat. "You never learned, did you?" The words blasted out of my mouth, riding a torrent of raw anger. Lifting all two-hundred-plus pounds of Byron off his feet, I pivoted and slammed him onto his desk. His body rattling with shock, he stared back at me with wide eyes. He tried to say something, but I couldn't make it out through the gurgles of spit and mucus dribbling from his lips.

"What do I have to do, Byron?" I kept my firm grip on his neck, knowing that was my only hope of keeping him subdued. He had just enough air to breathe, but beyond that, he was caught off guard and was too surprised to defend himself. I leaned over him, nearly touching his forehead with mine. "You should be a better man than this, still picking with folks like a schoolyard bully."

"Sorry." Byron croaked out the apology through crusty lips slimed with his own slobber. "Please, for God's sake, Deacon, let go."

I jerked my hand away suddenly and stepped back as Byron gulped for air like a fish out of water. I couldn't muster a drop of regret. "Don't say I never did anything for you."

Hacking and wheezing, Byron pulled himself off the desk, grabbed his phone, and began dialing. "You're fucked now," he said, his eyes stabbing me as he held the receiver. "Yes, I'd like to report an assault." He paused to catch his breath and let loose with another cough. "This is Byron Collins, principal at Jackson Junior High. The assailant is Broderick Deacon Davis. . . ."

The metallic taste of shame in my mouth, I turned and flung the office door open. Candy and Dejuan were seated outside, just in front of Byron's secretary's desk. All three turned toward me immediately, their eyes full of fear.

I paused before them. "I-I'm sorry" was all that came out. With nothing to add, I continued past them, bolting toward the main office door. Chairs rustled behind me as the secretary flew from her seat to check on Byron, and Candy rushed after me. She was shouting by the time I was in the hallway, something like, "Don't leave it like this!" I heard Candy's shouts, felt her anguish, but like a drowning man witnessing an onshore robbery, I was powerless to help her.

3

Maria

When confronting new clients, I always start with the same sentence: *There is no cure.*

Now I know there are more sensitive ways to say this, especially considering the average stutterer wants me to snap my fingers, hand over a magic pill, or perform radical surgery to untwist his tortured tongue. And don't think I don't pray for the day when I can wave a magic wand. Until then, the cold truth remains. My clients have to earn every bit of fluency themselves.

There's no cure. Is that a cruel message? Come on. Is there a cure for life itself? I've got unsolved ills of my own. From the day I learned my daddy never wanted me and my mommy couldn't handle me, stubborn wounds have threatened my best impulses and sunk my fiercest dreams. I'm still standing, mind you, but I'm not special. I just keep getting up, whether life knocks me down or I've KO'd myself.

I kept that image of life as a boxing ring in my head this afternoon as I rode to meet my brother, Thomas, for lunch. Since my '96 Grand Am was in the shop, I caught a ride with Ramsey Folger, the nationally renowned speech therapist who hired me two months ago. True to form, Ramsey had eagerly locked me inside his luxury Volvo.

"Maria, Maria," he said, sighing, his baritone melting into the car's leather interior. "I just realized I'm taking you to lunch with someone else. Who's this you have time for, when you've passed on every lunch invite I've made?" He looked over at me again, flooding me with the full wattage of his smile. "I'd started to think the secret of your figure was that you just skip lunch altogether."

"Oh, Ramsey, I wish," I replied, rolling my eyes and huffing playfully. I had addressed him as Dr. Folger for three weeks, until he threatened to fire me if I kept it up. "My weight has been stubborn as a two-year-old the past couple years." Although I'm tall enough that my weight "looks good on me," as the old folks say, I'll never compete with Tyra Banks or Naomi Campbell. I plead guilty to being a "baby with back."

Ramsey shook his head. "So you do eat lunch—you're just dissing me."

"Please! We did lunch as part of my interview process."

"And not once since, in two months." Coming to an intersection, he braked gently and gazed at me again, adjusting the collar of his silk shirt. "Who do you think you're fooling?"

"I'm shy. Sue me," I said, trying to sound flip but feeling my brow tighten as the Volvo's dashboard clock flashed the time—11:33. Thomas is frighteningly punctual. "You can't fault a girl for having lunch with her brother, can you?"

"It's a free country." Ramsey chuckled as our light turned green and he sped past the neighboring cars. "Just know that I've got big plans for you, Maria. I not only want you to help me run this summer's SRC—I want you to get every benefit you can from my reputation."

The Speech Recovery Clinic, or SRC, was Ramsey's annual intensive summer program for adult stutterers. Although he had spent most of his career treating children, Ramsey's SRC had put him on the national map. Using a mixture of tried-and-true therapy techniques, innovative exercises culled from his own research, and good old-fashioned ass-kicking motivation, Ramsey had put nearly two hundred stutterers on the road to fluency, or a pretty effective imitation. On top of that, he trained each client—whether a college athlete, a medical student, or a corporate executive—to go home and wow the local media with their improved speech and stories about the guru who'd made it all happen. Small wonder the brother had received hundreds of thousands in grant money, along with regular calls from regional and national media.

I kept the good doctor's national platform in mind as the jangle of his gold wrist bracelet told me he was on the prowl. A second later, I felt his warm right hand rest on the knee of my linen slacks. With thirty thousand in school loans hanging over my head, I couldn't afford not to have Ramsey in my corner, but the challenge would be keeping him out of my bed at the same time. At forty-two, Ramsey's almost fifteen years my senior, but the brother's not exactly a mud duck–short, sleek, and stylish, with high cheekbones and a well-groomed goatee, he reminds me of an aging Taye Diggs. Unlike the Taye in my daydreams, however, Ramsey is married with two teenage daughters.

I slid my knee away from his palm, smiling all the while. "That's it up there, next block," I said, pointing toward the Starbucks shop where I'd agreed to meet Thomas. I glanced at the dash clock again– 11:36. Six minutes late. This was not going to be fun.

"I'm familiar with this spot," Ramsey said, grinning. He pulled to a stop right in front of the store and clicked his hazard lights on. "Maria," he continued, placing a hand on the top of my passenger seat, "relax. Your face muscles are as tight as the skin on a drum. Don't disrupt God's beauty with all that stress."

Feeling my eyes drop from his, I exhaled as Ramsey dropped his hand from my seat and gripped his gear shaft. "I'm fine, but thank you. I'll see you after lunch."

"You need a ride when you're done, just ring my cell phone. I'll be running errands nearby."

I climbed out of the Volvo and stood with my back to the Starbucks for a second, watching Ramsey speed away and wishing I had time to check my look in a mirror. My boss had me worried now; I thought I'd looked fine a few minutes ago on campus, when I ducked into the ladies' room to check myself. I had pulled my coiled curls into a conservative bun for the day, forgone my favorite eye shadow, and outfitted myself in deep purple linen slacks, a matching vest, and a white short-sleeve blouse. I was a little more plain Jane than usual, but today I had to meet Thomas's standards, not mine.

My brother stood in line, about six people away from the counter, when I walked through the front door. From behind, he cut an oddly striking figure: five feet eleven, broad-shouldered, bald-headed, and dressed in a dark gray wool suit with well-shined leather shoes. He stood amid the usual Emory crowd of students, academics, and peaceniks, looking tense and out of place. A fish out of water, he gave off a vibe as corporate as it was stiff. I inhaled deeply and sidled up to him, touching a tentative hand to his left elbow.

"There you are." He looked at my hand on his elbow just long enough to convince me to remove it, then gave me a quick side-arm hug. He'd snatched his arm back off my shoulder before I realized he'd even touched me. "I was starting to think I had the wrong date or time, little sister."

"No, you had it right." I planted my feet next to his and played at studying the menu. Did I owe an explanation for my late arrival? I knew Thomas wanted one.

We stood in silence, hemmed in on every side by the shouts of completed orders coming from behind the counter, the aimless conversation of fellow customers, and the sidewalk traffic waiting outside the opening-and-closing door.

In seconds, the silence got to me. "I got hung up on a case review at work," I offered, playing with the silver locket around my neck as I spoke. "I'm meeting with a new client this afternoon and had to review his application. When I looked up from my desk, it was almost eleven thirty. I got over here as quickly as I could."

"That's why I always show up early for engagements," Thomas replied, his eyes still on the menu. "We could just have met over at the house next weekend, Maria, like I said." He had agreed to this meeting only after I insisted we fit something in this week. Though he lived and worked out in Stone Mountain, he had agreed to meet me since he was in the area, on his way to the airport. "Meeting today was tough for me. Clearly it was a strain on you, too."

I let his little rebuke go and made small talk while we ordered. Thomas was handling business as usual on his job, where he was global manufacturing director for a large Coke supplier. His wife, Lucille, didn't work, but she had her hands full decorating their new home and keeping up with their "adopted" son, Jamil.

In a few minutes we had picked up our food, a Caffè Mocha and raspberry Danish for me and a large decaf and chocolate-chip muffin for Thomas. We grabbed the only open seats and settled into the small circular table.

"Lucille wants to have you over for dinner, by the way," Thomas said suddenly, before taking a long pull from his coffee. "When I get back into town Sunday night, I'll call you, and we'll figure out a time."

"What about you or Jamil?" I tried to coax a smile from myself, let my lips spread. Thomas was my only living adult family member, but it was Lucille who wanted to have me over? My sister-in-law is a perfectly sweet, traditional lady with whom I have no qualms, but the girl's not exactly my soul mate. I preferred the idea that Jamil had suggested the invitation, but I knew Thomas would never admit that.

"Well, of course Jack and I both want to see you, too," Thomas replied, chuckling faintly and fondling his coffee cup. "It's just that Lucille runs the household, so all invitations come through her."

Dialing up my response, I edited the Georgian lilt out of my words; it was a reflex action whenever I was with Thomas, who had long ago shed his. "I would love to come over soon," I said. "Once you and I come to an agreement, we'll all be spending more time together anyway."

Thomas pulled his hands away from his cup, straightening his back. "An agreement about what?"

"Thomas, I couldn't wait any longer to tell you. I'm ready to tell Jamil that I'm his real mother. I want a more active role in his life."

Thomas cleared his throat and leaned back in his chair, throwing one leg over the other. "Go on."

"I don't want to shake things up all at once," I said with a strained smile. "You and Lucille have done a wonderful job raising him, and you will always be central to his life."

Thomas's eyes grew colder, more opaque. "Go on."

"You know I have my master's degree now. By the time I finish running this nationally renowned clinic with Dr. Folger, I'll be ready to get certified and write my own ticket. By this time next year, I could go into practice for myself."

"Go on."

"I have my act together. I plan to get a house next year, something with a decent-size yard and in a safe neighborhood with kids Jamil's age."

Thomas finished another sip of coffee, then held up a hand. "Do you want to compare the house you have in mind with mine, Maria?"

His smart-ass question popped me out of "professional" mode. "I ain't competing with you," I said, hearing a touch of my accent return as my chest grew pimply with goose bumps. "I'll never make two hundred thousand like you, but I'll be able to provide very well for any children I raise."

"And you want to raise Jack."

The clamp on my emotions popped open. "Stop calling him that!" I rooted my eyes to my brother's. "Jamil is still my son, and I never agreed to a legal name change."

"You see, right here," Thomas said, his voice filling with gravel as he shoved his coffee aside and began tapping the table with a long index finger. "This is why you're still not ready to raise your son, Maria. What businessman in his right mind is going to hire a *Jamil*? You might as well stamp the word *ghetto* on his forehead. You're an academic—haven't you heard about the recent employment studies? Résumés with ethnic-sounding names get tossed!"

A familiar wave of nausea swept me as I stared back at Thomas. "That's what I named him, and since you've never made the name change official, his name is still *Jamil*."

"What the hell were you thinking anyway, coming up with that name? Mee-maw probably rammed a fist through her coffin when you stuck that child with *Jamil*. We have called him Jack since the day you dropped him on our doorstep, and that is what he answers to now."

"That doesn't make it right." I let my words hang in the air for emphasis and wiped a tear from my eye. "You don't think I know Jamil loves you and Lucille? I see it in his eyes every time I go over to your house. I respect that." It was true, even if there were nights I prayed Jamil would show more interest, more curiosity, more *something* in me. I longed for the day when he would ask me why we looked so much alike.

Not my baby, though. Jamil—who wears my clear, rich chocolate complexion; my wide, brown-gray eyes; and his father's button nose—loves Thomas and Lucille to death. In his young mind and safe little world, they are unquestionably Mommy and Daddy.

I inhaled slowly, picturing myself in the sanctified calm of my yoga studio. "I do want him back, Thomas, okay? I want him back with me, full-time, all the time. But I know better than to expect that right now."

"So what is your point?"

I started to pull at my locket again, the closest thing to a family heirloom I've got. "In addition to letting him know the truth, I want to start spending time with him again, that's all. Let me keep him one weekend a month. Or, what if I just have him for a week or two this summer? I can take several days off and take him camping, to the zoo, maybe take in a Braves game—"

"Jack's seven years old, in case you've forgotten. He's just started playing tee ball—he's not following professional teams yet. Camping? He hates the outdoors. He's a very intelligent, bookish boy."

"You make him sound like you." I knew my tone was dismissive, knew I was headed somewhere I shouldn't go, but pain had gripped my soul and forced my lips wide open. "He's not, Thomas. You do realize that, don't you? A history lesson: you and Lucille can't have kids. That was why I let you raise Jamil in the first place. But we agreed it would be a joint effort. That's all I'm asking for."

Thomas's head had dipped momentarily during my tirade, but he recovered quickly. "Very easy for you to be smug now, isn't it? You weren't so cocky the night you brought a three-month-old child to our door, crying about that sorry-ass nigger that knocked you up."

I felt familiar drops of rain splash onto the top of my head, ping off my shoulders, and sprinkle my nose, the way they had the night I carried a blanketed, squealing Jamil up Thomas and Lucille's driveway. I gripped the table's black lacquer, so strong was the recall of that moment. I could go days sometimes without it crossing my mind, then lose a complete night's sleep reliving it.

I could barely see straight that night. I had broken my pledge again, stopping by a convenience store on the way home from Jamil's sitter's house. First there had been my latest migraine headache, then Jamil's colic—then my boyfriend, Guy McCutcheon, made the day a hat trick of nightmares. A late-morning phone call from his probation officer confirmed that I was on my own with this parenting thing.

"I don't know when his ass is getting out this time," the raspy-voiced, older white man had said candidly. "First he's carting heroin around—then he has the nerve to pull a gun on the arresting officer? Don't plan your life around him."

I returned from Jamil's sitter that afternoon, placed my screaming baby into his shabby crib, and emptied a six-pack of beer, one can following right behind the other. My fourth "fall" in three months of motherhood, after staying clean and sober throughout an unplanned pregnancy. I had loved Jamil enough to abstain while he was inside me; once he was out, though, my resolve had gone bye-bye.

That hard truth drove me to Thomas's in a huff, self-disgust oozing from my pores. I needed time to get *me* together. Young and dumb, I pictured a day would come when Thomas would give me my baby back, once I finished school and at least hid my demons as well as he did. Seven years and I was still waiting.

Thomas scooted closer to me, leaning across the table and masterfully keeping his voice low. "What did I tell you, Maria? We would help out, keep you from having to drop out of college, but in return we would raise Jack as our child."

I tasted the bitterness of my own tears as Thomas continued.

"We've held up our end of the deal. You're the one breaking it by making demands now." His seat creaking under the shifting of his weight, Thomas stood. "You've finally made some strides in life, little sister. I suggest you don't throw them away by complicating your life with a lawsuit. I will not let Lucille's heart be broken by your attempts to steal Jack away." He looked down the bridge of his wide nose at me, as if he could squash me with his shoe. "Don't forget—unlike us, you can always have more children. You think very carefully before we talk again."

I reached for words and found none as Thomas whipped past me, then out the front door. Sitting there, a shaft of sunlight painting my face through the window, I blotted my tears with a napkin and shut my eyes, picturing our grandmother, Mee-maw. My angel.

Mee-maw raised Thomas and me a few miles west of downtown in her wood-framed, two-bedroom house. Raised us as long as she could, at least. She died when I was in seventh grade, as the combination of her diabetes, hypertension, and kidney failure caught up to her.

Tall, stooped, and hobbled by a bad foot, Mee-maw always pushed us to crawl out of the hole life had pitched us into. Her daughter, Rosie, who had abandoned me and Thomas shortly after my birth, hadn't been heard from since leaving Atlanta to flee robbery charges, and our father (or fathers, if you believed neighborhood gossip) was a complete mystery. I had my own reasons to suspect he had been an Afro-Cuban, but they weren't based on any birth certificate. The closest thing I had to a piece of him was my locket, a triangular piece of silver emblazoned with what Mee-maw believed was the image of a Yoruba priestess. It was a gift from my father to my mother, one she had left behind.

If not for Mee-maw, Thomas and I probably wouldn't even be in touch today. "Even iffin' it's only half a bloodline," she had said once in a nod to the rumors, "it's more than you'll have with anyone else you meet. Stay true to each other." The fact we had even met today showed Mee-maw's words hadn't gone totally unheeded, but in our own way, Thomas and I had spent the years since her death fleeing our shared past. Far as I could see, my brother had morphed into a robot—brilliantly rocking his intelligence and living the privileged life we'd never experienced as kids, but shutting everyone other than Lucille and Jamil out of his inner life. Especially me.

Who was I to judge, though? While Thomas had drowned his abandonment in textbooks and computer screens, I had turned for comfort to Guy, a spoiled, drug-soaked mess who hadn't seen his son since Jamil was a few weeks old.

What I didn't understand was why I had to keep paying for my sins, while Thomas went his merry way transforming my son from

Jamil into *Jack*. I had paid my dues, hadn't I? Made my way through college and grad school. Networked my way into assisting a leader in my field. What else remained? What would make me worthy of getting my child back?

You can always have more children. Thomas made it sound so simple, but unlike him, I had no Lucille, no solid partner waiting to help me raise a new life. Plenty of brothers I knew would gladly help me manufacture a baby, but I'd be on my own for the rest of the journey. I'd learned the hard way that I couldn't handle the pressures of single motherhood; with Jamil, I'd nearly repeated the cycle Rosie began with me and Thomas.

I'd seen enough in life to throw away my rose-colored glasses. Forget love—I had to get my career on solid ground, prove that I'd earned the right to reveal my identity to Jamil. I couldn't waste precious energy searching for a soul mate that clearly didn't exist anyway. Two years I'd been celibate, and I'd stay that way for five more before messing with someone who might threaten my ability to bond with my son.

I stayed there in my seat at Starbucks, losing all concept of time. There'd be no new children for me. I just wanted the one I already had.

4

Deacon

I beat up my kid's principal. Can you get any more ghetto than that? Any more of this, and I'd take over the black sheep mantle from Miles, my older brother. Feeling like I needed an owner's manual to this thing called life, I was desperate to get out of Chicago.

After fleeing Dejuan's school, I returned to my parents' old home and packed furiously after scheduling an earlier flight back to Atlanta. My sister Darlene was away studying at Northwestern for the evening, so I was on schedule to escape before she arrived full of nosy questions. I was sure Candy had probably called her already to complain about my attack on Byron.

A little before four, I grabbed my garment bag and laptop, shut off the upstairs lights, set the alarm system, and let myself out the garage door. I had shut it behind me and was locking it when a hand gripped my shoulder. "Don't move, Mr. Davis."

I inhaled on instinct, shut my eyes, and felt a stream of whispered four-letter words tumble from between my lips. Byron had said he'd get me, so I wasn't surprised the police had finally come. Granted, in a city like Chicago, you might think they had concerns more urgent than a nonfatal assault on a 250-pound grown-ass man, but Byron was an educator with connections.

My stomach muscles flexed tight, my brow wrinkling, I raised my hands overhead. "Can I see a badge, Officer? I p-promise, I won't resist."

The policeman, a lanky white guy around my age, stepped around in front of me and held his badge forward. "You are Deacon Davis, right? I thought I recognized you from the last time I caught you on ESPN."

"That's me."

"You can put your hands down, sir," the officer said, his expression still businesslike. "My partner and I here," he said, tipping his head toward a police car slowly cruising up my parents' driveway, "we're just here to ask some questions, document your side of the altercation that occurred between you and Mr. Collins."

"Oh, God." My hands on my knees, I bent over for a minute, trying to believe it had come to this. It looked like Byron wanted his pound of flesh, not that I could exactly blame him. Yeah, Miles–whose skeletons include a conviction for heroin possession and an embezzlement charge–had competition for family jackass now.

"Mr. Davis," the officer said as I reared up to my full height, "your uncle insisted on coming along for the ride. As long as you answer our questions respectfully, we'll be out of your hair shortly–then you can give him a ride home."

"Huh?" I looked at the police car again and saw my uncle James climb from the backseat, looking like the stately AME pastor and local power broker he was. Staying just a step behind the other officer, Uncle James habitually smoothed the fabric of his sharp beige suit and straightened his red power tie. Watching all six feet four inches and 250 pounds of him, I cooled out just a bit.

"Don't smile at me, boy!" Uncle James shouted as he bounded toward me. He was glaring right through me, had not one touch of levity in his voice. His presence was so powerful, both police officers stood mute as he stepped up to me, surveying my clothing. "You do realize you're nobody's football star anymore? You're a normal peon now."

I didn't appreciate his little crack on my worn, pockmarked Steelers jersey and sweatpants, relics from my glory years in Three Rivers Stadium, but you'd best believe I kept my mouth shut. I wasn't the only Davis with a temper.

Running a hand through my unkempt head of kinky curls, I tried small talk instead. "So you're back from Africa already." As chairman of my father's empowerment organization, Communities in Action, Uncle James had spent the past two weeks in West Africa, at the invitation of the Congressional Black Caucus.

My uncle planted his feet but kept up his unnerving stare. "The

congressional folk sent me home a couple days early, which was fine
by me. Two weeks away from a good hamburger was too long. Deacon, what are you doing assaulting Dejuan's principal?"

I stared over my uncle's head. "It's complicated."

"Well, you won't be explainin' it to me first. You may as well can-
cel your little flight for now. Let's go inside and educate the officers
about your behavior."

It wasn't easy, but I completed the task. I sat in the bright, airy
kitchen with both officers and detailed my side of things: Byron's inappropriate discussion of both my late father and my divorce during
the parent-teacher conference, his browbeating ways with Candy, and
his mockery of my stutter. The more I talked, the more annoyed I could
tell the cops were with being dragged into this, especially when Officer
Wetzel, the one who'd welcomed me outside, mentioned that Byron
hadn't suffered any real injuries. After twenty minutes or so, they'd finished their interrogations and stood from the table. "Okay, Mr. Davis,"
Wetzel said, "we'll ask you not to leave town until we've had the chance
to file the reports for both you and Mr. Collins tomorrow."

Uncle James, who had been somewhere else in the house during
my interrogation, reappeared in the doorway leading to the family
room, a cordless phone in his hand. "Gentlemen," he said, "you did
speak with Mr. Collins earlier, right?" When the officers nodded, he
smiled. "Great, then you'll recognize his voice." He held the phone
out toward Wetzel. "He's on the phone, wants to speak to you."

"Thank you," Wetzel said, taking the phone and retreating to the
family room. Before Uncle James and the other officer had gotten
past a minute discussing the weather, Wetzel resurfaced.

"He's dropping the charges," Wetzel said, a weary, amused look on
his soft-featured face. "He may have been swayed by what I shared of
your account, Mr. Davis, but I think his mind was already made up."
He grinned at his partner. "We're outta here."

Still trying to make sense of Byron's change of heart, I stayed
moored at the kitchen table while Uncle James glad-handed the cops
and saw them out. A minute later, the smell of my uncle's English
Leather cologne told me he was standing over me again.

"I helped Byron get that principal's job," Uncle James said, as if noting it was raining outside. "I got him to back off, especially when I reminded him of his own immaturity."

My mouth opened, but no words would come. My sense of shame was too great, I guess.

"With that handled," he said, still looking ready to strangle me, "you now get to deal with me." When I didn't reply, he asked, "What kind of devil spirit has crawled up into you?"

"I know there's no excuse for what I've done. I'll make it right."

"Well, you'd better," Uncle James replied, taking a seat across from me. "You ain't caused this much trouble since you married Mercedes."

With the exception of bringing Dejuan into the world, I had invoked my parents' wrath only one other time: the day I brought Mercedes into the family. Despite the fact that I'd found the apparent woman of my dreams—fly, fine, and ambitious—Mother was immediately skeptical, concerned by Mercedes's sketchy past. Orphaned in her childhood, Mercedes claimed to have been reared by several different foster families in the D.C. area. That little explanation had bothered me at first, I guess, but once I got Mercedes pregnant, I didn't see any point quibbling. I loved her, she was having my child, and I wanted to put a ring on that finger.

My father had backed off, but that wasn't good enough for Mother; she hired a private detective, who unearthed court records showing that Mercedes had filed for legal emancipation as a teenager. Turned out the father she'd sued to escape was Big Walter Chance, a notorious D.C.-area coke dealer. That made for some ugly days. If we hadn't revealed we were already expecting with my daughter, Liza, I doubt Mother would even have attended the ceremony.

Despite my occasional stumbles, though, I was into new depths now. "Uncle James," I said, my back straight and my gaze steadied, "you shouldn't have stood up for me with Byron. That was on me."

"I take care of my own," Uncle James snapped. "May you use your powers to help someone less fortunate someday. Now get me a glass of water."

I went to the sink, started running the filtered water tap, then braved a look over my shoulder. "Candy called you, right?" I knew she had, because since I had moved to Atlanta, Uncle James had been Candy and Dejuan's main source of moral support, serving as a surrogate father and grandfather, much like he'd done for me since my father's death.

"Yes, Candy called me," Uncle James said, pausing to drain his glass of water. "She actually called me around the time I heard about your resignation from the Dream Party. Let me get this straight, Deacon. First, you let Miriam Lloyd use one bad television performance to goad you into resigning your job. Then, you drive poor Candy into a panic by starting a fight at Dejuan's school. Son, I have a sad truth to tell you."

"What?"

"Your momma was apparently sleeping with the mailman the year you were conceived, 'cause no Davis behaves like this."

I laughed off my uncle's jab, relieved to see him wipe that forbidding frown off his face, but things quickly turned serious again. First he reminded me of all the accomplishments in my "young" life: speaking at the 1996 Democratic National Convention and the Million Man March, being voted onto three NFL Pro Bowl teams, even writing the most popular speech of my father's presidential campaign. Uncle James couldn't understand how I'd let Miriam and Errick pressure me into resigning over one failed media appearance.

I shrugged off my past accomplishments, especially the big speeches. "Scripted speeches are easy for me, just like how James Earl Jones never stutters when he's acting. Speaking off the top of my head has always been the bigger challenge."

Uncle James wasn't hearing it. He couldn't believe that Errick had sided with Miriam against me, but he was more disappointed in me for not fighting them both. The truth was that in the moment, I was too burdened by shock to fight back; the fight in me erupted in Byron's office.

"You may as well know," Uncle James said, wiping his furrowed brow, "I'm not letting Miriam or Errick get away with this. You know Miriam's giving him your job, don't you?"

"I'm not surprised," I said, my jaw muscles flexing suddenly. I had figured that my cousin, a former star salesman for Microsoft and a proven fund-raiser for Communities in Action, would make Miriam's shortlist. It wasn't until that moment that I realized I'd hoped family loyalty would keep Errick from accepting her offer. So much for blood versus water.

"You see," Uncle James said, shaking a thick finger in my face, "this is why your father's legacy will be in better hands with you instead of Errick." He sighed, settling back into his seat. "I love that boy as much as I love you, but he doesn't have your integrity."

"Yeah well," I replied, shifting in my seat, "Errick doesn't stutter."

"There's the mailman's whiny genes again," Uncle James replied. "Playtime's over, son. If you want to continue your daddy's work someday, Deacon, you better deal head-on with this stuttering thing. It's not that big of a deal—Moses stuttered for one, not to mention most of us preachers stutter on purpose when we're in the pulpit—but if you're so ashamed of it, you'd let Errick kick you out of your job, it's a problem."

"The damn thing's got me tied in knots, Uncle James," I said, my voice just above a whisper. "I'm tired of fighting it, hiding it."

"I understand, son. It ain't like I don't know it's a tough thing." Without mentioning his name, my uncle had referenced the elephant in the room: Granddad, my uncle's father, was found swinging from a makeshift noose of extension cords when I was thirteen. No one likes to talk about why, but I've always guessed the humiliations of his knotted tongue were involved.

Handing me his empty glass, Uncle James stood. "Confront this, Deacon. If there's any way I can help, you let me know. Once you get your hands around this, you're welcome to come work for me at Communities in Action, at least until I retire." Uncle James smiled ruefully as he sprang his surprise on me, saying he planned to resign from Communities in Action and pastor his church, Olive Street AME, full-time. "Someone's going to have to take my place in a couple years, and if you and Errick don't have your acts straight, Miriam Lloyd and her goons will gladly take over." As biased as Uncle James was toward Miriam, I knew he was right; Miriam had dated my father before he met my mother, and rumor was the dating continued into my teens. As a result, Miriam acted as if she had as much claim to Frederick's legacy as I did.

"There's another reason you need to get yourself straight," my uncle continued when I nodded silently. "Your brother's back on his conspiracy soapbox again. He just can't let your father rest in peace."

"It's not like we all don't have questions," I said, sinking my front teeth into the flesh of my lower lip, "but he doesn't need to go about it like this." Nothing my older brother did surprised me anymore. Frederick Miles Davis was that rare black sheep whose scandalous ways were matched only by the strength of his intellect. Only Miles could win my father's old House congressional seat at the age of twenty-six, then lose it three years later after being caught with a condo full of narcotics and call girls. Only Miles could survive that embarrassment to earn a master's in journalism from Columbia and emerge as an investigative journalist with bylines in the *New York Post,* the *Chicago Sun-Times,* and *Vibe.* His latest of many nutty crusades to come: proving that our father's death was an assassination, despite the fact that police and FBI investigations found no evidence of arson or other criminal intent.

"Have you heard he signed some book deal with Time Warner?" Uncle James shook his head as if he still couldn't believe Miles's antics. "I've already put a call in to your mother, pushing her to talk some sense into the boy, but you know she's pretty hands-off."

He was right. I love Mother dearly, but she's never really dealt with Frederick's death. We all looked up a few months after his funeral to see that she'd eloped with Roberto, a Dominican businessman. Even when we were children, she was a protective but distant caretaker, and once we hit eighteen, she seemed convinced we could fend for ourselves.

I raised an eyebrow. "You want *me* to put Miles in check—is that what you're asking?"

Uncle James shrugged, his hands upturned. "When you're ready, after you get some help for your own issues. Just don't take too long, unless you want me to handle Miles in my own way, which wouldn't be pleasant for him or for me."

"I'll handle him, Uncle James," I said, "once I find a good speech therapist. I'm through letting this thing rule me." As I stared into my uncle's concerned eyes, I felt my father's spirit lurking nearby. I had experienced many highs and lows in my young life, but none of them compared to the night Mother telephoned me with the news of Frederick's death in that fire. If it had happened a few weeks earlier, before his historic presidential campaign won 8 percent of the national vote, I would have lined up with Miles and the crackpots who claimed the fire was a cover for his assassination. As it was, it just felt like a cruel, pointless tragedy.

My head wasn't right for weeks after my father's death. I didn't just lose a father and a true hero; I lost a friend, as well. The rare father who demanded respect but insisted we kids call him by his first name once we turned eighteen, as a sign of our responsibility to interact with others as equals. It wasn't just show, either: Frederick was always busy as hell, but never too tied up to deliver a pep talk over the phone or have a famous friend drop by with words of inspiration.

The only thing that powered me through that loss was a sense of duty, a call to continue my father's work. I had no idea how to get back into position to fulfill that duty, but I had my wake-up call now. Uncle James had staked the Davis family legacy on a favor today, saving both me and Dejuan from the consequences of my attack on Byron. I wasn't exactly sure how, but I had to honor that.

5

Maria

After working ten-hour days for three straight weeks, I treated myself and left the clinic right at five, intent on getting to Jamil's baseball game. As I pulled out of the parking garage and headed for the expressway, I had plenty of food for thought. Just before I left, Ramsey had bragged about a last-minute client he'd landed for the Speech Recovery Clinic.

He'd hit me with the news after grilling me about last-minute details, including our arrangements with Clark Atlanta University, where we were hosting the clinic, as well as whether all the clients had paid their invoices in full. "I know we start the clinic in a couple of days, but it was worth adding this young brother in." He had leaned in close, his breath tickling my cheek. "Have you heard of Deacon Davis?"

I recognized the name immediately, though less from the man's days in the NFL than from a profile I read of his family in *Ebony* years ago. I'd also read about his father in my college political science course, and had a girlfriend who worked on one of Frederick Davis's congressional campaigns. When Ramsey started yapping on about Deacon's impressive football career, I shut him up by saying I hadn't followed the game since my first boyfriend worshipped Troy Aikman and the Dallas Cowboys. Ramsey's eyes jumped at my first-ever reference to a love life, and I held my breath. Discussing Guy, whose only positive contribution to the world was Jamil, was like gargling with castor oil. I was so determined to forget him that I hadn't even responded to the letters he'd been sending the last few years, since his release from prison. He had apparently moved to Macon, where he was working as a barber. Each letter claimed he'd turned his life around and begged for my forgiveness. *Not hardly.*

Ramsey let me off the hook for my ignorance about football, talking incessantly about all we could gain by helping Deacon. "If we can untwist the boy's tongue," he'd said, "the sky is the limit for this young man. Apparently he's helping rebuild his father's political party. Can you imagine the profile he'll have if he succeeds? He might eventually run for office himself." A dreamy look had glistened in Ramsey's eyes. "Yes, he's standing there announcing his exploratory committee a few years from now, in the well of the Capitol Building, just before some kook tries to assassinate him, and he's thanking Ramsey Folger for helping him control his stuttering. I can taste the recognition now."

I just stared back, a taunting smile on my face. "Doctor, some days there's not enough space to fit you and your ego in the same room."

Ramsey insisted he was serious, pointing out how a satisfied Deacon Davis could help expose the clinic to black power brokers across the country. "We could get enough funding to offer free treatment to underprivileged stutterers, especially young brothers and sisters," he insisted. "It's important we keep Deacon in line, make sure he gets the most from this program, okay?"

That's when he explained that Deacon hadn't exactly signed up for the SRC by choice. To hear Ramsey, Deacon was a "damn hothead," one who'd probably be our most rebellious client. Apparently, that's where I would come in. "I need you to use your feminine wiles with him, Maria. Keep him as passive as possible so we can reach inside that head and fix his wiring."

When I asked what exactly qualified me for this task, as opposed to the six other clinic staff, Ramsey smiled wide. "Word is, a nice-looking female will carry incredible influence." He frowned at the cocked eyebrow I threw him. "Look, I am not asking you to flash him your breasts or anything improper. Just sidle up to him every now and then, show that gorgeous smile, make small talk, encourage him. That sort of thing. Can you help me out?"

Replaying the conversation in my head, I turned Ramsey's request over in my mind as I came to the I-78 on-ramp. I felt a little offended, honestly, but by now I understood that my boss, who had developed the most effective intensive therapy program in the country, had not gotten where he was by being politically correct. On top of that, he'd revealed earlier in the week that his second wife, Wanda, had filed for divorce after he'd caught her having an affair. After losing his first wife, Brenda, to breast cancer, Ramsey would soon be a single father again to his teenage daughters. He had a lot on him. I could be Pollyanna and rip him up and down for his sexist request, or I could keep my focus on the facts.

The SRC had changed hundreds of lives; I had seen examples up close and personal the past few months. Most recently I'd met a twenty-one-year-old single mother. This poor sister stuttered from the day she could talk; in high school, it took her ten seconds to get each word out. When Ramsey found her, she'd just been stripped of her welfare benefits after losing her fourth fast-food job. By the time I met her, she was a beaming, confident lady with no more than a slight slur and hesitation to her speech. Before meeting her, I'd assumed women who looked like me couldn't stutter. In six years of schooling in speech therapy, I had worked with male clients of every race, plus a sprinkling of predominantly white women. I hadn't seen one sister with a knotted tongue.

Ramsey had that type of touch, though: no matter how rare or unique the case, he could usually treat it.

I replayed more examples of Ramsey's handiwork as I continued east down the highway. My apprehension about exactly what he wanted me to do with Deacon Davis melted; I would help the cause, but respect myself at every step.

As I pulled into a gravel lot in McCurdy Park, my resolve about supporting the SRC deepened. Love, persistence, and desperation flooded me, deepening my conviction. I needed to be the best speech therapist possible for two reasons: the goodwill of my clients and the love of my son.

On the baseball field across from me, Jamil stepped up to home plate. His plastic navy blue helmet sat awkwardly on his little head. Lopsided, it looked like it had been made for someone twice his age.

As my beautiful boy eyed the batting tee that sat on home plate, I chuckled at his round little belly.

Jamil certainly hadn't inherited any fat gene from his father. As a naïve high school junior, one of the things that drew me to Guy—in addition to his carefree, wisecracking charisma, his creamy high yellow skin and baby face, and his curly head of jet-black hair—was his bowlegged, wiry build. As a dark-skinned girl who bought into the "damn near white is right" myth for a while, I had seen a lot about Guy that appealed to me then, so much that I'd convinced myself he would outgrow his little hobbies. As if selling weed and robbing liquor stores in order to resell the alcohol were really "hobbies." That's young, dumb love for you.

I broke from my swim in history when Jamil took another swing at the tee. His bat smacked the ball into the dirt, where it hopped eagerly toward the tall, skinny first baseman. The fielder nabbed the ball with ease and stabbed the white square bag with his foot before Jamil was halfway down the baseline.

I stepped from my car as Jamil wrestled his helmet off his head and trudged back to the dugout. Trying to keep my smile in check, I walked up to the low fence lining his team's wooden bench. "Hey, how's my special man doing?"

Jamil, who had just set his helmet down and accepted a couple of back pats from his teammates, turned suddenly. "Auntie Maria!" His lips spread ear to ear, and he hopped over to the fence. "You see me hit that ball?"

"Yes, I did," I said, palming his head, which Thomas had shaved nearly bald. Another case of my brother stamping his personal style onto his "son."

"They got me out, but that's okay. I'm still one of the best batters on the team."

"Stop bragging, Jack." A big, beefy kid next to him punched Jamil on the shoulder, then looked up at me. "He's all right. He's just slow when he runs the bases."

"This is my auntie, man. I have to make her proud."

I smiled, pressing down my irritation at hearing the fat kid call my baby Jack. I'd never get used to that.

Jamil leaned against the fence, nuzzling his head near my face. "How'd you know I was here?"

"Well, let's keep this our secret, okay?" I had come only because I knew Thomas was out of town and Lucille usually had a church usher meeting on Wednesdays. "I just wanted to make a surprise visit to my favorite little man."

"Okay. Can we get ice cream afterwards?"

"Well, your mom is still coming to pick you up. I'll make you a deal, though. We'll take a weekend soon and do whatever you want, okay? I'll even make a special meal for you." I knew exactly what I'd make, too–a platter of my Cuban favorites, all aimed at encouraging Jamil's interest in his heritage: boiled, seasoned yucca; fried bananas; black beans and rice; and roast pork.

"Awesome. Are you coming over for Independence Day?" Before I could answer, Jamil looked over his shoulder as another ball cracked off a bat. On the field, a kid had hit into a double play, meaning his team's turn at bat had ended.

"We have to go back on the field," Jamil said apologetically.

"I'll be waiting right here," I said, hoping my voice didn't catch. At least I wouldn't have to answer Jamil's question. No way would I be welcome to celebrate July Fourth with Thomas and Lucille.

I stood there, still trying to catch my breath, when someone tapped my shoulder. I looked to my left and sighed plaintively at my old friend, Alicia Winters.

"Hey, girl," Alicia whispered, her braided red hair glistening in the sunlight. "Put a smile on that face. I didn't hip you to this so you could play sad sack."

"Alicia, please," I said, shaking her hand off my shoulder.

"I'm serious," she replied, her blue eyes narrowing. "What if Jamil sees you staring at him with that look on your face? Don't complicate the boy's life, Maria."

"I already did that the day I gave him to Thomas and Lucille."

"He looks perfectly well adjusted to me. That's why you ain't challenged them for custody."

Alicia's words flipped a switch in me, made me feel like a stove burner suddenly turned up to HIGH. Fingering my Yoruba priestess locket, I turned deliberately toward my white buppie friend. Love her or leave her, she was the closest thing I had to a sister in this life. When we were kids, Alicia's family lived two doors down from Meemaw's. Once my grandmother passed, the Lelands helped Thomas raise me; many of my days began with breakfast at their house and ended with dinner in the same place. Alicia's mom even bought most of my school clothes.

Looking into Alicia's eyes, I flicked a finger over my shoulder. "Let's go talk, at my car."

Alicia shrugged and followed me, her low heels clacking against the gravel lot. When I reached my car, I leaned against a window and pointed a finger toward her face. "For the record, you don't know why I haven't challenged for custody," I said, feeling my restraint slip. "So stop running your damn mouth about it."

Alicia crossed her arms over her short-sleeve silk blouse. "Take it easy. God, you need to get you some."

Alicia and I had a funny rapport, one that traced back to our teens. She was always the fast, flirty white girl sleeping with every brother on the block, while I was the more cautious, conservative sister sporting pigtails. While I kept my legs closed until senior year, Alicia had experienced every flavor of neighborhood boy (and man, if you count anyone over eighteen) by tenth grade. We usually respected each other's differences—we had even done each other's hair for years—but I was tiring of my "sister" and her flip attitude.

"Stop talking like we're in high school, Alicia. Maybe if you hadn't had those 'peanut butter' legs of yours, so easy to spread, you wouldn't be saddled with two kids already." I admit, I was tripping by going there on her. In candid moments, Alicia admitted to feeling like she and Trent had started their family too early. She was certain she'd lost her shot at a promotion to district sales manager while carrying Trent Jr., and having Brian eighteen months later had stalled her climb again. I met the sudden, defensive glare in her eyes and stood my ground. "This isn't about how much sex I've had. It's about you making light of my life."

Alicia twisted her neck, looking away from me before biting her lip. "If you're gonna act like this every time we discuss Jamil, I'll just butt the hell out."

My eye contact didn't waver. "Maybe that's best."

"Whatever." She began to walk past me—then I lost my nerve and put a hand on her shoulder.

"Look, can we wave a white flag or something?" I couldn't let her go like this; the girl had looked out for me today, hipping me to Jamil's involvement in this summer camp. Trent Jr. was in the same camp, and when he mentioned seeing Jamil, Alicia called me, knowing I hungered for any chance to see my baby without Thomas and Lucille lurking nearby. "I'm just sensitive right now, girl. I told Thomas I'm ready to tell Jamil the truth, even take him back if they'll let me, but I don't totally have my act straight yet. I'll be certified soon, but I've still got major college loans. Even if Thomas offered, I probably wouldn't be the best person to provide for Jamil full-time."

Reaching toward her shoulder, Alicia covered my hand with her own. "I know you're still pissed about Thomas rejecting you. You just have to be patient, girl, give him time to work something out with you."

The tight muscles around my mouth relaxing, I glanced at the gravel beneath my feet. "You're right, I just—"

Alicia looked over her shoulder with a swift jerk. "Um, get in your car."

"What?"

"I said get your bulbous little ass in your car. Trust me."

I looked over Alicia's shoulder toward the field just in time to see Thomas roll into the lot, pushing his gleaming new Ford Taurus. It was like hot lead had been poured down my throat. "Oh, God."

"Get in the car and move it, girl. I'll run interference." Alicia shooed me violently as I opened the car door and slipped inside. As I started the engine, I paused long enough to see Alicia run around behind Thomas's car. I knew she'd flap her gums or stand on her head for him, whatever it took to give me some cover.

That's when I heard a knock on my passenger's side window. My foot lingering over the gas, I couldn't help but reflexively glance toward the sound. Staring at me, her eyes blazing and her neck muscles flexing anxiously, my sister-in-law, Lucille, rapped on the window again.

I jerked my head back to the left, saw Thomas climbing out of his Taurus. He was shooing Alicia away, peering instead toward Lucille and me.

I looked back at Lucille, who was too prim and proper to look frightful, but now had her hands planted on her hips. It took me a second to make sure Lucille had stepped back a few inches, and that was all I needed. I punched the gas, zooming toward the park exit.

The Clinic

6

Deacon

Maria had just lowered herself onto me when we heard the knock at my door. Talk about a heart-stopper.

As someone's fist thudded against my dorm room's door, again and again, Maria pulled her satin-soft lips from mine and fixed me with wide eyes. Her eyes had already widened as I'd filled her with little Deacon, but that look of amazement had been replaced by horror. She didn't even whisper the word, just mouthed it: *Who?*

We froze in place, me with my feet on the thin shag carpet, she with her legs wrapped around my thighs. I looked over Maria's glistening shoulder, staring at the door and willing the knocking to stop. No luck.

"D-Deacon?" It was Norm, my suite mate. He and I were neighbors in this little hovel of a dormitory, the temporary home for everyone in Dr. Folger's speech clinic. "D-D-Deacon, c-come on, dude. I can't f-fucking sleep with that noise."

My hands melting into the moist flesh of Maria's precious hips, I turned toward the window, where my portable stereo hummed with the soothing tunes of a Jonathan Butler CD. The music should have provided some privacy, even saved Norm's virgin ears from the sounds of our lust. I'd miscalculated, though; whether or not he'd heard our pants and moans, JB's jazz alone had probably interrupted Norm's sleep.

I guess I'd been a bit of a bully to old Norm in our ten days at the clinic. A twenty-something flooring contractor from Decatur, Indiana, my suite mate had long, stringy, blond hair; a patchy beard; and a simple wardrobe of denim overalls and white T-shirts. His only other prized possession was his collection of Garth Brooks CDs, all of which drove me up the wall. I tried to be patient with him, but whenever I could hear Garth as clearly as if I had him on my own stereo, I would rap the wall between us, loudly. Norm always got the message and turned his stereo down, so he'd earned the right to come after me. His timing was just way off.

Maria still hadn't moved off me, and the renewed look of lust in her eyes hinted that she wasn't going anywhere. I pulled her face back to mine, and she whispered, "If you don't answer, he'll have to assume you're asleep."

I didn't see how the squeaking of my battered little mattress would match up with the impression I was asleep, but I let Maria's words rule for the moment. Norm had apparently given up, so I arched my back anew and ran my hands up and down Maria's soft waistline, firm breasts, and smooth neck as she bobbed up and down, sucking me farther into the warmth between her thighs. Our tongues, then our lips met again and we consumed each other calmly, intently. In the back of my mind, I heard the bed squeaking, heard springs popping, even heard a few gasps escape from Maria, but when passion's ruling, you don't stop to think about repercussions. You also don't figure someone else might be listening in.

"Deacon! Come on now!" A new set of bangs at the door, a new voice. "It's Hector, man. Don't play games. Open up or I'm gettin' my key."

I had barely processed Hector's words, but Maria hopped off me in a pop. A sudden, audible pop—she yanked herself off me so fast. Standing nude in front of my bed, the moonlight from my window coating her voluptuous figure, she looked truly scared for the first time. "Shit," she mouthed before stepping over to my closet quickly. The door stood ajar, and next thing I knew she had stepped inside.

Stuck there on the edge of the bed, naked as she was, I waved my hands in the air frantically. "What now?"

Maria read my lips, then pierced me with a nasty gaze before closing the closet door after her. I had known her for only a week and a half, and only *known* her for a few minutes, but I could read her mind already: *This is your fault. Don't ruin my career.*

She had a point. I was definitely in less danger than she was. For one, I still wasn't sure if I had the patience to follow Dr. Folger's program. Not to mention there was a very real danger of me killing him before the program ended. He was an arrogant little fool.

For Maria, though, this was a life-or-death moment. Hector, a mouthy Mexican, was one of her fellow SRC coordinators, a recent master's graduate working toward certification. He and Maria shared the role of resident assistant, making sure we clients respected Folger's ten thirty curfew and his various other dogmas. A key commandment forbade any "fraternizing" between clients. Folger believed that inter-clinic romance would distract clients from his great wisdom, so all lusts must be checked at the door. It went without saying that flings between staff and clients were out of bounds. Maria and I hadn't planned any of this, but now that it was on, we were in deep doo-doo. If push came to shove, I could probably survive expulsion from the clinic, but this was Maria's career on the line. I couldn't let Hector find her.

"Hector," I said, yawning for his benefit, "I'm coming." Scary thing is, that was almost literally true. Maria had worked me close to the edge just that quickly. It was going to take great concentration to keep from messing myself. Moving quickly but noiselessly, I shoved Maria's blouse, shoes, shorts, and panties under my bed. Where was her bra? I pondered this as I slid on my boxers and pulled my thin navy blue blanket over the sweaty sheets. It smelled like sex in here, and not the kind of solitary enjoyment most dorm rooms saw. Maria's natural peachy scent mingled with my burning incense and her perfume, hanging in the air thickly. I had no way to offset it, so I'd have to keep Hector in the hallway, even if that meant kicking his ass. I stood, took three steps over to the door, and stopped. My brain whirring, I prayed for inspiration as I yanked the door open.

7

Maria

The path that led me to Deacon's bed was full of surprises. Trust me—if I'd realized that first day of the clinic just how much he'd shake up my life, I'd never have crossed the sacred line between therapist and client.

I was in the main lounge of Clark Atlanta's Pfeiffer Hall, conducting a headcount of the SRC clients, when he finally walked into the room. The other fourteen clients—three women and eleven men ranging from age sixteen to forty-five—had arrived on schedule, between eight and eight thirty a.m. It was almost nine when Deacon graced us with his presence.

From his perch on the edge of a maple-colored wooden desk at the front of the room, Ramsey took a mock glance at his gold Rolex. "Well, we can begin now, everyone. Mr. Davis has made time to join us."

As he strode toward the rows of plastic chairs arranged in a circle around Ramsey, Deacon didn't break a stride or a sweat. I stood to Ramsey's left, checking everyone off my attendance list, but I couldn't take my eyes off this man as he approached. If the profiles I'd read in *Sports Illustrated* and *Ebony* were any indication, the man was not only tall, bronze, and handsome, but he also had a good brain sitting atop those impressive cheekbones. Live and in living color, Deacon didn't disappoint. Clean-shaved and ruggedly pretty, he'd be right at home on the cover of an E. Lynn Harris novel.

"Good morning," Deacon said as he reached an open chair. Dressed in a snug rayon short-sleeve shirt, a pair of matching navy blue shorts, and leather sandals, he took a leisurely stretch and slid his long, muscled frame into a seat. He searched Ramsey's face for a second before looking my way, but I shot my gaze back to my checklist before his eyes caught mine. I didn't need the distraction. "Well," he said, smiling as Ramsey stayed silent and stared him down. "Let's go. Cure me, Doc."

Ramsey exhaled, just loudly enough that I could hear, and squeezed my elbow quickly. I got the message: We had a live one here. "We took the opportunity of your tardiness to get acquainted informally, Deacon," Ramsey said, his arms crossed. He stood to his full, diminutive height and walked toward the circle around which the chairs were formed. "Now that you're here, though, I'd like to have everyone introduce themselves formally. Before I infect you with my wisdom, I want you to tell me why you're here." Ramsey flicked a finger toward a balding, pudgy gentleman sitting a few feet from him. "Dr. Bill, start us off."

"Okay," Bill said, wiping his hands on the knees of his khaki slacks. "W-Well, my name is—"

"Stand up," Ramsey said, with enough snap to startle even me. "You're going to take the stage while you're here, people. No more running, no more living in fear. You'll be speaking front and center, understand me?"

"Okay." Bill stood and walked to the center of the circle. "Well, as I said, my name is Bill McCarthy. I'm a pediatrician from Burlington, Vermont, and I—"

Pacing a small trail into the lounge's worn, oatmeal-colored carpet, Ramsey stuck his hand into the air. "A black doctor in Vermont? You must be a lonely man."

"W-Well," Bill said, chuckling, "it's not that bad. I don't find race to be a big issue in Vermont, really."

"That's because there's not enough of us to be scared of, Bill." Ramsey smiled wickedly and looked across the audience, nearly half of which was white. "No offense, folks."

Bill wiped at his forehead, his ebony skin glowing with a thin film of sweat. "What else should I say? Well, I have a wife and a ten-year-old son. We also have two pets—"

"You don't stutter much, Bill," Ramsey said, interrupting again. "Why are you spending five thousand dollars and a month of your life here?"

"Why don't you let him finish? If he didn't stutter before, he damn sure will when you're done with him." Deacon had hopped into the thick of things, unexpected and uninvited. I took a step in his direction, but Ramsey waved me off.

"Mr. Davis, you will have your chance to take me on—trust me." Ramsey walked over to Deacon's chair and took a seat beside him. "Why don't I sit right here, so you can keep me honest while Bill completes his account." He slapped Deacon on the back and didn't flinch when the larger man narrowed his eyes and stared him down. "Okay, Bill, it's all you."

Bill wasn't going to be the poster child for stutterers. First, his stutters were relatively mild—the most he did was press his lips together tightly when saying words starting with *m* or *w*. Second, a wealthy patient of his, who had heard about the SRC and suggested he attend, was paying his clinic tuition. Bill seemed at peace with his speech, but felt that if his patients saw it as a small issue, why not see if he could neutralize it with free help? He had a thriving practice and a new partner to pick up his slack, so he had made the sacrifice to see what would happen.

Ramsey had cultivated a diverse crowd. Some of the more interesting clients were Amberly, a blond college dropout and aspiring flight attendant with the figure of a *Playboy* bunny, who had violent, seizurelike stutters; Sharon, a tight-lipped, middle-aged Italian housewife who sounded like an asthmatic preacher when she hit bad patches; and Terrell, a fifteen-year-old juvenile delinquent whose rapid-fire repetitions disappeared only during his rap performances, which had made him a minor star in south Atlanta.

We had clients who had been homeless, others who'd earned graduate degrees, some who talked nonstop, and others that made you pull words out of them. On top of that, each client stuttered differently from the other. Take away their shared burden of talking differently, and these folks didn't have that much in common.

Deacon's turn arrived. Ramsey had saved him for last, and when his name was called, the fine man rolled his eyes before stepping into the circle. His hands hanging at his side, Deacon looked over all our heads and spoke, his powerful voice filling the room. "My name is Deacon Davis. I am a former football player with the Pittsburgh Steelers. I have degrees in education and public policy, and most recently I was employed as an activist with—"

Deacon interrupted himself and stared over at Ramsey, who sat with a fist in his mouth and his shoulders shaking with laughter. "Don't mind me," he said, waving dismissively and wiping a tear from his eye. "Keep right on, please."

His pupils hardening into coal, Deacon stuck his tongue under the top ridge of his gums before continuing. "I worked most recently as an activist with Communities in Action, an organization with chapters in twelve cities. I have two children, Dejuan and Liza, and—" He glared at Ramsey again. "What the hell is so funny?"

Ramsey looked around at the crowd, even tapped Bill, who sat to his left, on the shoulder. "Bill, do you think Deacon even hears himself? Did you hear what I heard, Bill?"

Bill glanced at the carpet sheepishly and shrugged. I couldn't blame him; I wouldn't have wanted to be on Deacon's bad side either.

Ramsey looked at me, winked, then stood and walked up to Deacon. "He doesn't even hear himself, folks," he said, confidently gripping Deacon by the shoulder. "God bless him, he can't even hear that he's talking—like—this." Ramsey started speaking in staccato, separating each word with a staggered pause. "He—doesn't—realize—that—he—sounds—like—a—robot. It's not natural!

"That's the sound of a man trying *not* to stutter, people, and to be honest, you're all guilty of it. Deacon was lucky enough just now not to stutter while using that trick," Ramsey said, popping Deacon on the back and making a shooing motion toward Deacon's chair, "but he wouldn't be here if that hadn't caught up to him plenty of times in real life. Not to mention, he sounded silly! When I'm done with you, none of you will want to sound like that." Ramsey paused for a moment, seemingly just realizing that Deacon still stood there, staring him down as if he had no plans on returning to his seat. "Go sit down, Deacon. Shoo," he said, waving toward the chair again.

"It w-wouldn't even be a fair fight, would it?" Deacon said, stroking his chin and circling Ramsey slowly. "Nah," he said, stopping abruptly. "You're not even worth it." Before I realized what he meant, Deacon pivoted and stormed out of the circle, passing the chairs in a beeline for the exit.

Ramsey shot me a glance, one requiring no elaboration. As he continued his performance, I jogged behind Deacon and followed him out the door.

I barely got a hand onto his left elbow as I stepped into the hallway. I couldn't actually slow him down, of course, but when he felt my skin against his, he stopped in his tracks.

Deacon turned and faced me abruptly, nearly pinning me against the lounge door. He leaned over so that our faces were parallel, getting close enough that his woodsy cologne and cinnamon-scented breath washed over me. "Are you just the messenger, or can I shoot you?"

"I'm the voice of reason," I said, drawing my back tight and raising up on my toes. At five feet nine, I'm used to being one of the taller women in most settings, so Deacon's height wasn't intimidating. "You and I both know that you're a big deal, Deacon." I clasped my hands together and motioned in his direction. "You've already accomplished things that most of the people in that room, me included, will never experience. If you felt disrespected by Dr. Folger in there, you have to understand, that's just his style, his way of—"

"His way of what? Motivating people?" Deacon stood back a step, pressed his lips together, and shook his head. "Save it, please." He took a fresh look at me, and I could feel him calming down. A little. "What's your name again?"

I held a hand out to him. "I think Dr. Folger was going to introduce the therapists after your introduction. My name's Maria, Maria Oliver."

Deacon rolled his eyes. "Pleasure."

"This will be a good experience for you, Deacon, if you can just be patient with Dr. Folger. I know he's a strong drink of water."

"That's an understatement, sister." Deacon reached up and toyed with his hair, a short 'fro that looked like it was being prepped for braiding or dreadlocks. It reminded me of a tamed version of the sexy singer Maxwell's famous do. "You're cutting your boss too much slack. Don't forget education is what I do, Maria. Even when I was in the NFL, I spent every off season immersed in my graduate course work and substitute-taught also. I know how to m-motivate kids to learn," he said, pointing angrily over my head, "and what he's doing in there is not—" Deacon interrupted himself, inhaled deeply. I sensed he didn't want to stutter on the same word again. "Motivational," he said, releasing the word carefully.

"Just trust me," I said. "Dr. Folger knows what he's doing. He's trying to jog everyone out of their comfort zones right now, and frankly he's probably harsher on you because you bring so much to the plate."

"Oh, thank you," Deacon replied, softly touching a hand to his chest. "That's sweet. I feel *so* affirmed right now."

"Look," I said, feeling my neck twist, "I'm just trying to help you put your emotions in perspective."

The look in his eyes told me I'd tripped a wire. "Trying to help me—what?"

"Don't let how you're feeling right now make you throw away your investment in this clinic. Don't forget whatever drove you here in the first place."

A distant look crept into Deacon's eyes, and he walked over to the metal railing beside the stairwell. He leaned against it and crossed his arms, then shut his eyes. I wondered whether tears were coming, but instead he was simply silent.

I hovered there by the door, a few feet away, and decided to leave him with his thoughts. I had turned back toward the door when I heard him whisper my name.

"This is not a game," he said when I turned back around. His voice stayed low, and while there were no tears, a pained look infected his gaze. "My grandfather's reaction to his stuttering may have killed him. Can you understand I don't want to fall into the same trap?"

I stared back, silent, my mouth just barely staying closed.

"I'm not going out like he did," Deacon whispered as he pushed off the railing and stood upright. "My kids deserve better, my mother deserves better, and so does my father's organization."

I took another step over to Deacon, feeling my eyes mist, and placed a hand on one of his solid, pulsing biceps. "I understand. We're here to help ensure that."

"Go on back inside," he replied, patting my hand gently before removing it from his arm. "The others need you. I'll be there in a minute."

I opened the lounge door and slipped back inside. My professionalism was still intact, but whether he'd meant to or not, Deacon Davis had me wondering about the rest of the story.

8

Deacon

I was minding my business, I swear, out for a late evening run on the clinic's third day, when I nearly stepped in it. By *it* I mean the war of words flying between two women. The sounds of flying fur and raised voices greeted me as I neared Pfeiffer Hall's back entrance. It wasn't until I was literally around the corner, hidden in the shadows, that I realized who was involved.

The other woman sounded older and more tentative, like she hadn't had a good argument in years. "You know you were wrong, Maria."

"I was honest, Lucille. He's your child, too, but he's also mine." The biting, sharp tone was new to me, but I immediately caught Maria's voice.

"We're his guardians, not you." Lucille sounded like an overheated engine, running way too fast and way too jerky to hold up. "Why are you trying to change everything now?"

"Lucille," Maria said, sounding like she'd clenched her teeth, "I'm not having this conversation here. I've called your house three times the last few days, and now you track me down *here* of all places? Just go home, please."

I was intrigued with a capital *I*, but I knew I shouldn't be hearing this. The raging emotions were a little too familiar; frankly, these two sounded tame compared to the knockout bouts I'd had with Mercedes. I wouldn't have wanted folk eavesdropping on us.

The women's voices growing louder, I took another second to wipe my sweaty brow, then pivoted and sprinted back toward the street.

9

Maria

I had my arms crossed. No, *wrapped*. Wrapped around me like a vise, holding me in place. It was the only way to keep from putting my hands on Lucille. I still couldn't believe she had confronted me at work, the one pure area of my life. The one place where my failure as a mother was irrelevant.

"I'm not leaving until you agree to back off, Maria," Lucille said. She yanked her hands from the pockets of her white cotton slacks, punctuating her words with gestures. "I won't have you upsetting Thomas with threats about taking Jamil back, nor will I have you stalking our son at baseball games and other events. That is not acceptable behavior."

A teenage response flitted through my brain: *Accept* this, *Lucille*. "Jamil is my blood. I'm not going to be deleted from his life."

"Thomas keeps cutting himself while shaving," Lucille said suddenly, raking a hand absentmindedly through her thick, bulb-shaped perm.

I was one of only a couple people who knew what that meant. Since Thomas had been in his teens, razor cuts had been a sure sign of stress: they'd popped up on his face when he first took the SATs, the week before his first date, and in the month before he proposed to Lucille. "I know this is hard on Thomas, and on you," I said, a pleading tone creeping into my voice. "I'm just being honest, though. I need to spend more time with my child. Is that so evil?"

"Maria," Lucille said, the whinnying and pitching in her voice easing, "we've never forgotten that you brought Jamil into this world. We want you to be in his life, but we don't think Jamil needs to know you're his birth mother."

"But—"

"Look, I admit that he's still young. At some point, it might make sense. But not now."

Not up for some okeydoke, I crossed my arms over my nylon sweatsuit. "So what would be a good time frame, Lucille?"

Lucille clasped her hands together and slumped against the light-post near the dormitory's back entrance. "What if we hired an arbitrator to draft a formal agreement? Something protecting me and Thomas's parental rights but establishing your rights to visitation."

What she had in mind felt as see-through as Lil' Kim's bras. "Visitation sounds pretty limiting. What if Jamil wants to live with me when he's older?"

"Now, Maria," Lucille replied, her tone frosty and her eyes looking like slits, "are you saying you deserve parental rights, as in rights giving you priority over me and Thomas?"

From the shadows, I thought I heard someone cough. My chest burning with fear that someone from the clinic had overheard us, I lowered my voice. "I'm saying that legally, I have rights as his biological mother, a biological mother who never authorized a formal adoption."

"I know," Lucille said, "but morally, you know Thomas and I have the strongest rights and claims to Jack. We're his legal guardians. We've fed, clothed, and nurtured him his entire life."

Jack. Shaking my head, I removed my sweat jacket, hoping that would dry my underarms. The summer evening had cooled nicely, but Lucille's presence had me feeling like it was still eighty degrees out. "I said I've always respected you for that, Lucille. Hell, I've *loved* you for it. But that doesn't mean all my rights go out the window."

"My sweet Lord," Lucille said, shaking her head wearily, "you just want to take him away from us."

"That's not true."

"You're deceiving yourself, Maria. If you just wanted to 'relate' to Jamil, be his friend, or whatever mushy reasons you keep stating, you'd be happy with visitation."

"You've just been trying to avoid a confrontation all these years," I said before I could stop myself. "None of you love me anyway."

"You don't love yourself." Lucille crossed her arms, seemingly daring me to come at her. "That's why we're the right people to raise Jamil, not you."

"I don't–I don't love myself?" My voice sounded hollow and tinny in my own ears, maybe because my heart was pounding so angrily. "You stupid, square . . . Go home, Lucille. Right now."

"Jamil doesn't need you to raise him," Lucille said, daring me again with her simple presence.

I took a violent step toward Lucille, but stopped short by an inch. "We'll see what the court says about that!" I whirled around and rushed toward the dorm's back door. As much as she'd hurt me, I loved my sister-in-law too much to completely go off on her. I didn't know what might burst out of me.

10

Maria

I was still trembling the next morning, still trying to figure how to stand my ground over Jamil without losing my mind. It didn't help when Ramsey pulled me aside suddenly, as I headed into the campus cafeteria for breakfast.

"Good morning, Ms. Oliver," he said, winking as he steered me away from the line of coeds waiting for their shots at toast, scrambled eggs, and corned beef hash. "I just picked up your cell message from last night—sorry I'm just now getting back to you. What's going on?"

"Oh, yeah," I said, feeling a frown infect my face, "my *other* problem."

Ramsey's nose curled up in concern. "What's wrong?"

"Nothing, nothing. I mean, I was calling you about my assigned client list." The previous morning, Ramsey had officially assigned each therapist three clients to counsel. This meant meeting with your clients, one on one, for a daily debriefing. It was a chance for the therapist to assess the client's progress, and for the client to register any complaints or concerns. I knew all about Ramsey's belief in daily counseling, had no problem with that whatsoever. My problem, especially after Lucille's sneak attack left me so emotionally frayed, was with one name on my list.

"Now, Maria, we had an agreement that you would handle Deacon for me," he said when I asked him to assign our "star" to someone else. "What's changed?"

I would have felt like a teenager if I'd told the truth ("I think he's cute"), so I took a guess and said, "I'm afraid he may find me attractive, Ramsey. Wouldn't that make it hard for me to counsel him effectively?"

Ramsey ran his hands down my shoulders. "Maria, Maria, you're a grown-up. I have no doubt Deacon finds you attractive. What man wouldn't? That doesn't mean he can't learn fluency techniques from you. If he steps out of line, I'm confident you'll keep him in his place."

"I appreciate the vote of confidence," I replied, stepping aside as a gang of students passed. "It's just that I thought it might be simpler to pair Deacon with one of the males. I can still serve as a cheerleader for him, but I don't want to get too close."

Ramsey placed a hand to his chin, surveying me with cool calm. "Nope," he said finally. "You're far too classy a woman to doubt yourself. I have faith in you."

By the time that evening rolled around, I had calmed down some. A little prayer and a bit of improvised yoga freed me of some of the morning's anxiety. Fearing my attraction to Deacon wouldn't solve anything. It was a fact, but it didn't hold any cosmic power over me. Besides, it wasn't likely that the interest was mutual. A man with his looks, not to mention his accomplishments, had his choice of women. He was at the SRC for the sole purpose of getting his speech under control, and I doubted I was fine enough to distract him from that mission.

Once Deacon had taken a seat across from me, at a table in the far corner of the now-deserted cafeteria, we discussed the day's exercises. With the smell of burnt tuna noodle casserole hanging in the air, we discussed Ramsey's overview of the program's strategies, which had incorporated his theories on the causes of stuttering.

When Deacon was uncharacteristically silent at first, I asked, "What do you think is the most common cause of stuttering?" I was hoping to get him talking about his own experiences, get him to connect his journey with Ramsey's theories.

"I think it's physiological, something different in our wiring," he said with no hesitation. "So many people want to make it about whether we're nervous, or weak, or emotionally screwed up, but I think that's way off base."

We talked about evidence that supported Deacon's belief, including some recent neurological studies, and then I decided to bring up a topic that had been on my mind. "Would you say that you and your grandfather's stuttering had the same cause?"

When Deacon's eyes grew cold and his forehead reddened, I was afraid the first words out of his mouth would be unfit for print. He sighed and grimaced, fiddling with his soda cup, then finally raised his eyes to meet mine. "The only thing I feel certain of," he said, "is that I inherited this from him, so I guess that would make it the same cause."

I clasped my hands respectfully, inviting him to open up. "What do you know about how your grandfather coped with the stuttering?"

Deacon shook his head, sighed again, then reached for his leather backpack. "Most of what I know, I know from the one letter he ever wrote me."

Deacon

I surprised myself when I pulled out Granddad's letter. I'd packed it the night before leaving for the clinic, but hadn't planned to show it to Maria or anyone else until I was farther along in the program. The emotions it raised were too raw, too private.

Maria looked at the yellowing, crumpled sheets as they lay in my hand. "When did he write this?"

"When I was in junior high. My mother gave it to me, with hardly a word spoken, on my twenty-first birthday. My grandmother had just passed on, and my parents discovered the letter among her effects. I guess Granddad made my Grandma promise not to give it to me unless I was still having speech problems as a grown man."

Maria leaned forward, tenting her fingers underneath her chin. "Did you read the letter as soon as you got it?"

"Not exactly. I'm embarrassed to say, I let the past eight years go by without reading it. I was too busy denying and hiding my speech problems to deal with Granddad's suffering, the fact he may have done himself in. It took my Fox News implosion to make me desperate enough to see what he had to say."

"So was it as bad as you feared?"

"Henry James Davis was ahead of his time," I said. "You know how Folger's big deal is desensitization, getting us to stop worrying about whether we stutter in the first place? Listen to the first sentence of my grandfather's letter.

" 'Deacon, the more you try not to stutter, the more you will,' " I read aloud, pausing to take a breath as I recalled my first time reading these words. I hadn't heard them in my own voice. Granddad had nearly materialized in the flesh again, with his full head of white hair, bushy eyebrows, and caramel brown skin, dressed in his favorite pin-striped white suit.

I don't know what happened, son. Somewhere in the family line, I suppose, somebody's wiring between the mouth and the brain got a little out of whack. I hear tell that my grandfather had the same problem with his speech, so rest assured you're just one of many Davises with this thing. Unfortunately your daddy, with his highfalutin, blowhard self, probably puts extra pressure on you, whether he means to or not. Well, listen to me. If your stammers keep you from living up to what Frederick and his fan club expects, you just be like me. I ain't never let this affliction stop me from moving forward. I owned four pieces of property by the time I was thirty, and I put all three of my boys through college. Maybe I didn't have the prettiest jobs—processing mail at the downtown post office, welding in factories on the side, working security these days now that the manufacturing jobs are drying up—but I covered my responsibilities. If you're reading this, it's because you may still doubt whether you can live up to yours. If I did it, so can you.

When I finished reading it to Maria, I blew my nose and collected myself. "He's so right, but it still doesn't add up."

"You mean," Maria asked softly, "the fact that he committed suicide?"

"He never even left a note," I said, fighting back the quivers in my voice.

"A man of his generation probably didn't want to expose his emotions, Deacon. Do you know for sure that his stuttering drove his suicide?"

"No," I replied. "I was in high school when it happened, and there was an instant veil of secrecy about the whole thing."

Maria nodded sympathetically. "So, in truth, you're assuming that his words in the letter weren't true, that more than any other problem he faced, the stuttering was the unbearable one."

"It's not a trivial matter," I said, quickly lowering my voice when I heard myself. "How can anyone who stutters stop worrying about it, when society sure enough gives a damn?"

Maria smiled ruefully. "Does society really care that much?"

I cleared my throat then said, "What's one thing almost all black movies, with the exception of serious drama, have in common?"

Maria shrugged. "Most of them make us look like buffoons?"

"How about, most of them poke fun at stutterers. Name me a movie, I'll show you the stutterer they played for a fool."

Maria rolled her eyes. "Deacon, it's not like I'm not aware that—"

"Name a movie."

"I don't know, uh, *Harlem Nights.*"

"There was a boxer, guy they usually called Champ. Couldn't get two words out straight, brought the house down."

"Okay, there's one," she said. *"New Jack City."*

"Bill Nunn played the 'Duh-Duh' man, a hitman who everybody kept telling to shut up because he couldn't talk. Hil-freakin'-larious!"

We went on that way for a while, me coming up with examples for films by Spike Lee, joints starring big-time stars like Sam Jackson, and just about every black comedy ever made. I told her about my gut belief that everyone—from employers, to single women sizing up potential mates, to congregations sizing up preachers—viewed stutterers as weak, troubled losers. Maria tried to point out flaws in my logic and worked to encourage more positive self-talk in me.

"Deacon, as you know, we're not psychologists at the SRC, but we do believe in promoting healthy thoughts," she said. "No movie can make you think negatively of yourself or your speech. You understand that, right?"

We went on that way for a while, me doing an emotional striptease for this woman. At times I couldn't believe the things spilling out of me, but in an odd way it made sense. Not only was Maria a patient listener and a reassuring counselor, but based on my little eavesdropping the other night, I knew she bore crosses of her own. The details were none of my business, of course, but simply knowing that her life wasn't a fairy tale helped me peel back my own false facade. I was actually disappointed to learn our time was up.

"Thanks for being so open, Deacon. I have to see Terrell now," she said, patting my hand lightly. "He should be out in the hall. Send him in on your way out, okay?"

And that's when the inevitable happened, just as I zipped up my backpack and rose from my seat. I took a last look at Maria and realized the sister was fine.

12

Deacon

A week into the clinic, and I was still there. It was a muggy, sunny late Saturday morning, and we were on our first off-campus "real world" excursion. From Monday through Friday, Folger and his staff had put us through paces equivalent to boot camp. First we spent a day being picked apart for every possible disfluency and secondary behavior. In my small group, led by Folger himself, the good doctor informed Amberly, the would-be stewardess, that she had a "stuttering posture." Whenever she hit a speech block, her knees knocked and her healthy breasts swelled. Bill the pediatrician had a habit of leaning to his left when he hit a speech repetition, and Terrell, whose voice ran through several octaves during a block, always shoved his hands deep into his pockets. Poor kid sounded like a high-pitched Luciano Pavarotti doing a warm-up. As for me, I was accused of breaking eye contact whenever trouble hit. Folger insisted we'd have to unlearn these and other bad habits before getting on the right track.

From there Folger lectured us on the history of stuttering research and the many therapy techniques tried through the years. My favorite was the one applied by the Greek orator Demosthenes, who gargled and spoke with stones on his tongue. I couldn't see trying that one. Since Thursday, we'd been learning the actual mechanics of speech— that is, learning how sounds are supposed to be made versus the way we actually made them.

In our first exercise, we learned how to speak without struggling against the stuttering. No sudden, deep inhalations of air, no saying "you know" or "like" to get through a difficult passage, and for God's sake no cheating by clicking the tongue or shutting the eyes. It made for some pretty long conversations around the clinic. If you followed Folger's instructions to the letter, it would take you thirty seconds to complete one sentence.

I had a chance to show my dedication when my cousin Errick rang my cell phone, as our little group neared West End Mall. Maria was behind me when I pulled the phone off the belt of my shorts. "Deacon," she said in a hurried tone, "do you have to answer that?"

"No choice," I said slowly before flipping the phone open. "Hey," I said, slowing my pace and letting Maria and the other clients leave me behind.

"What's up, man? Nice of you take my call finally."

"Whatever." I was still pissed with him, but everyone I talked to had convinced me that Errick wasn't quite the Benedict Arnold I'd thought. He hadn't told me himself, but initially Miriam Lloyd had assigned Dave Savage, the Dream Party's legal counsel, to deliver the hit on me. Word was, Miriam was bound and determined to drum me out one way or another, and had a series of political maneuvers, including blackmail, at her ready. By getting me to resign and fight another day, Errick had saved me some humiliation and bought me time to get my stuttering back under control.

Errick panted, his breaths coming in raw chunks. "I'm on the Stair-Master right now, at the gym. Bunch of new babes in the house today."

"That's nice. Don't forget you're married." My cousin being a bit of a ho, he needed reminding.

"Oh no, that's *you* who looked without touching while you were with Mercedes. This brother here follows a different system."

I ignored his juvenile stab. "Whatever. Did Benet call you?" My sister, who had kept my dog, Prince, since my departure for the clinic, was tiring of chasing my frisky friend around her house.

"Yeah, she caught up with me last night. I'm picking your nasty canine up tonight. Spanky won't be happy with the competition, but I guess these are the sacrifices we make for family." Errick's trash-talking cocker spaniel, Spanky, never appreciated Prince's intrusions on his territory.

"I appreciate the help," I said. "Now you just owe me a new job." Since he'd convinced me to walk the Dream Party's plank, I had e-mailed Errick, asking for help finding a new job. My story with the

Dream Party wasn't finished, but I obviously couldn't return anytime soon. Newly unemployed and newly in debt thanks to this clinic, I hoped to get a job quickly as a football coach with a local school, maybe even substitute-teach until I figured out my next step.

"I'm asking around," Errick said. Although I'd found a few listings in the paper, my charismatic cousin was plugged into the social networks that really determined who got hired and fired. "I can drop by later this evening with three job postings I got hip to. While I'm at it, let me take your rusty ass out for the night. I know you have to be dying, boy, stuck up in that clinic all week."

"There's one cute therapist here," I said, making sure Maria wasn't behind me, "so I've got a few sights."

"Ah, that's my boy. You hit it yet?"

"Errick!"

"Don't act like you're wet behind the ears now, Deacon Davis. I said, did you–"

"Look, I'm here to get my speech t-together." I slowed down again, stretching out my words. "I don't have time to be chasing booty."

"Well, you ask me, the longer you keep your juices backed up, the worse your stuttering will get. When's the last time you hooked up with anyone, anyway? You've been working too hard for months now."

"It's been a few weeks," I said, taking a seat on a bench just inside the mall's main door. "But you know what? My life's been a lot simpler."

"Yeah," Errick said, chuckling, "and a lot drier, too."

"Just help me find a job, please." I tried to ignore Maria, who stood a few feet away, impatiently tapping her left foot.

"All right, but you know both Uncle James and I have got your back. You need me to send Dejuan some money?" Since I'd paid off my house with my NFL nest egg, I was most concerned with how to cover my son's child support. Mercedes, who runs her own investment firm, long ago rejected my attempts to establish support for Liza. The typical independent woman.

"Dejuan's covered through the end of the year at least," I said, "even if I wind up eating beans and ramen noodles. Like I said, just help me find a job."

"Got ya," Errick said. "Now, about your brother."

"Oh no," I replied, just as Maria came walking toward me, her hands balled against her hips. "Did he call you, too?" Miles had left me messages every other day since I'd started the clinic, all of which I'd ignored. I didn't have time for his latest Oliver Stone–like theories about who'd "assassinated" our father.

"Yeah," Errick replied, "he said he was coming into town to conduct some interviews for his book, research on your father's enemies and stuff like that."

"Well, if he asks where I am, play dumb," I replied. "I've got enough problems of my own right now." By now, Maria had walked up to my bench, my insubordination having scrunched the smooth, striking features of her face into a nasty frown. "I have to go, cuz. You can drop those job postings off tonight."

"If I'm coming all the way into the hood, I'm taking you back out with me. We'll find some honeys and get your bottle uncorked." This was trouble. When Errick got in these moods, no attractive lady in reach was safe.

"Shut up and bring the damn postings." I closed my phone and matched Maria's stare. "Happy now?"

Arms crossed, she was still tapping that left foot. "You are not working with me here." Her wide, bright eyes sparkling against her smooth Hershey's chocolate–colored skin, she motioned two fingers between her eyes and mine. "Everyone else has been off doing their speech exercises for ten minutes, while you sit here on the phone. It's not setting much of an example."

I rolled my eyes and bit my lower lip. "I told Folger from jump that I'd have to be accessible," I said, turning toward Maria. "A brother needs a job."

She grabbed my right arm, clamping down on my bicep. "I understand, really I do. You need to minimize the phone calls, though, okay? Save them for the end of the day."

"Come on," I pleaded. "I don't make that many calls anyway.

There's my mother, my uncle, and my cousin. I haven't even talked to my sisters since I've been here."

Shaking her head, Maria ignored my defense. "Let's go, I'm going to match you up with—"

"Is that really necessary?" I flashed a playful glance at her hand on my arm. "Why don't you be my partner?" Flirtation lifted each word as it spilled from my mouth, reminding me that Maria and I were starting to play a dangerous game.

I was enjoying my daily counseling sessions with her for more than one reason. The more I took in Maria's large, oval eyes; smooth, rich complexion; and shoulder-length, red-tinted coiled curls, the less professional my thoughts became. Add in her taut but voluptuous figure and multiply by the sexy Southern lilt rounding off her words, and it was nearly impossible to avoid being aroused.

Not that the attraction blocked out my need for her therapeutic expertise. The night before, she'd coaxed me into talking about the role that Frederick and Mother played in shaping my attitude about stuttering. "Your assumptions about how people view you and others who stutter—did you get any of these ideas from your father? In his letter, your grandfather made it sound like Frederick was disappointed by your speech problems."

Her question had taken me where I didn't want to go, but I reluctantly admitted that my parents had always set high standards for us kids, pushing us to live up to my father's reputation. Before I knew it, I had told Maria about Frederick's rigorous rewards system, one he applied to all our school activities. In short, if we "won," by scoring the right amount of points in basketball or football, or getting the highest grade on a test, we earned trips to the ice cream store or to the movies. If not, we went straight home with zero fanfare. Me being a natural athlete, I went out with my father for treats all the time, while Miles, who was a little less athletically gifted, was left at home with Mother and my sisters many nights.

Maria pressed me even more about Mother's reactions to my stuttering, and I wound up sharing memories that I thought I'd repressed for good. My mother was not ready for a "broken" child; after surviving an abusive childhood in urban New Orleans, she had been swept off her feet by the handsome, eloquent, and powerful Frederick Davis. From there, she had set about building a storybook existence, and a kid with a knotted tongue didn't fit too well with her plans. Unable to help me herself, she'd pressured my father to bypass the school speech therapists and "fix" me by hiring a top professional from a world-class university. The only problem was that Frederick, too busy to get intimately involved, was more confident that I'd eventually grow out of the stutters. As long as I was scoring touchdowns on the field and bringing home A's, he was much more confident in me than Mother was.

Slowly, Maria led me to acknowledge that although my mother was obviously more bothered by my stuttering, Frederick's insistence on "winning" had also fed my desire to hide my speech struggles. It was a painful realization, but I knew it was my best shot at eventually getting a handle on things.

"Uh, Deacon, if you want me to be your partner, you'll need to look at my *face*, please." The sound of Maria's voice snapped me out of my reflections, and I realized my eyes had trained a laser onto her breasts. My forehead flushing, I snapped my eyes back up to hers. "Lead the way—I'm ready to do some exercises!"

Too classy to embarrass me further, Maria turned over her shoulder and winked as she dragged me to the entrance of the mall's obligatory Foot Locker. "Come on. We're going in here and ask the clerk for help picking out a pair of running shoes. Stutter purposely on every word, and watch the clerk's reaction. Like Dr. Folger said, you'll realize people rarely react as negatively as you might think."

Still holding on to Maria's hand, I felt a flash of anxiety rocket through me. It occurred to me that my attraction to Maria was a test. Could I resist the urge to have my way with yet another attractive woman, now that my life was a step away from disaster? My relationship with my son and my daughter, my ability to advance my father's legacy, and my hopes of carving my own niche in the world rode on my ability to focus.

Steering clear of my interest in Maria, an interest stoked by her beauty, knowledge, sensitivity, and intriguing history, was going to be a challenge. This wasn't just the usual case of lust that in the past had led to abortions, broken hearts, and variations on the truth: a part of me wanted to help Maria resolve her own problems, starting with this mysterious dispute over her child. As I followed her into the Foot Locker, though, I decided it was time to stop the love train before it got us into trouble. For my sake and for Maria's, I had to keep her at arm's length.

13

Deacon

That same Saturday night, Errick's black Range Rover bounced to a stop in front of my dorm, Pfeiffer Hall. Eager to escape the clinic's four walls, I started toward the truck with a bounce in my step, then stopped cold when the passenger's-side door swung open.

There, beneath the overhead streetlamp, stood my big brother, Miles. Looking casually disheveled in his wrinkled, short-sleeve denim shirt, a pair of faded khaki slacks, and leather sandals, he stuck his hands in his pockets and smiled lazily. "Who's that boy with my momma's eyes?"

Willing myself to continue my stride, I forced a smile. "Who's that dude looks like a clone of my daddy?" With his deep brown complexion, bald head, squared mustache, and broad nose, my brother was Frederick reincarnated. Once I reached him, I leaned forward and wrapped him in a bear hug. At six feet even, Miles was a couple of inches shorter than me, with a sleeker, more graceful build.

Once we had hugged, Miles drew back, the usual predatory, mischievous glint in his eyes. "I figured you wouldn't call me back, so I'd just come to you in person, make things easier." He looked past me, studying the dormitory. "Errick told me about this clinic you signed up for. Is it helping you?"

"So far, so good," I replied, still wondering what my brother was up to.

Once I'd climbed into the Rover and slapped Errick in the back of the head for not warning me about Miles, we sped out into the streets of Hotlanta, looking for trouble. With Errick's stereo system blasting 50 Cent at max volume and our heads full with visions of Atlanta's finest women, I limited Miles to small talk as we rolled out to Buckhead. I caught him up on my resignation from the Dream Party, the latest on Uncle James (who hadn't spoken to my brother since Miles cursed him out a year ago), and the latest on my kids and their many activities.

When I asked Miles about Chantal, his on-again, off-again girlfriend, he blew me off with a wave of the hand. "Same old, same old." He clearly had no plans to make an honest woman of the poor girl, whom he'd lived with at several points since their college years. "How about your love life? Seeing anyone new these days?"

Errick replied for me, clearing his throat belligerently. "Deacon's applied self-service lately, if you know what I mean."

"Shut up, ho," I said, chuckling as I punched Errick's arm. "I'm just chilling, Miles."

"Chilling. That is the way to be," Miles said, a faint smile on his face.

By the time we'd settled in at Taboo nightclub, our second stop of the evening, I was relieved that I'd kept Miles from going into his latest conspiracy theories. He'd talked some about an investigative article he was writing about a pharmaceutical company, but stayed off the topic of Frederick's death.

My time ran out as we exited the club with three beautiful sisters in tow. Miles and Errick had rapped to them throughout the evening, while I had largely minded my own business and eaten a plate of fried calamari, so I leaned against Errick's Rover as my boys tried to line up some action for the night.

Errick was in rare form, his keen facial features bathed in the white light of an overhead streetlamp. "Here's how you find it," he said, handing a printed slip of paper to the trio's leader, a tall, lean honey named Toya. "Just act like you're driving to the airport, then head toward East Point. Follow those directions, and you can't go wrong."

Toya stepped forward and snared the slip between flawlessly manicured fingers, but still asked, "I thought I heard you were married, brother." She turned to me suddenly. "Now Deacon, we all know *you're* single again. You going to be at Errick's condo, too?"

"Oh no, Errick's on his own," I said. "I got places to be." Since it was already after ten thirty, I'd given up on making the clinic's eleven o'clock curfew. Maria and Hector wouldn't be happy with a brother, but I couldn't get too worked up about it. Who was I hurting? There were no workshops on Sunday mornings anyway. That said, I wasn't trying to be out all night.

"You all don't need old, square Deacon anyway," Errick said. "I got all you ladies need." In our day, Errick and I enjoyed competing for the same girls, seeing which of our strengths they found most attractive—my height, muscles, and doe eyes versus his fine grade of hair, penny-red skin, and high cheekbones.

As Errick sweet-talked the ladies into a night of adultery, Miles grabbed my elbow. "Get in the car, little brother," he said, looking suspiciously to his left and right.

Oh, Lord. I didn't even fight him, climbing into the passenger seat as he walked around to the driver's side.

"I've been cool with you, man, easing into this," Miles said, settling into the seat. "We need to talk about my upcoming book, though. I want everyone's blessing before I release it—Mother, you, Darlene, and Benet."

I shook my head, ran a hand across my forehead. "Miles, come on, just—"

Miles shifted in his seat, turning toward me. "I have the closest thing to proof anyone's found yet, Deacon. Proof Frederick's death was no accident."

"Saying the words out loud doesn't make them true, man," I said, my voice low.

Miles's eyebrows jumped as he leaned toward me. "Really? Disabuse me of this notion, then. I see more than a coincidence when of all the supper clubs to inexplicably catch fire and kill most of its guests, it just happened to be one housing our father, the first brother to build a viable political party. Have you forgotten how many Republicans *and* Democrats were threatened by Frederick's success?"

My chest rose as I inhaled, hoping to slow my words and stay as fluent as possible. "Listen to yourself. You sound like you should be writing for *The Final Call*, not the *Washington Post*. You have to stop making these charges without any evidence, Miles. It cheapens everything Frederick stood for."

"Your ignorance is painful to behold, little brother," Miles replied, leaning in closer to me, the beer on his breath souring my stomach. "My publisher gave me a six-figure advance for this new book. They know I'm on the path to finding evidence, the sort of stuff that will make everyone think twice."

"They don't care whether you've got real evidence," I said, forcing myself to stay calm. "They just want a good show, man. And you bring a hell of a show."

Miles broke the awkward silence between us. "Okay, okay," he said, anxiously tapping a finger against Errick's dashboard. "How's this? There's a former D.C. crime scene investigator who filed a report that was buried and overruled by her boss. This lady insisted the fire at Frederick's club was caused by arson."

My pulse sped up a bit, just by a nanosecond. During the first year after my father's death, when every radical activist was circulating rumors, I wanted concrete proof of what happened more than anyone. As the years passed, though, I'd constantly been disappointed; every theory out there had nothing but innuendo and wishful thinking behind it. I finally decided that the absence of evidence meant there was nothing sinister behind Frederick's death. By that time, I didn't have a choice. My marriage had dissolved, my children were growing, and I needed to build a new career. I couldn't keep digging in the past only to be let down again.

I turned wary eyes toward Miles. "This crime investigator—is this hearsay, or d-do you have her specific identity? She willing to speak on the record?"

"She is now that I've found her. Her name is Brenda Lawson. You can do a Google search online—you'll see her name comes up in news articles from the mid-nineties about other investigations."

"How is it that no one has found her before?"

"No one else had a personal vested interest before, that's how. I've wound my way through the D.C. police, fire, and prosecutors' offices for the past three years, man. You help someone's kid get a job, help another one's get into a local college, turn another onto a good deal for a mortgage loan. Scratching backs, that's what I've been doing.

"This Brenda Lawson got bounced from her job a year or so after Frederick's death. They tried to discredit her for her work on another case, but she's got records proving she had her act together. She's convinced she was let go in retaliation for her arson finding on the supper-club fire."

Some of the flurries in my chest calmed down. This Lawson lady sounded like a simple disgruntled employee, about as credible as Miles himself. "It still sounds like this comes down to her word versus the rest of the department."

"It's not perfect, but I'm just getting started with that angle." Miles glanced out the window, where Errick had Toya wrapped in the sort of intimate hug that would not make his wife, Shanna, very happy. "There's a whole other side to the question of *who* committed the arson, little brother, and it took me of all people to uncover two suspects."

Miles explained as my head jerked back, my mouth opening in a silent *How?* "Don't ask how," he said, "but I got hold of the supper club's records. Those that survived the fire, of course. I took special interest in the list of employees who were on duty that night. Included were a Pharrell Haynes, listed as a waiter, and a Tisha Norris, listed as a dishwasher. Those names sound familiar at all?"

"You've lost me."

"Some of my old contacts on the Hill helped me run every employee's name and social security number through both the FBI's and the D.C. PD's systems. Pharrell's and Tisha's background checks were the most interesting—each was hired by the club a week before the fire, and each was previously employed by your father-in-law."

"No way," I said, my voice nearly cracking. Big Walter Chance's link to Mercedes's family tree remained one of my family's best-kept secrets. Even though he'd been capped by one of his own foot soldiers around the time Liza was born, the sound of his name still got my pressure up, as my grandma used to say.

Dead, Big Walter would never be gone. He lived on in Mercedes's trust fund, the same one she hid from me for years and used to start Phoenix Capital Management, her twenty-five-million-dollar investment firm. A savvy, well-respected entrepreneur, Mercedes still lived in fear of the day Big Walter might reach up from the grave and un-mask her as his daughter, bringing her charmed career to a crashing halt.

I slid my hands up and down my seat's armrests, trying to keep cool. I prayed Mercedes had no tie to these people. Any threat to her was a threat to my little Liza. I felt my voice shake as I glared back at Miles. "Is that all you have? This coincidence?"

"That may be all we need, little brother," Miles replied, his glare intensifying. "Somebody in what's left of Big Walter's organization has to know what's up. The trick, of course, is finding someone who will talk. When the big man was murdered, his gang dispersed pretty widely. Those who are still in D.C. aren't trying to talk. I haven't given up yet, though." He grabbed my shoulder. "We both know if anyone had a motive to go after Frederick, it was Big Walter."

I couldn't argue that. When my father won his Senate seat, the media proclaimed him the new voice of black America. Frederick had quickly used that influence to spur increased crackdowns on the drug trade, not only in Illinois, but also in his new D.C. neighborhood, where Big Walter's dealers reigned supreme.

I sat there staring at my brother, my mouth wide open. For once, I was rendered mute, and it had nothing to do with my stuttering.

"I hope you'll take me a little more seriously now," Miles said, of-fering me a hand, which I took with a firm grip.

"I can't argue with you what you've told me," I said. "Do me a favor, though? Keep Mercedes out of this. I c-can't imagine she knew this Tisha or this Pharrell character. Remember, she'd been long gone from her father's grasp by the time all this went down."

"I'll respect that request as long as the trail doesn't lead to her door," Miles said, shaking my hand again.

"I appreciate it."

Hoping the most unpleasant part of the evening was behind me, I rolled down my window and yelled over at Errick, who was still sell-ing his harem on the idea of a threesome. "Come on, E, we need to go!"

Errick hustled over to the Rover, leaned in through my window. "Look, fellas, it's gonna be on tonight!" He looked past me to my brother. "Miles, you want some of this or not? I know Deacon's old fogy ass ain't up for it."

"Appreciate the offer, kid," Miles said, shaking his head, "but at this point I'll pass. My belly's full of beer, I'm tired, and at thirty-four, I don't trust my ability to put it down with one of them young girls."

"Guess I'm the only man up to the test tonight," Errick said, shaking his head. He stepped back, reaching into his slacks, then chucked his keys at me. "You all take my ride. Miles, drop Deke off and drive it back to your hotel. I'll drive your rental over to the hotel tomorrow morning and we'll exchange cars."

I handed the keys to Miles but gripped Errick's wrist with my free hand. "You're not really taking all three of those girls to your love nest, are you?" This was one of the reasons Errick and I had grown apart in recent years: the Negro was a hell of a business executive, but had the sexual maturity of a teen rapper set loose in the *Playboy* mansion. Nearly thirty, married, and prosperous, Errick still saw no issue in a spontaneously scheduled threesome.

My cousin glanced at my hand and let his eyes do the frowning. "You gonna preach at me, are you, Deacon?"

"I've said my piece." As a man with a few skeletons in my own closet, and one who knew some of the baggage that played into Errick's antics—including his distant relationship with my uncle Art and a marriage scarred by the trauma of five miscarriages—I held my tongue. It wasn't like I didn't have problems of my own.

With Errick squared away, Miles and I exchanged seats, and a minute later I pulled out into traffic, heading for the expressway. The drive back to the Clark campus made for one of the most peaceful conversations I'd had with Miles in years. Talking openly about his investigation into Frederick's death had freed us of the usual tension and resentment. It would have been a nice end to the evening, if only we hadn't stopped off at that Taco Bell.

Miles asked me to stop at the place, soon after we exited the expressway. He hadn't eaten much at Taboo and needed a little something-something. As we idled in the drive-through lane, he told me what he wanted: chicken quesadillas, a bean burrito, and a steak gordita. A simple order it was, but for some reason I got a burning sensation in my chest as he shared it with me.

When I pulled up to the drive-in speaker, the speaker box squawked with the drive-through girl's hurried, limp greeting. "Welcome to Taco Bell. May I help you?"

In that moment, I felt my first few days of clinic training drain right out of me. "I'll have," I said, feeling my throat tighten as I inhaled. "I'll have an order of the ka-ka-ka—"

The speaker crackled back at me. "What you want? Quesadillas?"

"Yes," I said before rising in my seat, my chest puffing with new air. "Chicken, please. Also, let me get a b-b-b—"

"What? I can't understand you!"

"I want a b-b-b—"

"Burrito? What type?"

"A b-b-b—"

"You sayin' you want a bean burrito?" Speaker girl was having herself a good laugh now. Probably a teen single mom on minimum wage, laughing at *me*. A week earlier, I might have jumped out of Errick's truck and put the fear of God into homegirl, and as humiliated as I felt, the word *bitch* might have escaped my lips. Determined to leave that Deacon Davis in the past, I let out a long breath, ready to clarify my order one last time.

Before I could get my reply out, Miles grabbed my shoulder and leaned past me. "Young lady!" he yelled.

"Yeah?"

"Do I need to come in there and see your manager, or are you going to treat my brother, your damn *customer*, with some respect?"

"Look, I just can't understand—"

"That's no excuse. Get your manager, Shafika."

The speaker went silent for a minute; then we heard frantic whispering as speaker girl and someone else argued. Finally, a deep voice boomed out, "Sir, you have a problem?"

"Most definitely, brother," Miles shouted back. "Your employee just disrespected a customer trying to put money in your pocket! You need to send her packing–"

Clearing my throat, I turned to Miles. "Let it go, man. I appreciate it, but let it go."

Sighing, Miles shrugged and sat back in his seat. "All yours," he said.

"You know what," I said, yelling at the speaker box, "we just lost our appetite, and you just lost our business." The words hung in the air as I roared through the lane, past the pick-up window, and out onto the street.

By the time I braked to a stop in a lot near Pfeiffer Hall, Miles was chuckling gently to himself. "Don't worry about that silly girl back there, man."

"It's all good," I lied, a numbing sensation crawling over me. It was like junior high, and Fox News, all over again.

"Don't let a few flubs get you down," Miles said, the glare in his eyes softening. "You're about much more than moments like that. Mark my words, you're gonna replace Uncle James as head of Communities in Action someday, and really make Frederick proud."

I whispered a halfhearted thanks to my brother. There were days I thought I was kidding myself, thinking I could fill my uncle's or my father's shoes.

I wrote down directions to get Miles back to his hotel, then popped fists with him as I climbed out of the truck. "Peace, man."

"All right, then." Miles gripped my fist. "Deacon? Get everything you can out of this clinic. When you get out, we have some justice to seek."

My hand on the open driver's side door, I nodded wearily at my brother. I had no doubt: if he was on the right track, my life was about to get infinitely more complex.

14

Maria

Deacon Davis had picked the wrong damn night to play fast and loose with the SRC curfew. As I sat in my room, my door open so that I could hear any stirring in the hallway, I sipped anxiously from my cooling coffee mug. In front of me, on a classroom school desk I'd crammed into a corner of the room, lay the journal notebook Folger insisted each therapist keep. Each day, we had to note our observations of each client's apparent progress and provide our theory on what factors affected each one's performance. I had kept up with my daily notes, but hadn't had time yet to analyze them or draw up recommendations for those who were doing poorly.

I was almost done, now that it was just after one a.m. When Hector and I did the bed check at eleven, I drew the short straw. We had both agreed that Deacon was liable to stay out the better part of the night, given some of the rumors we'd heard about his playboy past, so I knew I was in for a long one. In the last two hours, I had summarized my observations of every client, saving Deacon for last. I was about halfway through his section when I heard the exit door on my end of the hall whip open and slam shut.

He didn't even break stride as he passed my door. Wearing a fitted red silk shirt and light gray slacks, he simply nodded in my direction and hurtled on by. Nearly snapping my pencil in two before throwing it down, I cursed under my breath before speaking loudly, firmly. "Deacon." I was both angry and disappointed at his behavior, given how well some of our counseling sessions had gone, but I was not about to chase him. He would either come to me or I'd stroll over to his room, use my skeleton key, and haul his cocky ass out of bed at my leisure.

I let my voice ring in the hallway for several seconds and continued writing my analysis of Broderick Deacon Davis. I had gotten through two sentences when I felt his presence in the doorway. I kept writing until he coughed purposefully. "Good evening, Maria."

"Try *morning*." I raised my eyes momentarily, then continued with my writing. "Are you going to tell me this is an honest mistake?"

I heard him shift in the doorway, cross his arms. "I'm not a child. I didn't plan on missing curfew, but it just so happens I did. I have no excuses."

"Very mature of you," I replied as I continued writing. The pain at the top of my spinal cord, a sensation similar to having a dumbbell planted behind my neck, spiked again. I placed a hand to the spot, despite myself.

"Are you okay?" Deacon's voice took on a plausible tone of concern, but I was too irritated to appreciate it.

"I'm fine." In reality, the pain had nothing to do with my rebellious client. There were two causes. First, running the clinic had seriously messed with my usual morning schedule, meaning I'd missed out on my yoga classes the past two weeks. If that wasn't bad enough, my stress level had ballooned after my recent dustups with Thomas and Lucille. Not only had I nearly had a catfight with Lucille earlier in the week, but Thomas had called the previous night, as well, challenging me to "bring on" my threats of a lawsuit. He claimed he was still in touch with Guy, Jamil's father, and wouldn't hesitate to have Guy testify about the weaknesses—the drugs, the alcohol, the shoplifting charge—that led to my decision to leave Jamil with my brother. My own flesh and blood was calling my bluff, offering me the chance to go broke hiring an attorney and have my every last skeleton yanked into broad daylight.

Deacon took two steps inside my room. "You need a massage back there, maybe?"

I felt my forehead bunch as I sat back suddenly in my chair. "You can stay right where you are, thank you very much. And in case you didn't realize it, you're talking too damn fast."

"Ouch," he replied, backing up against the far wall and crossing his ankles. "I'm feeling pretty violated by all the coarse language. Do I get to report you to Folger?"

"Are you kidding me?" I pushed back from my chair, breezed past Deacon, and stood in my doorway. "Get out," I said, hooking a thumb down the hallway, toward his room. "We're going to talk this out, but not here."

Once I had followed him down the dimly lit hallway and into his compact room, I slowly guided the door closed behind me. Still fueled by anger, it took me a minute to realize how good the air smelled, spiced as it was by an incense stick on the window ledge and the heavy scent of bottles of cologne, six of which lined the floor beside Deacon's bed. The smells flooded me, warming the pit of my stomach, but I leaned into my tirade all the same. "Do you even want to be here, Deacon?"

He hovered by his bed, feinting toward it for a seat before righting himself and crossing his arms again. "You don't see me packing my bags, do you?"

"Do you want to continue on with your life as it is, is that it?"

His eyes turned to slits. "What the hell's that supposed to mean?"

"I'm not going to give you another pep talk about how special you are," I said, lowering my voice. "At this point, it's a question of respecting the other clients' experience. If you set a half-ass example, it's bound to rub off on people who don't have the luxury of going back to work for Daddy's organization and living off of his legacy. Most of these people have to earn their own way."

Deacon covered the few feet between us in a flash, so quickly, I was afraid he had more in common with NFL athletes than I'd initially thought. He was in my face, but his hands were at his sides and his voice came at me in a calm, low growl. "Because you've been a help to me, Maria, I'll let that slide right off my back. You might be interested to know that my father was nearly broke when he died. His campaigns left him with a few hundred grand in debts, and he never drew any more than ninety thousand in salary from Communities in Action. He left no trust funds, okay?"

I stayed right where I was, my lips a couple of inches away from his bobbing Adam's apple. I tipped my head back, looked up into the heat of his stare. "Give me some space, please."

"Whatever you want," he replied, stepping back and then sitting on the bed. "Look, save us both a headache and just report me to Folger in the morning. I'll deal with him and save you the trouble of being in the middle."

"You didn't answer my question," I said. "Do you want to be here or not?"

"Yeah," Deacon whispered, as if I'd coaxed the admission from him at gunpoint. "I've just got a lot on my mind, Maria."

I reached back, rubbing at my neck as I shook my head. "Well, don't we all? You have to respect the process here. You're not as miserable as you try to pretend, Deacon. Why else would you do what you did for Terrell?"

Deacon's nostrils flared as I saw the incident from that afternoon replay itself in his head. After our speech exercises at West End Mall, Ramsey had chartered a bus to take the clients over to Greenbriar Mall, where we took in a showing of *Deliver Us from Eva,* the LL Cool J–Gabrielle Union movie. In one scene, the characters joked that Eva was so evil, she had turned one ex-boyfriend into a stuttering fool. A few frames later, the boyfriend in question popped up, sounding like Porky Pig and getting big laughs from the crowd.

Everyone loved it, except for most of us SRC folks. Doris, one of the teens, couldn't take the humiliation and ran out of the theater, yelling, "It's not funny!" as she fled down the stairs. When a teen heckler sitting a few rows back shouted a nasty response, young Terrell leapt from his seat and ran up to the kid's row.

It wasn't pretty. Before any of the SRC coordinators could reach him, Terrell had pulled the kid, who was taller and heavier, into the aisle. Pressing him against the railing, he punched the kid silly until Deacon flew up the steps and wrapped himself around Terrell. As Terrell's victim slumped against the wall and three theater workers raced up the steps, Deacon kept his arms around Terrell's struggling form and whispered in his ear. By the time the theater staffers reached our aisle, Deacon, Terrell, and the heckler were calm and still. I did the talking, explaining what had set Terrell off, the heckler apologized, and we got off with a simple agreement to leave the theater.

"You probably kept Terrell from violating his probation," I said. "You believe he has reason to be hopeful about life despite his stutter, right?"

Deacon's eyes were on the floor. "Sure." His voice was husky, low.

"What did you say to him that stopped his squirming?"

"You have the power."

"That was it?"

"Those were my first words. Beyond that, I just fleshed it out for him. Whether it's handling his speech or resisting the urge to knock someone out, he has the power to d-direct his path. God will always have his say, of course, but that doesn't mean Terrell shouldn't do his part to be responsible. That's all I meant. He had the power to walk away from that little asshole, and he has the power to stay out of prison."

"His social worker warned us about him," I said. "She said he was very resistant to guidance. Why do you think he listened to you so quickly?"

Deacon looked up, finally meeting my stare. "He knows I speak from experience. I mean, I haven't faced all of Terrell's disadvantages, but I've dealt with my share. Kids like him, those who've been abandoned by their parents, they don't ask for much."

The weights on my spine pressed deeper, and I couldn't stop myself. "I don't think that's a fair term, *abandoned*. You never know why kids were separated from their parents."

"Oh, I know about separation," he responded, tapping the two photos by his bed. I knew immediately they were his son and daughter. "You have any kids, Maria?"

I shut my eyes, rubbed at my forehead. "Would I be staying in a crummy dorm with all of you if I did?"

Deacon shrugged. "Just making conversation."

"You know something about kids who grow up without their parents, huh?" My heartbeat sputtered for a millisecond, but I couldn't stop myself. "With the kids at the schools you've reformed, did you see many who knew their parents but weren't raised by them?"

"It's tough on them," Deacon said, his eyes on the floor. "I've heard plenty of teachers talk about kids in those situations. Grandma or an aunt is raising them while Mom the crack whore drops in every few years when she's bored. Not good."

"You really shouldn't be so flip," I said, my voice growing hoarse.

"You haven't walked in those women's shoes."

"No, I haven't." Deacon stood and walked back over to me. This time his movements were more graceful, almost liquid. "It can't be easy," he whispered, thumbing a pool of tears from my eye. "Something you want to tell me?"

"No." The answer squeaked from my throat as I let him tip my chin in his direction. I moved closer, let the inflating tips of my nipples strain my blouse as I leaned against his breastbone. "I don't want to talk."

Two years had passed since I had made love, roughly nine months since I had let a man spontaneously kiss me. Some things I guess you never forget, though, because I knew instantly that Deacon Davis was going to kiss me, and in return I was going to flood him with everything I had been saving up.

I heard him inhale deeply, then closed my eyes and wrapped myself around him as our lips met. In seconds our tongues flitted together before swarming each other. I palmed his hips as I felt him finger the buttons on my blouse and slide it off my shoulders. When I heard the fastener on my bra pop open, I instinctively tinkered with his belt then yanked his slacks to his knees.

"Hmm," Deacon whispered as he turned and guided me toward the little twin bed. The look in his eyes asked what we were doing, but his years of experience had clearly taken over. After laying me down and leaning over me with a deep kiss, he stepped to the window and pressed the CD player to life, permeating the room with Jonathan Butler's vibrant jazz.

When he leaned over me again, I took his mouth with mine again, afraid of making any conversation or complicating things. After a few seconds, Deacon poised himself over me. After toying with my mother's locket wordlessly, he yanked his silk boxers off and let me remove his shirt. Now that we were on even ground, he began to cover my body with licks, sucks, kisses, and fondles. As the space between my legs melted, I reached down for his long, pulsing manhood and ran my hands up and down its majesty. Only then did I realize how long I'd been away. When Deacon had me ready to burst, I climbed on top of him and let him hoist my hips in his hands as he swung around and placed his feet on the floor.

"Go slow," I pleaded through clenched teeth, searching his face through the sweat dripping down my forehead.

Deacon's only response was to gingerly slide himself inside me, an inch or two at a time, until I flexed my hips, bore down on him and pushed back. His eyes hardening as he realized I was ready for a higher tempo, he arched his back and gripped my shoulders.

That's when Norm knocked on the door.

I don't know why we didn't just stop everything then, but when Norm slunk away, Deacon and I tried to keep the love train rolling, rolling down the track. It took Hector's banging on the door to bring reality home.

In seconds, I was hiding in the closet, sweat popping out across my brow as I heard Deacon yank his door open. I was too crazy with fear to even process what all was said, something about Hector saying, "Who's the bitch you hiding?" while Deacon acted like he had no clue what the problem was. A scuffle followed as the door banged against the wall, as if Hector were trying to push past Deacon and come inside. Finally, I heard Deacon shout at Hector. "You want in this room, bring Folger over here with you. Until then, mind your damn business!"

The door's slam echoed inside my head for the next several minutes, after which Deacon noiselessly slid the closet door open. "I'll go to the bathroom," he whispered. "Listen for my knock at the door. That'll signal the coast is clear."

Before he could step away, I reached a hand out and took one of his in mine. "Thank you," I mouthed as quietly as possible. Even though I knew I had to, I didn't want to let go.

15

Deacon

I was on my way to the campus cafeteria, trying to get my story straight for Dr. Folger, when my new friend Terrell rolled up alongside me.

"What's up, Deacon?" Though four or five inches shorter than me, the wiry kid was all legs, so he had no trouble matching my hurried pace.

"Good morning, Terrell," I said, glancing over and nudging him with my elbow. "You ready for another week?"

"I-It's all good, man, you know what I'm sayin'. F-Folger gonna see I'm serious 'b-bout getting my shit straight."

"Hey, hey, dial it back a few paces," I said, placing a hand on his shoulder. Terrell's rapid-fire delivery worked well when he was rapping, but for conversational purposes, it tripped the little bro up something serious. "What did Ms. Maria tell you about taking the time to feel each sound, instead of rushing your way through?"

Terrell's light brown pupils flashed angrily, then cooled. I was flattered by his restraint. "You right, I know."

I didn't pile on, just continued striding toward the cafeteria's double doors until Terrell suddenly said, "They said I should thank you."

"For what?" I said, holding a door open for him.

"You know," Terrell replied, turning toward me as we stood in the lobby, just beyond the hustle and bustle of the cafeteria. "For pulling me off that kid the other day, a-at the movies. My parole o-officer said I should be back in juvie already for that."

I stood in front of Terrell, who had let his eyes drop to the linoleum tile as he finished his sentence. "Terrell," I said, playfully popping him on the chin so he'd raise his eyes, "don't thank me with words, young bro. Thank me with your actions, by making the most of this clinic." I extended a closed fist. "Got me?"

"Got ya," he replied, smiling and popping my fist with his own.

Our little bonding moment ended abruptly when I felt a slap on my shoulder. I looked behind me to see Folger himself standing there, peering up at me impatiently. "Deacon. We need to talk, right now."

"All right," I said, turning back to Terrell. "See you after breakfast, big guy."

Terrell backed away from us slowly, a concerned look on his face. "Okay."

Folger had already headed back out the door, jerking a finger across the way. "Meet me over in the main lounge, after you go get Maria. She should be in there eating. Hector's waiting on us."

My cheeks stung as if Folger had actually popped me with his gruff, brief tone. Walking with leaden steps, I went inside the cafeteria and found Maria. She sat surrounded by clients, happily relating some story about her childhood when I walked up. Feeling like a heel, I leaned over and whispered the message into her ear.

Her shoulders shot up, and her plump little lips flattened as I delivered the bad news. Her mood completely flipped, Maria slid her chair back, ignoring me, and stalked off, leaving me far behind.

Following in her path, I reminded myself that Maria had every right to her attitude. Damn, it was her career on the line, all because I'd once again used my Davis charms for evil. I mean, sure, she was a grown woman and everything had been consensual, but I could've just given her some kind words and sent her on her way. She never told me to kiss her.

It was my fault we were in this mess, and I had to protect her. How could I do that and make peace with Folger and Hector? I'd barely been at the clinic a week, and Folger's principles were just now starting to make faint sense. I needed to deal with the demons that had brought me there in the first place.

When we took our seats on a couch opposite Dr. Folger and Hector, Folger leaned back and flipped open a manila folder with my name stamped on the outside. "Deacon, " he said, "there's been an unacceptable allegation leveled against you. Hector, Norman, and Maria have provided their accounts of the evening in question. Do you want to tell me your side of the story?"

I couldn't help but glance over at Maria quickly. I didn't care what she'd told Folger, but shouldn't she have clued me in, to make sure I didn't unwittingly trip up on any lies in her account? "I spoke to Hector Saturday night," I said. "He asked me a series of questions and then left my room. What's the p-problem?"

"Oh, come on now." Folger's eyes darkened, and his temples twitched. "This is about some nigger shit, that's what this is about. To hear Norman tell it, Deacon, you were shooting a damn porno movie in your room. What did your manual tell you about entertaining in the dorm?"

I coughed, cleared my throat. "Not allowed."

"You showed a complete disrespect for the type of atmosphere we're trying to foster here."

I wanted to respect this man, really I did, but the soapbox act was too much. "People hear the sounds of sex in the real world, Doctor. Aren't you trying to prepare us for the real world?"

Folger put up a hand to block Hector, who had leaned forward like he was going to shut me up. I'd have liked to see him try. "Did you or did you not break the rules, Deacon?"

"I did entertain a female in my room, if that's what you're asking."

Folger's eyes wandered over to Maria for a moment, but his question targeted me. "Who was the woman?"

"It doesn't matter," I replied as Maria shifted uneasily next to me. "You asked if I broke the rules. I did."

Folger inhaled deeply, then wiped his brow. "Look, we can work this out if you'll be forthright. The most important thing is that this wasn't someone from the clinic."

I met Folger's beady stare and kept my mouth shut.

"You're not willing to say anything more, are you?"

"I broke the rules," I repeated. "I'm at your mercy."

Folger looked at Maria. "Help me out again. You were on duty to watch for Deacon when he came in. Did you see who he came in with?"

"I already told you, Doctor," Maria said. Her lips were so tight, they barely moved. "I had an upset stomach and spent fifteen minutes in the ladies' room. He must have come in then."

"Yes, Maria," Hector said, his thick eyebrows dancing, "but you didn't hear anything coming from his room, when you came out of the bathroom?"

"I went back into the bathroom a second time," Maria replied. Oh, the girl was dancing. "I told you, that's why you and Norm couldn't find me when you first banged on Deacon's door."

Hector sat back against the couch, shrugging his shoulders and shaking his head at Folger. "It don't add up, boss."

I hadn't wanted to lie, but I was getting uneasy with their questioning of Maria. "The girl was a Clark student, a junior in the b-business school. Said she was here for summer session. I met her during my morning run."

Folger's brow furrowed as he processed my story. "You mean, you didn't bring in a girlfriend? You're sleeping with undergraduate students? You're nearly thirty years old, for God's sake."

"And what's-her-name was at least t-twenty. Nothing statutory there."

Folger sat still as if about to sneeze, then touched a finger to his nose. "Hector, Maria, excuse us." He began rolling up a shirtsleeve. "It's about to get ghetto in here."

As Hector hopped out of his seat, stabbing me with eyes full of contempt, I tried not to notice Maria's quick, graceful exit. It was done now; we'd both let passion get the upper hand at the wrong time, but I was the one falling on the sword.

Folger's next question hit me between the eyes, just as the door slammed shut behind Hector. "Okay, who was really in the room, Deacon?"

"I just told you."

Folger stood and took a couple of steps, stopping right in front of me. "Her name," he said, hands on hips. "Now. I want to run her through the university system, see whether we can find her. Students have been informed that the clinic's dorm is off-limits to them."

"This is none of your business," I replied, scratching anxiously at my neck and keeping my tone respectful.

"Deacon, you better level with me, damn you. This is a serious infraction, and if you don't lay out all the cards, I'll have to send you home. Don't try to protect *anyone*, hear me? Not even Maria."

He couldn't have chilled me more if he'd turned into one of the X-Men and shot ice water at me from his wrists. I eased back in my seat as I asked, "Why would I be protecting Maria?"

Folger's eyes grew even larger. "You tell me. Something about her sudden disappearance during all this doesn't sound right. It's oddly irresponsible of her."

"I've told you what I did, Dr. Folger. There's nothing left to say."

"Nothing left to say, huh." Folger turned his back to me, keeping his hands planted against his sides. "God, I didn't want to have to do this, Deacon, but I'm sending you home. You're not trustworthy or mature enough to get what the SRC is offering you."

I stood and walked past Folger, knocking him off balance as I passed him by but saying nothing in my defense.

Terrell was waiting outside for me when I stepped into the sunlight. He ambled over to me, his hands shoved into his pockets. "E-Everything okay?"

Trying to figure how to explain what had just happened, I threw an arm over the kid's shoulder. I wasn't sure I understood it myself. Folger was wrong about me, at least in all the ways that mattered, but there'd been no way to defend myself without harming Maria. For her sake, I was headed back into the real world without the treatment I'd so desperately craved. I could only hope she would thank me later.

Back to the World

16

Deacon

I met Errick for lunch the next day, after a last-minute interview for an assistant coaching position at Roswell High School. With my therapeutic experience suddenly aborted, I had decided to throw myself back into life, full-bore. Since lugging my duffel bag from the clinic into my house the previous afternoon, I had set up four separate coaching interviews.

In addition to stumping for a paycheck, I'd decided to fly Dejuan into town for the summer. Even though he was thirteen, Uncle James had insisted on accompanying Dejuan on his flight down, but I knew my uncle's main plan was to get on my case for leaving the clinic. I had called and explained that I'd left because I couldn't get along with Folger, but conveniently left Maria out of my explanation.

For her part, Candy had been happy to let Dejuan come stay with me. I knew she would appreciate the break, and I had plenty of plans lined up for the kid. Johnny Dawson, an old friend and former NFL star, had agreed to make Dejuan a late add to his local football camp. That way my son would get to sharpen his skills again—Candy had pulled him off the team last fall when his grades dipped—and we wouldn't be in each other's face 24/7.

Errick wasn't feeling my simple game plan. We'd barely taken our seats at Harvey's Barbecue, a popular hole-in-the-wall owned by our second cousins, when he laid into me. "You're letting them win, man," he said. "I understand you want to get a paycheck going and all, but you've got to keep fighting to get back on board with the Dream Party."

"That's funny, coming from the man who fired my ass," I replied, grabbing a chicken leg. Harvey's was always packed, but rarely with the type of folk who cared whether you licked your fingers.

"Deke, why you think I took your job?" Eyebrows arched, Errick set his plate of food to the side. "I mean, I want to prove myself and all, and get some kudos along the way. But this also gives me a chance to prove Miriam and the board were wrong to force your resignation."

I finished chewing before replying. "How you plan on doing that?"

"I've been thinking about this. Now that I'm running the party, I figure I have the right to use whatever independent contractors I want. I want to sign you up right now, let you put your best skills to work."

I swallowed my last bite of the leg's meat and took time to lick my fingers. "What you got in mind?"

"Well for one, you can finish what you started. Guess who's agreed to do dinner with me and Uncle James when he comes through town next week?"

Picking up a thigh slathered in bloodred sauce, I shrugged. "Who, man?"

"Oh, nobody." Errick enjoyed his pause, cheesing from ear to ear. "Just the only governor in the country who prefers Earth, Wind and Fire to Billy Joel."

I dropped the thigh, let it slap against the plate and spatter me with a little sauce. "I know Perry Hooks didn't call you, not after I spent all that time chasing him?"

"You best believe it."

"Don't play with me, Errick." Perry Hooks—Gulf War I hero, seasoned community activist, and the first black governor of Ohio—was the presidential candidate the Dream Party most wanted as its standard bearer. The man was thirty-eight years old, and we were hoping he was just crazy enough to risk his 60 percent job approval with Ohioans and run with our backing. I had discussed it with my staff, and the timing made perfect sense: get him out there while he was still popular, with the juice to garner maximum media coverage and wake people up at the same time. Given my experience writing speeches for my father's Senate and presidential campaigns, I'd even started drafting a platform and an announcement speech.

The only wrinkle had been getting the governor to return our calls.

I had reached out to Perry first, getting through his secretaries and spinmeisters on the strength of our family history. Perry still tells the story of how he wrote a letter to my father during Frederick's first term in the Senate, when Perry was just an ambitious seminary student. Apparently my father knew talent when he saw it. He flew Perry into Washington, allowing the budding activist to shadow him for an entire week. At Perry's inauguration two years ago, he credited Frederick for his belief that elected officials could transform real people's lives.

As a result, I guess, Perry had been very gracious during our conversations, but had delayed giving us any answer, asking instead that "my people call his people" for a while, until he had time to see whether a presidential run made sense. Given that I hadn't heard boo from the brother in my last six weeks at work, I had written him off. The fact he'd agreed to dinner with Uncle James and Errick had to signal a change of heart.

"He's not making any promises," Errick said, lowering his voice after we'd spastically high-fived each other. "He just called and said he wants to talk. But he wouldn't have ever called if you hadn't laid the groundwork with him." He leaned closer. "I want you to help me close the deal. You deserve to be there."

As Errick continued running his mouth, discussing the best polling data and historical research to put in front of Perry, my initial euphoria plummeted. In all my excitement, I had forgotten one thing. Convincing the nation's second black governor to run for president was a big-league task, and with my verbal baggage, I wasn't sure I was up for it.

"I don't know what value I'd add," I said. "Uncle James knows Perry better than either of us, and you don't need my help to suck up to him."

Errick went oddly silent for a minute; then he said, "Ah hell, this ain't about your stutterfest on Fox again, is it?"

"What do you think?"

"Come on, Deke. It was bad, don't get me wrong, but you hardly ever go out like that. You'll be fine, especially with me and Uncle James there for backup."

"You don't know that, and neither do I," I replied. "One thing I learned in that clinic, Errick, is that d-different types of stresses, and d-different types of situations, make it harder for me to stay fluent. The Fox interview was a high-stress situation, one I hadn't faced in a while. Now, I've had dinner with plenty of folks, from politicians to celebrities, but I've never sat toe to toe with a living legend and convinced him to risk his entire career."

Errick looked at me, disappointment in his eyes as he wiped barbecue sauce off his face. "What's your point, Deke? You don't think you can handle stressful situations, even after that clinic?"

"I left the clinic before I learned everything," I said. "That's the point. I'm trying to feel my way, get my confidence back, but I need to start small. You don't want to drag me into prime time, not now. Give me some time."

Errick plucked his wallet from his slacks and planted a stack of dollar bills in the middle of the table. "Make sure Sue gets that tip," he said, referring to the waitress. "I gotta run."

I heard the anger in his tone, acted like it didn't register. "I'll rap later."

"Oh, you'll be hearing from me." Errick was at the front door, his back to me, by the time I looked up.

I finished my lunch at a leisurely pace, threw a couple more bills onto the table, and sauntered out to my car. I knew Errick was losing patience with me, but he hadn't walked so much as a step in my shoes. There were times a disability like stuttering held the worst of both worlds. At its face-twisting, tongue-tying worst, it left you naked before the world, a ripe punch line for those seeking amusement. Tough as that was, it would never win the politically correct, sympathetic reactions afforded to the blind, deaf, and wheelchair-bound. It's like people figured speech problems were something folk like me should just "get over."

Even as a mild stutterer, I'd been told time and again that I could be cured if I would just speak more slowly. I noticed that advice never came from people who'd actually stuttered themselves. Then there were those who implied that any stammer was evidence of a character flaw, as if every serial killer known to man had the same problem. For years I had bowed to these and other assaults, but I was determined to free myself. One day I'd be ready to tackle the stress of hobnobbing with a Perry Hooks, but there was no sense jumping into the fray before I was ready.

After spending the afternoon completing teaching applications at the Cobb County School Board, I went to the gym. I'd been away during my clinic stay, so all the regulars welcomed me back. I knew I'd grown a little bit in the clinic when I told a few of them where I'd been and how I was working to avoid any more Fox-style stutterfests. In between conversations, I threw myself into one of my usual routines—a high-impact step class, twelve sets of dumbbells, and half an hour on the bikes.

When I let myself into my front door, I dropped my workout bag in the foyer and headed straight for the kitchen, where I freshened Prince's water and food bowls. Still pumped up with endorphins from the workout, I decided to call Mercedes, before anticipating all the ways our conversation could go wrong.

Dialing her work number, I got her answering service, and began to leave a message when she suddenly picked up. "Deacon?"

"Good, I caught you," I said. "I know you're probably headed out the door to pick up Liza, but I needed to catch you."

"Actually, I'll be here until eight or nine tonight. We're trying to get the firm's annual report approved."

"Who's picking Liza up, then?"

Silence from Mercedes, then she said, "Bob agreed to get her for me."

Her boyfriend was picking up my little girl, when I was available? "How long has this been going on?"

"Oh, God, Deacon, every few weeks at most."

"I told you b-before, when you work late, I should be your first backup for Liza."

"I know you said that, but I also know you've had your hands full lately." The sarcasm in her tone was wild and free, all up in my face. "I heard about your troubles, Deacon, all of them, from your fight with Dejuan's principal to your resignation from the Dream Party. Is there anything I can do to help?"

I bit my lip before replying. "I'm fine. Don't worry about it."

"Are you sure? I don't want Liza to open the paper someday soon and read embarrassing things about her daddy, Deacon. I have a hard enough time explaining Miles's problems with the law."

"She's too young to know anything about Miles's problems," I said, feeling my neck muscles tense.

"Well, we all know he'll have more," Mercedes replied. "Is he really going through with this book of conspiracy theories about your father?"

My right temple pulsed anxiously at the thought of Miles and his search for the truth. "He's not crazy, Mercedes. He may not turn out to be right, but he's raising some valid questions about what happened to Frederick."

A nervous-sounding laugh tittered out of Mercedes before she said, "Don't tell me he's converted you, too."

"Don't misunderstand me," I replied. "I hope he's wrong." I knew Mercedes did, too; the last thing she wanted was to have the authorities digging back through Big Walter's scandalous past.

"I *know* he's wrong," she replied. "Enough about that, though. How was your clinic? Are you stuttering any less?"

"I d-don't know. Wuh-wuh-what d-do you tha-tha-think?"

"Oh, you got jokes, huh?"

"Don't worry about the clinic, Mercedes."

"Still standoffish, even now, huh?" I could imagine her crossing her arms on the other end of the line. "You never let me help you when I was your wife and lover—now I can't even help you as a friend, huh?"

Mercedes's dig resurrected the day I moved out of our Decatur home. Liza was at preschool, and I chose my timing to make sure she wasn't around. What I hadn't counted on was Mercedes arriving home early. She walked in on me as I shoveled my two best suits into a garment bag, and it got ugly.

Bear in mind, I was newly retired from the Steelers at the time, after the nation's top arthroscopic surgeon insisted the risks of having my shoulder sewn up a third time outweighed the possible benefits. Newly unemployed, I'd also lost both my endorsement deals, after flubbing my delivery during a taping for a big car dealership. For her part, Mercedes was rightfully pissed at me for not wanting to discuss my struggles with her. When she'd asked me what I was doing moving out, then taken me to task for being so self-contained, I hit her with the straw that broke the camel's back for me: the secret bank account I'd found.

In the course of setting up a new investment account for me, my loan officer had come across an account in Mercedes's maiden name, or should I say the name she'd created for herself when she ran away from Big Walter. She had more than a hundred grand in there, this account she'd apparently opened while in college. When I told her what I'd found, she knew there was no denying that she'd lied to me about her finances. I'd always suspected that Big Walter had left some of his drug money behind, but Mercedes had sworn she'd walked away from every last dime when she filed for legal emancipation, after Walter had her first boyfriend killed.

That's how it went down that day—one accusation after another flying back and forth, with stifled anger and anxieties bubbling forth like lava. She blamed her secrecy on my mother's petty intrusions; I reminded her that no one forced her to lie to me. We might have stayed there all day going back and forth if Mercedes hadn't lost it and come at me with a heated flurry of long nails and four-letter words. As she removed a heel, like I'd actually let her do anything with it, I stared at my wife blankly before throwing my suit bag over my shoulder and striding toward the front door. Mercedes followed me out to our circular driveway, shouting obscenities all the way, but she kept her hands off me, so I didn't have to touch her. My truck full with clothing, a computer, and a toiletry bag, I'd fired up the engine and sped off.

As I sat on the phone with Mercedes two and a half years later, I refused to repeat the same arguments. "I called," I said, "to say that Dejuan arrives in town next week, through August. I hope you won't mind me having Liza more often during that time."

Mercedes paused, thrown off guard. "Regardless of what I think, I can't stop Liza from seeing her big brother." The memory of her own childhood wiped clean, Mercedes looked down on Dejuan and Candy, as if my son's working-class upbringing would reach out and infect our baby. "She thinks Dejuan walks on water."

We were each silent for another minute, trying to small-talk our way off the phone as quickly as possible. As we sat there playing games, I lamented what we'd lost, from our first night together, during a Freaknic weekend when I impulsively pulled her onto the dance floor at a club, to the day I proposed, which was the morning after I learned she was expecting with Liza, to our high-society, drama-riddled wedding day. Our saga had ended, but I couldn't regret the ride. Not only had we made a beautiful baby, but at moments we'd shared the type of bond that lives forever.

Regret piling up inside me, a faint vision dimmed the pain: the sight of Maria astride me, our bodies locked in a furtive search for solace. The look on her face was seared into my memory—a joyful smile, one I guessed had been all too rare in recent years. I knew our story wasn't finished.

17

Maria

After my last morning appointment, I retrieved my lunch from the office refrigerator and returned to my desk to check my home voice mail. I had two messages. The first was from Andy, my Alcoholics Anonymous sponsor, who was checking up on me after my latest blowup with Thomas and Lucille. The second call was from Jamil's father.

"Hi, Maria, this is Guy." A pause, then I heard him gulp nervously. "I know you don't want to hear from me, but Thomas told me about your argument. I'm not trying to get in the middle of it, so don't get ghetto, 'kay? If you would just respond to one of my letters, let me explain things in person—"

I pressed the appropriate button and smiled grimly as the automated voice droned, "Message deleted."

I had nearly finished off my lunch, a tuna sandwich, when Ramsey appeared in the doorway of my office. Dressed in a beige silk shirt with matching slacks, he pointed a finger in my direction. "So, I haven't had time to ask you. Wasn't Friday night something else!"

Friday had been the graduation ceremony for the clinic. It had been hard to believe that four weeks had already passed for Deacon's former classmates, but they had. To celebrate, each client gave a five-minute presentation on his or her experience, after playing their own introductory videotapes from the clinic's first day. In every case, the progress made from day one to the end had been phenomenal. Amberly, Terrell, and even Bill, whose affliction had been relatively mild, looked like inmates whose shackles had just been loosed. Between their beaming expressions and the looks of relief, pride, and appreciation flooding the faces of their families, it was a deeply emotional night. More than ever, I was convinced that I had chosen the right calling as a fluency specialist. We couldn't cure our clients, but we could definitely improve their quality of life.

"It was life-changing," I said as Ramsey hovered in the doorway, his eyes lit by a wide grin. "I was so proud of each of them! Little Terrell, I mean, he went from being unable to get two words out straight to sounding so at ease." I paused, caught my breath. "I'm curious about how long the effects hold, once they've been back in the real world for a while, but I really feel like we gave them a head start."

"Oh, you'll see," Ramsey replied, assurance bolstering his words. "We'll be contacting each of them on a monthly basis for the next year, plus we'll hold weekend refresher clinics every six months. Your research on environmental stress should be especially helpful, Maria. So get ready to put those statistics to work!"

"I'll be ready," I said, chuckling. Ramsey's enthusiasm was infectious.

Ramsey's laughter and mine died down in a few seconds, and he strode toward my desk. "With the clinic over, we can start integrating you into the regular practice now," he said. "But before we start that process, we have a lingering issue with respect to the SRC."

A wave of nerves warmed my stomach. "What?"

"I still don't feel right about Deacon Davis," he said, sitting back in a chair opposite me. "It bugs the hell out of me that we lost him. We could have gotten so much publicity if he'd stuck with us, made it through."

"I don't think it's worth your time to worry about," I replied, hoping to get off this topic as quickly as possible.

The morning after Deacon stormed away from the clinic, I had taken it for granted that he would call me. I wasn't stupid enough to think we were in love, but I at least figured he'd want some closure. I mean, our stolen moment had complicated his life far more than it had mine. By the following week, reality had started to dawn: I was just one of many PYT's who had momentarily crossed his path.

Now, two weeks after the fact, I just wanted to forget he existed. We hadn't exactly become soul mates in two weeks, we'd had only a few personal conversations, and as far as I was concerned, I could still point him out in a crowd and say "I did *not* have sex with that man. . . ." At least, as long as I used a layered, Clinton-style definition of sex.

"Shouldn't we focus on the clients who stuck it out?" I said to Ramsey. We had lost two others along the way. "They're the ones who took what they needed from the experience."

"You're probably right," Ramsey said, letting an index finger slide down his temple and then across his cheek. "I just wonder if I was too hard on him. In your time together, did he ever express anger toward me?"

"Well, no more than anyone else," I said, cracking a grin.

"Maybe I'm just feeling more self-aware these days, Maria. Going through a divorce can do that to you."

Though I was relieved at anything that got the subject away from Deacon, I was still shocked by the sudden slump in Ramsey's shoulders. It was so unusual seeing him like that. I leaned forward in my chair, mindful of the need to keep a professional distance, and said, "It's not easy, keeping family issues from infecting your work."

His eyes still heavy with pain, Ramsey peered at me, questions dancing behind his stare. "What's wrong with your family, Maria? I know you've mentioned a brother to me several times. Is he okay?"

"Oh yes, he's fine. We just don't get along very well, is all."

"What do you have disagreements about?"

Suddenly, I was just too tired to play games. Ramsey had been nothing but a supportive boss to me these past several months, and though I'd initially suspected a covert agenda on his part, a growing, friendly rapport had developed. It wasn't sexual chemistry, just a comfortable vibe I felt in his presence. A vibe strong enough that I answered his question honestly. "Our disagreements are about my son. His name is Jamil."

Ramsey didn't drop the pen in his hand, so I don't know for sure how quiet my office got, but for what felt like minutes, the only sound was our respective inhaling and exhaling. Finally he ran a hand over the tip of his nose and asked, "Jamil is your *brother's* son, or yours?"

My heart hummed anxiously, but I sat upright in my chair and looked straight ahead. "Mine."

"Whoa," Ramsey replied. "I just got an education." As he stood and began pacing a circle in front of my doorway, I could feel Ramsey's opinion of me plummeting. Watching him, I grabbed hold of every defensive thought available. *Fool's probably been waiting to get his hands on my young, innocent flesh, only now he sees I'm not so pure. Excuse the hell out of me.*

After a couple of laps around the chair, Ramsey eased his way over to my side of the desk, where he stood over me. "You didn't have to hide this from me, Maria," he said, his eyes probing mine. "Seriously. I mean, legally, I could feel you've wronged me by claiming no children on your employment applications, but a matter that personal is your business, no one else's. I assume you're not raising him?"

Maybe I should have just told Deacon everything when he'd first probed, or maybe I just appreciated Ramsey's understanding tone now, but the next thing I knew I gave him a history lesson in how Jamil came to be. The more things flowed out of me, the more they took on a life of their own. I realized I'd lost control when I mentioned my last dinner with Thomas and Lucille, where they'd threatened me with a bruising trial featuring Guy and my entire sordid history.

"They can't do that," Ramsey said, his eyes bulging, his mouth wide open. His usual veneer of assured arrogance had been replaced by naïve shock. "My God, Maria, what you did for that child was an act of love. Why would your own brother side with your ex-boyfriend, for any reason?"

"It's complicated." As angry as I was with Thomas, it wouldn't be fair to bring up his and Lucille's infertility. "They've had Jamil so long now, they can't fathom having to give him up."

"Well, between you and me," Ramsey said, caressing my hands gently, "they're doing you and your son a grave disservice. You don't have to take this lying down."

I shook Ramsey's hand gratefully, then released it and turned back to my desk. "I don't want to overwhelm you with my problems," I said, reaching for a manila folder with my latest research notes. "I'm counting on God to give me the right guidance eventually."

Ramsey stepped back from my desk and turned toward the door, but kept his eyes on me. "That's admirable, but when you're ready to let God work through an earthly vessel, you just let me know. My divorce attorney is the best, very experienced in all aspects of family law. I think you need to have a chat with him, explore all of your options."

I thanked Ramsey again and we agreed to meet in the afternoon so that he could brief me on some clients he planned to place in my care. Once he was gone, I sat at my desk, muttering under my breath as I dived into my research notes. Ramsey's offer had been nice, but given my financial issues, I couldn't even afford a diagnostic meeting with his attorney, much less a retainer to actually put him on the case.

Glancing out my window, I noticed the sky had darkened. The leaves on the nearest red maple tree fluttered violently, straining against a growing wind. With August ending, fall waited just around the corner, meaning this tree's leaves and others would soon lose battles with chilly temperatures and unwelcome rains. Considering the weather in my own life, I related all too closely to that struggling tree.

18

Maria

Deacon's call interrupted my evening conversation with Alicia, just as she was helping me make some sense of my life. I clicked back over to Alicia, told her who was on the line.

"Um, you know what I'm thinking?" she said. "Be nice to him, girl, but don't get tangled up. That boy comes with too much baggage."

"Now why would you say that? I'm not exactly Pippi Longstocking here."

"Look, it's not just that he has kids by two other mommas, and is so emotionally conflicted, he's got this stuttering thing going on—"

"Alicia, most stutterers' problems are physiological. They're not usually caused by emotional problems."

"Excuse me. Whatever the reason, he stutters, he's got a trail of women and kids coming after him, and he's from a high-profile family. Where's he gonna find time for you?"

"I'm not trying to marry him, I just want some closure," I replied. "Look, you're gonna make me miss the brother altogether. Bye."

"Whatever."

I clicked back over to Deacon's line, let a smile sweeten my tone. "And how may I help you, Mr. Davis?"

"Did you think I lost your business card?" This was my first time hearing his voice over the phone. His baritone felt even deeper and more melodious from afar.

"I didn't know what to think," I said, sitting back in my lounger chair. "I hope you didn't feel obligated just because I wrote my home number on there."

"I would've been offended if you hadn't," Deacon replied. "Don't let me front. A year ago I could make love to a woman, or start to, and simply walk away. That time has passed."

"I almost forgot," I said, smiling and eager to lighten the moment. "Your biggest fan made me swear to deliver a message on his behalf." I could hear the grin in Deacon's voice. "Terrell?"

"You know it. He was really upset when you left, but I calmed him down by saying he could be a good example for you. Now that he's graduated from the clinic, he wants to convince you to get back into therapy, too."

"Hey, I'll hear the little dude out," Deacon said.

"More than that, Deacon, I really think he wants a big brother figure, one who can relate to what he's going through."

Deacon sighed. "Well, we'll just ignore the fact that my life isn't exactly straight out of a textbook for success these days. Whatever I can do for him, I'll do."

I read off Terrell's number for him, then spoke my mind. "You could have leveled with Folger about what happened, Deacon. I panicked when everything went down, but I was ready to quit the clinic if you'd been up front with him."

"Why would you do that?" Deacon's voice went up into a slightly higher pitch. "One night you say your whole life rides on this clinic working out for you, then you're willing to quit two days later?" He paused in thought. "Why the change in attitude?"

A bead of sweat broke out just above my lip. Despite the fact we were miles apart, it was like Deacon had backed me into a corner. "Who says something changed, besides me growing up and being an adult? I lost control with you. I was ready to pay the price."

"Maria," Deacon said, "what we did was natural from where I stand. Maybe our timing wasn't the best, but you can't second-guess it. Now tell me, why are you so eager to throw away your career all of a sudden?"

Formulating my answer, I reached up and pinched myself on the cheek, working up the will to keep Deacon out of my real world. Who was he to want intimate details on my problems already? Didn't he realize we were still in the "fronting" stage, when you kept your dirty laundry at the bottom of the hamper? I wasn't ready to go into the truth about Jamil, Thomas, and Guy. About the hopelessness that had wrapped me in its arms. Not yet.

"There's really nothing more to it than I'm telling you," I lied. "What do you want, Deacon? I don't have all night." My evening really wasn't going to be that busy, aside from doing some laundry, but he didn't need to know that.

"I can tell when I'm getting the brush-off," he responded, "but I wasn't trained to give up easily. I need a duh . . . a duh-duh . . ." He trailed off, clearly frustrated.

"Deacon," I said, putting on my therapist hat, "you haven't been away from the clinic that long. Don't fight the word, just flow with the stuttering, feel your way through it. Release the tension."

"Got you," he said, his tone noticeably darker now. "I need a date, Maria."

I felt my eyebrows arch with skepticism. "A date for what?"

"Have you heard of the Greater Atlanta Disabled Children's Fund?"

"Yes. What about it?"

"Well," he replied, "I was on the planning committee for the fund's big annual benefit, which is Saturday. I just realized I have no one to take. Since I don't dare go by myself, I thought I'd invite the last girl I got naked with."

"There's that Davis charm, huh?"

"Seriously, Maria. My ex will be there with her man, and the last thing I need is to show up looking like the lonely loser."

"So I'm a placeholder. Very flattering."

"Come on," he replied, laughter filling his voice. "It's more than that. I didn't exactly simplify your life while I was in the clinic. Let me make it up to you. I'll treat you to a nice dinner afterwards."

I smiled to myself. "Why don't we go out with your ex and her man? That'll make for a fun-filled evening."

"Uh, no. But in case you're wondering, her name's Mercedes, and her man is named Bobby Joe—"

"That's his real name?"

"No, it's my shorthand for Robert 'Bob' Cooper. He just has that look of a white boy from the Deep South, whose parents probably called him Bobby Joe."

"He's white?"

"Yeah. Do I sound bitter?"

"Just a bit."

"Forget about all that," Deacon said, his voice dropping and nearing a whisper. His voice reached for my buttons, persuading but not begging. "This is about you and me. I could call any number of women to be at my side, Maria. I want you there with me. Say no, and I'll have to be a no-show for this thing."

Considering Deacon's offer, my brain quickly rolled the dice. There were so many ways that accepting this invitation could go wrong, the first being if Ramsey ever found out. Even though we were growing closer as boss and employee, I knew he still harbored a suspicion about my attraction to Deacon and my "disappearance" the night the shit hit the fan. Although my anxiety about Jamil had upset me enough for me to risk losing my job, the moment had passed. I still wanted to sue Thomas for custody, but I needed to keep this job. How else could I prove my fitness to the courts?

For the record, I'm not stupid; I was plenty aware of the vortex of potential problems surrounding Deacon. A true roll of the dice would have confirmed that the odds weren't in favor of my wading deeper into his waters, but my curiosity about this man won out. I leaned all the way back in my seat, closing my eyes and saying a prayer in my head.

"What time will you pick me up?"

19

Maria

The following weekend, as Deacon and I arrived in midtown and pulled up to the Woodruff Arts Center, he made a reluctant confession. Wouldn't you know—he forgot to mention that children were allowed to attend the benefit, given its cause, and that his ex, Mercedes, was bringing little Liza along. With the exception of his older son, Dejuan, I'd have the pleasure of meeting Deacon's entire little family unit. Oh, joy.

Once we had parked at Colony Square and made the short walk to the ballroom where the benefit was being held, I tried to focus on the beautiful decorations. Anything to keep my mind off Deacon's news.

Deacon filled me in on the history behind his involvement in the disabled children's foundation. The foundation provided aid to children with a wide range of organic disabilities—the blind, the deaf, the learning disabled, the mentally challenged, and thanks to recent advocacy by my profession, stutterers. Deacon had known some troubled children who'd been helped by the foundation, and had started volunteering his support a couple of years ago, before the board invited him to sign on.

Before we saw Mercedes and Liza, we ran into one of my people. Alicia had already been planning to attend the benefit with her husband, Trent, and had been all too eager to meet Deacon in person, though she'd promised to be on her best behavior. She was already acting the fool when we crossed her path, arguing with some Hulk Hogan look-alike who turned out to be a bodyguard for D'Angelo, the night's entertainment.

Sticking her fingers in the big white guy's face, Alicia insisted that she'd been promised she could meet D'Angelo backstage. A friend of a mutual friend had made promises, all that jazz. The guard just smiled lazily as Alicia switched her case, claiming she was the singer's number-one fan and even crediting him with the conception of both of her sons, which I knew was bull because Trent only makes love to jazz.

Once she was done saying her piece, and being rejected again, Alicia turned to us. She got her predictable digs in, eyeing Deacon up and down, oohing and ahhing at how "big" he was and telling as much of my business as she could. It wasn't long before I pushed her back into a corner where Trent stood with some partners from his brokerage firm.

Deacon and I grabbed glasses of champagne and began working the room carefully. We were enjoying ourselves, but really weren't sure how to describe our relationship to people, especially his many business associates and acquaintances. All things considered, we tried not to act too much like a couple—no public displays of affection, no hanging all over each other, and so on.

I suggested the cautious approach for a good reason. Even though I knew Ramsey wouldn't be there, I didn't need anyone else from the speech pathology community whispering words into his ear. Perhaps some day soon there'd be enough between me and Deacon to bring everything out into the open, but we had a few miles to cover before I could risk my career over him.

Those concerns faded when we finally ran into Mercedes, Liza, and Bobby Joe-what's-his-name. "Oh, boy," Deacon said, exhaling loudly as they approached. "If my stomach's upset, it's b-because Mercedes is headed this way. Let me handle this. If you don't make any sudden moves, you'll be okay." I couldn't tell if he was joking or not.

20

Deacon

A funny thing happened as my family approached Maria and me. Bob, knowing he didn't want none of this, veered off suddenly in another direction after patting Mercedes on the arm. Mercedes continued toward us, but Liza left her far behind as my little girl broke free and bolted toward me.

"Oh, she's even cuter than that picture in your dorm room." Maria, still shaken by my well-meant warning, looked absolutely radiant. Her hair wrapped in a tight chignon, she wore a black crepe cocktail dress with matching heels. She had acted nonchalant about my initial invitation last week, but it was clear from the "new-car smell" of her outfit that she took me seriously. Her style matched her persona perfectly: simple beauty.

As Liza reached me, I opened my arms, my chest warming with pride at the familiar sight of my baby. An even fusion of my gene pool and Mercedes's, she was a beige-skinned little ball of energy, her black ruffled dress trying to keep up with her fast pace.

"Daddy!" She let me kiss her on the cheek, then placed her hands on my shoulders and peered into my eyes. "I told everybody you were coming!"

I knelt down, setting her back on the floor, then ran a hand over her smooth little cheek. "You been behaving yourself?"

"Of course," she said, smiling back at me innocently. At seven years old, my baby could do no wrong in my eyes, but I wasn't stupid. Liza was a little firecracker, bright as all get-out but on her way to being a bit cocky. She had inherited her strong ego honestly—completely from Mercedes, of course—but it was getting to be time to teach the child some humility.

"Who's that?" Liza said, peering around me and twirling a lock of her pressed curls in her right hand.

I stepped back, placing a hand behind Maria's back. "This is my friend Ms. Maria. Say hello."

Liza looked up into Maria's eyes, squaring her shoulders proudly. "Hello, Ms. Maria. What's your last name?"

Maria glanced at me quizzically before answering with a smile. "Oliver, Maria Oliver's my name, Liza. That sure is a pretty dress you have on. Are you excited to hang with these grown folks tonight?"

"More excited than she should be," said a voice from over my shoulder. Mercedes Crystal Wallace slid in between Maria and me, placing a gentle hand on each of our shoulders. Her lean, muscular body draped in a black satin dress with a respectfully plunging neckline, a glistening gold necklace hanging toward her scoop-size breasts, Mercedes was ready for everyone's attention. Glancing at me through the frames of her black designer glasses, she smiled her blinding million-dollar smile, the same one that won new clients for her investment firm every day. "How are you this evening, Deacon?"

"Surviving, Mercedes," I replied, eager to move things along. "Look, I'd like you to meet—"

"Liza, you've been playing with your hair again, haven't you?" Mercedes focused her gaze on Liza's little head of twisty curls. "I swear, I turn my head one second, and she undoes an hour's worth of work." My ex turned away and bent over Liza, her intense hazel eyes glowing against her manila-colored skin. "I'm not fixing your hair this time," she said. "You're going to do it as soon as we can find a ladies' room. For now, straighten your dress."

Liza paused, looking to me for some type of defense. Ordinarily I would have taken up for her, but since we were in public and I had Maria with me, I wasn't up for a scene. When Liza realized I was staying on the sidelines, she huffed out an "Okay, Mommy," before straightening her dress, folding her arms, and leaning against me so she could sulk.

Mercedes turned back toward me, but trained her eyes on Maria this time. "Now, you are who again?"

"Maria Oliver," she replied, offering a hand. "A friend of Deacon's."

"Oh, isn't that sweet of Deacon to bring you out tonight," Mercedes said, flashing her impossibly white teeth. "Where are you all friends from?"

"It's smelling mighty nosy in here," I said, steering Maria toward our assigned table. No one needed to know about our clinic connection, definitely not so close to my expulsion. I turned over my shoulder to Mercedes as Maria and I took a step away. "We have an extra seat reserved for Liza. She can sit with us."

"She can sit with you, that's fine," Mercedes replied, spitting the words out through tight lips. "Why don't you let Maria take Liza over to the table?" She reached out suddenly, touching a hand to my wrist. "You still owe me some answers from the other night." She looked around me again, capturing Maria's attention. "I do have some rights, being the mother of his child and all."

Maria had a funny look on her face, like a cat trapped between dueling dogs. "Uh, yes, I suppose so."

Mercedes's eyebrows arched impatiently, as if she wondered why Maria still stood before her. "Seriously, do you mind if I speak with Deacon for a minute?"

Maria hesitated, looked in my direction.

Stuck in a momentary speech block, I was still mute when Mercedes winked at Maria and said, "I really appreciate it." Maria may as well have been one of her employees at the firm.

"I'll be right there," I assured Maria, stroking her shoulder lightly.

"Whatever," she sang sarcastically. In a flash, she dropped my hand, took Liza's, and headed toward our table, her beautiful round hips sauntering with attitude.

Nodding at a few passing familiar faces, I crossed my arms and drew Mercedes closer with the wiggle of a finger. "Why was that necessary? You can't call me later?"

"No offense, I just wanted to catch up." She looked at her handbag, which was vibrating, and pulled out a miniature cell phone. "I didn't want your friend to be intimidated," she said as she looked at the phone's screen then snapped it back shut.

I took a deep breath, let it out slowly. "What did you want?"

"Has Dejuan arrived in town yet?"

"No, I'm picking him up tomorrow morning. We can pick Liza up on the way home from the airport, right?"

"Who's *we*?" Mercedes stepped closer to me, the smell of her perfume, hairspray, and natural scent wafting through the air. "You're going to have Maria over, too?"

"No," I said with a slight roll of the eyes, "it'll just be me and the kids. Maria's just a friend."

Mercedes chuckled. "For now. What might she be next month, Deacon?"

I didn't know if my stunned silence had more to do with my anger at the question or at my inability to answer it. I really had called Maria because I wanted to end our clinic experience on a more positive note, but seeing her again had reminded me of the real attraction there. If only I felt truly ready for her.

Now Mercedes had her hand on my shoulder. "Never mind, Deacon. Bob's going to be pissy if I don't get over to our table. I'll find you all after D'Angelo's performance, so I can get Liza." She stepped ahead of me, then turned back suddenly. "I hope you and the girl hit it off, really I do. Whatever makes you a better daddy to Liza."

I stood there for a second, watching my ex walk off as the ballroom lights dimmed and the master of ceremonies stepped out on stage to loud applause. I was eager to get to my table and spend time with both Maria and Liza, but seeing my ex had already thrown a wet blanket over my mood. The more I considered the love we'd lost, the more I wondered if I was wasting Maria's time.

21

Maria

After the benefit, Deacon offered to prepare dinner for me at his place, to allow for more conversation and probably something else, if I had to guess. I appreciated his decision, though, because my head was swimming with questions. I played it cool during most of the ride to his house, which we interrupted with a quick stop at a Publix in his neighborhood. I kept things surface level, telling Deacon how well everyone from the clinic was doing, mentioning a few details about my research project, and quizzing him about his job search.

When we pulled into the driveway of his home, a one-level brick house on a corner lot, this poor little girl was impressed. Stepping from his foyer and into a huge great room with a cathedral ceiling, I swept my eyes over his black leather furniture, stainless steel fixtures, and recessed lighting. My gold-digging girlfriends would say it was "just ah-ight" for a former football star, but for me it was a dream pad. "Ooh, I'd be so psyched to have a place like this sometime next year. With more of a feminine touch, of course."

"Yeah, it's functional and, most important, it's paid for," Deacon said, whistling as he completed my tour of the three bedrooms, his home office, and two and a half baths.

"Must be nice."

"Well, let's just say I lived beneath my means while I was in the NFL. Most of the money I saved is in college funds for the kids. The balance I used to pay for this house with cash." Deacon crossed the floor of the great room. "Just one more feature of the house to introduce you to." Opening the back door, he stepped onto his covered patio. "Prince! Come on, boy." As he took another step out onto the patio's vinyl floor, a large black Labrador bounded up to him. "This is my partner in crime," Deacon said, looking at me over his shoulder as he ran his hands up and down the big dog's shiny black coat.

"I should probably let him in—he's been out here since I left to pick you up. You mind? I'll make him behave."

"Fine with me," I said, choosing to reveal later that I'm a cat person.

My pride didn't get the best of me until Deacon had washed his hands and started slicing and dicing tomatoes, celery, and cucumbers for the salad. Since he wouldn't let me help in the kitchen, I sat stranded at his breakfast nook, reading a copy of *Ebony* magazine while Will Downing serenaded us from the perch of Deacon's home entertainment system. "So," I said, clearing my throat and trying to sound nonchalant, "are you and Mercedes the type of parents who are friends despite the divorce, or the type who tolerate each other for Liza's sake?"

"It's not that easy to categorize our relationship," he replied, his tone even more vague than his words.

I knew I must be halfway feeling Deacon Davis, because I cared enough to keep pressing. "Did you file for divorce, or her?"

Deacon had his back to me now, a hand to his lips as he surveyed a selection of wine bottles stocked over his stove. "I filed." He'd morphed into the typical male on me.

I played nervously with my locket, wondering how far I could push him. "Why?"

"It's complicated. You don't want to get into this already, do you?"

I crossed my legs and trained my eyes on him, meeting his stare as he turned around with a wine selection in hand. "Why am I here, Deacon? You just want to finish what we already started, is that it?"

He set the bottle down on the counter, went back to the salad bowl. "Is that what you think of me?"

"Tell me what I should think of you."

"I filed," he said slowly, "because she lied to me."

I kept my tone calm as I stroked the back of Prince's head. He was pretty restrained compared with Labs I'd seen before. "Did she have an affair?"

"Not to say there weren't people tempting each of us, but as far as I know, no. At the time, we were in such bad shape that it didn't matter anymore."

"Were *you* cheating?"

"Oh, hell no," he replied, setting the completed salad into the refrigerator. He pulled out what looked like a Tupperware dish with marinating meat. "Not that I didn't mess up while we were dating and engaged, for that matter. Once the rings went on, though, I put myself on sexual lockdown. You eat sea bass?"

There was something I hadn't tried in a while. Too often, dinner for me was a bowl of Toasted Oats on the run or a Snickers. "Sounds lovely."

"Cool. I'll whip up some string beans with it. Anyway, our main problems revolved around work. I was with the Steelers during the entire length of our marriage, and no pro athlete makes a great spouse. The traveling, the knucklehead teammates clowning you for not banging the same groupies they do, the constant p-pressure to deliver and keep a hungry rookie or journeyman from taking your spot—it adds up. Then I lost my endorsement deals."

Deacon told me how he'd lived on pins and needles when taping commercials. By the time he entered the NFL, the only people who knew that he stuttered were his agent, who'd heard him hit a few bad patches over the phone, and two of his closest teammates.

"You were 'in the closet,' so to speak," I said. I knew many mild stutterers could successfully hide their affliction, but hadn't thought Deacon was the type to do so.

"I learned from a young age about the price of stuttering," Deacon said. "Some people in my family assumed I'd never be fit to follow in Frederick's footsteps. They at least acted out of love, unlike the high school debate coach who kicked me off the team when I fell apart during one match." Deacon turned back toward the stove, placing the fish on a grill and dropping the string beans into a pot of boiling water. "No, I knew I had to get creative in life, do what it took to keep people from figuring me out. I would substitute words I could say for those I might stutter on, stay quiet when I really should have spoken up, you name it. Whatever helped me pass as normal."

Deacon told me how everything had caught up to him, especially once he retired early and had to face life without the cover of a helmet and pads. I stood and approached him as he stirred the beans and monitored the fish. "So Mercedes couldn't help you through that time?"

"She tried, but she had her hands full building her investment firm, not to mention that I wasn't really asking for help. I withdrew from things for a while, even before I retired. I would show up at work every day for practices and games, but said as little as I had to, and went straight home afterwards. I even stopped doing postgame interviews, for fear I'd fall apart on the air and make a true ass of myself."

"That had to be a lot of pressure," I said.

"It was, on me and on Mercedes. She kept trying to get me into speech therapy, pyschotherapy, anything, and I wasn't having it. If I accepted professional help, I'd be admitting I was a failure, and I couldn't cop to that. I slowly shut Mercedes out, so much so that by the time I figured out the secrets she'd kept from me, we'd run out of anything to hang on to."

As we continued talking about Deacon's past, I was on uneven ground, straddling the fence of therapist and lover. So much more lurked beneath Deacon's moody exterior than I had imagined, and I was honored by his openness. The funny thing was, I was getting off easy, not sharing one bit of my own mess.

Meeting Mercedes had resurrected all sorts of insecurities lurking deep within me. As tall, striking, sexy, and commanding as she was, she would have fit right in with some of the girls who'd ripped out chunks of my hair in the halls of Washington High School, after I started competing for the attention of their boyfriends junior year.

Until then, I'd been the shy bookworm, wearing thrift-shop clothes that Alicia's family purchased for me and keeping my focus on getting into college. It had taken meeting Guy to loosen me up, and even though I didn't sleep with anyone else during those years, once Guy broke me in, something changed. I mean, I still wasn't trying to be anybody's beauty queen, but suddenly brothers were hollering at me daily, even in front of their supposed girlfriends. The attention flattered a sister's ego, but the price tag was humiliation at the hands of girls who knew their way around better than I did.

That's what Mercedes felt like to me, a sister who played the game of life better than I did. I was guessing she was a couple years older than me, but it wasn't just that. She oozed with all the things I'd hoped to have at my age: impeccable style, staunch self-confidence, and eye-popping beauty to match. By comparison, I was stuck in a time warp, still trying to reclaim my responsibilities as a mother and prove myself professionally.

I didn't share this with Deacon that night. By the time we talked more about his past, we had finished dinner and downed half the bottle of wine. After he put Prince back out on the covered patio, we moved to the leather couch in his great room. As I continued probing him mentally, I lay my head against his shoulder and placed a hand to his chest. By now his stereo had clicked over to Vivian Green's CD, and as "Emotional Roller Coaster" filled the room, I felt my hands go up, looked down love's steep drop, and screamed with delight.

Our lips brushed together lightly before the song was over; then things moved at warp speed. The memory of our aborted encounter hung in the air as we slowly undressed one another while kissing and taking breaks to massage each newly revealed shoulder, breast, thigh, and neck. When Deacon was down to his silk boxers and I had nothing but panties left, he picked me up with a swift, graceful motion and carried me to his master bedroom.

Vivian's strains reached through the walls, continuing the mood as Deacon laid me down and peeled back my panties. In seconds, he had slid up the bed and parked his head between my legs, loosening and limbering me up with an agile, nimble tongue. As I stifled screams of ecstasy, he let me remove his boxers, revealing him down to his every last robust, swelling inch. After rolling a condom down over his massive head, Deacon leaned over me and we kissed deeply, tonguing ferociously as I tangled with his penis, becoming more familiar with it by the moment. Then suddenly he was inside me, stroking with slow rhythmic motions that were just right. It was like he'd read my mind, knew that I was too green after years of celibacy to screw like some animal. Maybe it was just the change in setting; the frenzied rush of the dorm was gone, now replaced by the simple desire to please each other.

Between occasional naps, we carried on into the night, sharing our bodies, and I hoped, our souls, as well. With each kiss, each touch, I prayed I could give Deacon just what Mercedes couldn't. I didn't want to believe I'd surrendered my vow of celibacy for nothing.

22

Deacon

A pair of gruff hands shook me awake. "Dad. Yo, Dad. You mind clearin' out?"

Annoyed, I shot forward and peered through a haze into Dejuan's eyes. He stood over the couch I'd spent the night on, and just over his shoulder I could see Terrell, hanging back and trying to cover an impish grin with one hand.

"Dejuan," I said, sitting upright and adjusting the fit of my boxer briefs, "you just couldn't let me sleep, huh?"

"Terrell and I been up for the past hour already, Dad. We need the TV out here. It's the only one with Sega."

"Oh yeah, that's all that matters." I shoved my way off the couch and stood in the middle of the wood floor, trying to get my early morning bearings. I had driven Liza, Dejuan, and Terrell to the island of Saint Simons for the weekend, where we were staying in one of Errick and Shanna's vacation condos. Friday night we had gone out for pizza near the waterfront, then played miniature golf before hitting the pool. We'd spent most of Saturday on the beach, me swimming with Liza while the boys rode Jet Skis and went water skiing. Now that Sunday morning had rolled around, we planned to have a lazy breakfast, get in a final round of swimming, then head home.

"You all can play Sega for a minute while I wake Liza," I said, heading toward the guest bedroom. "But we're having Bible study in a few."

"C-cool," Terrell said, taking a seat on the couch and grabbing up a Sega joystick. Looking over at Dejuan, who was considerably less responsive, he shrugged. "My g-grandma been quoting Scripture to me since I was born."

Standing to Terrell's side, I chuckled at his story and palmed his head playfully. Since he'd called me the day after Maria gave him my number, we had talked every couple of days. Given his lack of home and family support, Terrell was struggling to maintain the fluency training he had learned at the clinic. I felt his frustration in my innermost core. He was finding it tough to apply Folger's positive self-talk and fluency shaping in the heated glare of teachers, classmates, and street hoods. My empathy for the boy inspired me to encourage his friendship with Dejuan. The more I saw Terrell's anger and confusion over his stuttering, the more I thanked God for shielding Dejuan from my recessive gene.

Dejuan started up a video game, respectfully ignoring Terrell's endorsement of spirituality. My son was annoyed by my renewed interest in church and the Bible. Candy had forced him to attend Greater Bethesda Holiness Church with her mother since he was four, and in the past his time with me provided a break from all the fire and brimstone. In the last few weeks, however, I had started to tiptoe my way back into the church culture Mother and Frederick raised me in.

Being unemployed for the past month had left me with some extra time on my hands, and the need for God's grace in my life was undeniable. On top of that, I was grateful for the new assistant coaching position I had just landed at Therrell High School in southwest Atlanta, so on this Sunday, even though church wasn't a good option, I was determined to show God some love.

I had just pulled Liza from bed and given her a kiss on the forehead when I heard my cell phone ringing out in the family room. After shuttling her into the bathroom, I ran to the couch and clicked the phone on just in time.

Errick was doing his best impression of a televangelist. "It's Sunday. Do you know the Lawwwd?"

"If you knew him, you wouldn't make fun on his day," I replied. "What do you want?"

"Just making sure y'all haven't lowered my property values this weekend."

"We've behaved ourselves. You won't even know we were here."

"All right, then. Thought I'd hit you with some good news. We had that dinner with Governor Hooks yesterday, man. He's on board. We got our candidate!"

"See, I told you," I said, a pang of remorse rolling over me. "You didn't need me."

"Well, we'll need you sooner than later. All Perry's given us right now is an agreement to form an exploratory committee. That means we've got a few months to prove whether we can build a nationwide network and help him build a viable campaign. We're gonna be registering voters and recruiting 'get out the vote' volunteers nonstop. You gonna step up now?"

I hesitated in thought then said, "You know it. Just t-tell me what you need."

"Well, praise God! I'll start you slow, don't worry."

After Errick and I discussed some of the upcoming ways I could help the Dream Party's cause, I got the kids cleaned up and organized. We sat down to Bible study, ate a breakfast of doughnuts, scrambled eggs, and juice, and went out to the beach. Just about the time I figured it was time to pack it in, Miles's phone number popped up on my cell's caller ID.

My brother didn't waste any time. "You sitting down?"

"Doesn't matter," I said. Actually, I was still lying on my back spread across a towel, watching Liza, Dejuan, and Terrell toss a Frisbee on the shoreline.

"I made you a promise, little brother," Miles said. "I have to revoke it now."

I exhaled heavily, feeling my chest heave. "Go on."

"I still haven't found those two employees of Big Walter, the ones who were working at Frederick's club the night of the fire. But I know somebody who can help us find them."

"Tell me this isn't about Mercedes."

"Bingo."

My pulse didn't just quicken—now I could feel my heartbeat crashing against my chest. "Explain yourself, Miles. Quickly."

"Deacon, listen to me and listen good, okay. I kept hitting so many dead ends with this thing, I had to take a closer look at our girl.

So I looked up old what's-her-name, Desiree." Desiree was a friend from Mercedes's Spelman days. Until they had a major falling out shortly before our divorce, Desiree and Mercedes were inseparable. Desiree had hung out with us so much, we'd even tried matchmaking her with Miles around the time we got married. Miles, who'd been on a break from Chantal, had wasted no time treating Desiree like a play toy, loving and leaving her in record time. Even now he couldn't remember her last name.

"Yeah, Desiree what's-her-name. Anyway, before I left Atlanta, I looked her up. I took her out for dinner, fluffed her ego a little, and got her talking about some of her heart-to-heart conversations with Mercedes. I was just trying to get a feel for whether Mercedes kept up with any of her father's gang members or not."

"Yeah, okay," I said, fighting the irritation creeping up my spine. "So after you slept with her, what did you find out?"

"Hey, I'm not into kissing and telling, young brother. That's Errick. Suffice it to say, I asked Desiree to pay a little visit to Mercedes, play at making up and apologizing for whatever they fell out over. I just asked for one thing: Mercedes's high school scrapbook. Desiree said she had seen it in Mercedes's dorm room in college and at you all's first house."

I sat up, fiddling nervously with my sunglasses. "Mercedes actually fell for this?"

"Hey, time heals all wounds. Desiree must have talked a good game, because yesterday, I received the scrapbook via FedEx. I have to return it to Desiree tomorrow, of course, so she can return it before Mercedes misses it, but I already got my answer."

I just waited, knowing my life was about to take another sharp turn.

"Tisha Norris's name is all through that scrapbook, Deacon. It looks like she was three or four years behind Mercedes in school, but grew up down the street. There's pictures of them together and everything." Miles paused, sounding newly sensitive. "This may mean absolutely nothing. Tisha may be perfectly innocent of the arson that killed Frederick, and Mercedes may not have seen her since she left home. Either way, though, it's time to get Mercedes's help. If anyone can help us find Tisha, she can."

"Hey, hold on now." Processing Miles's words, I seesawed between competing emotions: the desire for answers about my father's death versus the need to protect my daughter and her mother. I had comforted Mercedes on many late nights, after she'd awakened from nightmarish flashbacks to her years amidst Big Walter's violent, unpredictable world. I couldn't drag her back into that without an airtight reason.

"Deacon, Mercedes is our best bet of proving whether Walter ordered a hit on Daddy." Miles paused, seemingly surprised at his intimate reference to our father.

"Miles, I just don't know—"

"I know this is a lot to process," Miles said, cutting me off. "Dragging Mercedes back into her father's world isn't something anyone could be proud of, but it's got to be done." He took a beat. "Now, she's not the mother of my child. So do you want to handle this, or should I?"

23

Maria

Deacon was still inside me when I realized what had happened.

"What did you call me?" I grabbed his shoulders, started to shove him off me.

His face still contorting from the final spasms of his orgasm, Deacon shut his eyes. "Uhh," he sighed, his hands still gripping my calves, which he'd used to keep my legs in the air.

I kicked back and rammed him with my feet, knocking him on his butt so he finally slipped out of me. "Did you just call me Mercedes, Deacon?"

My bedroom filled with silence as Deacon lay sprawled at the edge of my four-poster bed. Now he had his hands over his eyes. "Maria, I–I can explain. I mean, it just slipped out." He lurched forward, his six-pack abs pulsing as he faced me. "It means nothing."

"Means nothing, my ass," I shouted, pulling the covers over my naked body. My head had filled quickly with anxious, jealous thoughts, but I stifled every four-letter word on the tip of my tongue. "Get out!"

The weekend after Deacon took his kids to Saint Simons, he invited me to attend Liza's piano recital at Greater Atlanta Christian School, a suburban private school in Norcross. Mercedes, who had selected GACS over Deacon's suggestion that they place Liza in a top-ranked Atlanta public school, was in Canada on business, so it was a stress-free evening. We'd cheered for Liza at the recital, taken her out for ice cream, then dropped her at Deacon's sister Benet's house. Benet, who had a little one of her own, had offered to keep Dejuan and Liza for the night. I wasn't sure if she wanted to help her brother get his groove on, or just treat us to some quality time, but it was a nice gesture.

As we pulled away from Benet's, Deacon offered to host me at his house again, but I suggested he just drop me at home. I had plans to get caught up on much-needed shopping in the morning, and I really wanted to keep a little physical distance from him anyway. I was enjoying his company, but feeling uneasy about the intensity of our chemistry. We'd closed every date so far with sex, and it was becoming too much of a preoccupation.

We had a short lull in the conversation when my cell phone rang. When I saw it was Alicia, I looked over at Deacon and smiled shyly. "I absolutely hate people who answer their cell phones on dates, but I haven't talked to Alicia in a week. You mind? I'll keep it quick."

As he nodded, I answered and let Alicia catch me up on her week. She was in Los Angeles for work, negotiating a corporate sales contract for her company. I tried to discreetly update her on my and Deacon's doings, then bit my lip when she hit me with a whopper.

"Girl," she said, whispering as if she were in the car with me and Deacon, "I did a bad thing."

"What are you talking about?"

"Well, there's this guy I know who lives out here, and well, we've been hanging out."

I frowned, inhaling with concern. "Alicia, I know you aren't being trifling." She and her husband, Trent, had their share of issues–the weights of parenthood (for which she had limited patience), Trent's preoccupation with his job, and his decreasing sense of romance–but I'd never known either one to cheat.

We had a pissy little argument on the line, me trying to get her to identify the guy she was messing with and she insisting that she hadn't let him past "second base" yet, so it wasn't a big deal. When I had tired of trying to convince her to stop playing with fire, I let her go.

As we pulled into the parking lot of my apartment, I touched Deacon's knee gently. "Anything you want to tell me? You seem a little preoccupied tonight." I wondered whether he was still upset about a run-in he'd had with his old boss at the Dream Party, Miriam Lloyd. She had been at Liza's recital, at the side of a gentleman friend whose granddaughter was in school with Liza. Miriam had tried to be cute, "congratulating" Deacon on his new coaching job and implying he'd thrown away his career by leaving the American Dream Party.

"It's nothing," he replied, shaking his head. "At least I hope it's nothing."

"Want to tell me what it *might* be?"

"Trust me," he said, shutting off his truck's ignition. "Unless it turns out to be an issue, you d-don't want to know."

I let him get away with the dodge long enough to walk me to my door.

"Here's the deal," I said, my hand on my front doorknob. "You get no good-night kiss until you tell me what's on your mind."

Deacon, who had already started leaning in for his smooch, froze in midmotion. Stepping back, he cleared his throat impatiently. "Well, good night then."

"Hey," I said, chuckling and grabbing up one of his hands as I swung the door open. "I'll give you one more chance."

Once we'd made ourselves comfortable on my couch, I leaned against his shoulder. "Does this have anything to do with your family?"

"It's just my brother," Deacon said, as if I knew exactly what that meant.

"What happened?"

Slowly, Deacon started talking, first about Miles and his continued insistence that their father had been murdered, then about the complicated relationship he'd always had with his older brother. It seemed like their father was the defining element in their lives, the litmus test that separated them. Deacon, who'd never been viewed as worthy to carry on his father's work, wanted to prove himself by keeping Frederick's legacy alive. Miles, on the other hand, had been given everything necessary to succeed Frederick—his name, his looks, his eloquence, and his charm—but felt too pressured to appreciate it.

"Dealing with big brothers can be tricky sometimes," I said. "Thomas and I probably wouldn't talk any more than a couple times a year, if not for—" I stopped myself, realizing I hadn't told Deacon about Jamil yet. I didn't know when I planned to, but for some reason I wasn't comfortable doing so just yet.

"If not for what?" Deacon asked, leaning over and gazing into my eyes.

"Nothing." As my eyes ran from Deacon's stare, I felt myself getting more defensive.

"Maria," Deacon asked, "why do you have so many photos of that little boy?"

"That's none of your business." But of course he would think it was. I was only too stupid to have thrown my pictures of Jamil into a drawer before letting him in.

"Oh, really? Despite your pep talk to me, I seem to be doing most of the talking tonight. Given my relative disadvantage at t-talking, that doesn't seem fair. When are you gonna open up with a brother?"

"No can do," I said, curling my lower lip anxiously. "We're not there yet."

"If I didn't know any better," Deacon replied, his words becoming more deliberate and his tone softening, "I'd say the boy was your son. Hell of a resemblance."

"He's my nephew, my brother's kid," I said, flinching as my voice cracked. "That's called family resemblance."

Deacon took a hand and stroked my neck softly before saying, "I overheard you the night Lucille confronted you at the clinic, Maria." As I gasped audibly, he pressed his heavy, powerful hands into my shoulders. "I know you have a child. You can tell me about it. I won't run."

For a second, I was angry he had kept this from me, but when I saw the sincerity in his eyes I couldn't keep my temper. Caught with my figurative pants down, I took Deacon at his word and took the plunge. I told him more than he could possibly want to know about Jamil, the long version I'd usually save for a girlfriend. I even talked about my past alcoholism and the weed and heroin Guy convinced me to try in college. We talked for so long, by the time I'd gotten everything out, we both fell asleep right where we were, melting into the couch. It wasn't until the early morning time when I stirred awake and instinctively reached for Deacon, pulling him to me and stroking his chest and lips. By the time his slacks swelled with a serious bulge, he was wide awake, kissing me and sliding me out of my dress before taking me into the bedroom. The very bedroom in which he called me *Mercedes*.

Fifteen minutes after Deacon had wordlessly dressed and slammed the door after himself, I lay naked in bed, one thin sheet over me. A beautiful Saturday lay stretched before me like a neatly wrapped present, but I doubted I'd be able to enjoy it. I didn't even feel like bothering with yoga class.

My phone, which I'd used to call Alicia as Deacon left, still lay in the crook of my arm. I reached for it, ready to sling it over to my nightstand, when it rang.

I brought the receiver to my lips, my self-defensive funk infecting my tone. "Yes?"

"Maria? It's me." Deacon's connection was patchy, which seemed odd, since he couldn't be more than a few miles away.

"Why are you calling me? I told you to *get out*. I don't recall saying anything about *get out and call me*."

"Hear me out," Deacon said, with the force of a command. "You didn't let me explain."

"There's nothing to explain, Deacon," I replied, sitting up and crossing my arms. The smell of his musky cologne, a lingering reminder of this morning's rendezvous, only added to my anger. "You got so excited, you thought I was Mercedes. These things happen in the heat of the moment, right?"

"Please," Deacon said, emitting something between a chuckle and a whimper. "You think I'm holding a torch for Mercedes? If I wanted her back, I'd have her."

"She looked pretty happy with ol' Bob to me."

"I know you're not saying I lost Mercedes to him. Give me some damn credit, Maria."

"I don't need you cursing at me," I replied. "I'll hang up before you'll do that again."

"You're right. Look, there's a lot on my mind—"

"Including Mercedes, apparently."

"Yes, but not for the reasons you think. Maria, I can explain every-thing—"

"You're not getting back in this apartment any time soon."

A pause on Deacon's end of the line, then, "If you won't let me come back over, let me explain it to you now."

I climbed out of bed and padded into the kitchen, my bare feet slapping the vinyl tile floor. Deacon's little slip-up had knocked me back into reality about him, but I still had to start my day. "I get it, Deacon. Don't waste your time," I said, sighing as I measured coffee grinds into my espresso maker. "I had no business making love to you this early in our relationship anyway."

"You don't need to go there, not yet." Deacon went quiet for a minute; then I noticed that the background noise on his end died down. "Okay, I pulled off the road. I'm sitting here, able to concen-trate on answering any questions you have. D-Don't write me off."

My mind already made up, I humored him. Deacon went on for a while about the pressures he was under. He went into more detail about how Miles was forcing him to probe into Mercedes's past, con-vinced that she had knowledge about their father's death. Maybe I should have been surprised by all the drama, but as Alicia had warned me, people from families like Deacon's rarely had simple lives.

"Tell me this," I asked when he took a break from his litany of ex-cuses. "Weren't you bothered by Mercedes's past before you married her? She doesn't sound like a good fit with the great Davis family."

"Mercedes was completely estranged from her family by the time we met," Deacon said. He talked about their years dating long-distance as college students, when she was at Spelman and he was at FAMU. Fine, ambitious, and fiery, Mercedes had opened Deacon's nose so wide, he'd given her a pass on obvious lies about her past.

"Before I could do my homework, I had bigger concerns," he said. "When I came up for air, she was expecting with Liza. I proposed the next day, so we could marry without revealing the 'shotgun' motiva-tion."

I rolled my eyes, even if only for my own benefit. "How quaint."

"It wasn't quaint—it was practical. My parents would have placed a hit on me if I'd brought another love child into the world. Besides, I was head over heels this time." Deacon told how his mother had hired a detective to investigate Mercedes's past, how that led to Mercedes's wedding-eve confession. "She laid it out for me," he said, "on the night when I should have been knee-deep in drunk friends and loose strippers." Listening to Deacon recount everything, I felt for him: how many people learn they're about to marry into the family of a coke kingpin with dozens of street pushers and a virtual lock on northwest Washington, D.C.?

"I can't believe you're telling me all this," I said as I poured my first cup of espresso. "You don't know me that well. How do you know I won't go running my mouth in the streets, especially considering how bitchy Mercedes was the one time we met?"

"You're not that petty," Deacon replied. "Look, I know I messed up this morning. It won't happen again, but I'll let you decide when you're ready to go out again. I'm not going anywhere."

I walked back into my bedroom and began pulling workout clothes from my closet, getting set for yoga class. "Don't call me–I'll call you."

"Maria?"

"What, Deacon?"

"I'm not exaggerating when I say this. I need you."

"Good-bye." The smart-assed tone in my voice gone, my hand trembling gently, I set the receiver down. *Almost got me,* I thought. *Almost.*

24

Deacon

Standing in front of the soundstage at downtown's Centennial Olympic Park, I met Governor Perry Hooks for the first time since his inauguration.

"Deacon, it's good to see you again," Perry said, flashing a grin toward the popping cameras surrounding us. We were standing in front of the park's main stage, where the great George Benson filled the air with jazzy rhythm and blues.

"My p-pleasure, Governor," I said, wincing at the sound of my stutters. I hadn't mixed it up in a high-profile setting in a while, but I had finally let Errick coax me out today.

"Please, I'll always be Perry to you," the governor said, slapping me on the back and reaching to accept a pair of sunglasses from one of his security guards. As a black man who knew just what a threat he represented to the powers that be, Perry was never without his security detail, a group of brothers with the build of linebackers and the stoic expressions of the Nation of Islam.

"This is an awesome setup Errick's put together," Perry said, surveying the thousands of people—black, white, Asian, and Latino—clogging the park. This was the American Dream Party's first official voter registration festival, an event that I had initially planned. Judging by the Labor Day weekend crowds, Errick had come up with a model the party could replicate nationwide. "Deacon, I'm feeling very confident about this party's ability to help carry my message," Perry said, "but I hear you sowed the seeds for everything I'm seeing now. Is that true?"

"What's true," I said, shaking my head softly, "is that my cousin talks too much."

"Come on now, just tell me," Perry said, a hearty laugh enriching his voice. "I know you're not working for the party anymore, but what about me?"

Narrowing my eyes, I looked into the governor's face. "What about you?"

"Would you be willing to work for me, Deacon? Remember, I may be the Dream Party's candidate, but I have my own separate campaign team. I'm still rounding it out as we speak."

"Governor, I'd be honored," I said, feeling my face flush, "b-but I really don't think—"

"Don't think, young brother, just say yes."

"I just accepted a coaching job—"

"Deacon, don't front on me now." Perry smiled. "I know all about you, boy. You were writing speeches for your daddy when you were in high school, and you helped run his Chicago-area campaign office during both Senate campaigns."

"Well, if you want to go there, I also drafted speeches for his presidential run," I said, grinning. "I don't deny that I got skills, but I can't back out on this new job."

"You won't have to. I just need help right now with my weekend activities—appearances at events like this. Monday through Friday, the voters of Ohio expect me to keep my behind in Columbus." He reached into his shirt pocket, handed me a business card. "That's my campaign chairman's info. Call him, please? I want you on board."

"All right," I said. "I'll speak to you soon, Governor."

"Perry," he said insistently, clamping my arm before turning away, his team of guards trailing close behind.

Now that I had my mingling for the day out of the way, I jogged back toward the north end of the park, where Errick and his staff had set up a makeshift basketball court, volleyball court, and baseball diamond. The Dream Party had organized a full schedule of activities, in an effort to keep the kids of registering voters busy. The idea was also to increase our image with the soon-to-be-eighteen audience. Errick had assigned me the responsibility of overseeing the whole sports enterprise.

I'd made it halfway to the courts when Rashida, Errick's executive assistant, came running up to me. "Yo, boss, we've got a problem over here."

"What's the matter?"

Rashida shouted at me over the sound of the hip-hop music blasting through the park. "Young punks," she said, standing on the toes of her gym shoes and speaking into my ear. "Some stupid gang's over on the basketball courts, running the kids and other volunteers off. They trippin'." Rashida scrunched her little pug nose, rotated her neck. "They act like they own the park or somethin'. If I wasn't saved, I'd say somebody needs to bust a cap in 'em."

I pulled Rashida closer so we could talk with less shouting, calming her down by asking more questions. It sounded like the situation needed some manpower. Apparently a half-dozen guys had bumrushed the courts, scattering the teenage kids of the voters we were registering and threatening the handful of elderly and female volunteers who'd tried to talk some sense into them. One of the female volunteers, who'd been shoved to the ground by one of the hoods, had even called Miriam Lloyd, asking the queen bee herself to step in.

"Ms. Lloyd called me," Rashida said, as she followed me over toward the courts. "You know her bourgie ass wanted to call security and kick these fools out of the park altogether. I got her to chill, though, told her you could calm things down without all that drama."

As Rashida and I pushed through the thick crowds, passing pavilions full of folk chowing down on barbecue and outdoor tables packed with registering voters, a warning siren bubbled up at the back of my brain. If Miriam and the board of directors knew about this flare-up, someone would eventually make their way over to the park, trying to second-guess my handling of it. I knew they'd love any opportunity to make me look ineffective, even now that I was just a simple volunteer. Even though that bothered me, it was really secondary. The real question was whether I could protect the Dream Party's mission, and right now my brothers from the hood were standing in the way.

When I reached the court, I found a group of eight guys, most of them in their late teens and early twenties, running and gunning between the baskets while clumps of kids and dumbfounded volunteers cowered on the sidelines. I quickly scanned the gang on the court, seeking a familiar face. When I had no luck, I inhaled deeply and told myself to talk slowly but forcefully. I couldn't afford to look weak: Stuttering was not an option.

Just as I stepped up to the white boundary line on the court's left side, Dejuan shuffled over to me. He was headed back to Chicago soon, and had been here long enough that I was getting used to having him around. Our rapport was still unpredictable, lurching forward in fits and starts, but spending time together had clearly rejuvenated our relationship.

"Dad," he said, his voice low and his words spilling out fast, "you gonna put these motherfuckers in their place?"

I wasn't so naïve as to think my son didn't curse, but I still shot him an irritated look. "I'll put these *guys* in their place, yes, Dejuan. I don't want you over here, though." I pointed over my shoulder. "Go to the main pavilion. I think they need help filing the registration forms."

Hoping he'd actually obey me, I turned away from Dejuan and stepped into the middle of the court just as a tall, lanky brother shot a pass over my head. Instinctively, I leapt into the air, palmed the ball, then pulled it into my chest as I landed. The crowd went wild, then grew silent as the players began to circle me.

"What the fuck you doing, man?" A brother who made me look short was on my heels suddenly, flooding my neck with hot breath. "Give me the goddamn ball."

"You'll get the b-ball," I said, "when you and your boys listen to what I have to say."

In seconds, they formed an orderly ring around me. Shifting, grimacing, and giving me the finger, they eyed me like a lion lusting over a glistening cut of prime rib.

"It's like this, brothers," I said, keeping my tone and pitch low, as if this were a personal conversation without dozens of spectators. "In case you didn't understand, the American Dream Party has rented this park until five p.m. That means we decide who gets to use this court until then."

A wiry brother with dreadlocks spat suddenly, leaving a thick goober of mucus at my feet before saying, "Fuck an American Dream. Y'all need to go somewhere with that corny-ass name anyway."

Still holding the ball tightly, I nodded in recognition of homeboy's judgment. "It's a bit much, I know, but we're keeping the name in honor of my father. He fought—"

"Your father wasn't like most of us, okay?" The brother with the spit knocked fists with a couple of his boys. "The first nigger senator in years. We ain't gonna have another one no time soon. What can your daddy tell niggers like *us* about an American Dream? We do well to make it home safe every night."

"The f-first step," I responded before inhaling suddenly, "is to take some p-personal responsibility. You think the A-American Dream is an illusion? What are you d-doing to change that?" By now, I was disgusted with the sound of every stuttered word tripping from my lips.

The big, bulky brother who'd first challenged me piped up. "We gonna break the system down—that's what we gonna do. We ain't some street hoods, dawg. Me and my boy Austin here done signed up with the New Black Panther Party. We *got* a plan."

"Since you b-brothers are here," I said, grimacing at the fractured sound of my words, "why don't you take time to hear about *our* plan? We have G-Governor Perry Hooks of Ohio as our p-presidential c-candidate. Who do you think has helped changed the system more, him or someone from the P-Panthers? Just c-come on over to the registration t-tables and—"

"Damn, man." The spitter waved his hand dismissively and turned away. "I can't understand what this motherfucker's talking about. 'Uh, duh-duh, uh-uh.' " He walked off, raising his voice as his boys' laughter flooded me. "Gonna tell me how to live my life when he can't even goddamn talk! Ain't that some shit!"

I was too stunned to do anything but stand my ground, gripping the ball as all eight of them rolled off the court, imitating my jerky speech patterns. I didn't know if my words or my stuttering had driven them away. I turned from the court, evading the pitiful stares of numerous volunteers, and bounced the ball to the nearest kid on the sidelines.

Rashida grabbed my arm as I stepped off the court. "Hey, you got the job done–that's all that matters," she said, smiling gently. She looked away before I could figure if that was really pity in her eyes. "Ready to pull in some more voters? They just let a new busload of folks off out front."

"Give me a minute," I said, my voice nearly a whisper. My head was full of visions of my time in Dr. Folger's clinic, my heart weighty with regret for my failure to complete the experience and emerge with skills that could have saved me from this latest humiliation. Wasted opportunities, driven largely by my desire to protect Maria, who was now in the process of writing me off.

As I walked back toward the pavilions, I suddenly noticed an echoing set of footsteps. I stopped and pivoted to find Dejuan walking a few paces behind me. He stopped when he saw me staring back at him.

I crossed my arms and looked down at him, feeling a frown spread across my face. "Dejuan. You didn't go back to the pavilion before, did you?"

"Naw. I saw everything," my son said, stuffing his hands into his pockets and walking toward me again. "They weren't 'bout nothing, Dad. Talked all that stuff about you, but their asses sure stepped, didn't they?"

Laughing, I put my boy in a light headlock and lovingly rubbed his prickly head of cornrows. There'd be time later to lecture him about his filthy mouth.

25

Maria

In the weeks since Ramsey's initial offer to hook me up with Peter Hedges, his family attorney, I hadn't said boo about it. Ramsey, however, was determined that I would accept his help. Monday morning he had informed me that he'd set up a Wednesday-night dinner for the three of us at Morton's steakhouse. Out of gratitude, I took him up on the offer and headed downtown after work on Wednesday.

Peter, a light-skinned, burly man with wavy gray-streaked hair, was witty, professional, and powerful. I had my heart fully shielded, ready to be told that I had no hope of winning any legal rights to Jamil, but after I poured out my entire history, Peter assured me all was not lost. He wasn't ready to make any specific promises, but given that no formal adoption was ever processed and given my improved economic circumstances, Peter felt my case had potential. To do more, of course, he'd need money. As in $350 an hour, discounted by 30 percent because I was Ramsey's friend. Real helpful. Either way, I could plan on going bankrupt. Bye-bye, dreams of my first house.

"Maria," Ramsey said, patting my hand after Peter rushed off to another appointment, "don't get distracted by money right now. What's more important to you, some dollar figure or Jamil?"

I ignored the question, since it was insulting enough that I'd have to slap him to give a proper response. I reminded myself that Ramsey's heart really seemed to be in the right place. The sly winks and nods, the occasional lingering hand when he was within inches of me—all that had pretty much disappeared. We had settled into a comfortable, friendly rapport, like an older brother and sister. In a way, we were connected by our personal struggles. He was hacking through the weeds of a nasty divorce just as I braved this jungle of a potential custody battle. Sweeping aside Ramsey's insensitive question, I let him convince me to stick around for dessert.

Once we'd refreshed our coffee cups and ordered apple pie, Ramsey turned his seat so that he was facing me. "Let's talk about something else for a minute. I heard you ran into Deacon Davis the other day."

I frowned, my heartbeat thumping in my ears. "Oh, you mean at the Disabled Children's benefit? He was there, I'd almost forgotten."

Ramsey stirred some more Sweet'n Low into his coffee, took a sip. "You think he's finally realizing that half a clinic won't do the trick with his problem?"

"It's hard to say," I replied, shrugging. Deacon didn't really seem to stutter much from what I could see, but I knew he was still bothered by certain situations and stresses. I was definitely monitoring him, ready to nudge him into accepting help again when he was ready, but frankly I'd been a little distracted by all the sex.

An informal counseling session with my pastor, Dr. Wicks, had helped me realize the sex had been part of the problem. I had been pretty frank with my man of God, even detailed the circumstances under which Deacon revealed his subconscious obsession with Mercedes. As I sat there trying to dodge Ramsey's questions, the final minutes of Dr. Wicks's counsel rang in my ears.

Dr. Wicks said that my fornication with Deacon, though a sin, wasn't the main issue. He felt the root cause was my frustrated desire to play a bigger role in Jamil's life. He said my preoccupation with that kept me from spiritual peace and from the ability to choose men wisely. He counseled me to pray fervently for the best way to resolve my disagreements with Thomas and work something out. "God will show you a way," Pastor said. "You may not even like the resolution, but he will provide you one." He'd had a strong opinion about Deacon also. "Leave this young man alone for now," he said. "Just be still, Maria. Pray, fast, and *listen*. For a beautiful, vibrant young woman like you, there's plenty of time for marriage and romance once you've addressed this situation."

I could still hear Pastor's words as Ramsey peered at me intently. "Did you and Deacon exchange information, you know, keep the lines of communication open?"

"Would that be a problem?"

Ramsey's eyes flickered knowingly. "Why would it be a problem?"

I slid my pie plate toward the middle of the table. "Ramsey, is there something you want to ask me?"

Ramsey took another sip of coffee. "Absolutely not. You and Deacon are both young, attractive people. Anything that's happened between you two was probably inevitable."

My forehead grew hot as I processed Ramsey's accusation. This was the last thing I needed. Not after I'd realized Deacon was not Mr. Right, and while I faced a legal battle that would test my character. Had Ramsey caught me with my hand in the ethical cookie jar? I couldn't just sit there, my butt frozen to my seat, so I finally said, "We are friends, if that's what you're asking. I seem to recall a boss of mine encouraging me to cozy up to him in the first place."

Ramsey smiled, and my heartbeat slowed for the first time since he'd mentioned Deacon's name. "Exactly. Your history with Deacon, whatever it is, is your business. I just hope we can help him 'be all he can be' someday."

"I think we can hold out hope. We're just friends now, but I expect we'll hear from him eventually." Damn, I felt like a politician for real. *We're just friends* now. At least I wasn't lying, and if Ramsey wasn't asking more questions, I wasn't going to answer them in advance.

As my boss walked me to the parking garage, his cell phone rang. He flipped it open as we stepped into the dimly lit garage. "Hey, hey, what do you mean, jelly bean?" I knew from the playful tone, it had to be one of his daughters, probably sixteen-year-old Rachel. "Yeah, I'm on the way home now, assuming my 'date' doesn't try to have her way with me," he said, winking in my direction. "No, I haven't decided whether we're doing Vegas next weekend. I told you Daddy's work schedule might be changing." He sucked his teeth for a minute, listening, as we neared the row where I'd parked. "Rachel, we'll handle this when I get home, okay? Love you."

Pulling my car keys from my purse, I glanced over at Ramsey. "Young bucks giving you a hard way to go?"

"Adolescence must be God's revenge on every parent," he said, sighing and leaning against the Grand Am. "I don't hold it against Rachel or her sister, though. They didn't ask for what life's thrown at them: first, losing their wonderful mother, then seeing their knuckle-head dad marry a lying whore who treated them like they were in the way." He cleared his throat, scratched briefly at his neck. "I owe them some respite from all this divorce drama, so I'll keep my promise and take them to Vegas again."

My driver's side door open, I turned back toward him. "Are they big casino spenders already?"

"No, if anything, I'm the one who gets tempted to hit the slots every now and then. They just like the gaudy spectacle—the hotels, the indoor amusement parks, the never-ending selection of all-you-can-eat buffets. I figure, why not humor them."

I rested a hand on Ramsey's shoulder, impressed again by his loyalty to his girls. I wanted to tell him so, but found myself strangely speechless. Slowly, I'd come to see him in a new light. Looking at this short, trim man in his navy blazer, collarless silk shirt, and tailored cotton slacks, I felt a glimmer of attraction stirring. Yes, he was old enough to be my young uncle, and on top of it he was my boss, but he was not without appeal.

I patted Ramsey's shoulder and removed my hand quickly, ready to climb into the car. "You be good to those girls, now. I'll see you to-morrow."

"Maria." Ramsey leaned down and held my door open as I took a seat. "I forgot to tell you one thing about Peter and his legal services. Don't let money stop you from deciding whether to work with him." He leaned in farther, nearly on his knees now. "Don't tell him this, but I'm going to pay whatever he charges you."

I wasn't so stupid, nor so blinded by my love for Jamil, that I didn't flinch at the sound of his offer. "I couldn't let you do that, Ramsey. We're colleagues—it wouldn't be right. No, I appreciate it but—"

"No *buts*. If you appreciate the offer, you'll accept it."

I looked directly into his eyes, noticed that our lips were inches apart. "I don't want to feel obligated if I accept your help."

Ramsey smiled, just enough to reveal his tiny dimples. "The only thing I'll be looking for in return, Maria, is a continuation of your great performance on the job. This is a business investment for me. If you have peace about your relationship with Jamil, you'll be more productive for Folger and Associates. It's as simple as that."

I shook my head, trying to deny the excitement stirring in my stomach.

"Maria," Ramsey said, dropping his voice even lower and scooting closer to me, "we'll make it a loan. Okay? That way there's no strings, but it's still an investment from my perspective."

Ramsey was right in front of me now, but in his face I saw Jamil's, and at that moment I felt closer to redeeming my relationship with my son than I ever had. Almost as if watching from afar, I saw my hands shoot out and grab Ramsey by the neck, guiding his lips to mine. His breath was still relatively fresh from a dinner mint, and though his lips were a little chapped, he knew what to do with them, even dipped me a little tongue as if he knew what he was doing. I lapped my tongue against his one time, savoring the moment, then released his head and sat back.

Ramsey backed away and stood to his full height finally, his knees shaking. "Oh," he said, looking in my direction without really focusing on me. "Oh *God*, Maria." His cheeks glowing, his eyes dazed, Ramsey licked his lips, as if trying to keep some of me with him. "How should I interpret that?"

My eyes on my dashboard, I shut my door, started the engine, then rolled down my window. "It's gratitude, Ramsey," I said, smiling at him before averting my gaze. "Just gratitude. Drive safely." We exchanged waves and then I took off, backing out and quickly heading for the exit signs.

When I pulled into my apartment's parking lot, I stepped out of the car and found my own knees as weak as Ramsey's had been. Why in the world had I just kissed the man who signed my paychecks?

I had a bad habit, going back to the day I left Jamil with Thomas, of looking before I leapt with guys. I would meet a guy, go out with him, get tangled up physically, then cut things off without warning.

Most of my victims had been knuckleheads, but there were a few who probably could have changed my life.

Of course, they were all side orders on my plate of life anyway; it all came down to Jamil, and my determination to someday be worthy of him. I couldn't risk having another lover morph into Guy on me, the type of partner who leeches your spirit and sucks the ambition out of you. I had to get my degrees and become a worthy citizen. No judge would pay me any mind until I did so.

But here I was again with Ramsey, leaping forward physically without an ounce of thought or common sense. My gratitude for his help was fine and all, but now I'd probably left the brother sprung. I hadn't meant to be a tease, and it would be career suicide to actually mess with him. I was already feening for another counseling session with Pastor Wicks.

Among my messages was another voice mail from Guy, sounding more insistent about how I should back off Thomas and Lucille. I prayed for strength to refrain from hiring a hit man to visit Guy in Macon, and again deleted the message.

I took time to meditate on everything as I ran a hot bath and slid in a few minutes later. The heat caressed and relaxed muscles that had been tight for too long, and I sighed loudly as I sank deeper into the water. I shut my eyes and relished the respite until my doorbell rang.

"Maria, what have you done?" The accusation from my own lips lingered in the air until I finally stood, climbed out, and toweled off. Once I had slipped on my aqua terry-cloth robe, I hustled to the door, trying to calculate who it might be and whether it made sense to even open the door. I had a bad feeling about my visitor: Ramsey could easily have come calling for another kiss, and more.

I peered through the peephole and pulled my robe tight around me when I recognized Deacon's broad shoulders and probing eyes. The next thing I knew, I had run back to the bathroom, where I danced in front of the mirror, torn between adjusting my silk head wrap or ripping it off and quickly teasing some sense into my hair.

The doorbell rang again, and I marched out of the bathroom with the wrap still intact.

Leaving the chain lock on, I eased the door open, just enough to see through the crack. "You're not welcome here. Please go home."

Dressed in black nylon sweatpants, a worn, faded Steelers jersey, and a backwards black baseball cap, Deacon did a quick double take at my getup before crossing his arms. "What's wrong?"

"You didn't get the memo? You're still on my shit list."

"I know," he replied, grabbing the door and coming so close, his breath tickled my skin. He had bags under his eyes as if he hadn't been sleeping, but his lips curved into a warm, tentative smile. "This isn't p-personal, though. It's about business. I need a therapist, Maria."

"Wait right here," I said, starting to shut the door. "I'll get you Folger's number. He'll be thrilled to put you on his schedule."

"That's not cute," he said sternly, keeping the door cracked by pushing back with his shoulder. "I'm not crawling back to Folger's smart ass begging for help. If I can't have you as my therapist, Maria, I d-don't know if I'll get through this."

Trying to will strength from within, praying for some Holy Spirit power, I eased the door open and stood aside.

26

Deacon

By the time I stepped inside Maria's apartment and shut the door, she already had her back to me. "Wait here," she said, her voice low and dull as she hustled back to her bedroom.

Removing my ball cap, I took a seat on her bright red, puffy couch, the same one we'd poured out our hearts to each other on, turned on her television, and flipped through her basic cable channels until she resurfaced. "Okay, let's hear it, Deacon," Maria said, stalking into the room dressed in a pair of loose jeans and an oversize T-shirt.

"I told you," I said, letting more silence hang between us.

"Spell it out for me. You want speech therapy again. Why?"

I sat there on the couch, looking at Maria as she stood over me. I wanted to tell her how beautiful she looked, but knew I couldn't. I shut my eyes, fighting the dual motivations coursing through me. "I just need help, is all."

"Help with what, exactly?"

"I just don't have it all t-together, not yet," I said. "I've tried to apply the concepts from Folger's manual on my own ever since I left, but I keep getting tripped up." I told her about my recent showdown at the park, how the gang of hoods had humiliated me like an elderly invalid.

Maria was quiet for a few seconds after I finished; then she spoke slowly, with caution. "Was this the first time you've had this much trouble, since leaving the clinic?"

"Definitely," I said. "I mean, obviously I'm only working with half of Folger's lesson plan, but what I learned was helpful. Feeling my way through each sound, breathing with my diaphragm, even stuttering on purpose here and there has helped me loosen up in most situations."

"Tell me this. What was unique about that situation at the park, compared to ones where things went better? Were you tired from the heat? Did you feel physically threatened? What were the stressors, Deacon?"

"Tell me if this is crazy," I said, leaning forward in my seat. "I think what was toughest about this time was, it was a public-speaking situation, given that so many people were watching, and it was totally unscripted. It wasn't like a speech setting, where I come in the door with all my points planned out."

"Okay, that's a good observation," Maria replied. "Were you more worried about impressing yourself, the guys you were arguing with, or the crowd that was watching? And you know the right answer."

"It was the guys, those damn guys," I said, smacking fist against palm. "I couldn't make myself stop and use the speech techniques I'd learned, no matter how much I knew I should have. I wanted to win them over, educate them, and I knew I could only do that by appearing strong. I had to speak fluently, normally, like a strong black man."

Maria's gaze had softened. "What about slowing your speech, feeling your way through each word?"

"I didn't have time for that," I said. "Having slurred speech, using all the training, that would just make me sound odd to those brothers."

Maria paused a second before saying, "So, where did trying to act like you don't stutter get you?"

I couldn't even defend myself.

"Look, Deacon," Maria said, "it's really not appropriate for me to have these types of conversations with you, not unless I'm going to become your formal therapist. Is that what you want?"

I cleared my throat, wiped my nose. "Yes."

"Well, let me talk to Dr. Folger tomorrow and see if he's comfortable with Folger and Associates taking you back on as a client."

"I don't want that jerk's help, Maria. I want you as my therapist."

"Oh, really?"

"Yes. Did I stutter?"

"Oh, that's real funny. Deacon, you do understand that if I become your therapist, we have to officially grow up. Our relationship becomes strictly professional."

Subconsciously, I knew that's the way the world was supposed to work, but Maria's warning was nails to my chalkboard. "No, no, why are you bringing our relationship into this? These are separate issues."

"No, they're not. I've already compromised myself with you three times, and after that Mercedes incident, you've struck out. Even if you work with Dr. Folger instead of me, I cannot have a relationship with you. It wouldn't make me a good steward of my profession. So you go home, think long and hard, and call me tomorrow."

I sat there crouched over, shaking my head in frustration. Was there anything else I could tell Maria to soften her heart toward me? I wanted to hold out hope, but it was clear her emotional walls had risen, clicked, and locked into place.

I tried a sympathy plea first, a totally honest one. "You realize what this means, don't you?" I said, looking up into her hardening stare. "The stutters win again, blocking my way to a meaningful relationship. It's always like this," I continued, shaking my head. "I mean, I wound up getting Candy pregnant because I fell back on sex as a way of communicating, instead of getting to know her as a person, as someone I might have fallen in love with."

The look in Maria's eyes softened but now she had her arms crossed, as if anchoring herself against any sympathy for my words. "Life's not fair, Deacon. You're not having your cake and eat it too."

I wanted this woman as both my healer and my lover. She was offering me an impossible choice, but it was clear I'd have to make one. "Maria, please," I said, waving toward her love seat, "sit down. I'll take your help for now." I'd have to win her heart later.

Some of the defensiveness seeped out of Maria's posture as she took a seat. "Okay, don't keep me up all night, but what are some of the issues you think our therapy should address?"

I opened my hands to her, shrugged. "I just want to pick up where we left off."

"You know it's not quite that simple, right?" Maria read me with weary eyes, sighed. "We're going to have to do some reprogramming. And you're going to have to be patient in adapting to the clinic strategies, Deacon. That's the only way this will work."

For a good half hour, Maria helped me analyze my confrontation with the gang through the lens of the clinic. We talked some more about my early experiences with stuttering, broke down more of my self-talk, and even laughed a bit. I was already feeling better when she tapped her watch. "Oh, look at the time. It's nearly eleven o'clock. Don't we both have to be at work in the morning?"

"All right," I said, rising as she did and wishing I could get a nice, warm hug. I decided not to press my luck.

"For the record," Maria said as she led me to her door, "this is our one and only 'session' at my place. Call me tomorrow and we'll schedule a weekly time for you to meet me at my office."

"Okay," I said, sighing.

"One more thing," she said, turning to me as she opened the door. "When's the last time you talked to Terrell?"

"I just spoke to the whippersnapper this morning," I said. "Errick has some friends in the music business who are helping him record a rap single, can you believe it? Kid'll have a record deal before we know it."

Maria's mouth stayed in a straight line, but her eyes were smiling. "Just make sure Terrell doesn't get drawn in too quickly to that lifestyle," she said. "He's young, still learning right from wrong."

"Yeah, but this has to be awesome for his self-confidence."

Maria nodded, then jerked a finger toward the hallway. "Get out of my crib," she said, a mock tone of dismissal in her voice.

"Whatever," I replied, content to end on a light note. Suddenly adventurous, I opened my arms to her, my heart pounding. "How about a hug?"

Maria shook her head playfully, but looked away as she inched the door closed. "Good night, Deacon."

27

Deacon

With Labor Day behind us, it was about time for Dejuan to start school, so I hopped a plane to Chicago with him that Tuesday. It was a nice way to see him off, while solidifying the bond we'd strengthened during his time with me. Between shooting hoops, playing with Liza, and discussing my many personal missteps, all of which I hoped he could avoid, our relationship had definitely improved.

I hadn't made the trip back with him for pure father-son reasons, however. Now that I had decided to accept more help with my speech, I had to cut to the chase with my family issues, as well. I couldn't let Miles's accusations about Mercedes and her family's involvement in Frederick's death linger any longer.

When our plane landed at Midway Airport, I stayed with Dejuan at baggage claim until Candy showed up. Things were pleasant enough with her. It did my heart good, seeing the grin on her face as Dejuan talked enthusiastically about our time together. Candy offered me a ride, but I assured her I was fine with the rental car I'd reserved.

I had told her and Dejuan that I was in town on business, and that was true in the technical sense of the word. I wasn't drawing a check from Communities in Action or the Dream Party anymore, but if I could snuff out Miles's conspiracy theories, it would save both organizations months of nightmare publicity and distractions.

I had discovered the truth about Mercedes's history mainly due to the efforts of Phil Keys, a private investigator and family friend. When I decided to follow up on Miles's allegations without confronting Mercedes head-on, he was the first person I called.

Phil had turned me on years ago to the fact that Mercedes had just one sibling that anyone knew of, an estranged younger half brother. Walt Chance Jr. was now an auto mechanic on Chicago's west side, far removed from the D.C. remains of his father's drug operation. Word was that his hands were clean, even though he was still in touch with some of his father's former employees—the few who hadn't sold Big Walter out. Junior sounded like the best possible source—informed enough to be dangerous, innocent enough to be open, and unlikely to tell Mercedes about my visit.

My former brother-in-law was underneath a late-model Ford Escort when I rolled into his shop. It was an unsophisticated operation, a simple garage with four grease-stained bays and a small office partitioned by cracked glass. There didn't appear to be a receptionist or clerk, just three mechanics doing their thing.

A bald-headed brother walked up to me, his shirtsleeves rolled up to reveal arms full of tattoos. "What up. Can I help you?"

"Yeah," I said, pointing to the feet under the Escort. Phil had provided me with photos of Walt, so I knew neither this brother nor the other mechanic were who I was looking for. "That Walt under there?"

"Yeah." The mechanic, who wasn't even six feet tall but probably outweighed me, shifted into a more defensive stance. "This business, or personal? We don't take to niggers starting up shit round here."

"Why all the drama, brother?" My hands instinctively curled into fists, but I kept them at my side. "Just let me speak to him, please."

The mechanic took a step toward me. "Hold up your damn hands, then."

"Don't start something you can't finish," I said, complying as he patted me down quickly.

"All right, wait here." He turned back toward the Escort. "Yo, Walt! Speak to this nigger before we have to rumble."

The feet underneath the car kicked about for traction, then braced against the greasy floor and slid the tray out from under the Escort. Not paying me any real mind, the short, skinny man slowly stood before looking up at me. As our eyes met, I could see Mercedes's features in his face—high yellow complexion, narrow hazel eyes, high cheekbones. I was guessing she got her height from her mother's side of the family, but other than that, the two of them had probably pulled their looks from Big Walter.

Walt stayed where he was, a few feet from me. "I know you, right?"

"I imagine you know of me," I said, closing the distance between us and sticking out a hand. "D-Deacon Davis." I fought the twinge of embarrassment at my repetition. *Don't fight it.* Maria would have been proud.

Walt hiked his eyebrows at the sound of my name. "Stop fuckin' with me."

"Where else would you know my face from?" I knew Walt had at least heard of me when I married Mercedes, despite the fact he wasn't invited to the wedding.

Walt was silent for a minute, the gears of his brain churning before he asked defiantly, "What you want from me?"

I shifted in place, reminding myself not to reach out and break his pencil neck. "When's the last time you talked to your sister?"

"Man, she on her own," Walt replied, looking away and wiping his forehead with a greasy hand. "What I know about Mercedes, I know the same way I know what I know about your bourgie ass: from the TV."

I crossed my arms, glanced over my shoulder. "This can't be an easy topic for you, Walt. Is there somewhere we can speak privately?"

"We don't need no privacy, Deacon," Walt said, his nose wrinkling violently, "seeing as how I ain't got nothing to tell you. I ain't seen that girl since she was sixteen and I was a nine-year-old brat living down the street."

"I hear you, Walt," I said, patting his shoulder as if we were boys from way back. "Let me meet you back here at closing time. I'll explain everything then."

"I got a girl to get into tonight," Walt said, sniffing and wiping his forehead again. "Won't be available."

"Come on, a pretty boy like you can get laid any night." I reached into the back pocket of my jeans, pulled out two tickets. "You gonna pass on the Bears game with Denver tonight?"

Walt's eyes bugged out, at least as much as his narrow ones could. "Oh, snap. That's all right." He looked me up and down. "What if we go rap somewhere now, soon as I finish up this Escort? The price is, you let me have both tickets. I owe my boy a favor."

"Deal," I said, gripping his spindly hand. "I'll hold the tickets for now, though."

Walt handled his business while I took a seat in the little office and checked my cell phone for messages. Out of the three I had, one nearly knocked me for a loop.

"Hello, Deacon, this is Ken Nixon, campaign manager for Governor Hooks. I received your call, as well as your application materials. Deacon, it goes without saying that I'm an admirer of your father, and I'm impressed with your personal record. I'd like us to do a personal interview tomorrow, if possible. I'll be in Atlanta to help the Dream Party establish the Georgia headquarters office for the campaign. I'm thinking you might be a good member of that team. Say we discuss it over breakfast, around eight o'clock at the Airport Hilton?"

"Shit," I whispered before coaching myself into a calmer state and leaving Ken a message that I could meet him. I had planned to wait and return home in the morning, so I could see Uncle James and visit with Darlene at the family home, but that would have to wait for later. I was suddenly happy that Walt had muscled me out of the chance to see tonight's game. The tickets were free anyway, a gift from a former teammate who worked in the Bears' front office.

A few minutes later, Walt came by the office for me. Trying to loosen him up, I insisted we escape his newfound hood and get a taste of the downtown Loop. It was funny how family characteristics sometimes transcended socioeconomic class. Although he was blue-collar, Walt shared Mercedes's sense of thrift and financial stewardship. He was saving up for a house, and as such restricted his discretionary income to the occasional greasy burger and hoochie momma. As a rule, he refused to even go into downtown for fear he'd be tempted to waste money in the fine stores and restaurants.

I paid for us to grab a meal at the ESPN Zone, which knocked Walt's block off. After an uneasy, largely silent ride, I made use of the sports paraphernalia surrounding us and got Walt talking. By the time we were seated and placed our orders, we'd deconstructed every NFL team's shot at the Super Bowl and argued over the Kobe Bryant rape case. Coddling my freshly opened bottle of beer, I eased the conversation toward weightier matters.

"Walt, when you and your dad heard Mercedes was getting married, back in the day, did you ever try to contact her?"

"Naw," Walt replied, after swooshing another sip of his beer in his mouth. "I asked Big Walter about it, *once*. That was enough."

"Why?"

"He beat my ass, that's why. Told me I didn't need to ever bring her name up again. Said she'd chosen her path, and if she ever reentered our world, she'd probably wind up dead."

I had heard some of this before. "He told her she'd be a liability if she came back, right?"

"Yeah, my pop felt like he couldn't trust her once she called him out for being a gangster. Said she'd probably be the type to sell him out to the cops, in return for a college scholarship or some shit. He said that's why he just paid her off with that fat check."

I shook my head, reminded again of all my ex's lies. "So you know, when she and I first talked about you and your father, I wanted her to at least contact you somehow."

"She did the right thing," Walt said, sighing. "No good would have come of it, if we'd hooked back up." He looked into my eyes, an unashamed look on his face. "I was following in Big Walter's footsteps, you know."

"That was all you knew," I said, shrugging. "I don't think she would have judged you."

"It ain't about her judging me," he said, grinning oddly. "I would have had to judge her ass, man. Naw, she did the right thing, staying away."

I waited as our waitress, a cute sister with a small waist, long legs, and rope braids, set our order onto the table. When she was gone, I grabbed a chicken wing and asked, "If Big Walter was still alive, would you have stayed in the game?"

"Man," Walt said, sighing, "I ain't got time to worry about that. Only thing I knew for damn sure, I wasn't crazy enough to live the life without my pop around to watch my back. I mean, you never knew who to trust, who you had to take out before they turned on you. Until those fools got the jump on him, my pop was the master of that shit. When they got him, though, I had to get out of Dodge."

I finished off a few more chicken wings and let Walt knock off half his plate of cheese fries before I slid a slip of paper over to him. Licking cheese off his fingers, he looked at me quizzically before opening the slip. I watched him as he read the names of Pharrell Haynes and Tisha Norris, each written in Miles's handwriting. The names of the two people who'd been there the night my father died.

When he stayed silent and returned to his plate of fries, I pressed him. "You remember either of those names from your days in D.C.?" I couldn't tell him why I wanted to know—no way he'd talk if he knew that.

"I mean, I recognize both names, yeah. Why you asking?"

"What can you tell me about them?" I said, almost disappointed that he recognized the names. I wanted to believe Miles was loony.

Walt grabbed at a napkin and wiped another string of cheese off his chin. "What's it matter?"

"D-Do you want the damn Bears tickets or not, Walt?"

"Okay, shit. Uh, this Pharrell Haynes brother, he was, like, a ground troop. Did deliveries mostly, plus he helped out with the 'back to school' crew. He wasn't a key player or nothing."

"What's the 'back to school' crew?"

"Oh," Walt said, chuckling dryly, "that was Big Walt's nickname for the crew that schooled store owners who held back on their protection money. If some fool didn't pay up, the 'back to school' folks paid a visit, and usually that store wasn't standing afterwards."

I nearly choked on my drink before saying, "They were setting stores on fire?"

"No one will ever prove it," Walt said, nibbling on another fry. "Most of the merchants caught on and never involved the authorities. They chose life over justice, know what I mean?"

Miles's arson suspicions had just gone from loony to likely. Balling a fist but breathing slowly to keep my cool, I kept my eyes on Walt. "What about Tisha, Tisha Norris? What was her role in the gang?"

"Bruh," Walt said, rolling his eyes, "we could stay here all damn day discussing Tisha. Girl was in demand, you know what I'm sayin'."

"Was Big Walter pimping her?"

"Come on, dog, why we gotta call it that? Some things just happen naturally. Big Walter serviced a lot of high-rolling tourists, and sometimes they wanted someone to snort alongside them. Those girls got paid for their time."

"Was Tisha involved in the crew that set the fires and stuff, too?"

Walt frowned. "Uh, Tisha was a little . . . tender emotionally to get her hands involved in that stuff. She was a lover, not a fighter."

I chugged the rest of my beer down, a sinking sensation washing over me. D.C. was calling me. "Do you recall," I asked, once I'd finished the beer, "why they left Big Walter's organization?"

"Now you over my head," Walt replied, sipping again from his beer. "They would have left, like, when I was fifteen or somethin'. I don't even recall hearing about Pharrell leaving. With Tisha, only thing I heard was something about her gettin' knocked up and not wanting to kill the baby. Kind of made her worthless from my pop's view."

I backed off, letting Walt enjoy the rest of his meal in peace. We finished off our food, had another round of beers, and watched some *Sports Center* before heading back to my rental car. When we pulled into the lot of his shop, we exchanged a brisk handshake. As Walt opened the passenger door, I was seized by sudden guilt. Not only was this my former brother-in-law, but he was Liza's uncle, as well.

"Look, Walt," I said, placing a hand on his shoulder as he turned to exit the car, "don't rule out reconnecting with your sister. It's a lonely world out there without family."

"When I need family in my life," Walt replied, "I'll dump my rubbers and start making some babies. You be cool, Deacon."

28

Maria

"Just so you understand, I play hardball." Peter Hedges, my new attorney courtesy of Ramsey, sat next to me in the conference room adjoining his law office. "The best thing you can do today, Maria, is sit back and let me work. You'll thank me later," he said, winking.

I glanced over at Ramsey, who sat on the other side of me. Seemingly feeling my stare, he turned toward me and placed a hand on my shoulder. "I have seen this man at work," he said, his voice low, his hand caressing the skin beneath my blouse. "It's not always pretty, Maria, but it will be worth it." He leaned closer to me as Peter continued jotting notes on a legal pad, acting like he couldn't feel the faint chemistry bubbling between us. "I know I can't stick around for the discussion, but I'll be in the next room, okay?"

I patted Ramsey's hand gratefully but avoided his gaze. I was still confused about where things were headed with our relationship. Things were still strictly professional for now, but ever since I'd kissed him, there had been something new between us. It was like the kiss held a promise of a lurking *something* calling for exploration. That, or maybe the strong smell of Lemon Pledge emanating from the table, had me a little dizzy.

Exploring was what had gotten me mixed up with Deacon, and where had that left me? Stuck serving as a platonic therapist to a man who had everything I thought I wanted in Mr. Right: looks, ambition, sensitivity, and responsibility. Of course, he had his speech issues, not to mention the burden of being a Davis, but I knew enough about the market in men to know everyone's stuff stank in some way.

No, there was a good chance that if I'd just kept a cooler distance from Deacon, we might have grown together gradually, free of all the drama that got him kicked out of the clinic and now had him floundering through life.

I refused to make the same impulsive mistake with Ramsey. Since drawing my line in the sand with Deacon, I had taken to tending to my own needs in the bedroom, if you get my drift. I felt like I a kid again, but if it helped me avoid hopping in bed with the wrong brother at a weak moment, so be it.

When a knock came at the conference room door, Peter sprang to his feet, buttoned his suit coat, and walked over to usher Thomas and Lucille in. When I first saw them standing there in the doorway, a fleeting wave of nausea assaulted me. They looked so uncomfortable. Thomas, dressed in one of his standard-issue navy wool suits, had a pained but angry look on his face. Lucille oozed discomfort, running her hands up and down the front fabric of her flowery dress. It had been over two months since I had seen them, shortly after July Fourth. I knew they'd be upset with me, but I sensed more than that. They just looked tired.

Peter hovered over them as they took seats opposite ours. "Did my secretary already offer you coffee, tea, water?"

"Yes," Thomas replied, clearing his throat but not looking in Peter's direction. "We're fine." He scratched at his neck suddenly, and I noticed he had small bandages in two spots where he'd nicked himself shaving.

"Good," Peter said, checking his watch with a concerned expression. "We can wait a few more minutes on your attorney–"

"She's not coming," Thomas said, looking first at Peter as he returned to his seat, then turning toward me. "Maria, we came here to try and work out something reasonable. We won't make this ugly–"

"Let me understand this," Peter said, interrupting. His voice went from tenor to soprano for a second, he was so surprised. "You want to negotiate without your attorney present?"

"This is still a negotiation," Thomas said, his jaw twitching. "We have that right. I'd personally feel better just speaking directly to my sister."

I hadn't quite processed Thomas's words yet when Peter responded. "You forfeited that option, sir." He glanced at me, sending a reassuring look. Remembering his earlier words as well as the nasty nature of my last conversation with Thomas, I eased back into my seat, nodding.

"As I understand it, sir," Peter said, continuing, "you've made clear your view that Ms. Oliver should have no formal rights to custody of her son."

Lucille broke from her apparent trance, searching me anxiously. "Maria, where did you get that idea?"

"You can direct all questions to me," Peter said, his gruff tone sending Lucille's eyes back to the table. "I'm aware that you have already tried to trick Ms. Oliver into signing away her rights. You may as well understand, we intend to file for joint custody." I had agreed to this strategy earlier, after Peter first advocated filing for sole custody. He felt that we had to go for the whole enchilada in order to state an aggressive case, but after all Thomas and Lucille had done for Jamil, I couldn't stomach that.

"*Joint* custody?" Thomas shook his head, looked at me again. "Maria, you're going to turn Jamil's life upside down like that?"

Peter placed a hand on my shoulder, keeping me from responding. "The time for discussion has passed, Mr. Oliver. We will file and let the courts decide the most equitable solution. Be warned," he said, shaking a finger in their direction, "that we will not tolerate smear tactics."

Thomas and Lucille each blinked, as if Peter had accused them of sleeping with a goat. "What smear tactics?" Thomas looked at me again. "What we said about having Guy testify? That was emotion, Maria. We wouldn't let him tear you down."

"Again, speak to me," Peter said, gesturing wildly between Thomas and himself. "I know better than to trust anything someone says before we've taken the first step into court. Just know that if we even sense you're going to make an issue of Ms. Oliver's past, we stand ready to do the same with yours."

At first I thought I had heard Peter wrong, but he had my family's attention. Thomas's eyes snapped shut, and Lucille's lower lip drooped.

"What is that supposed to mean?" His eyes open again, Thomas chuckled nervously, though his shoulders seemed tensed for a blow.

"For starters, Mr. Oliver," Peter said, his back straight and his face betraying no emotion, "my private investigator had a few discussions with your coworkers, who shall remain nameless, of course. Is your wife aware of your relationship with one Phyllis Dobbs?"

As dead air silenced the room, a squeaky "Huh?" popped from my mouth. "That can't be right," I said, turning to Peter. I glanced at Thomas, who sat fidgeting in his chair. "My brother is a devoted—"

"I fell into a brief affair," Thomas said, his eyes on the table, his panicked smile gone. "My wife and I were under enormous stress then." As Lucille pulled out a handkerchief and began blowing her nose, Thomas flicked a glance at me. "You wouldn't have known, Maria—this was shortly before you brought Jamil around. We had just been through hell."

"Yes," Peter replied, "you'd both learned that you were infertile, right? We don't need to go into the details of who had the problem. Either way, it was one more reason you were desperate to make your nephew into your own child, wasn't it?"

"God have mercy on your soul," Lucille said suddenly, looking at Peter with eyes full of tears. "What kind of devil spirit is in you? Thomas's affair happened before Jamil was in our lives, and I've long since forgiven him."

"Ah, religion," Peter said, lowering his voice just barely. "The last refuge of scoundrels."

"Stop it," I said.

"Maria," Peter replied, pressing a hand against my shoulder, "we can talk in a few minutes. I just want your brother and sister-in-law to understand what's at stake here."

"I suppose," Thomas said, grabbing for one of Lucille's shaking hands and letting her lean against him as they stood, "you'll want to expose my wife's subsequent depression and treatment with antidepressants."

"We will do what we must," Peter said, unashamed, "because we intend to win."

Thomas pointed a finger at me, his breath coming in gasps, his voice fluttering with emotion. "You don't know what we've been

through, Maria," he said. "To even let this man treat us like this . . .
you can forget seeing Jamil again." He turned back to Peter. "You'll
hear from our lawyer *today*." After sending us both a menacing look,
my brother whipped around with Lucille in tow and burst through
the door.

29

Maria

"Girl, are you pulling my leg? That fool's crazy." Alicia was as wowed by Peter's tactics as I was. I had called her on my cell phone while driving home. It was actually my first time catching her in over a week. We'd been playing phone tag since she first left town for another supposed business trip.

"Alicia, there's nothing you can say that I didn't tell that fool myself. I felt like I was making up words, and they all had four letters."

"Why didn't he tell you in advance that he'd found that dirt on Thomas?"

"God only knows, and I'm not sticking around to figure out why. I told Peter he was fired, and told Ramsey I'll just take out a loan and repay him immediately for the fees. I want Jamil back, but not like that." As many years as I'd spent longing to get my child back, Peter's harassing treatment reminded me life hadn't been a cakewalk for Thomas and Lucille either. We were all flawed—it wasn't even about that. It was about my biological connection to Jamil meaning something, something more than just being the aunt he saw once a month.

Alicia sighed, employing unnecessary drama. "That sounds smart, girl. Have you told Thomas this?"

"I left a message on his voice mail this morning, one at home and one at work. I didn't say anything specific, just that I want to talk about what happened."

"See, that's how y'all should have handled it from jump. It was that skirt-chasing boss of yours that started this, hooking you up with that fool attorney."

"Alicia, he may be misguided, but Ramsey's not that bad."

"Whatever you wanna believe. I hear talk, girl. His second wife? Supposedly she wasn't the one who started the cheating."

"You know what? I couldn't care less," I said as I rolled to a stop at a red light. "At this point, I think I have to apologize to Thomas and hope he forgives me."

"That's probably best," Alicia said, "but you may want to give the boy a few weeks to cool down. I know I'd need the time, to keep from kicking your ass."

"Mmm-hmm. Now speaking of cheating, when are you hopping off the express train to disaster?"

Alicia went silent for a minute, then hit me with, "I know you're not trying to dip into my business again."

"Alicia, please. It's me."

"My husband's boring, Maria. The most romantic gesture he makes these days is brushing his teeth before he hops on top of me. Hell, if he could hop around for more than a few seconds, maybe I wouldn't mind. A girl needs more, you know?"

I sighed, checking myself before I got too harsh. "Have you told him all this? Given him a chance before you wind up in bed with this mystery man?"

"Trent doesn't hear me anymore, Maria," Alicia replied. "I miss that."

"You can get it back."

"Or I can let another man in between these thighs, in a way that makes him forget all those that came before."

"Alicia," I said, sighing my girl's name slowly. "What if Trent Jr. or Brian heard you right now?"

"Well, they don't, do they?" Alicia got quiet. "Maria?"

"What?"

"I know you want to judge, but you know me. I don't wanna go back to my single years—getting pumped and dumped by a new brother every week. Can't you just trust me, that I need to have some fun, but know I'll do the right thing in the end?"

Sending up a prayer for my girl even as I replied, I braked at another stoplight. "Alicia, I'm trying to trust your judgment. I think it's better than you even know."

30

Deacon

The Saturday morning after my formal interview with Ken Nixon, Perry Hooks's campaign manager, I reported to the campaign's Georgia headquarters, a refurbished warehouse in Little Five Points. Ken and I had agreed that I could perform two key roles. First, I would act as the formal liaison between the Hooks campaign team and the Dream Party itself. Although Ken had one staffer, Katrina Majors, dedicated to that task, the young sister was having a difficult time resolving major disputes. Since I was only available to work part-time, I would handle only those issues that she couldn't resolve. Given my years of experience with Communities in Action and the Dream Party, plus my close relationship with Errick, I'd be a natural troubleshooter.

I had also been invited to be a speechwriter. Under the guidance of campaign strategists and pollsters, I'd be writing drafts of speeches the governor could deliver as he traveled the country registering new voters and building a sense of excitement around the campaign. The best thing about the arrangement was the way it allowed me to prove my skills apart from the withering eyes of Miriam Lloyd and the Dream Party folk who'd deemed me unworthy.

Around eleven that morning, I had settled into my office and started discussing the latest Dream Party disputes with Katrina when someone knocked at my door. "Come in," I said absentmindedly. Given that it was a Saturday and much of the staff hadn't been hired yet, the offices were a ghost town. I figured anyone stopping by had a valid reason for doing so.

The door creaked open, and Mercedes stood on the other side. "The security guard said you were up here somewhere," she said, her voice flat and chilly.

I saw no point in faking the funk. "Katrina," I said, standing and stepping around her and my desk, "can you wait here for a minute? I'll just be a few minutes."

"That's fine," I heard her say just before I slammed the door behind me.

I stood with my back against the door, Mercedes damn near standing on my toes. "Is Liza okay?"

"She's fine. With your sister, actually." Mercedes looked up at me, her eyes open and unmoving, no blinks.

"So what's up?"

Her tailored pants suit wrinkled as she crossed her arms. "Why are you snooping around in my past again, Deacon?"

"You really want to do this here?"

"Yes," she said. She still hadn't blinked. "Let's."

"Go home," I said, feeling my blood pressure rise with each word. "I'll be there in an hour."

That got a blink from her. "Go—no. We're handling this now."

"One hour," I said, opening the door and stepping back inside the office.

When I pulled into the circular drive of Mercedes's rambling, three-story home, I hit the brakes, parked, and stifled the flood of questions filling my head. Since seeing Walt Jr., I had already booked a flight to D.C. for next month, when I'd try to track down Pharrell and Tisha and see if I'd finally hit a dead end. I had held Miles off by admitting I had found something but needed more time, but he was impatient by nature. It was bad enough that I'd started dodging his phone calls. As I ascended the front cobblestone walkway of Mercedes's new "estate," I prepared myself for whatever was waiting inside.

She opened her massive oak door before I reached the front porch. "I saw you coming down the street from my library," she said. She stepped aside as I crossed the threshold, then clamped the door shut behind me.

Standing in her high-ceilinged, airy foyer, we stared blankly at each other for a moment until she broke the silence. "Let's go downstairs," she said, motioning over her shoulder and heading for the steps that led to her finished basement. I wasn't sure, but I didn't think I'd been down there since Liza gave me a tour at their housewarming party.

I followed behind Mercedes, determined to ignore the perfect fit of her capri pants and tight white silk blouse. We walked past her personal fitness room, Liza's home theater, and the family room with wet bar before coming to a wide oval room at the end of the hallway. "This is where I take care of business while your daughter sleeps," Mercedes said, gesturing around before taking a seat in a maroon leather executive chair. Seated in front of her three-tier cherry wood desk, she flicked a finger toward a low maroon-and-black sofa sitting opposite her. "Have a seat."

Keeping my eyes on her, I slid down onto the couch, which was clearly not made for a brother of my height. I felt like a high schooler trying to scrunch into an elementary kid's desk, my knees tucked into my chest.

"I didn't want to go into this with anyone else around," Mercedes explained, "and I didn't want to talk someplace that might be monitored."

"Monitored?" Eager to relieve my tension, I had no choice but to scoot back and lay across the sofa.

Mercedes gazed away from me, her eyes seemingly searching a painting over my head. "Deacon, you know that regardless of all we've been through, I remain one of the Dream Party's biggest donors, right?"

"And I've always appreciated the loyalty," I said. Between her personal wealth and investments in several well-known entertainment and fashion companies, Mercedes rolled with some major players. Her connections had helped Errick bring any number of celebrity donors aboard.

"You're right, I have been loyal to your family, and that's exactly the way that I think of it. I'm not technically a Davis anymore, but I respect all of you. Can you say the same about me and my family?"

"I never knew your family," I said, finally growing tired of the odd little couch and standing up. I paced away from her, showed her some back. "What's your point?"

"One thing my little bastard brother knows," Mercedes said. "That's that if you or anyone from your world ever contacts him, he's to let me know immediately. How stupid did you think he was?"

"I didn't think Walt was stupid at all," I said, turning to face her. "I just figured he had less to lose than you. Thought he might be straight with me as a result."

"Why are you interested in these people who worked for Big Walter, Deacon?"

Caught in the crosshairs, I saw no point in running. "Miles has some theories about them. They were at Frederick's supper club the night he died." Since she'd called me out, I pulled her onto the plank with me. "You know their names, Mercedes?"

"Walt said you asked him about Pharrell and about Tisha," Mercedes said, shaking her head.

I tried to pierce her soul with my stare. "You know Tisha at all, Mercedes?"

"Jesus," Mercedes said, almost under her breath. "Deacon, it so happens I was friends with the girl when we were kids. She was from the neighborhood; there's nothing unusual about her winding up working for Big Walter. He pimped half of the local girls at one time or another."

"But you weren't in touch with her at the time of Frederick's death?"

Mercedes leaned forward in her chair, rested her head in open palms. "That's irrelevant, Deacon. Leave it alone. You're only going to get one warning."

"See, that's not helpful." My voice rising, I stood over Mercedes. All thoughts of managing my speech melted away. "You want me to t-tell you what you can do with your warnings?"

She looked up at me, her back straight and regal. "Have you lost your mind?"

"I let you lie and keep secrets from me for seven years," I said, flecks of spit spraying from my lips. "This has to stop now. Don't lie to me again, not when it comes to my father's death."

She stayed seated, looked at me again without blinking.

"Did someone kill my father?" I hovered over her, shaking with rage. I wanted to squeeze the answer from her if that's what it took, but I couldn't do it. Beneath her defiant snarl, I still saw the beautiful, familiar features of Liza's face.

"Deacon," she said, standing now with her hands on her hips, "how many times did we have this conversation when your father first died?"

"I've thought about that," I said. "I realized, all we ever did was discuss everyone else's conspiracy theories. And none of those theories ever fingered your father."

"What?" Mercedes twisted her neck, backed a step away as if in fear of me. "I don't know who's crazier, Deacon, you or your brother. When has anyone *ever* suggested Big Walter wanted your father dead?"

"Frederick was trying to help put him out of business," I replied. "It's not out of the question, is it?"

"First, it's not like I would have a damn clue," Mercedes shot back, jamming a finger into my chest. "When I severed ties with Big Walter, I was cut off from everyone in his inner circle, my brother included."

I wrapped a hand around the finger Mercedes still had against my chest, guided it and the rest of the hand back to her side. "That's why I went at Walt Jr. for the information."

"Deacon, just leave it alone," Mercedes said, turning and stepping toward her desk. "If you love Liza, and the life I've built for her, you have to know what you're doing threatens that."

"Yeah," I replied, "I know the world revolves around you. God forbid if in the course of figuring out why I lost my father, your fake little world gets shaken up a bit."

"Oh, please," she said, stalking back toward me. "You think this is just about what happens to me?"

The knowing glint in her eyes felt like an open mockery. "You really d-don't give a damn, do you?" I said. "My entire family's walking around wondering whether my father died or was assassinated. Liza will never know her grandfather. But for you, it's just a distraction."

"You know what," Mercedes said, turning toward the office door, "I can't help you. If you and Miles want to make up for your failure to fill Frederick's shoes by playing detective for the rest of your lives, go right ahead." She stopped in the doorway, glaring a hole through me. "I am not getting mixed up in this shit with you."

"I'll see myself out," I said. "Just stay out of my way."

"You haven't learned a blessed thing since we were together," she said, crossing her arms and blocking my way. "I mean, Jesus, you never wanted my help, but you're more than happy to go running off on a witch-hunt with your cokehead brother." She paused as if in thought. "I mean, who's to say Miles didn't dream this whole thing up during his latest high?"

"Just stop it!" I shouted, grabbing both of Mercedes's wrists and looking into her eyes as we struggled. Why was she so dismissive, so nasty? In the pit of my stomach, I knew I was getting close to some truth about Frederick's death, and I couldn't afford to just walk out.

Our hands were still intertwined, but as our glares softened and our foreheads nearly melted together, I knew where this was heading. Mercedes and I hadn't "slipped" since she had started dating Bob, but that had less to do with her feelings for him than with the increased distance I'd placed between us. By now, we were barely separated by an inch.

We stood there without speaking, mock-wrestling, until I broke the silence. "What?" I said, letting my head rest against hers. "What?"

"You tell me," she said, pulling back just a bit. "Bob's on his way over—"

I didn't let her finish. Guiding her chin up toward mine, I attacked her with a fierce kiss, the type that precedes screwing, not loving. Mercedes, up for the challenge, proceeded to lash the inside of my mouth with an angry tongue. The next thing I knew clothes were falling around us like snowflakes: her blouse and pants, my polo shirt, her bra and panties, then finally my jeans and skivvies.

The emotions were so raw, so empty, we didn't pause to calculate or consider the aftershocks. Mercedes shoved me against the little couch and worked my stiffening penis like a joystick before licking it up and down with increasingly intense strokes. When she'd nearly tipped me to the point of no return, I pulled her off me and threw her onto the couch.

Crouching over her, I massaged her familiar figure, reminding her of everything I'd done in past years to each spot. "This is mine, right?"

My words were breathless, devoid of real emotion, but my ex responded in kind. "Yeah, no one else knows it like you," she whispered through gritted teeth.

It wasn't until I was poised at the edge of Mercedes's private folds that Maria flashed through my mind. A shower of disappointment doused me, but the memory of Maria's own words left me suspended between plunging ahead and stepping back. *You've struck out. We're strictly professional now. We cannot have a relationship.*

"Come on!" Mercedes, her legs hiked in the air, her most private treasure awaiting my arrival, looked up at me with fire in her eyes. Impatience oozed from her every pore.

Stepping back slowly, I hiked my boxers back up over my slowly softening sex. By the time I had turned around and fastened the belt on my jeans, Mercedes's voice crept over my shoulder in a low growl. "Oh, so it's like that. Get out, then! You're a punk, Deacon." When I stayed silent, she added, "You wouldn't know what to do with it anyway!"

I grabbed my shirt, shoes, and socks and marched out of Mercedes's office. That last little shot was so laughable, it didn't deserve a response.

Maria

By the time I sat down with Deacon that afternoon for his therapy, I was struggling to keep my family troubles outside my office door. It was even harder to do with Deacon, of all people, sitting across from me in "client" mode, but I had no choice but to act like a professional.

"So," I said, shutting the notebook in which I was tracking his progress, "are you comfortable with this week's assignment?" Since Deacon had already learned some of the basic fluency techniques during his stay at the clinic, I was focused on his self-talk, the messages he sent himself that contributed to the severity of his stuttering. For the next week, I had instructed him to sit down after each noticeable bout of stuttering and write down the thoughts that preceded it.

Still sitting across from me, Deacon gave a thin smile. "I usually try to forget about my stutters when they happen," he said. "You mean I have to write every time down?"

"Yes, write it down, but more important, make sure you understand the thoughts that made you more tense, or that made you inhale too deeply, press your lips too tightly, et cetera."

"Okay," he replied, stretching the word out. "I'll do my best."

"Good."

He looked over my head, his eyes on my wall clock. "So, now that I've had my therapy, can we put our 'friend' hats on?"

"Okay. What's new?"

"Not much," he said, looking away momentarily. "Things are picking up with the Dream Party and Governor Hooks's campaign, though. I just turned in my draft of Perry's—I mean, the governor's—speech for an upcoming appearance he's making with Bill Cosby, Reverend Jackson, and Coretta Scott King."

"All right now," I said, my tone lightened by a chuckle. "I'm scared of you, Mr. Davis."

"I'll admit, I'm excited," Deacon said. "Plus, there's some cool stuff going down with Terrell."

"What's up?" I asked.

"You remember the demos he recorded? I guess some labels are already making him offers."

"Well, like I said, let's just hope for the best," I replied. "You're making a real difference in that boy's life."

"Hope so," Deacon replied. He leaned forward in his chair. "What's on your plate these days?"

"Not much," I said, "except for a weekend trip coming up."

"Where you headed?"

"Vegas," I said. "I'm leaving Friday afternoon."

"Cool," Deacon said as he rose from his seat. His forehead wrinkled with what felt like curiosity. "Going with some girlfriends, someone besides Alicia?"

"Sort of," I said, my reply light and breezy. "Just going along with a friend and his teen daughters."

Deacon raised an eyebrow and stopped in his tracks. "Just what type of friend is this?"

"Oh, just a friend like your 'girl' Mercedes," I replied without fighting the sarcasm in my voice.

"Oh. Okay, damn." Deacon turned away, his hand on my doorknob. "Your son? How's that situation?"

"I've decided I'll have to entrust it to God," I said. "I tried investigating my legal options, but too much drama lay that way." I had a feeling that despite my best efforts, the drama wasn't over either. I had left two additional messages for Thomas and Lucille in the past week, and still hadn't heard back.

"Too much drama?" Deacon turned toward me again. "Maria, there's no such thing as too much drama when it comes to your child—"

"Tell Mrs. Hill I'm ready for her, please," I said, waving absentmindedly and shuffling through the notes on my desk. "See you next week, Deacon."

32

Maria

During my flight Friday, as I sat next to Ramsey and across the row from his daughters, Rachel and Justine, I still wasn't sure whether I should feel guilty about the way I had brushed Deacon off. I wasn't trying to be bitchy; we were both too old to act like we didn't have strong feelings for each other, even if we had to keep them in check for now. That said, I wasn't prepared to go into the details of my relationship with Ramsey with him, and I was even less comfortable letting my guard down about Jamil with him. Either action would do nothing but stir up our already complicated relationship. And where Ramsey was concerned, I hadn't let the good doctor see so much as a square inch of my private parts, so I didn't need Deacon nosing around and getting jealous of our Vegas trip.

"You okay?" Ramsey had gently placed a hand onto my wrist. He laid his magazine, a professional journal, in his lap. "You've been awfully quiet."

"I'm fine," I said, smiling for his benefit but still tugging at my locket.

"I want to thank you again for accompanying us, Maria," Ramsey said. "I know the last place you want to be is with me, after the disaster Peter turned out to be for you."

"You know what," I said, turning to face him directly, "Peter wasn't the problem. I was. I thought I was willing to do anything to assert my rights to Jamil, but Peter helped me see that's not true. He was just doing his job, but I shouldn't have hired him in the first place."

"Very mature of you," Ramsey replied. "You're too sweet, really, if you ask me. But I respect your principles. I wish I could say you've rubbed off on me, but I've still got Peter gunning for Wanda's every weakness," he said, his face wrinkling at the mention of his ex. "As far as I'm concerned, I hope he shames her into moving out of the country altogether."

"Maybe you'll come around," I said, nodding across the aisle toward his girls, who were both fast asleep after spending the first hour of the flight flirting with the male attendant. "Look how blessed you are with those two. There's only so much to be bitter about, Ramsey."

"Keep working on me." Ramsey reached around me, squeezing me in a hug. "I'll learn yet."

Once we arrived in Vegas, I was glad I had let Ramsey talk me into accompanying them. It had been his way of apologizing for Peter's treatment of Thomas and Lucille, but all I cared about was the chance to finally experience the gambling mecca. The place lived up to its rep. If the idea was to surround gamblers with so much spectacle that they forgot they were spending real money, the casinos had executed it flawlessly.

Everywhere you looked, you saw ostentatious hotels, ridiculously underpriced all-you-can-eat buffets, and entertainment designed to keep the family busy while Mom or Dad handed a month's paycheck over to the casinos.

Ramsey let Rachel and Justine walk through the city's interconnected maze of hotels and amusement parks, so we spent Saturday on our own, dabbling in the casinos, wasting food at one buffet after another, and window-shopping up and down the main strips.

For Saturday evening, we had already purchased tickets to catch Gladys Knight's show. The girls had grudgingly agreed to go along, so around five we returned to our rooms at the Camelot to get dressed. Ramsey had put the girls, himself, and me all in separate rooms, a touch I appreciated. It's not like he had a choice, of course.

When I stepped into my room, ready to grab a quick bath, I realized I hadn't checked my cell phone all day. When I picked up my messages, they included voice mails from Alicia, one of my college sorority sisters who was in Atlanta for the weekend, and my favorite client, Deacon himself.

Alicia sounded pretty pissed with me on her message. Apparently a college friend of Trent's had spotted her kissing the mysterious man at a bar in L.A. She hadn't returned from the West Coast yet, but Trent was calling her with a lot of questions, and she wanted me to call him and cover for her, buy her some time before her return flight home. Alicia was going to have to understand that saving her marriage was her responsibility this time: I had counseled her and Trent through numerous marital crises over the years, and I had to focus on my own needs for once.

I played Alicia's message a second time, then called Deacon as I sat on my bed, removing my low heels. When he answered his cell phone I said, "Okay, make it quick. I'm charging you for every minute."

Deacon chuckled. "What happened to the 'friend hat'?"

"You don't get to interrupt my vacation weekend and use me for free," I replied, grinning to myself. "Plus, I put off calling Alicia for you, since you sounded like you needed to talk."

"Don't do me any favors," Deacon said. "You didn't want to talk to Alicia anyway."

"Very perceptive," I replied. "How did you know that?"

"Male intuition. Look, thanks for calling."

"So what's up?"

Deacon paused for a minute before answering. "So I was prepared for a weekend of chilling, right? Then I get a call early this morning from Ken Nixon, the chairman of Governor Hooks's presidential campaign."

"They want you to be his running mate," I said. "In 2008, once you've turned thirty-five, that is."

"Okay, I get your point, it could be worse. But check this out. Apparently my cousin Errick and the Dream Party convinced Perry to hold a formal press conference in the next couple of weeks, so he can officially announce his candidacy. Guess who he wants to write his speech?"

"Deacon, that's a great honor."

"Well, there's more. Everyone on the campaign is so anxious about Perry's announcement, they want the speech to be pitch-perfect. So not only do I have to draft this speech in the next thirty-six hours, the campaign leadership team wants to vet it with me and the governor on Monday."

"You should be proud," I said, seriously impressed.

"Yeah, I know," Deacon replied, "but now my mind is filling with all the ways this could go wrong. I mean, I won't be appearing on television or anything like that, but I've got to defend every word in this speech in front of the entire Hooks campaign leadership team. We're talking about people like Andy Young, Earl Graves, Tavis Smiley, and Congresswoman Maxine Walters." He paused, and I could hear him inhaling. "I'd be lying to say I'm not scared. What if I fall apart in front of them?"

"Deacon," I said, "when have you ever fallen apart when it mattered? You're just swimming in negative self-talk, you know."

"I know, d-don't think about the stuttering," he said wearily. "Think about what I'll do *besides* stuttering."

"And that will include what?"

"Feeling my way through each word, exaggerating the first sound of any word I may stutter on, softening my speech articulators, and when in doubt, telling my audience that I stutter and asking them to be patient. As if they'll give a damn."

I shook my head. "You'll never know if you don't try, will you?"

Deacon was quiet for a minute, then asked, "What if the answer's no, if people won't wait on me to get words out?"

"You tell me," I said, trying to keep my voice calm. "What's the worst that could happen, Deacon?"

"I could get kicked off the campaign team."

"And what would you lose?" I asked.

"No money, that's for sure," he said. "I'm just an unpaid volunteer for now, though Perry is working on getting me a part-time salary."

"Okay, so you wouldn't be out any money. What would you lose?"

"Well, hell, I'd lose the chance to be on a campaign team that may make history, Maria. That's not peanuts."

"Let me get this straight. You think Perry Hooks walks on water and would make a historically great president, right?"

"Sure."

"But you think he'd let his advisers drop you from the team because you trip over your words every now and then."

Deacon drawled out his reply. "So you're saying—"

"That any campaign, or any person for that matter, that writes you off because of how you speak isn't worth your time, or anyone else's. Think of it this way: if you do stutter during your discussion of the speech, you'll be giving Hooks and his people a chance to show their true character."

"Hmm." Deacon sighed, sounding like he was chewing over my words. "What the hell, I'll buy your logic. You've got me feeling I should throw in a few 'duh-uhs' and 'ah-ahs' just for the hell of it."

Walking into the bathroom, I smiled as I yanked back the shower curtain and started running hot water. "I'll expect a report next week, okay?"

"Thanks, Maria. I'll let you go. Can I ask you a question?"

"What?"

"Is Folger about to get into that bathtub with you?"

"Oh, Deacon." I had started to step out of my slacks, but his little jab stopped me in middress.

"Surely you didn't think we were so platonic that I wouldn't do some snooping."

"Who says you have any right to snoop in the first place?"

"Couldn't help myself. I stopped by Folger's secretary's desk when I left your office the other day. We made some small talk, and I mentioned how much I love going to Vegas. She mentioned the coincidental fact that Folger was headed there this weekend."

I walked back toward my bed, reaching back with one hand to start unfastening my bra. "Well, now that that's out in the open, you probably feel less guilty about Mercedes and whatever other women you've been seeing."

Deacon hesitated as if I'd drawn blood before saying, "You're the one that drew a line in the sand, not me."

I felt a twinge, realizing he hadn't touched my implicit accusation about Mercedes. "I'm glad you weren't sexually traumatized by our breakup, Deacon."

"I'm not going to lie to you, Maria," Deacon replied, his voice growing huffy and heated. "You have questions, you're free to ask them. You're the one that put this wall between us."

"Deacon," I said, "you have a stressful next few days coming up, and you're about to piss your therapist the hell off. I'm hanging up now."

I clapped my phone shut, finished undressing, and walked into the bathroom. Just before I slid the shower curtain back, I looked over my shoulder at my nude reflection. Seeing my image there, pure and unvarnished, I couldn't deny the tears pooling in my eyes, or the rubbery sensation in my knees. I was sick of kidding myself. An evening with Ramsey lay ahead of me, while my mind was fixated on Deacon. Deacon and Mercedes. Had he started sleeping with her or anyone else? He hadn't lied to me, but he'd been coy, and I hated the fact that despite being his therapist, I'd be tossing and turning all night, tormented by visions of him with another woman in his arms.

Growing Pains

33

Deacon

When I returned to Atlanta from my short trip to Columbus, Ohio, where I had successfully defended my draft of Governor Hooks's campaign speech, I had a disturbing invitation on my voice mail. Mercedes wanted me to join her and Liza for dinner Tuesday evening.

As I drove to Mercedes's house, full of suspicion and loathing, sweat rolled off my forehead despite the fact it was barely a sixty-degree day. It hadn't been a full week since Mercedes and I had violated each other in her home office, and I didn't like the idea of putting Liza between us at such an awkward time. I would have loved nothing better than to make up an excuse about how I couldn't make it, but I figured for Mercedes to involve Liza, she must have her heart in the right place.

When I arrived at the house, I felt like I had taken a time machine back to the early nineties. A beaming Mercedes met me at the door, wearing an apron wrapped around her peach-colored blouse and matching slacks. She asked no searching questions, made no smart-ass observations about me or anyone I loved, didn't even question why I hadn't called since our little dustup. She had already set the large oval table in her dining room, so in minutes she, Liza, and I were eating and conversing like a family again.

I was in the midst of quizzing Liza about her day's lessons when my cell phone pulsed against my waist. I grabbed it up, checking the number on caller ID: MILES.

I excused myself, pushed back from the table, and walked out into Mercedes's airy family room. I wanted to stay close enough that I wouldn't look like I was having a secret conversation. "What's up, man?" I said, my tone loose and light.

"I know you're over there, Deacon," Miles said, nearly biting the ends off his words. "When are you going to get the truth out of her?"

"Hey, let me remind you," I said, taking a seat on one of Mercedes's white leather chairs. "I told you, things are coming along." I had told my brother the blow-by-blow details about my confrontation with Mercedes. "Can I have a few more days?"

"No. The point wasn't for you to bang her, Deacon. You think a woman like that is going to come straight with the truth, just because you make her feel good?"

I pressed my right thumb and forefinger together, slowed the boiling of my blood. "I can't just access what you need, not without easing the door open." I had nearly confused myself with the coded language.

"I've been waiting on you for weeks now," Miles replied. "You do what you have to and get some evidence, little brother. Otherwise I'll kick down her door tomorrow and get it my damn self."

I swallowed, trying to contain my anger. It looked like Miles was on to something, but I wasn't going to let him run rampant. "Don't talk crazy," I said, my voice low. "I'll call you when I have something, okay?" I shut the phone off before he could answer.

To shield Liza from her uncle's wrath, I decided to do what I had to. After we ate, Mercedes had her housekeeper clean up the kitchen while we took Liza biking. When we returned, I spent an hour teaching my little girl the basics of chess, then led her to bed with Mercedes's blessing.

Mercedes was seated on her couch in the family room, typing on her miniature laptop PC, when I returned from putting Liza to bed. She glanced my way without letting it slow her fingers. "Thanks for coming by tonight. I hope it makes up for how foul we were with each other."

"It was my fault," I said softly, taking a seat next to her but keeping a few inches' distance. "I'm sorry, Mercedes." I meant it.

"I think deep down," she said, her head focused on the PC's flat screen, "I was trying to express what I really wanted, Deacon."

"We were in love once," I said. "I guess that doesn't change overnight."

"Look," Mercedes said, laying her PC next to her spot on the couch, "I already told Bob what happened. We were pretty blah anyway. We've agreed to end our little relationship."

"I hope that wasn't on my account," I said, my honesty getting ahead of me.

"No, you were just a symptom," she replied. "I'm just saying, if you want to stay the night, there's nothing stopping you on my side." She turned to face me. "Is the same true for you?"

"If you're asking about Maria, she's my therapist," I said. "She draws a very clear line, so I'm definitely not spoken for."

I drew Mercedes's head to my shoulder and began speaking to her in hushed tones, as we talked in depth about Liza—her progress in school, her lingering dream that we would someday reconcile, and her increasingly headstrong ways. It felt like we were married parents again, facing the world with the knowledge that the other had our back. Of course, it helped that we both ignored the subject of our fathers.

When we were ready for bed, I ran a bath for Mercedes in her Jacuzzi and let her soak and soothe her muscles while I cased her home office. By the time she had toweled off and climbed into bed, dressed in an aqua-blue silk short set, I had my night planned.

We agreed we didn't need to complicate things with sex. I don't know if I was more relieved out of loyalty to Maria, or out of fear of Liza hearing us. I showered, threw on an old pair of my boxers Mercedes hadn't thrown out yet, and climbed into the bed. She snuggled up against me but turned her face in the opposite direction. We talked until she fell asleep.

Mercedes could be a light sleeper, so I waited until she had been snoring for fifteen minutes before sliding out of bed. When the time came, just after midnight, I padded down the hallway on bare feet and tiptoed my way down the wooden steps. Fortunately the wood was so new and sturdy, there were almost no squeaks at all. I had been worried about tripping in the dark, but the stairwell and hallways were dimly lit by track lighting.

Once I descended to the basement level and reached Mercedes's home office, I eased the door closed behind me and flicked on the banker's lamp sitting by her computer. I didn't begin to believe that someone with Mercedes's savvy had anything in this office that would tie her to the people from Big Walter's gang, but I hoped to find a safety deposit box key, or something comparable. I didn't know what I was looking for, but I'd know it when I saw it.

I lost track of time as I pulled out one desk drawer after another, rifled through reams of file folders, and meticulously reviewed the contents of the office's closets. I knew I was getting desperate when I found myself reading through a pack of old greeting cards that sat in the back of the closet. There were at least a couple of hundred of them, bound with a dozen or so rubber bands, but curiosity kept me opening and closing each one, then setting it back into the pile. It was like every card my ex had received was in there—birthday, college graduation, birthday, engagement, wedding, birthday, baby shower, more birthdays, and so on.

About halfway through the stack, I reached one that gave me pause. It was a sparkling white thank-you card with a Scripture from the book of Ephesians on the front. On the inside, it was inscribed with a handwritten message:

> *Mercedes,*
>   *Girl, I can't thank you enough for everything. I know you said not to contact you, but I mailed this before I crossed the border, so ain't no way the return address could be traced to me.*
>   *God has blessed you so, I can't even express it. You helped me believe in me when I was ready to give up. Me and my little one owe you. Please keep this note, at least until we can repay what we owe you.*
>
>

God bless,
Tisha

Seated just outside the closet door, my back to the wall, my mouth suddenly dry and parched, I reread the name. Tisha. Big Walter's employee. One of the two working in the supper club the night my father died.

The next thing I knew, I was standing over Mercedes, who was still fast asleep. Leaning over, I grabbed her shoulders and shook her briskly.

"Hmm?" She opened one eye halfway first, then the other before her vision came into focus. "What do you want, Deacon?" She was nearly alert, just that fast.

I flipped the card onto her chest and stepped back from the bed, my hands in the air. "What is this?"

"That's what I should be asking you," she replied, yawning and flipping the card open like she'd never seen it before.

"No more lies," I said, my voice shaking. "Tell me everything you know, now."

"You're still playing cops and robbers," Mercedes said, shaking her head sorrowfully before sitting up in the bed. "Why don't you trust me, Deacon?"

"How the hell can you expect trust, when you never tell the truth!" My heart racing, I paced back and forth alongside the bed.

"Deacon," Mercedes said, her tone calm and deliberate, "Some things are too messy to share with anyone else." She looked up into my eyes, her gaze rock-solid. "I severed ties with Big Walter, but some of his former employees, like Tisha, were like family to me."

"So you're admitting now that you were in touch with Tisha at the time Frederick died, and you probably know where she is now."

Mercedes reached out and grabbed my elbow, her eyes pinning me in place. "Tisha helped me escape from D.C. when I was a kid," she said, her voice low. "You remember how I told you I packed up in the dead of night and hopped a bus to Atlanta? Tisha drove me! She was only fourteen, but already had boyfriends with cars. She took one guy's ride for the night and drove me to the bus station. So, did I stay in touch with her for a while? Hell yes!"

"You know what, I really don't need an explanation of all your lies," I said, yanking my elbow from her grasp. "Just tell me, why

were Tisha and Pharrell Haynes working at Frederick's club the
night of the fire? Don't forget, I already know Pharrell was a trained
arsonist."

Instead of answering, Mercedes climbed from the bed and briskly
walked up to me. "Deacon," she said, reaching up and stroking my
right cheek, "you don't want to do anything that would disturb Liza
and wake her, do you? Listen to me, because I'm not going to say this
again. You're playing in deep waters that neither you nor your family
need to mess with. Just trust me, let me keep the lid on this Pandora's
box. It's what's best."

I slapped her hand from my face. "Was my father murdered?"

"It was Frederick's time," she replied, a hint of a plea in her voice.
"There was no great conspiracy, Deacon, nothing involving the Man
or Big Walter, that caused his death."

Ignoring Mercedes's response, I went to her closet and retrieved
my clothes and shoes. I stood in the middle of the floor and began
dressing as Mercedes watched me. "Go ahead and say it. 'To hell with
you, Mercedes.' That's what you're thinking, right? Just keep it up,
Deacon. You're not the only one who's involved here. Miles still
doesn't have his shit together, do you realize that?" She smiled at my
involuntary pause. "He's still snorting coke, if the D.C. grapevine's to
be believed. And as for your hero, Governor Hooks, he's no saint either."

I stared at her, wishing my eyes could spit lead. "What, you've
been doing three-ways with him or something?"

"Oh, that's good. Let's just say that he's not the best family man,
and he's keeping some secrets of his own. You want all this hitting the
papers? Keep chasing Tisha and see what comes out."

Fully clothed now, I shook my head as I walked toward the bedroom door. "Mercedes," I said, turning as I grabbed for the brass
doorknob, "I'm leaving now, but I'll be back once I get the truth."

Mercedes's voice nearly dropped to a whisper. "I really don't think
you want it."

"I tried to p-protect you," I said, pointing a shaking finger in her
direction. "Didn't want to endanger the mother of my child. You've

spent your mercy points, though. If you were involved in this at all, you're going to jail. I'll raise Liza my damn self."

I knew I'd hit the breaking point, because I didn't feel an ounce of guilt when I slammed the bedroom door shut. I had probably interrupted Liza's sleep, but the way things were looking, her little world would soon be turned upside down anyway.

34

Deacon

As soon as the city prison guard shut the cell door after us, I shoved Miles from behind. My superior size, along with the element of surprise, sent him sprawling to the floor. A few feet away from a group of brothers huddled in one corner of the holding cell, he struggled to his feet.

"Damn!" A short, chubby brother with a salt-and-pepper beard roared with laughter. "That boy ain't even been in here two seconds, and already punked!"

"Kiss my ass, motherfucker," Miles said, growling as he brushed himself off. His words were harsh, but his tone was still proper. His oxford shirt was wrinkled and torn, and the knees of his dress slacks were stained, but he stood proud and tall. "You want some of this?"

The brother who'd picked at him smiled and exchanged glances with the two guys closest to him. All three of them were wearing sweatpants and had do-rags for hats, but they didn't come off like hard-core players. That, and I could tell they weren't sure just how crazy Miles might be.

They still hadn't said anything to my brother when he turned back to me. "You want to take me on in a fair fight now?" He raised his fists, striking the pose he'd made famous in college, when he nearly made the Olympic welterweight boxing team.

An hour after our arrest, I still seethed with anger at my brother. When I'd stormed out of Mercedes's house, I had driven directly to see Miles. I had stopped by to see him several times at his and Chantal's room at the Embassy Suites downtown. Chantal had only been there once, due to her busy schedule of research, interviews, and partying.

Surprisingly, Miles answered his door before I'd completed my first knock. He was dressed in a nice oxford shirt and dress slacks, looking neat and orderly like it was three p.m. instead of three a.m. "What you got for me?"

"Didn't think you'd be up," I said, sniffing the stale air of his suite.

"I was up writing," he said coolly.

Standing in the suite's front room, where Miles had a laptop computer and reams of paper strewn across a coffee table, I looked toward the bedroom. The door stood open, and it looked like all the lights were on. "Chantal up, too?"

"No, she's sleeping somewhere, probably at her Aunt Marcy's over in East Point," Miles said, his tone growing more dismissive. He ambled back over to the couch and sat down in front of the coffee table. "Grab a seat," he said, gesturing toward a chair with plump cushions.

Feeling depressed about the Davis men and our relations with women, I sank into the chair. "What'd you do to her this time?"

"She just keeps pressing my buttons, Deacon. She's still convinced I have a secret plan to marry her someday."

I had heard this song before, had argued with Miles countless times about the way he took Chantal for granted. I knew exactly where resurrecting this discussion would lead. First, he'd remind me of his belief that no Davis heir could live up to the example Frederick had set as a husband, father, and leader. Then he'd remind me how my failed marriage proved his point.

"You may as well know, you're on the right track," I said, getting into what really mattered.

He looked up at me, his eyes widening. "Oh?"

"Yeah," I said, unable to look him in the eye. "I found proof that Mercedes has been in contact with that Tisha Norris for sure. She didn't even deny it."

"But she didn't tell you shit else," Miles said matter-of-factly.

"Right." I took in a deep breath, stood and treated myself to a yawn. "We're gonna have to go to D.C., I guess, find this girl ourselves."

"I already tried that, little brother," Miles said. "Everyone I found that knew her swore she had moved away but didn't know where to. Her trail ran cold." He stood up, motioned toward the door. "Mercedes is our best shot, man. Come on, let's go back over there."

"Not so fast." I stepped in front of the door, crossed my arms. "Maybe when Liza's away from home, sometime tomorrow. I'm not letting you go over there half-cocked with my baby in the middle."

Miles squinted at me, his head tilted in surprise. "Deacon, cut the heroics—"

A loud rapping shook the door and we both grew silent. I searched Miles's face. "Chantal leaves for one night, and you already got some freak coming over?"

Miles shrugged, a wary look rolling into his eyes.

Another set of raps to the door, followed by a loud voice. "Mr. Davis, Atlanta police. Open up now, sir."

When I turned back from the door, ready to quiz Miles again, he had disappeared, but I heard him scurrying around in the bathroom. The door was shut, the only sound being the flushing of the toilet.

That's when I connected the dots. Mercedes had claimed Miles was back to his old tricks, and though I didn't want to believe it, I knew from the past that nothing was out of the question where my brother was concerned.

With Miles still in the bathroom, the voice on the other side of the door slapped me out of my thoughts. "Final warning, we're coming in now!"

I had spent too many years as a black man on this earth to let the Atlanta PD burst in on us with guns drawn. I had no interest in going out like that, so I yelled back through the door. "Okay, chill! I'm opening the door now, slowly."

I flipped the lock and let the door swing open on its own power. Willing myself to stand still, I held my hands in the air and searched the officers' faces. I wanted them to see I was cool, calm, and collected. As cool as possible, that is, for someone whose brother was hastily flushing cocaine down the toilet.

The officers were an Oreo trio, a tall, middle-aged white woman with two young, slim black males. "Up against the wall," the woman, a brunette with craggy skin, said.

I complied quickly, hugging the wall as one of the brothers frisked me. I was glad I wasn't carrying my gun. I owned only one, and usually kept it locked away at home for emergencies. I had considered keeping it on me lately, though.

I let the officer complete his search on me and tried to keep calm as the other two officers raced through the suite. They quickly focused on the closed bathroom door and shouted warnings to Miles.

"Come out of there right now, sir!" The female officer barked the words, sounding ready to back up every inch of her threatening tone.

"We gotta move," the other brother with her said. He stepped back to kick the door open just as I heard Miles fling it open.

Miles had no contrition, no embarrassment as they dragged him over next to me and spread-eagled him against the wall. "What the hell is this about? Do you know who we are?"

"We know someone called the front desk, saying a woman was being raped in this room," the officer who'd frisked me said. He grabbed Miles by the collar, turned him around. "According to your wallet, you're the Miles Davis this room's registered to?"

"What do you think, Officer?" Even though his hands were cuffed, Miles stood toe to toe with the policeman. "Tell me, do you see any woman in here looks like she's been raped?"

"You got other problems now." The lady officer emerged from the bathroom. She had several dripping-wet plastic bags in each hand. "You tried to flush too fast, Mr. Davis. The toilet backed up." I could hear the laughter edging into her voice, and in seconds she had her partners cackling along.

Facing off with Miles in the holding cell, I remembered the officers' amusement and laughed at him, too. "I'm not fighting your stupid ass," I said. I took my arm, cuffed him around the neck, and pulled him up to the front of the cell, inches away from the bars. Trapped amidst a bunch of convicts, Miles didn't need to call extra attention to himself. With my size, I could handle myself, but as an average-size man talking mess, he was asking for an eventual ass-kicking.

"I hope you're happy," I said once I'd released him and we were facing front, looking down the hall for signs of my attorney, Allen Pryor.

"I'm human, Deacon," Miles said, staring ahead coldly. "My life is a mess—you don't think I know that? I can't be the great, responsible Davis heir every day. Sometimes it's just too much."

"You d-don't think I can relate?" I leaned forward slightly, grabbing the bars before me. "We grew up in the same house, you know."

"Yeah, well, everyone bears his own particular cross. The coke, the escape—that's what gets me by."

"Dammit, Miles," I said, gritting my teeth. "Make your own fate, but don't get me mixed up in it." I shook my head, rage coursing through me. I had just started to prove myself to Perry Hooks and the Dream Party. My visit to Miles's room might cost me every bit of progress I'd made in recent weeks. Miles and I were grown-ass men, still finding ways to stain Frederick's legacy. When this got out, Errick and everyone who believed in me would catch hell from Miriam and the other Dream Party board members.

"Let me handle this, okay," Miles said. "If Errick can post my bail, too, I'll get my attorney on the case tomorrow. We'll get these charges thrown out. You can't search someone's room for drugs without a search warrant. I'll bet Mercedes is the one that called in that rape allegation, and she'll never be willing to back that up in court with testimony."

"Miles, once the officers got into the room, you made the search fair game with your bathroom antics."

"No way," Miles said, sniffing rebelliously. "No way."

We went silent, staying near the front of the cell and silently watching each other's backs. When Allen arrived an hour later, he debriefed me on the night's happenings and promised to get our initial court appearances moved up as early as possible.

Around noon the next day, we got into court. Miles's attorney hadn't returned his calls yet, so Allen represented us both. Allen was a smooth talker, and given the low-priority nature of our charges in a city with Atlanta's crime problems, we each got bonds below five grand. I was a little surprised Miles's wasn't higher, but if I had to guess, his heroin arrest had probably been scrubbed from the public record.

Errick showed up after the hearing and posted both our bonds. Once he'd handled business, he blew down our cell's hallway like he was the warden, shaking guards' hands and even nodding conspiratorially at a few guys in other cells, like he was at home among the prison population. In short order, Miles and I were released to his custody and followed him out to his Range Rover.

Starting his truck's engine, Errick glanced over at me, then back at Miles. "I remember when I was the irresponsible one among us. You Davis brothers better squash this craziness."

Sitting in the back, Miles snorted, then sighed. "Errick, shut up and take me to the Embassy Suites."

"Miles," I said, barely able to keep my eyes open, "they're not going to let you back in, not after the hell you raised."

Errick looked at me, his mouth twisted in a frown. "He ain't stayin' with me."

"I know." I said. "Just take us to my crib. I'll handle him."

Wheeling his truck through the streets, Errick ranted under his breath. "Talking like he's still somebody's 'big cousin.' Irresponsible bastard."

"Hey!" Miles leaned forward in his seat, poking his head between Errick's and mine. "Watch your tone with me, Errick, I'll knock—"

"You ain't doing shit," Errick said, sticking a right hand in Miles's face while steering with the other. "Aunt Leah called when I was on the way to get you." His eyes darted my way, but he saved his nastiest glare for Miles. "She's flying into Atlanta tomorrow morning. Momma's gon' knock your ass out."

35

Maria

Thursdays are the only mornings I don't see clients, so I get to start my day a little later. That's why I was still in bed when my phone rang at 6:37. Lazily, I grabbed my remote control, muted Channel 5's morning news, and pulled my cordless phone to my ear. I was so out of it, I forgot to check caller ID.

Not that it mattered. I recognized Deacon's voice immediately. "Maria?"

"Good morning," I said, yawning as I sat up in bed. "Where did you get the impression I'm at your beck and call? Or don't you have a clock?"

Instead of the snappy comeback I might have expected, all I heard was silence before he replied, "I thought you should know, I won't make my appointment today." His voice had the drag of a kicked puppy.

"Is everything okay?"

"I'll survive," he said, chuckling weakly, "but probably just barely. I g-got into a bit of trouble yesterday."

"What happened?"

"Well, I spent some time in a small cell full of funky men, most of whom looked like me."

"You were in jail?" A vein of anxiety snaked through me, but I kept cool, staying on the right side of the therapist-lover line.

Deacon rewound the tape of the past days, recounting his fight with his brother as well as the drug charges involved. The police released him on a small bond and had a preliminary hearing scheduled in a few days. The more he talked, the more Alicia's early warnings wove through my brain. *That boy's got too much baggage.* Not that I hadn't had a brush or two with the law myself, but at least those troubles were firmly in my past. Besides his speech struggles, I'd thought

Deacon had conquered his emotional demons. Was that just wishful thinking?

"I swear, Maria, I've never touched an ounce of any illegal drug besides weed, and that was a few times in college," Deacon said, his voice insistent.

I knew how it would sound, but my concern had turned into a defensive shield. "Tell me again, why were you in Miles's hotel room?"

"I had to see him last night—it was urgent. Between you and me, it had to do with our father's death."

"I don't understand—what was so urgent about something that happened seven years ago?"

"It just—I had learned some disturbing information from Mercedes."

"Oh," I said, feeling my eyebrows jump with indignation. "So late at night, you just happened to be at Mercedes's house when you found this information?"

A pregnant pause, then Deacon replied, "You have to trust me, it was innocent—"

"You don't have to explain yourself to me, Deacon," I said, lying through my teeth. "I'm your therapist, nothing more."

"I—look, let me explain myself later, when things get a little less crazy. Bottom line, I went to see Miles and we got set up. Now my mother's flying into town to chastise us. Maria, I'm not up for that emotional circus."

"I understand your concern," I said, stifling my first thought. *What you want me to do about it?* "Is there some way I can help?"

"You've done enough, just by answering the phone," Deacon said. "I already know what I need to do when I see Mother, but I knew hearing your voice would help me get through it."

I patted my chest a couple of times, trying to slow the flurries Deacon's sweet words had stirred. "Deacon, are you sure you don't need more help? There's no harm in seeing a psychologist, someone who can help you deal with the emotional side of things exclusively. I can recommend some good people."

"No, I know what I need to do," he repeated. "Again, I just needed to hear your voice. When I get myself fixed, Ms. Oliver, I'm firing you as my therapist. I've got a new role in mind for you."

"Stop," I said, though an ear-to-ear smile swept my face.

"Is everything okay with you?" he asked. "Did you ever patch things up with Thomas?"

"Not quite," I said. "My brother can be pretty stubborn. Not only has he never returned my messages, he hasn't responded to the letter I wrote last week. He's left me no choice but to stalk him."

"Watch yourself," Deacon said, laughing gently.

"All I'm going to do is stop by his office, probably tomorrow during my lunch hour," I explained. "I'll be perfectly civil, but it's the only way I can corner him without putting Jamil and Lucille in the middle."

"Well, sounds like we both have some big confrontations coming," Deacon said. "I hope things go well, Maria."

"Thank you. I'll keep you in my prayers. Maybe I can reschedule you in for a makeup appointment tomorrow?" I was really hoping he would call me before then, but my pride wouldn't let me dangle that little admission.

"I'll update you soon," he said. "Thanks again, sexy." He hung up before I could scold him.

By eight thirty, I had put in a yoga tape, showered and dressed, and had my first espresso of the day. Just about ready to gather my purse and work bag, I sat crunching my way through a crusty cinnamon raisin bagel when my doorbell chimed.

I looked through the peephole, saw Ramsey's inquisitive eyes staring back at me, and felt my shoulders slump. This was not a good sign. Not that Ramsey wasn't welcome at my home—in the three months since we had become real friends, he had come by for coffee and conversation a half dozen times. That said, as a couple we were still pure as the driven snow—nothing beyond the unplanned kiss I planted on him the night he introduced me to Peter Hedges. He hadn't gotten any and wasn't about to, so he really didn't have "popcorn" visit status; he should have called a sister first.

I opened the door and blocked his way, keeping a hand on the doorknob. "Good morning," I said, forcing a smile. "I was just headed to the office."

"Yes, I was hoping I would catch you," Ramsey said, smiling and glancing to his left and right. "I wanted to take you to breakfast. Neither of us is seeing clients this morning, and my evenings are booked all week with the girls' afterschool activities."

Wondering what could be so urgent, I tried not to sound too dismissive. "It's late notice, Doctor. Why don't we look at doing something next week?"

"Well," Ramsey said, scratching at the tip of his nose, "I don't know if this can wait that long. Maybe we could go out for dinner Saturday?"

"Ramsey, I don't know if that's a good idea," I said. Even though I wasn't sure I'd ever act on the attraction, my conversation with Deacon had reminded me that Ramsey didn't have a chance in hell with me. It was past time to make sure he and reality were well acquainted. "Saturday dinner gets to feeling too much like a real date, don't you think?"

Ramsey smiled brightly, as if he hadn't heard me. "Why don't I just come in?"

"Okay," I said, sighing, "but I've really got to get going."

When the door had swung shut behind him, Ramsey leaned against it, arms folded. "Now tell me, why would you use such harsh language, Maria? Would it be the end of the world if we went out on 'a real date'?"

I stepped back toward my love seat and took a seat on its arm. "Ramsey, I'm just starting to acknowledge some feelings and issues that I've been struggling with. I've been dodging some complex realities, and it's time I stopped doing that."

"Oh," he said, rubbing at his chin, "and the first complex reality is that you're not attracted to me?"

"I wouldn't put it like that," I said, seeking out his eyes. I realized I hadn't had to let a man down easy in a while, and felt my way gingerly as if doing it for the first time. I guess in recent years, I'd become so good at swatting brothers down before they got to the plate, I'd never had to reject someone who deserved any civility. "Ramsey, you are attractive, accomplished, everything I could want on paper. But I have to be honest with myself about who I'm really attracted to."

"It's Deacon, right?" Ramsey reached me before finishing the sentence. He stood over me, reaching for one of my hands. "Maria, he's your client, for God's sake. Even if you remove the ethical conflict, why would you want to complicate your life with someone who's still trying to figure out his own?" When I looked away from him but didn't resist the hand he had laid on top of one of mine, he continued. "I am not stupid. I know you fell for him during the clinic. But I also know women. The bad, troubled boy is always intriguing, but eventually you start to think practically. And you, Maria," he said, his voice now a humming purr, "are a level-headed, practical woman. You know I'm the one who helped you develop the will to fight for your son. You know I'm the one who can open doors for your career."

I didn't know what to think of Ramsey's full-court press, but he had hit a nerve with his slams on Deacon. As undeniable as my feelings for him were, a part of me felt increasingly naïve for wanting Deacon. I couldn't deny it: the little girl in me, the good-as-orphaned single mom done wrong by Guy, wanted nothing more than to see Deacon Davis be my knight in shining armor. There were moments I even fantasized about having his children, something I hadn't let myself do about any man in years.

Sensing he'd captured my attention, Ramsey leaned closer to me. "Deacon is a big kid, Maria. I'm a man. Your man, if you so choose."

"Ramsey," I said, feeling my brow warm but thinking plenty clearly, "please, don't. It wouldn't be good for either of us. I don't know that you've even processed your divorce yet."

"Let me worry about that," he snapped suddenly. He stepped around me and eased onto the love seat before pulling me down next to him. Before I knew it, he had cupped my chin and drawn my face to his. "Just," he said, leaning in and letting his words ease out, "let me handle everything."

"No." I took my hands and firmly scooted him away from me.

"Think carefully, baby," Ramsey said, reaching out for me again and easing me against the love seat's cushions. "If you're telling me I can never make the most of our relationship, well, we both know it's not that simple."

"What is this?" I didn't hold back this time. I straight-up shoved Ramsey with enough force that he flew to the other end of the love seat.

Just like that, he was back in my face, hands gripped against my shoulders. "Oh, you won't be suing me for harassment, Maria. If you only see me as a neutered friend, that's your right. But it's my right to share what I know about your family problems with whomever I choose." He smiled wide at the shocked look that must have covered my face. "You wouldn't want little Jamil to get a visit at school from a stranger like me, would you? You know, someone who puts a bug in his ear about the fact that his Auntie Maria is really his *mommy*, and the people he thinks are Mommy and Daddy are just extended family?"

The weight of his words left me blurry-eyed, but I could see well enough to slap the taste out of his mouth. "Shut up!" I screamed, my hand shaking as I withdrew it from his bleeding lips. "Don't even think about it, Ramsey!"

"Why don't you think about this," Ramsey said, standing quickly and wiping blood from his mouth. "You don't get something for nothing in this life, Maria. Either you behave like a lady and give me a chance with you, or deal with the consequences."

I grabbed my phone, dialed 911. "I'd leave if I were you!" I shouted, walking into the kitchen. An entire rack of steak knives sat ready and waiting.

By the time I reached the knife rack, my front door had creaked open and slammed shut. That didn't stop me from grabbing the largest knife with a jittery hand, before going back to check the door.

When the door popped open suddenly, when I was a few feet away, I raised the knife and spoke loudly and forcefully. "Go home, Ramsey."

"No, try again." Alicia popped her head around the door, craning her neck. Her eyes bulged when she saw the knife. "Damn, I guess it's not a good time."

Dropping the knife, I collapsed against the wall. "Shut up, and shut the door behind you."

After I summarized my morning for her, I poured Alicia some espresso while she brought me up to speed on her latest attempts to patch things up with Trent. Thank God he had agreed to attend counseling with her, once she convinced him she hadn't slept with the mystery man, who was apparently the president of her company's L.A. division.

Staring at her over my coffee table, I crossed my legs. "I think you're finally doing the right thing. Trust me, you don't want to wind up single in this world if you don't have to. The scene's just full of a bunch of players, fools, and secret-agent types."

"I want my marriage to work," Alicia whispered, raising her eyes to meet mine. A trail of tears dotted her face. "I've told Tom I can't see him anymore. We were headed for trouble anyway. I gave him head last week." She looked away again, confirming she caught the disappointment on my face. "Help me, please?"

I stood, went to Alicia, and folded my arms around her. After twenty years of friendship, I knew that was all the answer she needed.

36

Deacon

I think if Miles had imagined for a second that his drug habit would bring Mother back into the picture, he'd have left the blow alone. It was too late now.

By the time Mother arrived in Atlanta with my Uncle James, who'd been visiting her and my stepfather in Florida, it was late afternoon. Errick, Miles, and I picked them up at the airport and made uneasy conversation while driving to Buckhead, where we had an early dinner at a Greek place Mother loves.

I hadn't seen my mother in almost six months, so throughout dinner and the trip back to my house, we killed time talking about everything except the obvious. Mother, who hadn't seen either of my kids since Christmas, was full of questions about them, especially Liza and, by extension, Mercedes. I talked plenty about Liza's progress in school and her new interest in ballet, and skimmed over my jacked-up relationship with Mercedes. I was pretty sure I wouldn't be able to see Liza again until I'd made my trip to D.C., because after the past twenty-four hours, my anger at Mercedes's betrayals meant I had to keep as much distance between us as possible.

The main event didn't kick off until Miles, Uncle James, Mother, and I stepped into my great room. "Deacon, bring me an ashtray, please," Mother asked, though the *please* wasn't exactly heartfelt. She stood in the center of the room and stretched her willowy arms over her head. Uncle James had already taken a seat on my couch, his sport coat and tie lying at his side. He sat there rolling up the sleeves of his white oxford, preparing for what he knew would be a bloody battle.

I locked Prince out on the covered patio, ignoring his anguished howls, then got an ashtray for Mother, who stood in the hallway teasing her feathery, shoulder-length waves of coal-black hair. When I returned to the great room, Miles lay sprawled across from her and

Uncle James on the love seat. I set the tray down in front of my mother, who had finally taken a seat, then crossed over toward the fireplace. "So," I said, easing down into my leather rocking chair, "I guess you're looking for some explanations from me and Miles."

"We're grown men," Miles snapped, to no one in particular. "We don't *explain* ourselves to anyone."

"Oh, I don't want explanations," Mother said, a freshly lit cigarette simmering between two fingers. Adjusting her silk dress, she crossed her legs. "I simply want you boys to get your lives on the right track. I don't need to know why you're making a mockery of me, and of your father's memory. I just want it to stop."

"Now, Leah," Uncle James said, his voice just above a whisper but still forceful. He let a hand rest on Mother's shoulder. "Remember what we prayed about?"

Mother didn't fight Uncle James off, just ignored him. "This is simple. I have thought about this for months even before this latest embarrassment, but I held my tongue. Now you are going to hear it." She opened out one hand and began ticking things off, finger by finger. "First of all, Miles, this is proof that you have to reenter the Betty Ford Clinic. You thought you were fooling all of us these last couple of years, but the joke is on you. Whatever happens with these charges—and I expect Deacon's to be dismissed, when you admit the drugs were all yours—I insist that you get some real help. I will pay for it."

She ticked off another finger. "Second, Miles, I am putting my foot down. This nonsense of spreading conspiracy theories about your father's death? That ends, now. I expect you to call your publisher and tell them you cannot deliver that book. If they take your advance back, which I doubt they will, your stepfather has agreed—"

With Prince's sudden barks banging against the patio's glass window pane, Miles shut his eyes and held up a hand. "That man is not my father, in any sense of the word."

Mother's nostrils flared. "Roberto," she replied, stressing the name proudly, "has agreed to reimburse you so you can pay the publisher back."

"Well, God bless him." Sinking lower into his seat, his eyes glazing over, Miles acted like he hadn't even registered Mother's demands. I wondered if he'd sneaked a hit of weed while no one was looking.

"Now, Deacon," Mother said, turning toward me. Just that quick, I was in the spotlight. "I know you weren't using any of these drugs with your brother. But it's not like you to be out with him late at night. Something's obviously wrong."

"If you want an explanation, it's simple," I said, anxiety and defiance battling within me. "Miles has always been right. Something's not right about the way Frederick died."

"Oh, Lord—not you, too," Mother replied, shaking her head and chuckling grimly. She elbowed Uncle James, who sat tapping one foot nervously. "You hear this, James? Miles has corrupted my baby boy now."

"Somebody t-tell me I'm wrong," I said, leaning forward in my chair and looking more at Uncle James than at my mother. "Tell me you know for certain that the fire was a pure accident." I paused, searching Miles's face to see how much, if anything, he had ever shared with them. "Tell me there's no reason to be concerned that former employees of Big Walter Chance were working at the supper club the night of the fire."

"I've heard most of the same rumors you boys have," Uncle James said, his face drooping with grief. "That's all they've proved to be, though. Rumors. What do you think most honors your father's memory—continuing his work or trying to find malice where it probably doesn't exist?"

"I'm tired of that argument," Mother said, waving a hand in Uncle James's face before turning back to me. "Son, it's time for you to live your life for Deacon, not for Frederick or anyone other than you yourself, and your children. You're a good father to Liza and Dejuan, honey, but your lives could be simpler if you'd find a good woman and get a real job."

"A real job," I said, feeling my chest muscles tighten. "What would that be?"

"The world is full of business opportunities," she replied, stabbing her cigarette out in the ashtray and then lighting up another one. "Certainly you could get on as an investor in some of your old team-mates' business ventures. If not, Roberto would love to have you expand his franchises into Georgia." My stepfather owned dozens of fast-food restaurants in the Southeast, including Burger Kings, Sub-ways, and Dairy Queens. He was also an irritable, controlling little man. I swore his main goal in life was to make my mother forget my father ever existed. I'd be homeless before I'd go to work for him.

When I made it clear that I had deeper goals than selling burgers and shakes, Mother didn't let up. "You think you're achieving some great purpose in life by working with the Dream Party and Perry Hooks?" She shut her eyes tight and shook her head, seemingly trying to believe my naïveté. "Like any American of color, Perry doesn't have a snowball's chance in hell of becoming president, not now and not ever. All you'll help him do is throw away his political future. But I'll never convince you, will I? This is all part of your belief in Fred-erick's *dream*." The mockery in her voice was unmistakable. "The dream that was nothing but a nightmare for me."

"Leah." Uncle James raised his voice this time. He rubbed Mother's back lightly, but the look in his eyes was steely. "We agreed not to say things we'd regret later."

"Too late," I said, springing to my feet and walking to the mantel over my fireplace. "Why don't you respect Frederick's work, Mother? I know life with him was hard, with him traveling so much, always being underpaid. You never had him to yourself, he was in such de-mand. Didn't you believe in what he stood for, though?"

Mother stabbed out another cigarette and looked down before staring back at me. "Your father's mission was honorable, and I sup-ported him publicly every step of the way. But the mission ended when he died, Deacon. It's not your place to continue it." The res-olute pride in her eyes softened a bit as she said, "Didn't getting fired after that Fox News failure show you that?"

A cloak of silence fell over the room as I replayed Mother's in-sulting words. I realized in that moment I'd never discussed the de-tails of my resignation with her. When she resigned from her positions on the board of both Communities in Action and the Dream Party, the year after Frederick's death, Mother had made it clear that she was getting on with her life. She had respected our right to stay involved in Frederick's organizations, but insisted she wanted no part in them. As a result, when Mother and I had our quarterly phone calls or occasional visits, I left the subject of the Dream Party off the table.

She had brought it up now, though, and I was ready for her. I folded my arms and looked into her eyes, piercing coal-black pupils that looked just like mine. "Who said I got fired?"

"I know, I know," she replied, stabbing her latest cigarette butt in my direction. "You weren't actually fired—you resigned at Miriam Lloyd's suggestion. It's the same difference, dear. Your father's fan club doesn't respect you, because of the stuttering, Deacon." She paused, glancing at Uncle James as if she hoped he would step in, but then barreled on. "I know how they are. Your uncle's not the problem, of course, but the rest of the people running your father's organizations, they can't see all your gifts. They judge you by that one weakness. They treated me the same way, whispering that I was a bad wife because I wouldn't campaign and play political games to help your father's career. They're very small-minded people."

I stood my ground, continued staring at Mother. "What do you think?"

"What do I think about what?"

"About me," I said, after inhaling too deeply. I wasn't sure I really wanted an answer.

With lightning speed, my mother rolled her eyes before giving me a patronizing smile. "Deacon, I think your heart's always been in the right place, if that's what you mean."

"No, I mean, d-do you think my stuttering makes me less of a man, less of a potential leader? Do you think Miriam Lloyd was right about me?"

"What?" Mother looked away from me over to Uncle James, then at Miles, her forehead creased from a sudden frown. "Why would he ask me that?"

"Speak to me, Mother," I said. "I already know the answer. When I was away at that speech therapy clinic, we did some exercises examining the way we were raised to think about our stuttering. You know what I realized?"

Her tone turned more chilly than usual. "I'm sure you'll tell me whether I want to know or not."

I took a deep breath, sat down in my chair again, but held every inch of my mother's stare. "Do you remember the arguments you used to have with Frederick about whether I needed professional speech therapy?"

"Oh, Deacon," she said, sighing and flexing her hands, "if I had to guess, I think we only sent you to a few sessions, then stopped when we saw it wasn't helping. Money was tight then."

I let my gaze intensify. "You may as well know, I overheard at least one of your arguments about me."

My heart's pounding growing louder, I took Mother back to that night. After an eighth-grade basketball game, my classmate Mike Spicer and his mom dropped me at home. After letting myself into the kitchen via the back door, I had rushed to the refrigerator, my stomach screaming for leftover fried chicken, when I heard my father's voice boom from the living room.

"Dammit, Leah, I'm not going into this again! We don't have the money."

I had eased the refrigerator door shut and pressed up against it, keeping still as I heard Mother's response. "Frederick, look, I know you can only give a few hours a week to raising your *own children*, but you're not the one who has to face his teachers and the other parents. They think Deacon's an imbecile, the way he talks. It scares me!"

I heard my father sigh, then, "There's no cure for it, Leah. I know what I'm talking about. Look at my daddy. God will help Deacon manage with this burden. He might heal him miraculously, for all we know."

"Blind faith won't save him, Frederick!" Mother had shouted in reply. "In fact, I think letting him see a school speech therapist isn't enough. You need to find the best in the field, get one of your fat-cat donors to cover it. Do you want your son living life as a second-class citizen? Step up and help him fix this. You're Frederick 'Second Coming' Davis, aren't you?"

I ended the story there because that was the last I had heard before bolting out the back door and leaving it open behind me. I had run the streets for several hours, returning home with the story that Mike's mother had never shown up to give me a ride and I'd had to walk. Mrs. Spicer got cursed out by Mother for no good reason, but I preferred that to confronting my mother's view of me as a verbal cripple.

"Sometimes," I told her now, as she stared at her hands in her lap, "I think if I'd let myself process your words that night, I would have gone completely off the deep end. Instead of letting myself feel the pain, I tried to deny it. There were times I tried to pretend I didn't even stutter."

"You always had some really good stretches," Mother replied, firing up another cigarette before flashing me a sympathetic look.

"Mother, the good stretches just masked the hell going on inside," I said. "A hell driven by my knowledge that every stutter I made disappointed you, or worse, made you ashamed of me."

"Oh no," Mother said, standing. "You are *not* going to turn this into some mother-bashing session, blaming me for your problems." She glanced at my uncle again. "I came down off the cross when I quit Communities in Action's board and married Roberto, didn't I, James?"

"Sit down, Mother." Miles's command blasted from out of nowhere. "You owe Deacon the respect of hearing him out—then you get to hear me."

A rare look of shock on her face, Mother stared quizzically at her oldest son. "Miles, I already told you what you need—"

"I heard your advice, and I'm not taking it," he said, standing and crossing my rug so that he was standing over her.

"Miles." Uncle James's voice carried a promise of intervention.

"I'm cool," Miles said, his hands flying over his head. "Disabuse me of this notion, Mother. Would it not be crazy for me to enter rehab while my heart's not in it? That's madness. If I go now, I'll never take it seriously because it won't be my idea."

Mother was unbowed. "Oh, you're going, Miles."

"Watch it, dear Momma, I'm fragile," Miles replied, his eyes popping all the way open. "I mean, I've got issues. I wonder whose fault that is?"

"So I was an imperfect mother. Is that what you want me to admit?" Mother stood and took a step toward Miles, a small tear forming in one eye. "But your father wasn't perfect either."

"Yes, I know, blame the dead man," Miles said.

A ghost may as well have slapped Miles, it happened so fast. I heard a loud crack and looked up to see him rubbing his cheek. Mother was in his face, right hand trembling at her side. "You will show me some respect," she said, her voice cracking.

Uncle James and I surrounded them as they lunged at each other. I grabbed Miles from behind and muscled him toward the fireplace as Uncle James pulled Mother back down to the couch.

Mother and Uncle James calmed down quickly, but Miles continued to wrestle me, forcing me to tighten my grip on him as we lumbered around like elephants locked in mortal combat. "Chill, man, damn," I said through clenched teeth.

"She's the problem!" Miles was inconsolable, even though he'd let me pin him against the wall and had stopped struggling. He pointed over my shoulder. "She left us alone to deal with all this shit, Uncle James! Daddy died and she ran away from the mess left behind!"

"Oh, God, James!" I glanced over my shoulder at the sound of Mother's bloodcurdling scream. She was bent over, still seated, her shoulders rattling with sobs. "Tell them, please!" She looked up suddenly, her hands pawing away at her carefully coiffed hair. "They should know, they have to know, but they won't believe me." She turned to my uncle again. "Tell them!"

37

Deacon

Once I put Mother to bed, I stumbled back into my great room and plopped onto the couch. I had already dropped Miles and Uncle James at Errick's house for the night, so for the first time in twenty-four hours, I had some privacy. The weight of the night's arguments hit me, and my eyes filled with salty tears. Clumsily wiping at the signs of my sorrow, I blamed both Miles and myself. By standing our ground with Mother, we had provoked her revelation.

We never knew it, but my mother's grief at losing my father was complicated by their agreement to divorce, a week before Frederick died. Truth told, it wasn't hard to imagine how they'd hidden this from us. At the time, I was consumed with my second year with the Steelers, Miles was serving his one and only term in Congress, Benet was cramming for her MCATs, and Darlene was a typically rebellious, self-absorbed high school senior.

The divorce wasn't even the worst of it. According to Mother, the whole thing started one night as she separated dirty clothes and a folded sheet of paper slipped from my father's favorite pair of slacks. Once she'd opened it up—she still wasn't sure why she had—she recognized it as the results of a paternity test. As a former nurse who volunteered at clinics across Chicago during our childhood, her instincts were pretty trustworthy. Based on her read, it looked like Frederick had brought another life into the world, without her help.

That's where it got really bad. When confronted, Frederick refused to answer her. Mother didn't specify, but I'm sure he reminded her that she had tolerated his occasional "female friend" before. Apparently he refused to explain anything, saying only that the truth wouldn't solve anything between them.

Before that night, Mother had followed the "out of sight, out of mind" rule with my father's affairs. As long as he didn't leave behind any evidence, she wasn't going to stress out. Robbed of that one consolation, she had prepared to shut the Davis family down. Frederick had insisted that she was biblically bound to honor their marriage and forgive his weaknesses, but when he saw the only way to stop her was to tell the whole truth and nothing but, he backed down.

"It was probably Miriam Lloyd's daughter, Charlene," Mother had sighed as Miles and I sat there in shock. Charlene, the Dream Party's press secretary, was a forceful, witty presence around the office, admittedly wise beyond her twenty-five years. The grapevine had long implied that her birth came on the heels of Miriam's affair with my father. At Mother's prompting, we Davis kids had always treated these rumors like salesmen ringing the front doorbell; ignore them, and they will go away.

"I know you boys have heard the rumors," Mother had continued, "and like you I tried to ignore them. But once I saw that Frederick had fathered *somebody*, I figured it had to be Charlene." Her logic made sense. Charlene had been seriously ill around that time; it was possible that Miriam had talked my father into confirming his identity, in order to provide insight into his secret daughter's health problems.

As I wiped the last few seeping tears from my eyes, I did something I hadn't done in a long while. I prayed for my mother. Tonight's revelation, which Uncle James had firmly but sorrowfully backed up, didn't totally absolve Mother's years of distance and neglect, but they definitely put her in a new light. I almost felt guilty for the way I'd attacked her reaction to my stuttering, though the emotional release had been long overdue.

With nothing but the settling of my house surrounding me, I closed my eyes and prayed that Mother could be freed from the bitterness and pain that drove her to marry Roberto and separate herself from her family. I prayed for Miles's overcoming his drug addiction, for Errick's ability to honor his marriage, for Benet and Darlene, for Uncle James, for my children, and finally for Maria.

Praying for Maria brought me back face-to-face with my most recent struggles. I asked for the courage to continue with speech therapy, and for freedom from my long-nursed habit of running from my speech problems.

Once I finished praying, my eyes stayed closed, and I felt my neck tip back against the couch. All the talk about Frederick must have kicked in, because my mind replayed a scene from the year before he died. Freshly drafted by the Steelers, I had come home to work on my speech before the Democratic National Convention. Although my father himself was not welcome, given that he had left the Dems to found the Dream Party, the Democrats still wanted to be associated with the family name.

We were out on the backyard basketball court, playing a little one-on-one and arguing over the speech. I dribbled circles around the old man, who was still fit and trim but was nearly two inches shorter than me.

"I have some more thoughts about your speech," Frederick said, grinning as he tried to stay between me and the basket. "You need to be more confrontational, challenge the party to stand up for the people."

Bouncing the ball around my back, I smiled. "Confrontation, huh. How's this?" I faked right, then pivoted left and drove for the basket, where I banked a layup through the fraying net.

"Don't start smelling yourself," Frederick said, sweat shimmering on his brow as he grabbed a rebound. "A brother your age would've shut you down before you completed that weak little fake. Now listen to me."

"Come on, man." Chuckling, I leaned over and took a few deep breaths of air, my hands resting on my knees. "There'll be time to work the speech tonight."

"No can do," Frederick said, dribbling the ball at an increased tempo and motioning toward me with the fingers of his left hand. "Have to do an interview tonight. Larry King's doing some special program on minority issues and the election. I got invited to take part by phone. Jesse must have been busy."

"Hmm," I said, raising my hands and going into defense mode as he drove toward me. "All right, then."

He dribbled up to me, then planted his feet when he realized he wasn't getting around me. He tried to shake me, turning and twisting his upper body, then went for it. He flew into the air, turned over his shoulder, and let the ball fly free. To my surprise, it not only got by me, it swooshed through the net.

"Yes, praise God!" My father stood with his arms raised, exultant, seemingly forgetting he'd cut my lead to only thirteen points. "I'm happy now. Let's go inside and get on that speech. Larry comes on in a couple of hours."

I squeezed his shoulder as we stepped off the court. "Are you sure you want me to do this?" I looked over at him, trying to sound strong and hoping my eyes didn't betray the anxiety churning within. "I mean, if you'd rather t-talk Miles into giving the speech, I'll understand." Even then, Miles's "what the hell" attitude toward life was becoming increasingly clear, so I knew I needed to offer another savior. "Don't forget Errick, either. He's made for this type of stuff."

"Watch this," Frederick said as we descended the hill leading to the back porch. "I'm about to earn my title as your father, despite the fact you just spanked me mercilessly." He slowed to a halt and stood in front of me. "If I wanted Miles or Errick to speak, I would have chosen them, Deacon," he said, slapping his hands onto both of my shoulders. "I chose you to give this speech, to represent a new generation of leadership, because of what I see in *you*."

"Okay," I said, feeling embarrassed but holding his stare. "If you're sure."

"Deacon, I could have told the DNC that I didn't want to select a speaker at all. Ever thought of that? So know that when I chose you for this honor, it's because you alone earned it."

When I emerged from the dream, I was still crying. Prince lay at my feet, unusually quiet but looking up at me with pleading eyes, as if offering me his shoulder.

It took moments like these to remind me what Frederick had meant to me. He'd had plenty of shortcomings as a father and husband—aside from the infidelities, his love for the spotlight had pretty much made Mother a single mom. That said, in Frederick's presence, it was impossible to feel there were limits in life. Maybe he'd never had the time or money to help me "cure" my stuttering, but he had never doubted my ability to live up to his example, warts and all.

Once I had blown my nose and washed my face, I allowed myself a quick peek into the guest room before going to bed. Mother lay there sleeping peacefully, a welcome sight after the stresses she'd suffered a few hours earlier. Leaning there against her doorway, I realized that she had spent the last seven years trying to forget all she'd lost in Frederick, both before and after his death. I understood her reasons, but more than ever I knew I didn't dare make the same mistake. I had to make peace with Frederick's life and death, and the road to that peace ran through Washington, D.C.

38

Maria

The morning after my confrontation with Ramsey, I was still jumpy but trying not to stress over it. I knew I couldn't go into work; I had called in sick the day before, and no one had asked any questions when I called in again that morning. I needed at least a couple of days to process my boss's behavior before I could respond to it. Suddenly, Alicia's warnings about him, which she'd reminded me of when I spent the previous night at her and Trent's, made a lot more sense.

As I drove toward Thomas's office in Stone Mountain, though, my thoughts kept returning to how and when to resign from Ramsey's practice. I knew I had to make a tough decision, but the closer I got to Thomas's, the more I put it out of my mind. As crazy as things were with Ramsey and Deacon, in the moment I needed to focus on a simpler goal. I just needed a few minutes to apologize to Thomas for the nasty nature of my lawsuit. Even though I had clearly made a big boo-boo by hiring Peter Hedges, I was confident Thomas would understand once I explained how I'd fired the fat shyster.

When I walked into the lobby of his office, an attractive heavyset receptionist with a close-cropped blond haircut smiled my way. "May I help you?"

"Yes," I said, smiling as pleasantly as I could. "I'm here to see Thomas Oliver, please."

"Hold on a minute, I'll ring his extension." Waiting for my brother's line to pick up, the receptionist, whose name tag read SUE, let her eyes smile at me through her glasses. "No answer," she said. "He may have left for an early lunch; he's been doing that lately. Did you have an appointment with him?"

"Uh no, I'm his sister." My right foot tapped nervously against the lobby's wooden floor. "I really need to see him," I said, fighting the urge to chew on a fingernail. "Is it okay if I sit out here and wait for him to get back?"

"Sure," Sue replied, smiling wide. "I'll ring him every few minutes, how's that?"

At quarter after eleven, I still sat there with my figurative thumb stuck up my figurative butt, getting absolutely nowhere. I set down the incredibly boring industry magazine I was skimming and glanced over at Sue. "Still nothing?" I asked, trying to sound patient.

"I can ring him again," Sue replied, her smile thinner now. "Give me a minute—" She interrupted herself as a short, trim brunette stepped out into the lobby from the inner offices. "Mary, help me out for a minute."

"Hmm?" Mary, hurtling by at the speed of light, stopped in her tracks before flitting over to Sue's desk.

"Do you know when Thomas Oliver is expected back from lunch, or wherever he is?"

A mischievous smile broke out on Mary's face and she leaned in toward Sue. She thought her gossip was beneath my radar, but I heard every trifling word. "I don't know when he'll be back," she said through pursed lips. "You remember what Chrissy said about seeing him at the Motel Six on Bay Road? I mean, she saw him going in there *twice* last week. You know Chrissy lives right around the corner."

Looking at me over Mary's bony little shoulder, Sue whispered back to her friend. "Later, okay?" She raised her voice. "So, you think Mr. Oliver won't be back until one o'clock, maybe?"

Mary wasn't good at catching hints. She leaned back over her girl's desk, grinning wider. "Well," she said, a giggle bubbling up from her throat, "how long can an afternoon delight take?"

"Motel Six on Bay Road," I said, my words coming briskly as I stood and stared coldly at Sue and Mary. "Thank you. I'll just find my brother on my own."

"Oh my, ma'am," Sue said as I walked to the set of glass double doors. "Don't mind our little gossip. We don't know what we're talking about—"

"Thank you," I said, turning toward Sue as I swung a door open, "you've done plenty for now."

I had never stayed at the Motel 6 on Bay Road, but I had passed it plenty of times. In five minutes I was in the motel's parking lot. Sitting a hundred feet from the little registration office, I gripped my Grand Am's gearshift and prayed for a touch of wisdom.

The secretaries' silly gossip had reignited the feeling of betrayal I'd experienced when Peter first revealed Thomas's past affair. Even though it was really between him and Lucille, I had been disappointed in my brother. I certainly didn't want to believe he was still carrying on with someone else, now that he was raising Jamil. If Thomas was that weak, maybe I really did need to get my son back.

That still didn't make it my business whether Thomas was locked away in one of these rooms, screwing some slut and breaking Lucille's heart again. But what about the impact on Jamil, if Lucille ever caught Thomas cheating again and left him? Sitting there, tension hammering my entire body, I decided I had no choice. I had to go in.

I took the direct approach with the front desk clerk. I don't think he should have told me what room number Thomas had paid for, but given that his eyes never left my chest, he probably never got around to considering company policy.

Arriving at room 234, I gingerly walked up to the door, cringing in fear that the sounds of skinnin' and grinnin' would bombard me through the walls. Instead, I heard Thomas's voice, its low tone wafting through the door. He sounded slightly agitated, and his voice was growing closer, as if he were preparing to walk out of the room.

I stood back, crossed my arms, and waited on him. Better to take him on woman to man instead of involving whatever silly skeezer was with him.

After a few more seconds, the door flew open and Thomas stepped outside. He was fully dressed and looked as clean and well-pressed as he probably had when he left the house that morning.

I tapped his shoulder as the door closed behind him. He did a double take, then jumped a foot off the ground. "M-Maria!"

Looking him up and down, I crossed my arms over my chest.

"Your entire office thinks you're here fooling around. Are they right, Thomas?"

Wiping a trail of sweat beads from his forehead, Thomas jerked away from me. "No, of course not," he said, glancing back at the motel room's closed door. "What are you doing here?"

"I went to see you at work. Sue says you're spending your lunch breaks here lately."

"That gossiping piece of—" Thomas stopped himself and pressed his lips tight before continuing. "Maria, there's nothing for us to discuss. You made that clear with that lawyer of yours. Go home!"

"Thomas," I said, stepping up and placing my head as close to his as I could, "I'm not leaving until you tell me whether you're still cheating on Lucille! If I'm wrong, then I'll butt out—"

That's when the door to room 234 flew open, and I nearly peed myself. The face I saw made me wish a gum-popping, twenty-something named Shaniqua, or even a young, dumb blonde named Bambi had emerged.

Feeling like my spine had turned as limp as cooked spaghetti, I fought a gasp as I stared into my ex-boyfriend Guy's weathered face. He wasn't smiling, but his green eyes danced with excitement.

For what felt like minutes, none of us spoke—not Guy, me, or Thomas. Guy wasn't the same skinny kid I remembered; he'd grown into a trim twenty-eight-year-old man. As I took him in—wrinkled khaki slacks, smudged white T-shirt, bald head, olive skin with a tinge of beige to it, meticulously groomed goatee—the passage of time slammed into me.

"Hey, hey," Guy said, breaking the veil of silence and moving toward me with his arms open. "What's up, girl?"

Shock held me in place, just long enough for Guy to get his arms around me before stepping back respectfully. The stench of Fritos was all over his T-shirt.

"G-Guy?" Was this what Deacon and my other clients felt like during speech blocks? I grasped for words desperately. "What—what are you doing here?"

"That's supposed to be between me and Thomas," Guy replied,

reaching out to pat my shoulder before leaning back against the doorway. "Gotta ask him. You look good, girl."

I turned toward my brother, grabbed an arm, and yanked him farther away from Guy. "What's he talking about?"

"Maria," Thomas said, hot air streaming from his nostrils, "just turn around and go home. Your lawyer will be able to explain everything in a few days."

"My lawyer?" My vision blurring, I searched my brother's face frantically. "I don't have a lawyer anymore, Thomas. That's what I've been trying to tell you for the last two weeks, with all those messages. What the hell are you doing?"

"You know," Guy said, stepping toward us, "maybe it's better she caught us, Thomas."

Thomas turned back toward Guy. "Shut up."

Guy did a double take, shocked at being punked by Thomas of all people. "Cool out, Thomas. Was a time I'd have to fuck you up for that tone. All I'm saying is," he said, winking at me now, "you ain't got to ambush your sister like this."

"Ambush?" I stepped around Thomas and stood toe to toe with Guy. As I remembered, he was no bigger than me. He'd learned some manners, though; as I closed in, he meekly let me back him up against the motel room's door. "You have some nerve, Guy." Tears squeezed from the corners of my eyes. "You're the reason Jamil wound up with Thomas in the first place. It took me a year to lose the bad habits you taught me, but I've cleaned up my act." I got all the way into his face. "You have no say in this, none!" I opened a hand and slapped him square on the jaw. "Go back to whatever hole you crawled out of."

Shielding himself with a hand over his cheek, Guy leaned against the door. "Maria, check yourself—"

"You heard me!"

His eyes closed, Guy turned and pushed his door all the way open, then pivoted suddenly. His eyes bulged grotesquely, looking ready to ooze from their sockets. "You can be such a bitch," he said, his voice lowering to a growl. "You hear her, Thomas? Shit like that, that's why I'm testifying for *you*."

Guy was a few cards shy of a full deck when we were kids, but I'd been away from him long enough that his sudden transformation still frightened me. I didn't break his stare, didn't soften the flames shooting from my eyes, but I did take a step back.

"You couldn't even answer one letter, could ya?" Guy wasn't advancing back toward me, but his eyes said he wanted to. "I've turned my life around the past three years, Maria. For the record, I'm not just a barber no more. I'm about to be an entrepreneur. My boss is opening up a new shop in Macon, and I'm gonna be manager and part owner."

For a few seconds, I almost felt guilty that I'd never responded to Guy's letters, but the memory of his alliance with Thomas quickly erased those emotions. "I hear you, Guy, okay? Happy now?"

The same green eyes that seduced me into giving up my virginity grew as dark as the eye of a tornado. Guy pointed a finger in my direction, stabbing the air. "You fucking bitch—"

"That's enough, Guy." Thomas lurched forward and shoved Guy far into the room. He reached for the door and slammed it shut, leaving himself outside to deal with me.

His hand gripping the door, keeping it closed as Guy tugged hard from the other side, Thomas planted his feet and spoke to me through clenched teeth. "You started all of this, little sister. I suggest you apologize to that lawyer instead of me. You'll be needing him."

39

Deacon

Writing furiously, I jotted down the names and phone numbers falling from Miles's mouth. Struggling to hold my day planner steady, I cradled my cell phone against my right shoulder and continued writing. "Say that last one again, man."

"Harris. Carlene Harris. She's in the D.C. prosecutor's office."

I took down Carlene's number and glanced at the dwindling line of people waiting to board my flight. "All right. You sure there's no one else?"

"I told you, that's everybody I've spoken to the past two years." Miles paused, and his tone turned mournful. "I never could connect the dots, little brother. I hope you can."

"I won't stop until I've found either Tisha Norris or Pharrell Haynes," I said. "Bet on that."

"My money's on you, man."

"Mine's on you, too," I replied. "You be cool to Mother and let her help you get yourself straight, all right?" With some calming words from me and from Uncle James, Miles and Mother's fiery battles had started to cool. Mother had agreed to stay in Atlanta with Miles until he had his preliminary hearing next week. They were staying at my place, where they'd be until Miles's charges would likely be sent to a grand jury, which would give him a couple of months before being indicted. Mother had promised to call in some favors as long as he agreed to return to Florida with her and enroll in a rehab program, but she'd made clear this was strike two, and if there was a third, he'd be spending his middle-aged years behind bars.

"All right, little brother," Miles said. "Just remember one thing for me. If you have to choose between learning the truth and getting yourself jacked up, err on the side of getting back home in one piece. Remember, you got a hearing of your own next week."

Even though my attorney, Allen, was confident that my clean record and Miles's testimony would get my charges dropped for good, I knew I had to be back in town for the hearing or my problems would quickly get more intense. "I hear you, Miles," I said, before pausing as Maria's phone number popped up on my caller ID. "Miles," I said, "I'll talk to you soon, okay?"

I clicked over to pick up Maria's call. "Yo."

"Yo to you," she said, her tone saucy with irritation. "That's the best you can do, after leaving that ominous message?"

"I tried to reach you several times," I replied. "Where've you been?"

"Oh, Deacon, my life makes about as much sense as yours. You remember I was going to see Thomas at his job?"

As I stood and grabbed my shoulder bag, I tripped off Maria's news about the new alliance between Thomas and this Guy character, Jamil's father. "How does this work?" I asked once I was in line to board the flight. "A drug-addicted deadbeat dad gets to judge your character?"

"It's complicated," Maria said. "Trust me, I got the full lecture from my attorney, Peter, yesterday. I had to rehire him, so you can imagine he's even more obnoxious than usual now."

"Damn," I said, lowering my voice while handing my boarding pass to the Delta attendant. "Sounds like homeboy's a necessary evil at this point, though."

"Yeah, I guess so." Maria paused, leaving the line silent as I took my first few steps down the carpeted ramp leading to the plane's mouth.

I stepped inside and nodded at the two flight attendants before heading toward the coach seats. "Why so quiet? They're gonna make me hang up in a minute, you know."

"I know," she replied, sighing. "I'm just torn, that's all."

"Torn?" I asked, pausing in front of my seat.

"Yes. I know you need to make this trip."

"But?"

"Deacon, it's just . . ." Maria sighed again, and her voice weakened.

"Please don't create more problems for yourself. I want you back in one piece."

I guess that's what did it. I was settling into my seat, surrounded on all sides by fellow passengers, but the words popped out. "Maria, just so you know, I haven't slept with Mercedes since I've met you. I haven't slept with anyone else. And if these folk around me weren't looking at me funny, I'd probably go into more detail."

The laughter in her voice put plenty of wind in my sails, enough to last my entire trip. "Just get back here, Mr. Davis. I'll be waiting."

40

Maria

Monday morning, I finally returned to the office. My very first meeting was with Ramsey, who rushed over as soon as I turned on my office light.

I hadn't talked with my boss since Thursday, when he'd acted like he had date rape on his mind, but after some prayer and reflection, I was ready for him. When he came to the door, knocking tepidly, I crossed my arms and took a seat at my desk. "Good morning, Ramsey. Please come in."

"I was worried about you." Still resting in the doorway, Ramsey had his head down and his hands deep in his pockets. "Is it okay if I shut the door behind me?" His eyes flitted up long enough to beg, then sought out the carpet again.

"That's fine." With Ramsey's back to me, I calmly removed my microcassette recorder from my slacks. Punching the record button, I let it rest in my lap, well out of his sight.

"We can talk about what happened, Maria," Ramsey said, his back now plastered against the closed door. "I mean, I think we both bear the responsibility."

"The responsibility for what?" I needed him on the record, just in case. "The fact that you behaved like a bitch in heat, pawing at me and insisting I view you as more than a friend?" Trying to maintain my cool, I shuffled some papers on my desk. "You're my boss, Ramsey. The way you talked the other day, I didn't know if I had a job to come back to."

"No, no," Ramsey said, waving his arms frantically. "I'd never hold that over your head. I just lost myself in the moment." He sighed, shook his head. "Have to admit, I haven't been single in a long time. I'm not used to getting rejected, but I'd never bring that into the office."

"Well, I would hope not," I replied. "Paint a picture in your mind, Ramsey. Take any man you know, replace him for yourself the other day, and insert Rachel or Justine in my place." I paused, letting the image sink in for him. "I don't expect this to ever come up again."

"Thank you, Maria," Ramsey said finally, after sighing and shaking his head for several seconds. After mumbling something about checking in with me later about office business, he grabbed the door handle and was gone.

This was what made sense, I reminded myself as I prepared for my first client of the day. Between Ramsey's apparent shame and my bit of recorded evidence, I should be safe from any harassment and keep on track with my certification and experience. As long as he respected me for the next year, I could tolerate Ramsey long enough to get what I needed from his reputation before setting up my own practice. It might not fly with your hard-core feminist, but if I'd learned one thing in life, it was that no one and no situation was perfect. I had to get mine.

The morning and early afternoon flew by without incident. At three o'clock, I had a new teenage client, Sam, whose main problem was in saying sounds made with the hard palate—*s, z, ch, j, r,* and *y.* He closed his eyes a lot and even cried a couple of times during our session. It was the type of session that reminded me why I started doing this in the first place.

Sam and I were almost finished when Ellen, the office secretary, rapped at my door. Annoyed, I yanked the door open. "We're almost finished. Can't this wait?"

"Um, no," she said, her blue eyes wide and her forehead wrinkled with anxiety. "Your sister-in-law's on the phone, Maria. Says it's an emergency." She eased my door all the way open and nodded toward Sam. "Why don't I bring the young man back out to the lobby, to wait on his parents?"

I was instantly short of breath, struggling to keep my mind from going to the worst places imaginable. I explained to Sam that I'd see him next week, then ran to my desk phone as Ellen and Sam shut the door behind them.

"Lucille?"

"Maria." Her voice sounding dry as the heart of the Sahara, Lucille stated my name like it was a dreaded disease. "Where is Jamil?"

"What?"

Lucille's voice jumped to a high pitch, the words shrieking out of her mouth. "Maria, do you have him?"

"No, God, no," I replied, trying to steady myself against my desk. "What's wrong?"

"I don't know yet," she said, her voice sounding as shaky as mine felt. "He wasn't at his usual spot when I went to pick him up today, and the teacher on duty thought he'd already been picked up. Thomas hasn't left work all day and doesn't know where he is. Oh, God."

"Let's not panic yet," I said, just barely getting the words out. There had to be a mistake. "Lucille, are you sure you didn't arrange for someone else to get him today, maybe a parent of one of his classmates, someone he's spending the afternoon with?"

"No!" Lucille spoke in a hurried whisper now. "Thomas and I will call you later." She hung up before I could offer any help, assurance, or prayers.

My heart pounding, my brain grasping for some easy way to find Jamil, I struggled to recall the names of Guy's old friends, people I might somehow track down. My desperate thoughts were interrupted by the next ring of my phone.

"Hello?"

"Maria, it's Guy."

A primal roar erupted from me. *"Where is he?"*

"Watch your tone with me, girl. You'll know where he is when I want you to know. For now, just know the boy's safe."

Warm, bubbly tears blurred my vision. "Why, Guy? Why are you making everything worse, again?"

"I'm making things worse, huh?" Guy tittered suddenly, as if my question were laugh-out-loud funny. "Not hardly. I'm proving my love for this boy, even my love for you. I know I'll never get to raise him, and I know you'll never take me back, but I'm the only one who

can stop this legal madness. I mean, Thomas is trying to paint you as an unfit mother, you're trying to crucify him for that little affair he had, and all the while Jamil's living a lie. It's gotta stop, Maria."

"Guy," I said, my chest muscles coiling anxiously, "you're just digging a deeper hole for yourself. Just listen to me. Take him back to his school. I'll tell Lucille to go get him—"

"No one sees him until I say so! You'll hear from me when I'm ready."

When I realized the line had gone dead, I slammed the phone down so hard, I was sure I'd broken it. Grabbing my jacket and slamming my office door shut behind me, I ran through the office, sweeping past the stares of surrounding therapists and clients. I had to get outside, somewhere away from all the prying eyes, before I wilted in front of them all. As much as I wanted to blame Thomas for this hell, he wasn't the one who'd set it in motion. I had only myself to thank.

41

Deacon

Twenty-four hours into my D.C. trip, I already knew I'd landed in the right place.

Miles's friend in the prosecutor's office, Carlene Harris, had put me in touch with a police detective who pulled the records from the investigation into the supper-club fire. It turned out that although none of them were ever formal suspects, every surviving employee had been subjected to a detailed interview.

Tisha Norris and Pharrell Haynes had come off like innocents. They were no different from the other employees working in the kitchen that night; they had all survived while several employees in the dining room—waiters, waitresses, and busboys—had been trampled by panicked crowds or been cut down by smoke inhalation. The fire had started near the ovens where Tisha and Pharrell worked, so they had joined most of their fellow staff in rushing out the kitchen's two back doors.

Tisha, who'd been a new single mother, had admitted to bolting for the exit, but police reports showed Pharrell had helped drag two elderly women from the dining room. Each was interviewed and sent home without arousing any suspicion. Apparently Walt Jr. had been right about Pharrell's well-hidden history of setting fires for Big Walter; there was no mention of it anywhere in the police files.

From the files, I got the most important information: Pharrell's and Tisha's addresses, as of that November day in 1996. Carlene had other contacts that tried to help me find current address information on the two, but it appeared neither one lived in D.C. anymore. In order to do a wider search, I would need the help of someone with federal pull. Miles had a few suggestions, but I already knew it would take a lot of begging, charming, and dumb luck.

That's why I decided to work with what I had first. It was already after seven p.m. when I pulled out of D.C. police headquarters onto Indiana Avenue, but I drove straight to Pharrell's old neighborhood. He had lived on U Street in Northwest, a few blocks from Howard University's campus, on a street lined with narrow row houses. I parked two streets up from his old address and zigzagged toward his place, darting back and forth across the street. The average exchange, at the homes where someone answered the door, went like this:

HOMEOWNER/TENANT: Can I help you?
ME: Yeah, what's up. I'm an old friend of Pharrell Haynes, who used to live at 524. I understand he moved. Any idea where he's living these days?
HOMEOWNER/TENANT: (No response, as they slammed their door in my face. Or) Never heard of him.

It went on that way for the next ninety minutes, as I worked my way down three complete blocks. I finally gave up when I crossed into blocks that were nothing but white yuppies who raised their hands and swore they'd been in the neighborhood only a couple of years. Gentrification had done its job, sweeping the hood's long-term residents out to low-rent areas of Virginia and Maryland. It was also pissing all over my makeshift investigation.

Before continuing with my work, I ducked into the Florida Avenue Grill for dinner. After checking up on Miles and Mother, I called Maria to let her know I hadn't gotten myself killed yet. I was sitting there, slicing into my catfish, when she told me about Guy and Jamil.

I dropped my silverware and nearly knocked my plate off the counter, I was so shaken. "What is he thinking?" I couldn't believe it.

"It's all my fault," she replied. Her voice was steady but full of self-loathing. "Guy would've forgotten about all of us, if I hadn't pushed my luck trying to get closer to Jamil. I scared Thomas—do you understand that, Deacon? And his fear drove him to seek Guy's help with the custody case. I've done nothing but harm that little boy, all over again!"

I could hear the tears in her voice. "Maria, the only thing you know for sure is that right now Jamil's with his biological father. Leave it at that, and focus on getting your son home safely."

She was silent.

"D-Do you want me to come back to Atlanta now? Because I will." I meant every word. I was going to get to the bottom of my father's death, but it had waited seven years already. It could wait a week, or however long it took to help Maria find Jamil. She didn't need to be alone.

"No, you keep up your work there," Maria replied, sniffling, her voice regaining strength. "I don't even know if they're in Georgia at this point, anyway. Based on what Guy said this afternoon, he'll probably wait until they're out of reach to call again."

"Well, look—call me later tonight," I said once I'd made sure that Alicia could keep her company for the night. "Whether you hear anything more or not. And, Maria?"

She hesitated, possibly sensing what was coming, maybe just being too out of sorts to respond right away. "What, Deacon?"

"I love you." I hung up before she could feel pressured to answer, and as I finished my meal, said a new round of prayers.

Around ten, when I rolled past Tisha Norris's old housing project, things looked more encouraging than they had over on U Street. Tisha's old stomping grounds, a weathered series of low-rise tenements off Rhode Island Avenue, were clearly ruled by the same folk who had reigned supreme seven years ago.

As I approached the middle tenement, the one that Tisha had lived in, Maria's earlier warning coursed through my thoughts. *Don't create more problems for yourself.* I had considered calling it a night, retiring to a hotel and coming back first thing in the morning with the cover of daylight, but my adrenaline was pumping. As long as I kept my cool and took the Lord with me, I figured I was as safe now as I'd be later.

As I walked up the sidewalk, the increasingly chill night nipping at me, a group of middle-aged brothers stood to my left trading loud jokes and insults. I could feel them sizing me up. I imagined I was noteworthy more for my size than for my clothing; my cotton Adidas tracksuit, which I was wearing over my Steelers jersey, looked a lot like the sweats some of these brothers were sporting. I had combed my 'fro out to its full height, and I stepped with a relaxed but authoritative rhythm. I glanced toward the brothers before they had stopped staring at me. "What's up, y'all."

"What up, partner." Some variation of that cascaded from the small crowd as I slowed my pace.

I broke stride and eased into my question, throwing in some voluntary stuttering. "You bruh-brothers know a lady named Tisha Norris?"

They went silent for a minute, several of the brothers looking away while puffing on their cigarettes, a couple more taking the opportunity to sneak another swig from their beer bottles. Finally, someone piped up from the midst of the crew. "What you know about Tisha Norris, fool?"

As I balled and un-balled my fists, my arms and legs prickled, itching to lash out in self-defense. The crowd parted and a bald-headed pipsqueak of a guy rushed forward, stopping just outside of my reach. "Make yourself known, dog. What you want with Tisha?"

"I'm not looking for trouble," I said, surprised by the calm washing over me. I'd already stuttered in front of them; there was nothing to hide now. I didn't even mind the little pug's attitude; at least he clearly knew my prey. That was all that mattered. "I knew Tisha back in high school. We have a friend in common, maybe you know her. Mercedes Chance?" It didn't feel right throwing Big Walter's last name behind Mercedes's, but I knew I'd get a reaction with it.

"Mercedes?" The little guy's eyebrows jumped and he nodded at his crew, as if to say everything was good. "Walk with me, man," he said, taking me by the shoulder and stepping toward the tenement.

I played along, staying at his side as we walked toward the building. "So, what's up?"

"What's Mercedes want from Tisha?" He stopped as we reached the building's front door.

I put out a hand. "What's your name, brother?"

"Rip," he said, offering a low fist, which I popped with one of my own. "And you be?"

"Jay, Jay Richards," I replied, figuring a guy traveling in Rip's circles didn't watch much ESPN or CNN. "Mercedes and I are business associates. You know she keeps her distance from the old neighborhood, so I'm here on her behalf."

Rip smiled, showing off a mouth full of bleeding gums. "You tryin' to get a message to Tisha, then?"

"Yeah. Would I give it to you?"

"Naw, I don't know enough about that girl. But I can tell you who does. Go to the third floor," he said, hooking a finger toward the front door. "Second door on the right when you come off the stairwell. If she likes you, she'll get a message to Tisha for you."

When I came to the door Rip had directed me to, I braved a quick breath—the air was rank with the smell of urine, vomit, and smoke—and knocked. It took another three knocks before a tall, long-legged sister with a blond natural answered the door. A screaming, wrinkled baby wriggled underneath her right arm. "Yeah?"

"Rip suggested I come see you," I said, shouting over the baby's yells and the pop and sizzles of grease coming from the fried chicken on her stove.

"Who are you?"

"Do you know Tisha Norris?"

The blaze in her eyes went out and she gripped the baby tighter. "What you know about Tisha?"

"I'm not with the cops, if that's what you're thinking," I said. "I just need to get a message to her."

"I ain't talked to Tisha in weeks," she said, lowering her eyes. "I cain't help you."

I fought the spasm of excitement her admission sparked. *A few weeks?* "Look, I'm friends with Mercedes Chance. The message is from her."

"Oh, no," the woman said, blocking the doorway as much with the shirtless, drooling infant as with her body. "I convinced Tisha to cut ties with that heifer a long time ago. She don't want nothing to do with Mercedes."

"How would you know?" I said.

"Look, who are you? Tell me now or I'm shutting this door."

I was too close to keep lying. "My name's Deacon Davis," I said, noticing the way the woman's shoulders drew up and her eyes flashed. "I'm trying to understand what happened the night my father, Frederick Davis, died. Now, can you tell me how you know Tisha?"

"Oh, Lord Jesus," the sister said, the words tumbling breathlessly from between her lips. She leaned against the wall, cradling the increasingly calm baby against her chest, and shut her eyes. "I always prayed I'd be strong if you showed up."

I didn't know what to do with that one. "Say what?"

"My name is LaShundra," she said, looking into my eyes with a longing, pleading stare. "I'm Tisha's sister." LaShundra looked me over, at least twice, as if trying to match me to a previous vision she'd had of me. "Brother, I think you should come inside."

42

Maria

The night of Jamil's disappearance, I slipped out of my apartment feeling like a fugitive. It was early morning, and I wanted to scoot before the police detective who'd met with me, Thomas, and Lucille called again. Though Jamil hadn't yet been missing for twenty-four hours, Thomas had called in some favors through his company's CEO, and the police already had a mini-team on the case. Even they didn't have the inside track that I did.

Guy called just after eleven, as I sat listlessly watching *BET Nightly News*. Alicia, who'd spent most of the evening at my side, making sure I didn't have any alcohol on hand and forcing me to take a long bath, had just left. My home phone, which was the only number I had ever given Guy, had been tapped with the hopes of tracing any call he might make. That wasn't the phone that stirred me to life, though. It was my cell.

Imagine my surprise at hearing Guy's voice on that line. "Hey, beautiful."

"How—how did you get this number?"

"Weren't expecting me on this line, huh? Surprise! Jamil knew all of your numbers by heart. Boy worships you. Deep down, he knows who his mommy is."

I fought the tremors in my voice, knowing I needed to sound calm. "Guy, I hope you didn't tell that child anything about—"

"The truth? You really want to keep the lies alive, don't ya? That's not right. Before this boy goes back to Thomas and Lucille, he will know who his real parents are, that we love him, and why we failed him. Don't you think he should know that, Maria?"

"Eventually, yes," I said, wishing I could pull Guy through the phone's receiver and strangle him. "But not like this. It's not right."

"I've had about enough of you implying I'm a screwup. *Watch your tone.* Ya know, Jamil's gonna come through this fine, but you keep up the smart-ass talk, and you sure as hell won't."

"Let Jamil go, Guy," I said. "You want to make up for the past, settle up with me, take me on!"

"Oh, there'll be time for that." Guy went silent for a minute, and I could picture him punching the air, wrestling with years of self-hatred and weakness. "We're in Philadelphia, okay? Why don't you get your ass here by tomorrow night? I'll call you on your cell phone around six, and we'll sit down with Jamil. There'll be no more lies clouding our boy's head."

"Why should we go all the way to–?" I stopped myself when I remembered who I was dealing with. Guy must have taken Jamil straight to the airport after abducting him, so that he could get through security before any authorities were notified. He was a bum, but he wasn't entirely stupid. "Okay," I said, "I'll meet you there. Just let me talk to Jamil first."

Guy laughed, a sound so hoarse and high-pitched, it sounded painful. "You don't call the shots here."

"You want me to come to Philadelphia, the least you can do is let me speak to Jamil." I paused, weighing my next words but knowing they made sense. As unstable as Guy was behaving, having the police involved would probably just lead to a bloody showdown. "If you let me speak to Jamil, so I know he's fine, I swear I won't tell Thomas or the authorities about this."

The line was silent for a second; then I heard the phone being handed to someone. "Auntie Maria?"

My heart melted at the sound of my baby's voice. "Hey, how's my handsome little man?"

"Who is this Mr. Guy? Why won't he let me see Daddy and Mommy?"

"Mr. Guy is a friend of the family," I said, carefully handpicking my words. "He means well, Jamil, but he's a little confused. Just be nice to him, honey, and tomorrow I'll be there to–"

Suddenly Guy was back on the line. "At ease now? Tomorrow night." The line went dead again, and I ran toward my bedroom.

43

Deacon

When Maria opened the door to her room at the Holiday Inn, an old, drably renovated high-rise smack dab near downtown Philadelphia, I pulled her into my arms. We were both silent, staring into each other's eyes and speaking volumes. We hadn't had the freedom to hold each other like this in months: our relationship as therapist and client had forced us into separate corners that never felt natural. As I took her soft, precious chin in one hand, maneuvering her full lips closer to mine, I knew I was ready for a new therapist. Assuming I still needed one at all.

I shut the door behind me as we joined at the mouth, kissing softly, then with increasing force as I backed her up against the nearest wall. My mouth tingling with pleasure, my nostrils expanding with the sweet scent of her body perfume, my hands wandering slowly down her lovely body, I felt ready to relive our earlier months of passion.

Then I remembered, and judging from her weakening grasp on my shoulders and the sudden pause in her kiss, so did she.

We separated enough to regain control of our senses, and I asked the most important question. "Did Guy call yet?"

"About twenty minutes ago," she replied, backing up against the little desk opposite the room's only bed. "He didn't give an exact location, of course," she said, awkwardly trying to smooth her hair back into place.

"So what's the plan?" I had taken a seat on the bed, but was keeping my distance.

"He told me to take a cab to Fairmount Park, near the Philadelphia Zoo. Said to be there at seven thirty, just outside the zoo's main entrance."

"I still don't believe this," I said, standing again and walking to the room's window.

"Do you have better news?" she asked, her words rushing from over my shoulder.

"I don't know if I'm being t-teased or what," I replied, turning back to face Maria as I rolled up the sleeves on my sweatshirt. "The woman I found last night was Tisha Norris's half sister. She's got a different last name, which explains why Miles found no evidence of her existence when he searched police records. LaShundra swears she doesn't know where Tisha is exactly, but that Tisha wrote her from Canada a couple months ago, saying she was coming back through D.C., maybe to stay for good. Guess she thought the coast was finally clear."

Maria frowned. "Did LaShundra say why her sister moved in the first place, least of all to Canada?"

"I want to believe she was being straight with me," I said. "Apparently LaShundra got saved at some Holiness church a few years ago, and came out of there a real holy roller. She said that although she helped Tisha move away after the fire at my father's club, she's always known God would require her to confess everything someday."

Still resting against the desk, Maria crossed her legs. "So what does she know?"

"What she told me she knows is that Tisha did have a hand in that fire. Or should I say arson." I began shuffling my feet, anything to redirect the energy and anxiety flooding me. "Can you believe Miles was right all this time?"

"My God, Deacon. What are you going to do?"

"I can't think beyond finding Tisha right now. She's the only one who can confirm anything."

"Why did she set the fire? Are you sure your father was the target?"

I paused in thought, still trying to believe that my conversation with LaShundra had happened. "Her sister says my father was the target, but won't say much more. She says Tisha should explain the whole story instead of me hearing it secondhand. LaShundra seems to think I'll take pity on her sister if I hear everything from the horse's mouth. As if there'd be any acceptable reason for what she did."

"Well, I guess it's just a matter of time before you find Tisha."

Maria walked back over to me and placed her hands on my shoulders. "Thank you again for interrupting all that."

I resisted the urge to pull her closer, just answered. "I wouldn't be anyplace else. We should probably get going, right?"

A few minutes before seven, we hopped into a cab and rode a few miles to the corner of Thirty-fourth and Girard, the zoo's main entrance. The zoo was closed, but some sort of street festival was going on, and the zoo's front walk was crowded with vendors selling T-shirts, hot dogs, and popcorn to groupings of families and strolling couples.

Once I had paid for the cab, we split up and stood at opposite ends of the block. Maria didn't want Guy to spot me with her, for fear he'd run off again. Trying to keep my cool, I took a seat on a large rock and tried to keep Maria in my line of sight.

Once seven thirty had come and gone, I waded through the vigorous crowd and found Maria again. Grabbing her hand, I kept my eyes straight ahead. "You sure he said seven thirty? It's almost quarter till eight now."

"Maybe he's just running late," she replied, turning away from me as if I were a complete stranger. "He'll be here—I know he will." She paused in thought. "You think maybe he saw you and recognized you somehow, maybe got scared?"

"I'm not that famous, Maria," I said, stepping back toward my end of the block.

She looked at me with soft, mournful eyes. "Give him a few more minutes?"

"All right." I turned away and went back to my rock. Before I took a seat, I turned back toward where I'd last seen Maria. I couldn't make her out in the crowd anymore.

Five minutes later, I still didn't see her, not in her original spot or anywhere else. After another ten minutes, I said to hell with it and began pacing the entire block, circling in hopes of seeing anybody who resembled Maria, Guy, or Jamil.

By the time the surrounding crowds had thinned out, I checked my watch to see it was eight thirty. Anxiety raced up my legs, gushed through my stomach, and clouded my brain. Either Maria had deserted me for some reason, or Guy had already taken off with her.

Unwilling to give up the ship, I burst out further into the park, searching frantically for Maria and nearly knocking over every person in my path. I yanked my cell phone from my jacket pocket and began dialing her number, when my phone beeped with a message prompt. When I checked my voice mail, I stopped dead in my tracks.

"Deacon, it's me," Maria said. "Please understand, I have to do this alone. I love you, too."

44

Maria

I wasn't proud of what I'd done, but as my cab bounced toward South Philadelphia, I knew I had made the right decision. I wanted more than anything to have Deacon with me in my hour of need, but it just hadn't felt right.

As my driver slammed to a sudden stop at a red light, spurring a blast of urgent honks from the cars behind us, I summoned images of Jamil and Guy, reflecting on their meaning in my life. Even if I had other children someday, Jamil would always be most precious to me, while Guy would always symbolize my youthful failures and foolishness. They were joined at the hip in my psyche: for years after being abandoned by Guy and giving Jamil over to Thomas and Lucille, I had felt unworthy of true love. Not just unworthy of love itself, but even of the right to pursue it. How many men, of all stripes and colors—choirboys, dogs, nice guys, and players—had I turned away, all because I was still obsessed by what I'd done wrong with Guy and Jamil?

I didn't believe it was a coincidence that I had been lured away from Atlanta, away from everyone else in my life, in order to finally deal with Guy, and by extension, Jamil. With Deacon being so close by in D.C., I had welcomed his offer to drive up and provide moral support, but every minute of my flight from Atlanta to Philly, I had known this battle was mine alone. Hopefully the last one I would have to face on my own, but mine alone all the same. I couldn't wish it away no matter how hard I tried.

Then there was the nightmarish thought of what would happen if Guy even guessed I had brought Deacon or anyone along for protection. As much as I loved Deacon, and as certain as I was that he had much better control over his temper, I knew he'd be pure kindling to a hothead like Guy. The wrong stare from either one of them, and things could get bloody all too quickly. I wasn't putting Jamil in any additional danger; I'd already done enough damage where he was concerned.

In a few minutes, the cab left downtown's sprawling network of one-way streets behind and we coasted into a run-down residential neighborhood. After a few more blocks, the driver pitched to a stop in front of an old shopping plaza. It was more of a shell of a plaza from what I could tell, given that the only thing in it was a Walgreens pharmacy that had already closed for the night. The rest of the stores were boarded over with white wooden planks. The only light in the entire lot came from a lamp poised at the front curb.

"You sure this is where you wanted?" The driver, an Arab-looking gentleman with no accent, a bald head, and a graying beard, glanced back at me, concern in his eyes. "Not much of a place to be hanging out by oneself, miss."

"I—uh—yes, I know." The same adrenaline that had pushed me forward from the minute I boarded my plane that morning was thinning out now. It hit me that I was walking blindly into a situation with one certainty: that Guy was straight-up crazy. "I'm supposed to meet someone in the back of the lot," I said, thrusting a fifty-dollar bill at the driver. "Is this enough for you to stay here and wait on me? I should be back out front in a few minutes."

"Miss, miss." He shook his head as if pitying this silly country girl who thought a cab would actually wait at her beck and call. Then he sighed. "Okay. The extra twenty-five, that gets you about another fifteen minutes." He turned back toward me, his eyes seeking mine in the dark car. "Hurry back."

"Thank you." I climbed out of the cab and pulled my suede jacket against me as I passed the Walgreens and turned the nearest corner. Immediately, I found myself facing the abandoned back lot, a wide-open space with no working lamps or lighting. All I could make out in the pitch black were the silhouettes of two cars, one a few spaces away, the other toward the right far corner.

My phone rang, and even though I saw it was Deacon's number, I answered it.

"Tell me where you are," he said with no introduction.

"Deacon, let me call you back in a minute. I think I've found them."

"Maria, it's not safe. Tell me where are you, dammit."

"Did you get my message?"

"Yes, I did, but—"

My phone beeped with another incoming call, another number I had memorized. "That's Guy—I have to go." I made a split-second decision. "1648 South Roland Street, okay? Don't come here for me, Deacon. If you don't hear from me in fifteen minutes, just send the police over, okay?"

"Maria," he said, "I'm—"

God help me, but I had to let him go and answer Guy. "Yes?"

"I'm the car near the back of the lot," he said, his voice a growl. "Come on over, love of my life."

"You can see me coming, then," I replied. My heart pounding louder with each step, I reminded myself of the one weapon I'd brought along and began whispering prayers for strength, calm, and Holy Spirit protection.

When I was within a hundred feet of the car, whose make and model weren't clear to me given the darkness and my nervousness, Guy walked out to me. His arms were crossed, and he had a large knife on display in his right hand. I wouldn't be reaching that car until he was good and ready for me to. "Looks like you followed instructions to the letter, Maria. Amazing what a little fear'll do to ya."

"I'm alone," I said, rubbing my arms to fight off a shiver. "Where's Jamil?"

"He's in the car. You'll see him in a minute." Guy fished in the pockets of his jeans, retrieved a crumpled sheet of paper, and held out what looked like a miniature tape recorder. "Let's go back over to the sidewalk, under that lamp, so you can read this out loud for me." He pointed the knife blade at me. "You first."

When we reached the sidewalk, I frowned at the chicken scratch on Guy's sheet of paper. "What is this?"

"This is your way of explaining to the cops that I didn't harm Jamil, that I'm his biological father, and I was trying to do the right thing by taking him away from you and Thomas's legal battle." He held out the device to me. "This will record your statement. I just turned it on—just read into it. You owe me that much, Maria."

Like it would make a difference. This wasn't a battle worth fighting. I dutifully read Guy's ridiculous statement, correcting his misspellings and grammar along the way.

When I handed the tape recorder back to him, he smiled. "Cool. Now some good news. I'll let you leave here with the boy. The pigs ain't shooting me down 'cause they catch me hauling him around. Make me a promise, though."

"Whatever you ask, Guy." That was a flimsy plank to step on, but how could I rule anything out where my son's safety was concerned?

"It's simple," he said, an actual smirk on his face. "You can't have him. You don't deserve that boy any more than I do. You walked away from him just like I walked away from you, Maria, and if nothing else comes of this, you're going to admit that you're just as guilty of bad parenting as me."

"So that's what this was really about, wasn't it?" I shook my head impatiently, even as a voice in my head begged me to back off for Jamil's sake. "What do you know about why I gave Jamil to Thomas, Guy? You were nowhere to be found at the time, remember?"

"Hey, we can argue all you want," Guy replied. "We argue, then I disappear with Jamil again. Your call."

"Not that you care, Guy, but I'm way ahead of you," I said, my voice quivering anew with bottled anger. "What I want stopped mattering a long time ago. Thomas and Lucille have earned the right to Jamil. Let him go now, and I'll never challenge them on that again."

"That's my girl," Guy said, stepping closer to me. He reached around his back, removed a leather cover, and slid the knife into it. Stuffing the sheathed knife into the waist of his jeans, he took his newly freed hands and began stroking my face. "One more deal, baby, and we're finished, okay? This one's not as simple, but we'll work it out."

I gently reached up and removed his hands from my face. "What is it?"

"It's time. Time for us to tell this boy the truth about who his parents are. I know we can never raise him as a family, especially since you froze me out these past few years, but we gotta do the right thing by him."

I couldn't help myself. I shook my head again, looking away from Guy so as to keep from slapping him silly.

The narrowing of Guy's eyes told me he'd picked up on my reaction. "I know what you're thinking—just shut up, you stupid, uneducated Guy. I'm not stopping until we tell this boy the truth, Maria. It may be painful for him, but it's the right thing to do."

I had sensed this was coming, but there was only so much I could do, even with the stakes as high as they were. "Guy," I said, "we can't do that without Thomas and Lucille being present. Does Jamil need to hear the truth eventually? Yes. Should he hear it in a strange city, in a dark, scary parking lot, after spending forty-eight hours trapped with a lunatic, not to mention when neither of his parents are here to help explain? No."

Guy's temples twitched and he flexed his hands. His lower lip dropped as he began to respond. "You just never listen," he said, his breath growing shallow.

That's when he shot a hand around his back.

I knew what Guy was going for, so I went for mine. Light bounced off the blade of my pocketknife as I yanked it from my slacks already unsheathed. As Guy's hand closed around his own knife handle, I screamed out and plunged the blade into his left cheek.

I wasn't fast enough. "Shit!" He screamed, his cheek shooting blood. Before I got a second cut in, he dropped his knife and slammed a fist into my forehead, sending me crashing to the cold sidewalk.

On my knees, waiting for my vision to come into focus, I realized I had no idea what Guy was capable of. Before he'd reached for that knife, I didn't believe he would actually harm me or Jamil. Now, all bets were off. Shivering with sudden fear, I had visions of Guy's long, sharp knife penetrating my skin and ending my lifelong search for forgiveness, peace, and love.

When I didn't feel anything, I looked up to see Guy scurrying across the parking lot toward the car, the large knife in his right fist. Jamil! Another surge of adrenaline bubbling through me, I rose and gave chase.

When I reached the car, Guy had opened a back door and pulled Jamil out. They turned quickly and stood facing me, Jamil pinned against Guy, who held the knife in his free hand.

"Let's just get to it," Guy said, squeezing Jamil's shoulder while staring at me. "Here's the deal, Jamil. Look at me." As I stood a few feet away, afraid of what he might do with the knife, Guy tipped Jamil's face up toward his. "I'm your father. You hear me? The man you call Daddy? That's your uncle. The woman you call Mommy is his wife, but your real mommy is your Auntie Maria."

Jamil, his teeth chattering, his eyes squinted, shocked us both with his response. "Stop lying," he said, his nostrils flaring in anger. "I don't even look nothing like you." He stared up at me, a nervous look returning to his eyes. "Why's he lying, Auntie Maria? When can I go home?"

"Jamil," I said, willfully ignoring his first question, "we're going home very soon. Just be still and let me talk with Mr. Guy, okay?"

"But he's lying, right?" Jamil's little eyes started to sag. "I don't want him to be my daddy!"

"Who cares what you want?" In an instant, Guy's switch had flipped. He pivoted suddenly and slammed Jamil against the door. "Shut up and get back in the car!"

"Guy," I said, taking a step closer, "stop it. You're scaring him. I told you, this is something for Thomas and Lucille to handle."

Guy pointed the knife at me again and said, "This is your last warning." Then he turned and slammed Jamil against the car again, his voice getting louder, shriller. "I made you, you little bastard, and I'll—"

With Guy's back half turned to me, I rushed forward and ran my knife blade along the side of Guy's neck, leaving a trail of blood dripping onto his shoulder. His eyes crossing, Guy shouted in pain and released Jamil. As he stumbled around, trying to gain his bearings, I pulled Jamil to my side before slamming the open car door against Guy's back. The force of the blow knocked him half into the car, his knees on the pavement.

I couldn't stop there; Guy had made it clear one of us wouldn't be walking away if he didn't get his way. For a period of time—don't ask me whether it was seconds or minutes—I had an out-of-body experience. I saw a woman who looked like me grab the car door, swing it back open, and slam it, again and again, into Guy's bent-over frame. He screamed in agony with each blow, but I wasn't satisfied until his cries turned to whimpers. After numerous blows, his legs kicked violently and he went silent.

I stood over Guy's battered body, my own breaths coming in wheezes and gasps, when I realized I'd lost track of Jamil. Before I could get too anxious, he was at my side, tugging at my sleeve, then grabbing me around the waist.

"Auntie Maria," he said, his wide eyes wet with tears though his voice was strong and somber, "is he dead?"

Patting Jamil's head, I kicked Guy's knife underneath the car before answering. "No, honey," I said finally, grabbing his hand and backing away from Guy. "Come on, we've got a cab to catch."

45

Deacon

In a week where I was closing in on my father's killers, losing Maria was not an option I could stomach. The sight that greeted me as my cab neared 1648 South Roland struck more fear into me than I'd experienced in a long time.

The street blocked off by three police cars, the cab dropped me off a block back from the crime scene. Not only did their red and blue sirens fill the air with sound and fury, but up ahead sat an ambulance with both doors open. Inside, I glimpsed one occupied stretcher and a paramedic.

I ran desperately, passing the empty police cars and stopping only when a huge officer who made me look puny stepped from out of the dark. "That's close enough, sir," he said, gesturing across the street. "You can continue on, just use that side of the block. We've got a situation here."

"I know," I replied. "A friend of mine came here earlier—Maria Oliver?"

"Hmm." The officer's eyebrows lowered and he looked me over skeptically. "More complications we don't need. Let me go get her."

My heart lifting a bit, I clamped a hand to the officer's bicep. "Sir?"

He looked back at me like I had five seconds to let him go. "Yeah?"

"Was the little boy, was he okay, too?"

"Deacon!" We both turned to see Maria step out from behind the ambulance, flanked by Jamil and two police officers. I hadn't seen such a precious sight since the day Liza was born, after Mercedes's incredibly complicated and frightening labor.

I put my sense of betrayal aside for the next hour, as Maria completed her statement for the officers and let a paramedic patch her forehead up.

It turned out that Guy was in the ambulance, after Maria had housed him pretty thoroughly. The cabdriver who'd taken her to the shopping plaza had apparently called the police and even waited with her until everyone showed up. For an East Coast cabbie in 2003, the dude was a veritable Good Samaritan.

As we waited on Maria, I sat in a police car with Jamil and took the opportunity to get acquainted. I didn't know what portions of the truth had been revealed to him during this nightmare, so I kept things surface-level and let the officer who sat with us probe him for details. Given that everything had started in Atlanta, the Philly police were mainly taking notes before handing off to Atlanta and possibly federal authorities.

Once we were back at the hotel, we ordered a roll-away bed for Jamil and a second room for me. Only when we'd put Jamil to bed did I give it to Maria straight. "You ever do that again," I said, standing over her as she lay on the bed, a hand over her eyes, "and we're through, do you understand?"

She lowered her hand from her eyes and stared up at me wearily, a smile creeping into her gaze. "Who said we'd begun anything, Mr. Davis?"

I sat down and ran a hand over the smooth surface of her hair, which she had pulled into a conservative bun. In the center of her forehead, a gauzy bandage reminded me of just what she'd survived. "I understand, okay? But we've spent enough time facing life alone, don't you think?"

She looked away before sighing, "Yes."

I reached down, pecked a kiss onto her forehead and both cheeks. "I'm going to bed now," I said, patting her hand. "See you in the morning. I wrote my room number on the notepad."

She held on to my hand. "Where are you going?"

"Uh, Ms. Oliver," I said, a smirk creeping across my face. "I've jacked up too many relationships by focusing on the physical. It was always easier to lead with sex than with t-talk. I'm through with that mistake."

"I know you are," Maria replied, chuckling softly. "You think I'm getting busy with my baby sleeping ten feet away? Keep your clothes on and get over here."

46

Deacon

It may sound trifling, but I purposefully didn't shower the morning I hopped back onto 95 South, headed to D.C. I had just dropped Maria and Jamil at the airport, but I wanted to keep them with me in spirit. By doing nothing more than washing up—hitting only the underarms and groin area with soap—I had retained the comforting smell of Maria's sweet sweat and her fruity perfume, while removing my worst personal funk. My travel bag in the back, I had on the bare minimum—clean boxers, a pair of jeans, cross-trainer gym shoes, a turtleneck, and of course, my Steelers jersey.

I gunned my rental down the highway, weaving in and out of traffic and refusing to anticipate exactly what I might find. By noon, I was on an exit ramp for North Capitol Street.

Tisha Norris's sister, LaShundra, had given me the address of New Life Baptist House, a small apartment building run by a storefront church with the same name. The place specialized in transitional housing for poor unwed mothers. Tisha had supposedly told her sister she'd squatted here for several months since returning to the States. LaShundra had called the place several times and been told her sister wasn't available, but it was the only lead she could provide.

The only thing I knew for certain was that LaShundra was the one who had a conscience: As far as I could guess, Tisha would not be happy to see me. That's why I'd decided to spend the next few days on a civilian stakeout, parked across from New Life with nothing but some of LaShundra's photos of Tisha and a copy of Deion Sanders's autobiography to keep me company.

I knew it was her the minute she stepped out of the apartment house. It was just after five o'clock, as dusk clouded the sky and my stomach rumbled with a request for dinner. Tisha looked a lot like her sister and not much different from the girl in the photos I had—long, lean, and leggy, with a full head of curls now dyed red. Even in a baggy navy blue windbreaker and bland khaki slacks with gym shoes, she stood out from the six or seven sisters surrounding her.

The women were lost in conversation, talking and joking amongst themselves, so they paid me no mind as I climbed from the car. Taking another quick glance between the woman across the street and the top photo in my hand, I leaned against the car as they crossed the street. They were headed straight at me. Tisha was so into her conversation with a taller, tattooed sister that I barely had to move to tap her on the shoulder.

"Tisha, right?" Maybe it was the fresh memory of Maria's courage in the face of Guy's wrath, but any temptation to get tongue-tied was far from me. My words flowed out smooth as butter. "Can we rap for a minute?"

Every little conversation, every joke ping-ponging amongst the sisters stopped in an instant. The street grew so quiet, it seemed even the birds stopped their singing, the crickets ceased their chirping.

Her shoulders drawn back defensively, her face hardening, Tisha broke the silence. "I don't know you. Don't want to know you."

A short, round-faced girl with a pregnant belly peered around her, eyes trained on me. "This one of them niggers used to beat on you, Tisha?"

"I've never met her before," I said, keeping my posture relaxed since Tisha still hadn't moved away from me. "She knows my name, though. Knows my family." I swung my eyes back toward her. "I'm Deacon Davis. Frederick's son."

Tisha's reaction reminded me of those *Tom and Jerry* cartoons, the ones where the cat's eyes jump out of his head. She slapped a hand over her mouth, mumbled something, and took off down the street.

One of the girls ran after Tisha, but the others stayed right there with me. Surrounding me. Necks twisted, hands went onto hips, and the air filled with harrumphs and belligerent obscenities.

"Don't make me push you sisters down to chase her." My hands hung loosely at my sides as they circled me. "I'm not going to hurt her."

"Get in your car, sir." A thin, middle-aged woman stepped forward. She adjusted her glasses before continuing in her calm, reasonable tone. "I run this house, and we get people like you here every day, harassing these women before they can fix their lives. Now in the name of our Lord and Savior Jesus Christ, I ask you to get in your car and leave Tisha alone."

This sister didn't know the first thing about me or why I was there, but I couldn't blame her for being skeptical. "Okay." I put my hands up, turned around and slid a key into my car door. "If you only understood the full story—"

They were off balance, now, thinking I'd given up. When I pivoted suddenly and burst through the crowd, not a hand touched me. Gritting my teeth, I blazed a path in the same direction Tisha had run. Behind me, the air filled with yells, and I heard footsteps of those who thought they could cut me down, but they'd probably never matched receivers like Jerry Rice yard for yard. I was all alone.

I hurtled down the block and into the next, my ears tuned into the noises of the street. I broke stride at each alley, just long enough to make sure Tisha hadn't doubled back toward the apartment house.

Rushing down the third block, I heard two women arguing up ahead. At the next alley, I made a hard right and nearly ran over Tisha and one of her friends. They stood facing the brick wall of the first house on the alley. A couple of fat stray dogs, probably mutts, lay a few feet away, looking half-asleep.

Tisha's friend, a willowy sister with bloodshot eyes that had probably survived every possible nightmare, turned on me. "Ain't y'all done enough!" She came at me like a hellcat, her long, sharp nails flailing. I caught one of her hands, then the other, and stood there trying to figure out my next step.

"Stop it, Sandy, stop it!" Tisha, cowering up against the wall, screamed so loud, she froze me and Sandy in place. "Don't fight him, girl. He might kill your ass. Just stay here, don't leave me."

"I'm not here for revenge, Tisha," I said, my voice cracking as I turned to face her. In my peripheral vision, I saw Sandy shift into a crouch, but she stayed put. "I just want the truth, any truth you have, about why my father died in that fire."

"I don't know, I don't know!" Tisha clamped her head with both hands, her chin pointed at the pavement. "What do you want from me?"

I forced myself to stay where I was, sensing her fragility. "You worked for Big Walter Chance, then you showed up working at my father's club," I replied. "My father and Big Walter weren't exactly friends. He tried to shut Walter's dealers down." I took a slow step toward her. "Did Walter use you and Pharrell Haynes to set the fire?"

Tisha's eyes filled with angry tears as she stared at me defiantly. "Why you got to give Walter the credit?"

Her words, or maybe it was her tone, froze me in place. A part of me wanted to bolt from that alley and return to my previous years of blissful ignorance, but momentum pushed me forward. "Who deserves the credit then, Tisha?"

"Pharrell may have done the hard part," she said, glaring at me still. "But it was my idea."

"What are you saying?" Six inches separated us now. My mouth was so dry, I felt like I could drink a full canteen of water. "*You* put Pharrell up to the arson? Why would you do that? Was it your way of getting in good with Walter?"

"No!" Tisha began crying violently, her shoulders shaking, her breaths coming fast and furious. "It was about my baby," she said, before suddenly lurching forward and vomiting all over my shoes.

Barely registering the sour smell, I fell to my knees and leaned Tisha back up against the brick wall. I let a few beats pass as her breathing slowed, then said, "What?" The word barely escaped my rapidly tightening throat.

"I wasn't in my right mind," she said, looking into my eyes with a terrified stare. "I hadn't never been pregnant before, Mr. Davis. At least, I'd never kept no child long enough for it to live."

I wanted to ask her what the hell she was babbling about, but something, someone held my tongue.

"I thought your father was different," Tisha continued, her voice dropping to a whisper.

Now it was my turn to throw up. As if she'd shot me, I slumped against the wall next to Tisha, staring ahead blankly. My mother's revelations about the divorce plans cycled through my thoughts. A wave of dry heaves racked my body; then I got out a response. "You got a p-paternity test, didn't you."

"Yeah," Tisha replied, her voice still shaking. "The senator lectured at my school, Benjamin Banneker, when I was a senior. Because I'd already been busted for spending time in one of Big Walter's nightclubs, I was in this group of 'at risk' kids that got a special session with Frederick—I mean, your father. When I heard him speak, it did somethin' to me. I started calling his Senate office all the time, posing like a grown woman and stuff. I couldn't believe when he said he remembered me from his visits to Banneker. From there, things just happened.

"He'd send some man from his office to pick me up from school, and we'd meet at one of those hotels near the Hill. The whole time I was carrying Santonio, Frederick—I mean, your father—promised to help raise him once we took the test and proved everything. I was young and stupid, Mr. Davis, but even I knew he'd never leave your momma for me. But he said we'd be important to him, that he'd be there for his son. Then, when Santonio was born and I mailed him the test results, well, I just never heard back.

"Your father had ignored my ass for three months when Big Walter fired me from his gang. I'd told him I was through hooking for him. Walter never knew who my baby's daddy was, but he hated me for getting knocked up, and when I said I was through selling myself, he wasn't having that. He beat me black and blue before tossing me in the street.

"The only thing I could think about, Mr. Davis, when I moved into a homeless shelter with Santonio, was how your father started everything. If he hadn't gotten me pregnant, Big Walter wouldn't have got pissed at me, and I'd still have a good job and a place to live." A fresh round of tears poured from Tisha's eyes as she turned away. "Your father called himself doin' me a favor when he finally got me a job at the supper club, but by then it was too late: I wanted him to pay, to feel pain like I'd felt."

"All you had to do was get Pharrell hired on at the club, so he could set up the arson for you," I said, not even recognizing the voice that produced the words.

"Yeah." She began sobbing again. "Oh, God, I should have kept my ass in Canada."

I had no words for this moment, but through my own haze of tears, I reached over and pulled Tisha's head onto my shoulder. Patting her hair and stroking her shoulder, I stared vacantly at her friend Sandy, who stood there speechless. "Is her son back at the house?"

"Um, yeah," Sandy said, toeing a circle into the cement.

"Go tell him Mommy's coming home soon."

47

Maria

I took one last look into my nephew's eyes as he sat between Thomas and Lucille. It was frightening because the next time I looked at Jamil, he'd know I was looking at my own son.

Seated next to me on Thomas and Lucille's plush love seat, Deacon reached over my shoulder and offered a hand. Gripping it tightly, I stared into my lap for a second before I found the courage to meet Jamil's gaze again. "Honey," I said, "what Mr. Guy told you was true. When God brought you into the world, you came out of my body." The effort of expelling the words wiped me out, and I slumped against Deacon's solid shoulder. I'd spent days comforting my new boyfriend; now it was my turn to lean on him.

The night Deacon returned from D.C. confirmed that we were both turning a new emotional corner. We had walked alone for too long, and the last few days had proved we were ready to face our tests together.

After Deacon's drug charges were dismissed at his preliminary hearing, we went out for a long lunch and tried to absorb the ugly truths he'd learned about his father. Still holding to my renewed celibacy pledge, I held Deacon against me that first night as he quietly mourned. Despite what he'd learned about his father's behavior with Tisha Norris, he still loved Frederick fiercely, but the halo was gone. We talked about whether anyone else—from his mother, to his uncle James, to family friends like Miriam Lloyd—might have known the truth all along and hidden it out of respect to his father's legacy. There were no easy answers.

Deacon hadn't told anyone—not even Errick or Miles—about his discoveries. We agreed that I would help him host an informal reunion as soon as possible. The truth had to be aired before it ate him up.

Before we could get to that, though, there was the matter of Jamil.

The weekend after his return, Deacon and I drove to Thomas and Lucille's. As Deacon zoomed his truck down the highway toward Stone Mountain, he listened patiently to my rehearsed comments. The whole thing felt like a dream one minute, a nightmare the next. I couldn't believe I was going to finally tell Jamil the truth.

The police department's child psychologist had encouraged me and Thomas to directly address the things Guy had told him. Although the little man had told Thomas he didn't believe Guy's claim to be his father, he had told the psychologist that he always wondered why he didn't look more like Lucille. Confusion and betrayal were already setting in. We had to go ahead and get things out sooner, not later.

With my confession still hanging in the air, Jamil looked longingly between Thomas and Lucille, the frantic look in his eyes breaking my heart.

"It's the truth, honey," Lucille said, patting Jamil's head and wiping tears from her eyes. "Your Auntie Maria gave birth to you. Daddy and I asked her to let us raise you, though, because we loved you so much."

Jamil stared at me as if seeing me for the first time. "You—you're my mommy?"

"Your mommy is sitting right next to you," I said, pointing toward Lucille. "Jamil, a mommy is the woman who feeds you, clothes you, and keeps you safe. God used me to bring you into the world, but he wanted you to be raised by your parents."

Jamil glanced up at Thomas, who still hadn't said a word. Embarrassed, Thomas looked away and wiped his nose before coughing out, "We love you, Jamil; this doesn't change any of that."

"But if I came out of you, Auntie Maria," Jamil said, swinging his gaze back to me, "shouldn't I live with you?"

Deacon began massaging my hand and rubbing my back as I fought for the right words. "Oh, Jamil, there's nothing I want more than for you to live with me. But again, you're already living with the mommy and daddy who love you most. You don't want to change that, do you?" I cursed myself for the question as soon as it slipped out. Not only was it inappropriate, but it reminded me of what I really wanted.

Jamil looked down at his lap, his fingers intertwining, his short legs kicking against the couch. "I don't wanna move, Auntie Maria," he said, glancing up at me sheepishly. "God wants me here, right?"

I knew it in the depths of my soul, after years spent running from this simple fact. "Yes, Jamil," I replied. My eyes spilled over with tears, betraying the pain caused by letting go. "God wants you right here." I released Deacon's hand, pecked a kiss onto his cheek, then opened my arms for Jamil. "Come here and give me a kiss."

As Jamil ran into my embrace and I stroked his head and kissed his cheek, Thomas spoke, his voice increasingly husky. "Jamil, you'll be spending more time with your Auntie Maria, okay? Maybe you'll come up with a new nickname for her even."

Lucille flashed a tentative but sympathetic glance my way. "*Mommy Maria* sounds cute."

"Whatever you're comfortable with, son," Thomas said, before clearing his throat. "But we'll always be your parents."

"I love you, handsome." I released Jamil and stood. Deacon was at my side instantly. "I should go," I said, barely able to make eye contact with Thomas and Lucille. I swayed in place watching the three of them, looking like model subjects for a family portrait. "Really, I better go. I don't have a good excuse. I'll be in touch soon."

"Please do, Maria," Lucille said, her voice soft and assuring. "If we don't hear from you this week, we'll come looking for you."

Deacon and I left them sitting there, whispering and hugging one another, and walked back out to the foyer. We were searching through the hall closets for our jackets when Thomas popped up behind us. "Let me get those for you," he said, glancing at the floor as he squeezed between us and slid our jackets off their respective hangers.

As I accepted my jacket, I struggled to meet my brother's gaze. "Thanks, Thomas."

"Maria," Thomas said as he handed Deacon his coat, "I don't want you to adapt to this arrangement on your own."

"Oh, she won't be alone," Deacon said, drawing me to his side again.

"I understand that you'll be there for her," Thomas said, good-naturedly punching Deacon's shoulder, "but I want to be there for you, too, Maria. I want our entire family to weather this together."

I can't tell you what it meant to hear Thomas use me and the word *family* in the same sentence. It had been so long since I had felt a part of anyone's family. I was rendered speechless, curious to hear Thomas expound.

"I've been told we need to get counseling for Jamil," he said finally, his fists in his pockets. "But I suggested to the therapist that you and I should see her first, so we can put some of the past behind us. You know, my bad habit of treating you like you're still my baby sister, your habit of writing me off as an out-of-touch square. Dr. Lowry thinks that will make for a smoother transition as we integrate you into Jamil's life."

As emotionally drained as I was, I couldn't withhold a big hug from my brother. "Just call me before you set the date and time. I'll work it into my schedule."

"Will do," Thomas whispered. He winked as he pulled back from me. "Mee-maw would be proud."

As Deacon helped me into my jacket, the best I could do was flash a genuine smile and a *mm-hmm*. Once Deacon had my jacket on and we stepped outside, though, I collapsed into my man's warm, encompassing embrace.

48

Deacon

I couldn't dodge her forever. She had called ceaselessly, leaving urgent messages on my voice mail the entire time I was in D.C., and in the several days since I'd returned with Maria. Besides, I had to go through her to see my daughter.

Mercedes was in the midst of a staff meeting when I walked past her secretary and rapped on the front glass wall of her private conference room. After making my presence known, I stood there, hands in the pockets of my suit pants, as her eyes met mine. Determined to be cool, my ex nonchalantly set her laser pointer down and excused herself.

The door snapping shut behind her, she sized me up with fire in her eyes. "We've been worried sick about you."

"Liza knew I was okay." I had called my baby each night I was away, assuring her Daddy was traveling on business and was just fine. Whenever Mercedes grabbed the phone from her, though, I always hung up.

"We may as well go to your office, or wherever you think's least likely to be bugged," I said. "You know what this is about."

"Tisha?" The name stumbled out of Mercedes's mouth, and she looked as frightened as I'd ever seen her. Lips clamped together, she pivoted suddenly, briskly leading me to her office.

"So she didn't call you?" I said as I stood by her office door, which she had immediately slammed behind us.

"Deacon, there's a perfectly good explanation—"

I raised a hand. "Did you hear me or not? I already talked to Tisha. She told me everything. I just want to know one thing, Mercedes. Did you set Miles and me up with the cops at his hotel?"

Her arms crossed, Mercedes maintained rigid eye contact. "I told you to let things be, didn't I?" Her voice lost some of its edge as she asked, "Why couldn't you have just listened?"

"Is that a yes?"

"I wanted to slow you and Miles down, get you off of Tisha's trail, so your answer is yes."

"Well, for the record," I said, thinking of Miles's drug treatment, "your evil may have been used for good in that case. What happened to the threats you made about Governor Hooks, destroying his candidacy?"

"I guess I was bluffing," Mercedes said, her arms still crossed. "As you see now, I wasn't hiding anything for my own benefit, Deacon."

"I think we both know that's a lie," I replied. "The last thing you wanted was to be embarrassed by Big Walter again. If the police had ever suspected Tisha of this, they'd have torn your father's gangs apart looking for answers."

"Maybe I felt that way subconsciously." Mercedes was still hugging herself, but hadn't looked away yet. "But if I was protecting myself, I was really protecting all of us—you, me, and especially Liza."

Standing before the woman who had once meant so much, I slipped my hands deep into the pockets of my slacks. "Did you have any idea, any idea at all, that Tisha was capable of murder?"

"If you're asking whether I could have stopped her or Pharrell, the answer is no. I knew your father had messed around with Tisha, and I knew she was upset. But I never thought she would pull something so sick. She always had problems, but I never saw them going that far."

I didn't tell Mercedes that Tisha had already confessed everything to me, including the ways she and Pharrell coordinated the arson at my father's club. Pharrell had done his homework; even though most of the fires he'd set for Big Walter had used homemade napalm-type bombs, at my father's club he had apparently rigged a relatively sophisticated commercial explosive, something harder to trace. Tisha claimed ignorance of the details, aside from the step they took to ensure Frederick didn't escape the fire. Just before kicking things off, Pharrell had personally followed my father into the men's room, knocked him out with a napkin dipped in chloroform, and laid him down in a locked stall.

At this point I had to take Tisha's story as gospel, because Pharrell had vanished into thin air. Tisha believed he'd crossed into Mexico, but without any details, such a lead was too ambiguous to be useful. As horrific as the truth was, I had no plans to chase Pharrell. Bringing Pharrell to justice would unavoidably mean charging Tisha with the murder also, and now that I'd confirmed little Santonio's lineage, I couldn't put his mother in prison. God would have to judge Pharrell and Tisha, not me. I had no doubt Frederick would understand.

Tisha had told me one more thing: she had never shared her murderous thoughts with Mercedes. It was hard to imagine why she would lie for someone else after being caught.

"One more question," I said to Mercedes, stepping so close to my ex that the scent of her perfume rushed up my nostrils. "I know why you didn't want the public to know the truth, for Frederick's sake as well as Tisha's. Damn the p-public, though, Mercedes. Why couldn't you trust *me* with the truth?"

"I was protecting you," Mercedes replied, tilting her head back to meet my gaze, "and I was protecting the memory of my child's grandfather. I thought about telling you, more times than you'll know, but Deacon, he was your hero just like he was a hero to the man on the street. I didn't want to rob you of that."

"Some of this was my fault," I whispered, my chin tipping toward my chest. "I never opened up with you like I should have, but then you weren't much better." Still gripping Mercedes's hand, I squared my shoulders and traded gazes with her again. "Maybe if I'd taken the first step, let down my guard about my stuttering and everything, you'd have trusted me with the entire truth—from Big Walter to Frederick."

"We could try it again," Mercedes said, her voice softer than I'd heard it in years. "We're not who we were when we divorced, Deacon. Maybe we'd do better today."

After all we had been through, and all that lay ahead as we continued raising Liza together, I didn't have it in me to tell Mercedes the hard truth. That even though I respected her reasons for keeping the truth about my father's death a secret, I could never trust her as a life mate again. Especially not when I'd already found Maria, a woman with whom I could always be myself and expect the same in return.

With Mercedes awaiting my reaction, I did the only fair thing I could. Releasing her hand, I rebelliously wiped my misting eyes and reached past her, opening the office door.

49

Deacon

By simply showing up tonight, Governor Perry Hooks had proved that he was foolhardy, half-crazy, and courageous. In five minutes, he'd be formally announcing his candidacy for the presidency of the United States.

I sat with the governor in his limousine, enduring yet another round of his revisions to the speech I'd written for him. Palms, cell phones, and BlackBerry devices beeped and rang all around us, as the other five aides crowded around us handled their respective business.

"Sorry, Deke, I'm not saying that," the governor said as he took a dreaded red pen to the speech's last paragraph. "I've prayed over it since this morning—" He frowned as Faith Meeks, his campaign manager, shoved a cell phone into his hand. He forgot me for a minute and began arguing with his head of security, something about them wanting us to enter Harlem's Apollo Theater from a different entrance.

Our motorcade had fought through classic New York City traffic, but finally we were here. The limo jerked to a stop about a block from the theater, and we emptied onto the crowded street, where we were swarmed by throngs of supporters. The governor and I were instantly surrounded by four security guards, who quickly hustled us through the main entrance.

By the time the governor and I were backstage, the first wave of stage fright hit me. When Errick bolted backstage, assuring us that the Dream Party had everything perfectly organized for the night, he collared me first. Apparently Miriam Lloyd and the Dream Party board were getting nervous, and they wanted me back. They knew if I continued working so closely with Perry, I might never return to the fold. I told Errick there'd be time to deal with Miriam later, and he left me alone, pulling Perry off into a corner with a quick question.

Left alone, I tried not to let nerves get to me. As the auditorium filled with the excited introductory remarks of a parade of black America's finest—congressmen and -women, famed entrepreneurs, notable philanthropists, star athletes, millionaire rappers, big-time movie stars, and popular singers—I felt a prick of the same fear that brought me down in that infamous Fox News interview. Why, I thought, a sudden wave of sweat thickening below my hairline, had Perry entrusted me with his formal introduction?

Then I heard my name called, and the curtain opened. No more time for positive self-talk, no more indulgence of fears. It was time to deliver.

Flashbulbs popping, hands clapping, the Isley Brothers' "Fight the Power" bumping out of the speakers, I stepped to the center of the stage, where a large wooden podium with a ridiculous bank of microphones awaited me. It felt like a party, like another hot night at the Apollo, so I took time to work the crowd, reaching down to shake hands with the gaggle of press below and waving at every familiar face in the crowd. There were many.

Maria was seated on the second row, just behind the reporters and to the left of the governor's family. Surrounding her were Jamil, Liza, Dejuan, Terrell, Uncle James, and my mother.

I blew a kiss at Maria, who chuckled with embarrassment as the kids teased her. I was so glad she had suggested bringing all three of them along. I had an easier time seeing Dejuan regularly now—about once a month, whether that meant flying him to Atlanta, or me jumping on the plane instead—but I knew at his pivotal age, it was helpful for him to see firsthand the many possibilities offered by this life.

My relationship with Liza really hadn't suffered any, despite the fact that Mercedes and I had only recently started talking again. Miles, who was still living in Tampa with Mother and Roberto, had been drug-free for three months and had proposed marriage to his girl Chantal. The revelations about our father's death, and the sordid circumstances, had obviously killed his conspiracy book, but he was determined to put his skills to better use. He was talking about starting a national black newspaper.

Both Mother and Uncle James had suspected just enough about the real cause of Frederick's death to bury their respective heads in the sand. By the time I'd confronted them with the truth, I had enough documentation and matching accounts from other folk to see the bottom-line truth. Despite all of his marvelous qualities and strengths, my father fell victim to a common weakness. We all agreed that while the family had to swallow that bitter pill, the thousands of lives Frederick had touched would not be helped by the news. We would keep it to ourselves, at least as long as we could. For all we knew, my baby brother, Santonio, might insist on telling his mother's story some day. In the meantime, my sisters, Miles, and I were determined to build a relationship with the boy. He hadn't asked for any of this, but he was stuck with us Davises now.

As the crowd quieted, I stepped up, angled the central mic up toward my chin, and gazed confidently over the crowd. And that's when I felt it more clearly than I ever had before—if Frederick wasn't perfect, why did I think I had to be, least of all when it came to how I spoke? I inhaled gently and released my first words with an easy whoosh.

"Good evening, my name is Deacon Davis. Today we celebrate the birthday of our beloved Dr. Martin Luther King, but we also celebrate another anniversary. Eight years ago today, my father, Frederick Douglass Davis, announced the start of an exciting journey for black America: his campaign for the presidency of the United States." I paused as the crowd filled the air with enthusiastic applause, then continued, recalling some of the highlights of Frederick's campaign, including his aggressive calls for tax reform, his plan to fund a national health-care system, and his advocacy of color-blind economic justice.

My knees weakened as I neared the most dreaded part of the speech. As if sensing my every emotion, the crowd's cheers quieted as I continued. "We all know my father's journey ended unexpectedly," I said, my mouth going dry. I looked up from my text, inhaled deeply and found myself struggling for words. For a few seconds, I was mute, then I got out, "B-But my father always b-believed that the causes he worked for were b-bigger than himself." With the theater now uncomfortably quiet, I looked into Maria's smiling eyes and righted myself.

"Whew! No, brothers and sisters, my name is not Porky Pig," I said, drawing a good-natured round of laughs and a couple of "That's all right, baby!" yells from the balcony. "You all be patient with me," I said, chuckling now. "I may take a while getting things out, but I promise it's worth the wait." It wasn't great comedy, but people who had started shifting uncomfortably were giving me their full attention again. "As I was saying, or trying to say, my father believed that his mission was bigger than himself. It was in that spirit that he made time fifteen years ago to mentor a young graduate student named Lincoln Perry Hooks.

"How appropriate that today that same young man, now a legendary leader in his own right, picks up the banner first carried by my father. For everyone here and for those watching on C-SPAN, let me assure you: As the son of Frederick Davis, I am supporting Governor Hooks because he exemplifies the values my father stood for. He is certainly his own man, but if you want a man in the White House who governs the way Frederick Davis would have, this is as close as you're going to get." I looked toward the left wing of the stage, where Perry stood with his back ramrod straight, his cool, spiritual gaze leveled my way. "Ladies and gentlemen, please welcome the governor of the great state of Ohio, Perry Hooks!"

I stood enveloped in the crowd's adulation as Perry expertly worked the crowd into a frenzy, walking across the front of the stage and leaning to shake every hand he could reach. As he pulled a few people onstage for hugs and singled out some of the crowd's many large signs as his favorites, I knew I had crossed a threshold. A new phase of my life was waiting around the corner, and I was excited about attacking it.

Everyone in the Dream Party and on Perry's campaign team, himself included, knew we weren't going to ever see the White House, but that wasn't the real goal anyway. If Perry had anything like my father's success at appealing to his own people, plus Hispanics and progressive whites, he'd have the Democrats clamoring for his endorsement, assuming he agreed to withdraw from the race. The influence he would wield over the next president's agenda could be unprecedented. The only question was whether instead of returning to finish his term as governor, Perry might wind up serving in the Cabinet of the next administration.

Either way, he was pressing me to join his staff full-time after the campaign. The thought of relocating to Columbus, Ohio, and being separated from both my kids, plus Maria, hadn't gone down well. Perry had promised I could support him from Atlanta, though I wasn't sure how that would work in practice. As long as the campaign continued the momentum it had gained in recent months, though, I'd have plenty of options.

Those concerns melted away as Perry pulled me into a bear hug before releasing me and stepping to the podium. Retreating back into the shadows but facing forward, I watched history unfold.

50

Maria

By the time the night before election day rolled around, ten months after Deacon and Governor Hooks wowed the crowd at the Apollo, I was having a hard time remembering what my man looked like.

Deacon had spent the past six months working in the governor's main headquarters in Columbus, on a Monday-through-Thursday schedule. He flew home most weekends to see me and Liza, at least when he wasn't going to Chicago to see Dejuan, or traveling with the governor to deliver motivational speeches to newly registered voters. In a word, my summer and fall as Deacon Davis's woman weren't much different from my single days.

What Deacon and I lacked in quantity, we tried to make up for with quality. Because we were practicing abstinence—when we weren't "slipping up"—we spent our few hours together each week focused on our respective inner journeys. Although he still stuttered from time to time, Deacon was shedding the self-consciousness and shame that had driven him to Ramsey Folger's clinic. It showed in his work—as a full-time staffer for the Hooks campaign, he was helping set policy, speaking to college students, and conducting live broadcast interviews. He had moments of self-doubt and fear, like any human, but every day a spirit of adventure drove him past those little dips.

I knew I'd need that same spirit myself pretty soon. Now that I was fully certified as a fluency therapist and had successfully managed another Speech Recovery Clinic with Ramsey, I was ready to spread my wings. I already had informal offers from several Atlanta-area therapists and hospitals. In a perfect world, I would have just stayed on with Ramsey, but our personal baggage made that thought pretty unattractive. It was time for me to go, but Deacon had convinced me to wait until he figured out his next career move. I couldn't imagine he'd actually leave Atlanta, but in case he did I didn't want to be caught flatfooted.

Outside of work, I was enjoying my relationship with Jamil. It was hard to explain, but with the truth out in the open, I was so much more relaxed around my little man. We were more like big sister and little brother now. I picked him up for church a couple of times a month, and Thomas was inviting me on family vacations now. Back in March, Deacon and I had actually flown out to Orlando with Thomas, Lucille, and Jamil for a long weekend at Disney World.

It wasn't all peaches and cream, of course. I still wasn't sure how to handle issues like discipline. Although Jamil's grades were still strong, his teachers were complaining that he had become more social in class, or should I say less attentive. Thomas and Lucille had cracked down hard, scooting up his bedtime and taking away his video games until his attitude improved. To me it had seemed like an overreaction to a child who was just trying to fit in with his classmates, but Deacon reminded me weekly to keep my thoughts to myself. For better or for worse, I had sacrificed my two cents a long time ago.

As many reasons as I had to be grateful, I was feeling irritable that evening as Alicia and I returned to Columbus's Hyatt on Capital Square. After withdrawing from the presidential race and throwing his support—national polls showed him at 15 percent at the time—to the Democratic nominee, Governor Hooks and his campaign team had spent the past two months crisscrossing every pocket of black folks in America, meaning every major urban area and a good piece of the South. Right now they were sweeping through Georgia, the Carolinas, and Florida, shoring up turnout there before returning to Columbus to vote in the morning, do some national media spots, then retire to suites in the Hyatt to watch election returns. It was a great effort, but Deacon had gone along for the ride, meaning I'd barely laid eyes on him since September.

Once we took the elevator up to our floor, Alicia and I walked briskly to our hotel room. I was planning to stay with Deacon once he arrived tomorrow, but tonight was our girls' night out. As I impatiently jammed my room card into the door, Alicia tapped me on the shoulder. "Slow down, sis, be cool."

Leaving the card lodged in the closed door, I looked back at Alicia, a frown breaking out on my face. "What are you babbling about?"

"In case you didn't realize, you're murmuring under your breath, girl." She slipped me an evil smile. "I know you miss your man. Just be patient. Once the votes are in tomorrow night, you'll be sharing a room with him." She winked. "Maybe you'll have an 'accident' and get busy even, who knows?"

"Listen, She-Who-Has-Just-Patched-Up-Her-Own-Marriage," I said, wagging a finger in her face. "Don't hate. We do the best we can. I'm just ready to have Deacon to myself again."

"All fine and well," Alicia said, chuckling as I swung the door open. "Are you sure he's gonna stay in Atlanta after all this? He's got plenty of options."

Nursing a game face, I sank onto the bed nearest to the window. "I don't totally kid myself. It's not all about me. Liza's in Atlanta. He doesn't want to be separated from both of his kids, Alicia."

"I hope you're right," she said, walking to the closet by her bed and yanking out her garment bag. "Well, there'll be time to worry about Mr. Man when he hits town. Right now we need to decide which parties to hit tonight—" She was interrupted by the jangling of the phone sitting between our beds.

I slid over and grabbed the receiver. "Hello?"

"Yes, may I speak with Deacon, please?" I recognized the smooth, confident rush of Miriam Lloyd's voice immediately. I guess I'd spent more hours in Deacon's world than I realized. When I told Miriam he wasn't in yet, she said, "This would be Maria then, right?"

"Yes. Hi, Ms. Lloyd."

"Hello, dear. Would you be a sweetheart and have Deacon make a note to call me in a couple of days, whenever he's recovered from the campaign?"

I toyed with telling her Deacon would have zero interest in returning her call. "You just want to give him that general message?'

Miriam paused, then hummed in amusement. "Oh, you mean should I explain why he should call me when he can't stand me?"

"Your words, not mine, Ms. Lloyd."

"Tell him I said the Dream Party won't let him get away again. When he's ready, we'll get him back on board. Errick has already said he wants to try his hand running one of Communities in Action's programs, so if Deacon wants the executive director job back on his terms, it's ready for him, just in time to build our slate of candidates for the 2006 congressional races."

"Well, I'll pass the message along, Ms. Lloyd."

"Thank you, dear. I'll see you at the reception tomorrow night. We've all got hands raised to heaven and fingers crossed, right?"

"Amen." As excited as I was for Deacon, Miriam's call wasn't going to feel real until we had this election behind us. I started jotting down the message for him when the phone rang again.

Alicia grabbed it up this time. "Yello." Her eyes darkened in confusion as the voice on the other end ranted. "Okay, okay. She's right here." She raised an eyebrow as she thrust the phone into my hands.

"Maria?" It was Miles. I had only hung out with him in person a couple of times, including the weekend of his wedding to his long-time girlfriend, Chantal, but we talked on the phone a couple of times a month, whenever he called Deacon. Back to work in D.C., he was a senior editor for a new black newspaper. "Hey," he said impatiently, "where's my little brother?"

"He's on the trail with the governor," I replied. *Duh.*

"No, he's not," he said, snapping the words out like a teacher correcting a student. "This is important, Maria. There's rumblings rolling through the D.C. press corps about Hooks, something embarrassing. It sounds bad."

Feeling chastened, I squinted at Alicia, who sat across from me trying to dip. "All I know is, he's supposed to be with the governor."

"I just spoke with the governor's campaign chairman," Miles replied. "They said Deacon was here. I called the front desk for his room, and they directed me to some room where another chick answered. That's when I called the desk again to see if a room was registered in your name." He took a breath finally. "Now, if your man's in the same hotel you are, shouldn't you know about it?"

"He's not—" I stopped myself. "Did you ask the woman in the other room if that was Deacon's room?"

"I asked for him by instinct, Maria. The woman said he was in the shower and would call me back on my cell." He paused again, and I thought I heard a muffled gasp. "Hey look, I must have just been confused. Don't sweat it. I'm sure he'll turn up."

"Um, yeah." I hung up and blew air through my lips as Alicia stared at me quizzically. When I replayed the conversation for her, she grabbed her cell phone and began reading and punching in the hotel's main number as printed on the room phone.

"Yeah," she said a few seconds later, "can you ring the room of Deacon Davis for me?" She sat there, her legs crossed and pumping nervously. I heard a voice answer on the other end of her phone, and it sounded like a female.

"Yeah," Alicia said, her voice turning cranky around the edges, "is this Deacon's room?" She shook her head as the woman responded. "Why don't you just answer my question? If you're in the man's room, who are you to him anyway?" She looked up at me suddenly, her face turning crimson. "You want to take it there, we can go, okay, trick?" She uncrossed her legs and stood, the veins in her neck popping out as she shook her head. "Oh, you gonna be bold and tell me the room number, even? Stay right there, how about that? We'll see how bold you are face-to-face." She snapped her phone shut and looked down at me, her eyes growing weary. "Maria, don't panic, but something's not right."

"What room are they in, Alicia?" I wasn't drawing any conclusions yet, though I probably had the right to. Whatever was going on, I had to see for myself.

I was out the door, slamming it shut behind me, seconds after Alicia told me the room. It was just a floor up on eight, so I walked past the elevator and stormed the steps, heels and all. Just in case I had to get ghetto, I'd be well equipped.

I blew into the hallway and headed for room 857. When I reached the high oak door, I noticed it was cracked. I knocked forcefully all the same. "Hello?"

That heavy door creaked open behind my little bit of force, slowly revealing an unblemished room that looked like a honeymoon suite. Every possible detail had been accounted for—a table alongside the bed was appointed with an ice bucket and two bottles of champagne. The room simmered with the promise of sexual heat, as fostered by the floor's dimmed track lights and the recessed lights overhead, all bolstered by the horns, guitar, and percussion of a Miles Davis recording, and I don't mean Deacon's brother.

I hadn't yet decided what to think when a pair of forceful arms slipped around my waist. My reflexive panic was quickly quelled by the familiar cologne filling my nostrils and the bass voice that slipped over my shoulders. "Looking for someone?"

Not wanting to see him right away, cherishing the deliciousness of the surprise, I reached a hand over my shoulder and reached for Deacon's smooth, clean-shaven face. "It's not nice to play with a sister's paranoia, Mr. Davis," I said, stroking his cheek.

He took me by one hand and turned me to face him. "I told the governor I was about to lose my woman," he said, pulling my chin up toward his. "He said at this point, there's nothing more I can really do anyway. You are so beautiful." Deacon leaned down and extended his lips until they brushed, then bonded with mine.

When we finally separated, I planted my hands onto his shoulders. "You go to all this trouble, you're liable to get a girl into trouble."

"Oh, no," Deacon said, guiding me toward the bed. Once he had deposited me there, he took a step back and clasped his hands in front of him. "I'm not perfect, but I'm not slipping again, baby. The next time we make love, your mind will be at ease. No more questions about whether I'll be there, whether I'll leave you like Guy or anyone else did."

Heat buzzed throughout my chest and I looked away momentarily, embarrassed at his loving words. As scared as I was, though, I believed every vowel, consonant, and syllable.

"I should warn you," Deacon said as he approached me and bent down on one knee. "I have every intention of giving you a family, but as you know, both of my kids were 'oops' babies. If you say yes,

Maria, our wedding night will be the first time I've ever *tried* to make a baby."

I reached down and ran a hand through Deacon's lovely, freshly tamed mane. I wasn't moving until he asked the question flat-out, but I'd play along for now. "Well, you know a sister can't wait forever."

He smiled up at me as he reached into his pants pocket. "Just be patient. You can't rush perfection."

ACKNOWLEDGMENTS

Although this story was inspired by my personal experiences with stuttering, I believe Deacon's and Maria's respective struggles are universal. Maybe you've never stuttered a day in your life, maybe you've never been separated from your own child, but you've certainly tried to keep some secret from others or even from yourself. Some secrets are best kept that way, but many must be unveiled before they can be solved. I hope this story encourages you to consider the difference.

As a person who stutters, I have been blessed in many ways that differ from Deacon. I thank my father, Chester, a stutterer himself, for being a true role model. I don't know many others with my "thorn" who have a parent successfully dealing with the same condition. Dad, you have always shown me by example that a few flubbed words ain't the end of the world. For my mother, Sherry, I love that you never doubted my ability to succeed in spite of. Your unconditional love and constant cheerleading are invaluable to me.

One reason my romantic life has been more stable than Deacon's is the unblinking support of my wife, Kyra. Thank you for helping me understand that few people obsess about my speech more than I do.

While recognizing those who have provided ongoing support to my career—my immediate and extended family, friends, church family, the nation's black booksellers, TriCom Publicity, my agent Elaine Koster, my editor Kara Cesare, and every loyal reader—I also credit the many positive role models who have helped me persevere to this point, either directly or indirectly. These include the great actor James Earl Jones, my uncle Victor Robinson, the leadership of the National Stuttering Association as well as its individual members, and the legion of speech therapists who have counseled me since my early teens. There are far worse burdens than stuttering, but when you're caught in the midst of a speech block with an amused stranger staring back at you, it's tempting to lose sight of that fact.

God bless,

C. Kelly Robinson

The Strong, Silent Type

C. Kelly Robinson

A CONVERSATION WITH
C. KELLY ROBINSON

Q. How does The Strong, Silent Type *compare with your previous works?*

A. Although the initial inspiration for this book is my most personal one yet, I think the story is true to what my readers expect—an entertaining, true-to-life story with elements of humor, suspense, and romance. With that said, *The Strong, Silent Type* is probably my most ambitious work to date, because it involves some adversities I've experienced directly.

Q. You have a history of stuttering. Did you base Deacon and his difficulties on your life experience?

A. Deacon is his own creation. He and I have a few things in common—the stuttering, being from high-achieving families, surviving moments of self-doubt. The similarities pretty much end there. With Deacon, I wanted to create an attractive, heroic figure whose one shortcoming was this rare, misunderstood disability that he had the ability to hide. That was really never an option for me.

Q. Do you know many women like Maria, who are separated from their children?

A. When I began writing the manuscript, I knew I wanted to connect Deacon with a woman who had her own hidden battles, a fellow wounded soul. I don't personally know any women who are hiding their identity from their children like Maria is, but I know some who have put their children up for adoption or have lost custody for various reasons. When you consider the unique gift that all mothers receive in their children, I think being separated from them for any reason is an undeniable tragedy.

Q. Like many authors, you're on record about who some of your favorite authors have been through the years. Have you read anyone recently who particularly inspired you?

A. The past couple of years I've made strides in finally making time to read some authors whose names I've always heard but never experienced in print: Pearl Cleage, James Patterson, Richard Price, and Nick Hornby are good examples. I always like to challenge myself, looking for lessons across genres.

Q. Will we ever see any of the characters from The Perfect Blend *again?*

A. Count on it. I don't have all the details yet, but I predict that O.J. and Tony will appear in future works of mine, and you never know when Mitchell and Nikki will pop up as supporting characters.

QUESTIONS FOR DISCUSSION

1. Was Deacon's employer, the American Dream Party, right to remove him from his job? Should he have fought them and sued for discrimination? Why or why not?

2. Do you know anyone who stutters? Why do you think they stutter? Would you hire them to work for you? Why or why not?

3. When Deacon felt disrespected by his son's principal, how should he have handled the situation? Have you ever had a tense meeting with your child's teacher or principal? How did you handle it–similarly to or differently from Deacon and Candy's response?

4. When she couldn't get her drinking under control, Maria gave Jamil to Thomas because she feared she'd be as unfit as her own mother had been. Did she make the right decision by giving Jamil away?

5. Once she gave Jamil to Thomas and Lucille, should Maria have insisted they raise him with the knowledge that she was his mother? Why or why not?

6. Because Deacon's stuttering was relatively mild, he managed to hide it during most of his young adult life, until it caught up with him. What types of secrets have you attempted to hide from others until circumstances forced you to be open about them and/or seek help?

7. When Deacon and Maria were nearly caught in their affair at the clinic, should they have just confessed? Why or why not?

8. Discuss Deacon's father and Deacon's evolving view of him. Was Frederick just another "failed" black leader or a sincere hero with a few human flaws? How have your own views of your parents shaped your life?

9. Should Maria have even entertained filing suit to get custody of Jamil? Was she right to blame herself for Guy's reappearance and kidnapping of Jamil?

10. Why do you think Deacon's marriage to Mercedes didn't work out? Should he have considered her offer to reconcile?

11. What do you think of Deacon's mother and the ways she walled herself off from her family after Frederick's death? Was she protecting herself or being selfish?

12. Considering the many ways Ramsey tried to help her, could Maria still have maintained a working relationship with him?

13. Was Maria right to meet Guy and Jamil on her own, without Deacon's help?